THE STATIONMASTER'S FAREWELL

THE STATIONMASTER'S FAREWELL

EDWARD MARSTON

Allison & Busby Limited
13 Charlotte Mews
London W1T 4EJ
www.allisonandbusby.com

First published in Great Britain by Allison & Busby in 2012.

A CIP catalogue record for this book is available from
the British Library.

First Edition

ISBN 978-0-7490-4021-5

Typeset in 12.25/16.6 pt Adobe Garamond Pro by
Allison & Busby Ltd.

Paper used in this publication is from sustainably managed sources.
All of the wood used is procured from legal sources and is fully traceable.
The producing mill uses schemes such as ISO 14001
to monitor environmental impact.

Printed and bound by
CPI Group (UK) Ltd, Croydon, CR0 4YY

*With love and thanks
to Dr Janet Cutler, former President
of the Railway and Canal Historical Society,
who provided me with a base in Dawlish from which
to explore South Devon and whose knowledge of its
railway history was an invaluable source.*

CHAPTER ONE

November 4th 1857

Joel Heygate was not only a highly efficient stationmaster, he was immensely popular in the community. He was a stout man of middle height with a flabby face decorated by bushy eyebrows and a walrus moustache. In his frock coat and top hat, he was a striking figure and seemed to be a permanent fixture at Exeter St David's railway station. Those who met him for the first time were impressed by his cheerful disposition and his readiness to offer help. None of them would have guessed that tragedy had entered his life in dramatic fashion. A few years earlier, Heygate's wife and daughter had been killed in a freak accident on the track outside Plymouth station. Other men might have been embittered by the event and blamed the railway for the death of their loved ones. Heygate steadfastly refused to do that. If anything, his passion for the railway system was intensified and he described himself as having the best job in the world.

Because he had such a legion of friends, he was never lonely. Living in the house provided by the South Devon Railway, he shared it with a canary called Peter and with his warm memories of a happy marriage. When he was not tending his little garden, he spent his spare time birdwatching, making constant use of a telescope bequeathed to him by an old sailor. It was not the only gift that came his way. Local landowners would often drop off a brace of pheasant, and an obliging fishmonger would sometimes slip sole or mackerel into his hand. The railway station was his kingdom. During working hours, he would stride up and down the long single platform with an air of supreme contentment. Heygate would make regular visits to the refreshment room.

'Good morning, Mrs Rossiter,' he said.

'Good morning, Mr Heygate,' she replied.

'Good morning, Dorcas,' he went on, turning to the waitress who was wiping the tables with a cloth. 'How are you today?'

'Very well, thank you, Mr Heygate,' she said.

He checked his pocket watch. 'The next train will be here in twenty minutes.'

'We'll be ready for it,' said Mrs Rossiter, sweetly. As she looked at Dorcas, her voice hardened. 'You always forget that table in the corner, Miss Hope.'

'I'm sorry,' said Dorcas, moving across to it.

Mrs Rossiter rolled her eyes. 'I have to watch her all the time.'

Railway companies employed a large number of women but the vast majority were invisible as they toiled away in laundries, washing the never-ending stream of towels, tablecloths, sheets and antimacassars that were cleaned on a weekly basis. Mountains of sacks had to be made or repaired by an army of seamstresses. Female employees were more in evidence in railway hotels but Exeter St David's was unusual in having two of them on duty in the refreshment room. Pretty waitresses like Dorcas Hope were in a vulnerable position, likely to be ogled or groped by lecherous male passengers. She escaped both these fates, thanks to the protection offered by Heygate and, even more so, by the basilisk stare of Agnes Rossiter.

The manageress was a widow in her forties, a thin sharp-featured martinet who made even the bravest and most inebriated of men shudder at the thought of ogling or groping her. Mrs Rossiter's fearsome reputation was enough in itself to keep men on their best behaviour and restrict them to sly, wistful glances at Dorcas, a shapely young woman whose patent lack of education was outweighed by her willingness to learn. It irked Mrs Rossiter that the stationmaster showed the waitress an almost paternal affection, using her Christian name while keeping the manageress herself on surname status. This was especially demeaning to a woman who had a secret fondness for Heygate and who nursed the faint hope that she might one day be able to arouse his interest in her. For the moment, however, their relationship was one of polite formality.

'Will you be going to the bonfire tomorrow, Mr Heygate?' she asked.

'Of course, Mrs Rossiter,' he said, affably. 'It's an event I've been enjoying for over forty years now. What about you?'

'Oh, I'll be there,' she said, beaming as if a tryst had just been arranged. 'I'll look out for you.'

'I may be difficult to find in the crowd.'

'Father's taking me,' announced Dorcas. 'He won't let me go alone.'

'Quite right too,' said Mrs Rossiter with a sniff. 'Passions can run disgustingly high on Guy Fawkes Night. No decent woman is safe on her own.' She smiled at Heygate. 'That's why I'll be grateful for your company.'

'Don't bank on it,' he said. 'The world and his wife will be there.'

'I'll find you nevertheless,' she warned.

Heygate winced inwardly. While he had the greatest respect for Agnes Rossiter, he had no wish to spend any leisure time with the woman. Her brittle voice grated on his ear and he took care to keep his distance because of her abiding aroma of lavender and mothballs. She was not unattractive. Indeed, some might account her handsome until they saw her in combative mode, when her eyes glinted madly, her teeth were bared and her whole body bristled like a wildcat about to attack.

The refreshment room occupied a long low space that was filled with small tables and an array of chairs. On the counter that ran the length of the room, food and drink were on display and the walls were covered with advertisements. The catering had been leased to a contractor to whom the railway company had guaranteed regular stops at the station by their passenger traffic. In addition to those waiting to board a train or to welcome someone alighting from it, Mrs Rossiter and Dorcas also served the mass of people who surged out of a train making a prolonged stop there to break a lengthy journey. At such times, it was hectic but they coped valiantly.

'How is your mother, Dorcas?' asked Heygate, solicitously.

'She never complains,' said the waitress, 'even though she's in pain.'

'Is there nothing that can be done for her?'

Dorcas shrugged. 'There's nothing we can afford, Mr Heygate.'

'Do give her my regards.'

'Yes, I will.'

'My grandfather was crippled by arthritis, so I know what a trial it can be. Your mother has my sympathy.'

'Thank you.'

'I get an occasional twinge myself,' said Mrs Rossiter, rubbing her hip as she made a plea for attention. 'It's agony in cold weather.'

'Ah,' said the stationmaster as two customers entered the room, 'I can see that I'm in the way. I'll let you get on with serving the travelling public.'

He tipped his hat to the well-dressed couple who'd just come in then shared a farewell smile between Dorcas and Mrs Rossiter before leaving. Straightening her white apron, the waitress went swiftly around to the other side of the counter. The manageress, meanwhile, appraised the two passengers through narrowed lids then took in the whole display of refreshments with a graceful sweep of her arm. She spoke as if bestowing a great favour upon them.

'What can we get for you?' she asked.

Exeter was a pleasant cathedral city with a population in excess of thirty-two thousand. In the reign of Elizabeth I, it had been one of the largest and wealthiest provincial communities in England but it was now in decline. The

11

Industrial Revolution that created the huge conurbations in the Midlands and the North had largely passed it by, allowing it to retain a semi-rural atmosphere. County and agricultural interest still held sway. Though its mayor spoke of the city with fierce pride, it was dogged by unemployment, destitution, poor drainage and woefully inadequate public health provisions. Only three years earlier, it had witnessed a bread riot in its streets, a violent outpouring of discontent that resulted in widespread damage and serious injury to citizens and policemen. While it may have died down now, the discontent had not gone away. It was still simmering below the surface and the man most aware of it was the Right Reverend Henry Phillpotts, incumbent Bishop of Exeter. The distant sound of exploding fireworks made him grimace.

'It's started already,' he complained. 'They can't even wait a single day.'

'We must make allowances for the impetuosity of the young,' said Ralph Barnes, tolerantly. 'Their excitement is only natural.'

'You don't need to remind me. I've been the victim of their excitement many times. The year that I was consecrated, they burnt an effigy of me.'

'It's traditional to burn effigies of clergymen on Guy Fawkes Night.'

'This was different, Ralph, as you will recall. It was not undertaken in a spirit of good humour. There was a collective antagonism towards me. It was the reason I summoned the 7th Yeoman Cavalry here as a precaution, and the reason that I always leave the city at this time of the year.'

They were in the bishop's palace at the rear of the

12

cathedral. Both men were in their seventies, yet their vigour and dedication were unimpaired. Bishop Phillpotts considered himself a prince of the church and acted with regal arrogance. He was a strict disciplinarian who ruled the clergy in his diocese with an iron rod. It earned him few friends and many enemies but he felt that seeking popularity was a sure sign of weakness of character. While his hair was silvered and his forehead lined, his eyes maintained their imperious sparkle. He turned his back so that Barnes could help him on with his cloak.

'Thank you, Ralph,' he said, adjusting the garment.

'When will we return?'

'Only when calm has been restored.'

They were leaving Exeter to avoid the celebrations on the following day, moving instead to the palace that the bishop had had built at Torquay. It was his preferred residence, with extensive gardens that stretched down to the sea. He felt safer there, well away from the hullabaloo of November 5th and the dangers that accompanied it. At an age when retirement might have beckoned, Ralph Barnes had continued to be the secretary to the bishop and clerk to the dean and chapter. A former solicitor in the city, Barnes was a slim, immaculate, well-groomed individual with a cool head and an unobtrusive manner. Beside a man of such arresting eminence as Phillpotts, he was rather insignificant but he played a vital role in the diocese and discharged his duties well.

Putting on his top hat, Barnes followed the bishop through the front door held open by a servant, then clambered into the open carriage beside him. Paradoxically, they were fleeing from an annual event that only existed because of ecclesiastical support. Guy Fawkes Day was a symbol of a Reformation that was held in high regard by the Protestant citizenry. The public were allowed to hold festivities in the cathedral close and the Church contributed funds to the building of a massive bonfire near the west door of the edifice. Essentially an occasion for the youth of the city, it was attended by people of all ages. Having sanctioned the celebrations, the bishop was now being driven well away from them. As the carriage rumbled into the close, they caught sight of the vast pile of timber and other combustible material.

'That will burn merrily for hours,' observed Barnes.

'There'd be even more merriment if I was sitting on top of it,' said Phillpotts, sourly. 'Someone who lives by the highest moral principles will never find favour with the common people. That's why I rise above their mindless disapproval of me.'

'Yet you still command a great deal of respect.'

'After over a quarter of a century as their bishop, I deserve it.'

'I couldn't agree more.'

'When I took charge of this diocese, the clergy were despondent and their respective ministries fell well short of desired standards. That is no longer the case. I have brought about a reformation of my own.' He permitted himself a rare smile. 'Fortunately, it does not need to be marked by an annual bonfire.'

Barnes grinned. 'That's very amusing, Bishop.'

'You know exactly how much I've done to revive the church here.'

'Nobody could have done more.'

While they were talking, squibs were being let off on all sides by mischievous children, filling the air with a series of pops and flashes. Someone threw a firework at the carriage and it exploded under the hooves of one of the horses. With a loud neigh, it reared up between the shafts. The driver needed time to bring the animal under control again. Meanwhile, other fireworks were being hurled in fun at the carriage and there was a whole salvo of minor explosions. Stamping his foot in exasperation, the bishop looked up at the driver.

'Hurry up, man!' he shouted. 'Get me away from here!'

Dorcas Hope was roused from her slumbers at four o'clock next morning when cannon fire boomed out from various quarters of the city to mark the great day. By the time she set off towards the station, the streets were already busy. Children were hawking rudimentary guys about and youths were carrying more fuel to the bonfire. There was a sense of corporate exhilaration and Dorcas was caught up in it. When a firework went off close to her, she simply laughed and continued on her way. It was her custom to peep into the stationmaster's house each morning so that she could watch the canary hopping about in its cage. When she reached the relevant window this time, however, the curtains were drawn. That was most unusual. Joel Heygate was an early riser and a stickler for punctuality. She'd expected him to have been at work an hour ago. Could he have overslept for once or – the thought was more disturbing – been taken ill? Dorcas was worried. She went to the front door and used the knocker. Though the sound echoed through the house, it evoked no response. She tried again but it was futile.

Heygate was either not there or too unwell to move. When she looked upwards, she saw that the bedroom curtains were also closed.

The irony was that she had a key to the house. It had been entrusted to her so that she could feed Peter on the few occasions when Heygate took time off to visit friends in Cornwall. Dorcas kept it hidden at home. It never occurred to her that the key might have been useful. There was no time to retrieve it now. If she was only minutes late, she would suffer a stinging reprimand from Mrs Rossiter and she wanted to avoid that at all costs. She was about to leave when she noticed that there was a chink in the curtains that concealed the parlour from view. If she stood on her toes, she might just be able to get a glimpse of the interior. Raising herself up to her full height, she peered through the tiny gap. The room was in shadow but she was able to see something that turned her concern into alarm. There was a cloth over the birdcage. The first thing that the stationmaster did every morning was to remove the cloth and welcome Peter into the light of day. The bird was still in darkness. It was ominous.

Dorcas hurried to the station as fast as she could, determined to report what she'd discovered. When she arrived, she found everyone in a state of agitation. Clerks and porters were asking each other what could possibly have happened to Heygate and Mrs Rossiter was weeping quietly into a handkerchief. Before Dorcas could speak, a stern voice interrupted the anguished debate.

'That's enough of that!' declared Lawrence Woodford. 'You all have jobs to do. I suggest that you get on and do them.' When they paused to gape at him, he wagged an admonitory finger. 'I'm in charge now,' he decreed. 'If you don't do as you're told, there'll be dire consequences.'

Obeying the order, they all dispersed. Only Dorcas remained.

'I just passed Mr Heygate's house,' she explained. 'The curtains were drawn.'

'We know that, Miss Hope,' said Woodford, irritably.

'What's happened to him?'

'Your guess is as good as mine.'

'He's never late for work, Mr Woodford.'

'There's always a first time,' he said, 'and this – evidently – is it. That's why it's fallen to me to take over as stationmaster.'

It was a role that he'd coveted for many years. Woodford was the chief clerk, a tall, stooping man of middle years with a mobile face and darting eyes. Dorcas had never liked him. He was officious, self-important and inclined to shoot her lewd glances whenever he caught her alone. Since he made no secret of the fact that he felt he could do the job better than Heygate, he was now glorying in the opportunity to prove it. He smirked triumphantly.

'You answer to me henceforth, Miss Hope.'

'I understand, Mr Woodford.'

'This station will be run properly from now on.'

'Mr Heygate ran it very well,' she said, defensively.

'Then where is he?' he demanded. 'A captain does not desert his ship.'

'He may have been taken ill.'

'Joel Heygate is *never* ill.'

'There's no other explanation.'

'I can think of two or three,' he said, darkly. 'The most obvious one is that he's absconded. He has the keys to the safe, remember, and could easily have emptied it before making his escape.'

Dorcas was horrified. 'He wouldn't do a thing like that!'

'You're too young and trusting, Miss Hope. I know the ways of the world.'

'And I know Mr Heygate,' she said with a hint of defiance. 'He was a good man and it's wrong to think bad things about him.'

'Get off to the refreshment room,' he snapped.

She held her ground. 'I want to know the truth, Mr Woodford.'

'You'll hear it at the same time as the rest of us. I've sent word to the police and asked them to collect Mrs Penhallurick on their way here. She cleans the house so is bound to have a key. Don't be misled by false loyalty,' he said, looming over her. 'There's something sinister in his disappearance. It's just as well that you have me to step into the breach.'

Dorcas looked around in bewilderment. Ordinarily, it was a joy to come to work. The stationmaster looked after her and she enjoyed meeting so many people every day. Any pleasure had now been snatched away from her. Instead of working under a kind friend, she was at the mercy of someone she disliked and distrusted.

Woodford asserted his authority. 'Don't stand there dithering, girl,' he growled. 'You have passengers to serve.'

She scampered off to the refreshment room with tears in her eyes.

Exeter had learnt from experience that it was wise to clear the streets of horses, carriages and carts on that particular day in autumn. Household pets were locked safely away but there were always stray animals on which the crueller youths could pounce. More than one dog went yelping across the cobbles with a cracker attached to its tail and cats were tempting targets for a lighted squib or two. An afternoon service was held in the cathedral but the main focus of attention was the close. It filled up steadily throughout the day. Children argued, fought, played games or paraded their guys – misshapen creations wearing tatty old coats, corduroy breeches and battered hats on the pumpkins or other vegetables that served as heads. Carrots were pressed into service as comical noses. Suspended from one arm was a lantern while a bundle of matches dangled from the other. The better examples of craftsmanship garnered pennies from passers-by, while the poorer exhibits aroused derision. Owners of rival guys sometimes came to blows.

Celebrations were not confined to the city. People came in from miles around, many of them arriving by train. There were well over a hundred pubs in Exeter and they were all working at full stretch. When they tumbled out to watch the lighting of the bonfire that evening, their patrons were drunk, rowdy and excitable as they swelled the enormous crowd in the cathedral close. The timbers were fired, the crackle of twigs was heard and smoke began to rise in earnest. There was a concerted cheer from the crowd but it was nothing to the volcanic eruption of delight that later greeted the sight of hungry flames around a guy that bore a distinct resemblance to the bishop. They yelled and hooted until his papier mâché mitre was destroyed along with the rest of him. Henry Phillpotts was burnt out of existence.

Police were on duty but their numbers were ridiculously small. There was no way that they could control any disorder.

They just hoped that it would not reach a level where they'd have to call on reinforcements from Topsham Barracks. Ever since police and soldiers had engaged in a ferocious brawl over a decade earlier, there had been bad blood between them. The general view taken of the police was unflattering and Guy Fawkes Night was seen by many as an excuse to settle old scores with them. Lest their hats were knocked off or they became embroiled in a fracas, policemen therefore tended to stay in the shadows. Even with the support of watchmen, they were hopelessly outnumbered. Yet the mayor and the justices of the peace had to make a gesture in the direction of law and order, so they occupied the Guildhall ready to offer summary justice to any malefactors dragged in.

While everyone around her was whooping with joy, Dorcas was strangely detached from the whole event. She was still preoccupied by the fate of Joel Heygate. At first she hadn't wanted to go to the bonfire celebrations but her father felt that they might stop her from brooding about the stationmaster. Nathaniel Hope had been upset to hear about the man's disappearance. Since he worked as a guard on the railway, he saw a great deal of Heygate and the two of them were good friends. Hope was a big, solid man with craggy features edged with a beard. In the jostling throng, he kept a protective arm around his daughter. To make sure that she heard him, he had to raise his voice over the cacophony.

'Try not to think about it,' he advised.

'That's what I've been trying to do, Father, but I can't put it out of my mind. I'm afraid that something terrible has happened to Mr Heygate.'

'We don't know that for certain.'

'*I* do,' she said, grimly. 'He's disappeared.'

'That doesn't mean he came to grief somewhere, Dorcas. When the police went into his house this morning, there was no sign of anything untoward. Nothing was touched and nothing was taken.'

'That's no comfort to me.'

'No,' he sighed, 'I can see that it isn't. Joel Heygate is a man in a thousand. I admire him. It was only because he was the stationmaster that I agreed to let you take that job in the refreshment room.'

'He was my friend.'

'He was also someone who could take care of himself,' he said, sounding more optimistic than he felt. 'If he did get into a spot of bother last night, I'm sure that he was able to cope with it.'

'Then where is he?' she wailed.

Hope had no answer to that. He was still struggling to suppress his own fears. Heygate was a methodical man. Over the years, he'd kept to a strict routine. Until now, he'd never once deviated from it. His absence was thus profoundly unsettling. Closing his eyes, Hope offered up a silent prayer for him.

The blazing bonfire didn't merely warm everyone up on a raw evening, it also lit up the whole area and painted the cathedral in garish colours. Flames danced wildly and the roar was deafening. The stench of smoke was everywhere and sparks were carried on the wind, singeing the overhanging branches of nearby trees or lodging harmlessly on roofs until they expired. Bawdy songs were sung, scuffles broke out and youthful exuberance had free rein. The cathedral close was a cauldron of heat, noise and abandon. Policemen stationed on the margins began to get restive.

Dorcas had seen enough. It was time to go. Before she could ask her father to take her home, however, she spotted someone coming towards them. It was Mrs Rossiter, barging her way through the crowd and looking in all directions as she did so. She was wearing her best coat and a new hat trimmed with ostrich feathers. When she bumped into Dorcas, she spoke with breathless urgency.

'Have you seen Mr Heygate?' she asked.

'No, Mrs Rossiter,' replied Dorcas.

'He promised that he'd be here. Well, you're my witness, Miss Hope. You heard him. He more or less agreed to meet me at the bonfire.'

'He's not here,' said Hope, resignedly.

'He *must* be, Mr Hope. It's not like him to let me down. It's not like him at all. Joel – Mr Heygate, that is – is so reliable. He's in the crowd somewhere.'

'I very much doubt that, Mrs Rossiter.'

'So do I,' added Dorcas.

'You're both wrong,' insisted the older woman. 'He's here. I sense it.'

'Then you're mistaken, Mrs Rossiter.'

'He *is* – I'd swear it.'

'You may be right,' said Hope, deciding to humour her. 'Who knows? He may have turned up out of the blue. Listen,' he went on, 'Dorcas and I are about to leave. Would you like to walk home with us?'

'What a terrible thing to suggest!' said Mrs Rossiter, indignantly. 'That would be an act of betrayal. I can't leave when I have to meet Mr Heygate.'

'But he's not here,' said Dorcas in despair.

'Yes he is, and I won't rest until I find him.'

Lifting her chin, Mrs Rossiter charged off, elbowing her way through the bellowing horde as she continued her search. Dorcas felt sorry for her. She'd never seen the other woman so close to hysteria. Mrs Rossiter had such self-control as a rule that her behaviour was troubling.

'Do you think we should go after her, Father?' she asked.

'Leave her be.'

'But she's wasting her time.'

'I know,' he said, sadly. 'One thing is certain. Joel Heygate is not here.'

A rousing cheer went up as the blaze suddenly strengthened and poked tongues of flame at the cathedral in blatant mockery. Smoke thickened and sparks fell in ever-widening showers of radiance. Fireworks exploded like a volley from an infantry regiment. The Bishop of Exeter had perished with the other guys tossed onto the bonfire and the inferno roared on. It would be several hours before it burnt itself out and exposed the charred body of a human being among the embers. Crazed she might be, but Mrs Rossiter's instincts had been sound.

The stationmaster was there, after all.

CHAPTER TWO

'Exeter!' cried Leeming in dismay.

'It's in Devon,' explained Tallis. 'In fact, it's the county town.'

'I know where it is, sir, and that's a very long way away. Why can't we simply investigate crimes here in London? That's where we live. Going to Exeter may mean leaving my family for days on end.'

Tallis was acerbic. 'I don't care if it's months on end, Sergeant. Duty comes first. If you wish to remain a detective, you must be prepared to go where necessity dictates.' He raised a menacing eyebrow. 'I take it that you are desirous of retaining your position at Scotland Yard? If not, you can easily wear a uniform instead and pound the streets in all weathers as a humble constable.'

'No, no,' said Leeming, recalling grim memories of his days on the beat. 'I'm much happier here, Superintendent.

It's a privilege to work under you. I'll go where I'm sent – as long as it's not to America, that is.'

Colbeck was amused. 'I thought that you enjoyed our voyage, Victor.'

'Whatever gave you that idea? The only thing I enjoyed was stepping back on to dry land again. Sailing the Atlantic was a torment from start to finish. For days afterwards my legs were wobbly.'

'But it was a *successful* venture. That's what counts. We caught them.'

'Exactly,' said Tallis, slapping his desk for emphasis. 'We sent a clear message to the criminal fraternity. No matter how far they run, they can't escape us.'

'Yet you opposed the notion at the time,' Colbeck reminded him.

'That's not true at all, Inspector.'

'You thought the idea impractical because of the cost involved.'

'That's right, sir,' said Leeming. 'You were against it. So was I.'

Earlier that year, Colbeck and Leeming had pursued two criminals to New York City in order to arrest them and have them extradited. Being apart from his wife and two children for several weeks had been an ordeal for the sergeant and he'd promised his family that he'd never desert them for that length of time again. He was not the only one who found the prospect of a visit to Exeter unappealing. Colbeck had even more reason to stay in the capital. He was due to get married at the end of the month and did not wish the wedding plans to be hampered by a protracted investigation in another part of the country. He pressed for details.

'What can you tell us, Superintendent?' he asked.

'A man was burnt to death last night in a bonfire in the cathedral close,' said Tallis. 'He's believed to be a stationmaster by the name of Joel Heygate. That's why the South Devon Railway sought my help.'

What he omitted to say was that the telegraph he held in his hand specifically requested assistance from Robert Colbeck rather than from him. The inspector had been so effective at solving crimes connected with the railway system that he was routinely known in the press as the Railway Detective. It was one reason for the latent tension between the two men. Edward Tallis both admired and resented Colbeck. While he freely acknowledged his brilliance, he was annoyed that the inspector's exploits overshadowed his own appreciable efforts. Tallis was senior to Colbeck, yet it was the latter who won all the plaudits. It rankled.

They were in the superintendent's office and there was a whiff of stale cigar smoke in the air. Seated behind his desk, Tallis stroked his moustache as he read the telegraph once more. He deliberately kept the detectives standing. As a retired major in the Indian army, he liked to remind those beneath him of their inferior rank.

'You are to leave on the next available train,' he told them.

Colbeck nodded. 'I can check the timetable in my copy of *Bradshaw*.'

'Won't I have time to go home first?' complained Leeming.

'No,' said Tallis. 'You keep a change of clothing here for just such a situation as this. Time is of the essence. We can't have you running back to your wife whenever you have to leave London.'

27

'Estelle will wonder where I am.'

'Send her a message, man.'

'It's not the same, sir.'

'I'll have to take your word for that,' said Tallis, coldly. 'Thankfully, I am unfettered by marital obligations. I had the sense to remain single so that I could pursue my career without any distractions. You know my credo. Being a detective is not an occupation – it's a way of life. Nothing else matters.'

'I could take issue with you on that score,' said Colbeck, levelly, 'but this is not the time to do so.' He extended a hand. 'Might I see the telegraph, please?'

'There's no need. I've told you everything that it contains.' Tallis slipped the telegraph into a drawer. 'I suggest that you make your travel arrangements.'

'Whom do we contact when we arrive?'

'The man who got in touch with me is a Mr Gervase Quinnell of the South Devon Railway. He'll be awaiting you.'

'What about the local constabulary?'

'Their investigation has probably started.'

'Then why can't we let them get on with it?' asked Leeming, peevishly. 'They know Exeter and its people much better than we do.'

'Mr Quinnell clearly has little faith in them,' said Tallis, 'or he wouldn't have turned to me. He views this as essentially a railway crime and knows my reputation.'

'But there's no proof that the victim is the stationmaster, is there?' observed Colbeck. 'If he was found under a bonfire, identification would have been very difficult. His clothing would have been destroyed and his face and body horribly disfigured. There's another thing,' he added. 'You say that he was burnt to death. Is there any evidence of that? A bonfire is a public event. The victim could hardly be hurled alive into the blaze in front of a large crowd. Isn't it more likely that he was killed *beforehand*? The body must have already been hidden under the bonfire when it was set alight. It's the most logical supposition.'

'That's idle speculation.'

'I think it's a fair point,' said Leeming.

'Be quiet, Sergeant. Nobody asked for your opinion.'

'It's not *my* opinion, sir, it's the inspector's and I agree with it.'

'Shut up, man!'

'What's the exact wording in the telegraph?' wondered Colbeck.

Tallis was impatient. 'All that need concern you is that our help has been sought. That's why I'm sending you to Devon, so please stop quibbling. As for you, Sergeant,' he said, reserving his sarcasm for Leeming, 'I will put an advertisement in all the national newspapers, requesting any villains intending to commit a crime on the railway to confine their activities to London and its environs. Will that content you?'

'It would certainly make my life a lot easier, sir,' said Leeming.

Colbeck took him by the arm. 'Come on, Victor,' he said, pulling him gently away. 'The superintendent is being droll. We are two of a pair. Both of us would like to keep the time we spend away from London to an absolute minimum and there's one obvious way to do that.'

'Is there?'

'Yes – we must solve this crime as soon as possible.'

He led the sergeant out and closed the door firmly behind them.

Exeter St David's railway station was a place of mourning. Even though there was still some uncertainty as to the identity of the murder victim, almost everyone believed that it had to be Joel Heygate. The one exception was Agnes Rossiter who insisted that he was still alive and who put all her energies into the smooth running of the refreshment room because it was 'what Mr Heygate would have expected of me'. It was not a view shared by Dorcas Hope. Stunned by what had happened, she walked around in a dream and had to be given a verbal crack of the whip from time to time by the manageress. Other members of staff were horrified by the news, finding it hard to accept that such a universally popular man had met his death in such a grotesque way. Passengers waiting to depart from the station had all heard the rumour and rushed to pay fulsome tributes to Heygate.

Rising above the general solemnity, Lawrence Woodford concentrated on the many duties that fell to a stationmaster, supervising his staff, keeping the platform uncluttered, inspecting all the buildings for cleanliness, ensuring the most economical use of stores, stationery, coal, gas and oil, noting the appearance of all passengers, answering their endless questions and – most important of all – taking care that trains left the station on time. Dressed for the occasion in frock coat and top hat, he lacked Heygate's physical presence but his calm efficiency was undeniable. It was almost as if he'd been rehearsing for this moment of crisis.

Dorcas discovered an unexpected streak of kindness in

the man. Slipping out of the refreshment room, she accosted him on the platform.

'Could I have a word with you, please, sir?' she asked, nervously.

'What's the trouble, Miss Hope?'

'I'm worried about Peter – that's Mr Heygate's canary. Somebody ought to look after him.'

'I quite agree,' said Woodford.

'Peter knows me. I've fed him in the past. Can I take care of him?'

'I don't see why not. We shouldn't let the bird suffer. The decision is not mine to make, of course,' he went on with a smile, 'but I can pass on your generous offer and recommend that we accept it.'

'Thank you, Mr Woodford.'

'You get back in there with Mrs Rossiter. Leave it to me.'

As Dorcas scurried off, Woodford strode along the platform with his head up and his back straight. He was in charge now. The sense of power and influence was almost dizzying. He savoured it to the full. When he got to the stationmaster's office, he entered it as of right and was in time to witness a raging argument.

'I should have been consulted, Mr Quinnell.'

'There was no point, Superintendent.'

'I'm in charge of the police force here.'

'And I represent the South Devon Railway. We want this crime solved.'

'Then let us get on with solving it.'

'With all due respect,' said Quinnell with disdain, 'it's way beyond the competence of your force.'

'I dispute that, sir.'

31

'I showed initiative and made contact with Scotland Yard.'

'It was an insult to me and I am bound to say that I resent it bitterly.'

'We need the best man for the job.'

'The murder occurred on our territory and it's our job to investigate it.'

Unaware of Woodford, they continued to bicker. Gervase Quinnell was the managing director of the South Devon Railway, a plump, pompous man in his fifties, with bulging eyes and mutton chop whiskers peppered with grey. Superintendent David Steel, by contrast, tall and square-shouldered, cut a fine figure in his police uniform. His handsome face was puckered by barely concealed rage. Appointed when he was in his late twenties, he'd run the Exeter police force for a decade and felt that his sterling work deserved more recognition.

'Inspector Colbeck is the person to take on this case,' said Quinnell, briskly. 'He comes with the highest credentials.'

'There's no need for him to come at all,' argued Steel. 'May I remind you that I, too, served in the Metropolitan Police Force before I came to Devon? When I left to take up a post in Barnstaple, I did so with glowing testimonials.'

'You do not have Colbeck's expertise with regard to *railways*.'

'Murder is murder, regardless of who the victim might be.'

'Success is success. That's why he's on his way here.'

'You might have had the courtesy to discuss it with me beforehand.'

'I'm discussing it with you now, Superintendent,' said Quinnell, airily. 'You're not being excluded from the investigation. You're simply being demoted to a supportive role. Look and learn, man. Inspector Colbeck can teach you a lot.'

'But he knows nothing at all about Exeter.'

'In that case, he'll turn to you for assistance.'

'What if the dead man is not the stationmaster, after all?'

Quinnell was testy. 'It *has* to be him. There's no question of that. How else do you explain his disappearance?'

'When we sought his next of kin, Mr Heygate's brother was unable to identify him with any confidence. He'd only say that the corpse *might* be him.'

'The circumstantial evidence points unmistakably to Heygate. Since he was a model employee of ours, I'm taking a personal interest in the case.' He inflated his chest and put thumbs inside his waistcoat. 'I *care* for the men who work on my railway.'

'Then why don't you pay them a decent wage?' retorted Steel. 'If the porters got enough to live on, they wouldn't have to work part-time for me on night patrol.'

Quinnell was scandalised. He was just about to issue a sharp rebuke when he became aware of Woodford, standing self-consciously in the open doorway and listening to the heated exchange. Steel also noticed the new stationmaster for the first time. He treated him to a long and hostile glare.

'Well,' he demanded, 'what do *you* want?'

Woodford cleared his throat. 'It's about the canary . . .'

When they caught the train in London, Colbeck was in his element. Rail journeys were a constant source of pleasure to him because there was so much of interest to see out of the window. Leeming, on the other hand, disliked the noise, the rattle and the sense of imprisonment he always felt on a train. Though they would be travelling first class for most of the way on the broad gauge of the Great Western Railway, the sergeant was not appeased. Uppermost in his mind was the fact that Exeter was the best part of two hundred miles from the wife and children he adored. Murder cases took time. It might be weeks before he saw them again.

Until they reached Chippenham, the compartment was too full to permit a proper conversation. It suddenly emptied at the Wiltshire station, allowing them to set off on the next stage alone. Colbeck tried to cheer his companion up.

'What did you do yesterday, Victor?'

Leeming was surly. 'I can't remember. It seems like an age ago.'

'Didn't you celebrate Guy Fawkes Day with the children?'

'Oh, yes. I'd forgotten that.'

'Did you have a bonfire?'

'Yes,' said the other, rallying. 'I'd been building it all week. I made them a guy as well. It looked a bit like Superintendent Tallis, now I come to think of it.'

Colbeck laughed. 'Did it have a cigar in its mouth?'

'Yes, it did – a big one. I carved it out of a piece of wood. The children loved it when the guy caught fire. They danced around it and so did Estelle.' He heaved a sigh. 'I'm going to miss them, Inspector.'

'It's an occupational risk, I'm afraid.'

'My wife has still never got used to it. What about yours, sir?'

'I'm not actually married yet,' corrected Colbeck, 'but Madeleine has known me long enough to realise that there'll

34

be sudden absences on my part. Fortunately, it's a price she's prepared to pay.'

'At least she understands what you do. I tell Estelle very little of what we get up to. It would worry her sick if she knew the kinds of dangers we face – best to keep her ignorant.'

'I can't do that with Madeleine because she's actually been involved in some of our assignments. She knows the hazards that confront us.'

'What if the superintendent finds out that she's helped us in the past?'

'I'll take great care to ensure that he *doesn't* find out, Victor. You know his opinion of women. He scorns the whole sex. Mr Tallis would never admit that there are times in an investigation when female assistance is vital. We've seen it happen with our own eyes.'

The detectives had first met Madeleine Andrews when her father was badly injured during the robbery of the train that he was driving. What had begun for Colbeck as a chance meeting had developed into a close friendship, then slowly evanesced into a loving partnership. Madeleine had been able to offer crucial help during a number of cases and it had drawn them even closer together.

'Did you send Miss Andrews a note before we left?' asked Leeming.

'It was rather more than a note.'

'She'll be upset that you're going away when the wedding is in sight.'

'That's unavoidable,' said Colbeck, flicking a speck of dirt from the arm of his coat. 'Madeleine will be too busy to pine, however. She has work of her own to keep her busy and, now that her father has retired, she has company throughout the day. Time will pass quickly.'

'It seems to be dragging at the moment,' muttered Leeming.

'Address your mind to the case in hand.'

Leeming obeyed and sat up. 'What do you think we'll find in Exeter?'

'I daresay we'll find a lot of commotion. A stationmaster is an important figure in a city like that. His death will have shocked everyone. The other thing we'll find, of course, is an unwelcoming police force. They'll object strongly to our barging in on their murder – and rightly so. We'll have to win them over.' He winked at Leeming. 'I'll leave you to do that, Victor.'

'My ugly mug will never win friends, sir.'

'It won the hand of a lovely young woman.'

Leeming smiled nostalgically. 'That was different.'

'I think you're unaware of your charms,' teased Colbeck.

'I know what I see when I look in the mirror to shave every morning.'

The sergeant had no illusions about his appearance. He was a sturdy, bull-necked man with the kind of unprepossessing features more suited to a desperate criminal. Though wearing much the same attire as Colbeck, he somehow looked scruffy and disreputable. Beside the inspector, most men would be outshone. He was tall, slim and elegant with exaggerated good looks and a stylishness that marked him out as the dandy of Scotland Yard. He might have been a minor aristocrat sharing a compartment with a bare-knuckle boxer who'd mistaken it for third class.

'There is something else we can expect,' predicted Colbeck.

'What's that, sir?'

'We'll get interference from the Church.'

'How do you know?'

'The bonfire was held in the cathedral close, Victor. A cathedral presupposes a bishop. He'll be mortified that a heinous crime was committed on his doorstep, so to speak. As well as a grudging police force, we'll be up against an angry bishop who'll be barking at our heels throughout.' An image formed in his mind. 'Try to imagine Superintendent Tallis in a cope and mitre.'

Leeming gurgled.

As soon as the telegraph was received at Torquay railway station, it was sent to the bishop's palace. Henry Phillpotts was taking tea with his wife and secretary when the telegraph was handed to him. When he read it, he spluttered.

'What's wrong, Henry?' asked his wife.

'Was there trouble at the bonfire celebrations?' guessed Barnes.

'Trouble!' echoed the bishop. 'I'll say there was trouble. Foul murder was committed. The body of the stationmaster was found among the embers.'

'That's dreadful!' said his wife, bringing both hands to her face.

'It's an unforgivable stain on the cathedral close, my dear. How dare someone abuse our hospitality in that way! It's a desecration. And there's another thing,' he said, handing the telegraph to his secretary. 'Why wasn't I told earlier? Why did Mr Quinnell wait until late afternoon before having the grace to apprise me of these distressing details? He should have been in touch at once. So should the police and so – I regret to say – should someone at the cathedral. Heads need to be knocked together over this outrage.'

'Calm down, Henry,' advised his wife.

'There'll be dire repercussions. We must return to Exeter immediately.'

'Is that necessary?'

'Yes, my dear, it is.'

'But I do so love having you here.'

Deborah Phillpotts was a gracious lady in her seventies with a poise and refinement that belied the fact that she'd borne eighteen children. She'd married Phillpotts when he was vicar of a parish in County Durham. It was not long before he was appointed chaplain to the bishop and she knew that he was destined for higher things. Married for over half a century, she'd been a devoted wife and mother, supporting her husband at all times and enjoying the fruits of his success. Belonging as they did to the clerical aristocracy, they lived in a style comparable to that of the Devonshire nobility. It gave both of them a patrician air.

Having read it, Ralph Barnes passed the telegraph back to the bishop.

'Heygate was a decent fellow,' he said. 'I liked him. When his wife and child were killed in an accident, he coped with the situation bravely. In some ways, I suppose it's a relief that they're not alive to suffer this terrible blow.'

'I'm more concerned about the terrible blow to us, Ralph,' said Phillpotts. 'It's deliberate. He was killed outside the cathedral for the express purpose of defiling consecrated ground and taunting *me*.'

'I'm not sure that you should take this too personally, Bishop.'

'How else can I take it?'

'We need to know more details of the case. All that the telegraph gives us are the bare bones, as it were. What have the police discovered and who is this Inspector Colbeck from Scotland Yard?'

'I don't know and I'm not sure that I want someone from London coming to lead the investigation. This is a local matter that must be sorted out promptly by local means. We don't want news of this horrendous crime to be disseminated throughout the whole country.' He rose to his feet. 'If only we had a police superintendent in whom I could place more trust.'

'I thought that the fellow had been doing quite well,' remarked his wife.

'He has,' agreed Barnes. 'Superintendent Steel has made the most of limited resources and achieved a degree of success.'

'Then why is Exeter such an unruly city?' challenged Phillpotts.

'It's no worse than many cities of an equivalent size.'

'It *feels* worse, Ralph. We have too many ruffians stalking the streets.'

'And too ready a supply of beer to stir them up.'

Phillpotts flicked a dismissive hand. 'That's a separate issue. What concerns me about Steel is that he's not a true gentleman.'

'It's difficult to remain gentlemanly when dealing with the scum of society.'

'You know what I mean, Ralph – he doesn't show me due deference.'

'That *is* reprehensible,' Deborah put in.

'However,' said Phillpotts, 'he's responsible for law and

order. It's down to him to solve this murder.' He waved the telegraph in the air. 'Then we can send this Inspector Colbeck back to London where he belongs.'

The first thing that the detectives saw when they alighted at their destination was an attractive young woman walking along the platform with a birdcage covered by a cloth. From inside the cage, a canary was chirping. Their attention was immediately diverted by the sight of a portly man, bearing down upon them with a mixture of gratitude and doubt. While he was pleased that the men he assumed were Scotland Yard detectives had finally arrived, Gervase Quinnell was not reassured by their appearance. One of them was far too polished and urbane while the other looked as if he should be wearing a collar and chain like a performing bear.

'You must be Mr Quinnell,' said Colbeck, offering his hand.

'I am indeed,' replied the other, receiving a firm handshake. 'Your telegraph warned me that you'd arrive on this train.'

Colbeck introduced Leeming, who was busy stretching his limbs after the long journey. The sergeant looked around and blinked.

'There's only one platform.'

'It's long enough to cope with the demands put upon it, Victor,' said Colbeck. 'Careful timetabling is the answer, as Mr Quinnell will attest.'

'Exeter St David's is one of our most well-organised stations,' boasted Quinnell, taking his cue. 'Until yesterday, it was blessed in having a stationmaster of outstanding ability. However,' he added, 'this is not the place to discuss the matter. Since you may be here for some time, I'd like to offer you hospitality in my own home in Starcross. It's only six miles or so away. I can supply you with all of the relevant details on our way there.'

'Thank you for your kind invitation,' said Colbeck, 'but we have to decline it. Much as I'd like to see Starcross because of its association with the atmospheric railway, I think it would be more sensible for us to stay in the city near the scene of the crime.'

It was not the only reason that Colbeck had rejected the offer. One minute in Quinnell's company told him that they were dealing with a conceited and overbearing man who'd be forever looking over their shoulder. Freedom of action was imperative. They would not get that if they were under Quinnell's roof, and the journey to and from Starcross every day would be tiresome.

'Very well,' said Quinnell, clearly offended, 'you must do as you think fit.'

'The first thing we need to do is to make contact with the superintendent of your police force,' said Colbeck. 'It's a basic courtesy. Also, of course, we need his cooperation. Local knowledge is indispensable and it's something we lack at the moment. Might we know his name?'

'It's Steel,' replied the other through gritted teeth, 'Superintendent Steel.'

'That's a good name for a policeman,' noted Leeming.

'He can be awkward at times and very stubborn. For instance, he's still claiming that the victim may not be Joel Heygate when everyone else knows that it must be.'

'He's simply keeping an open mind,' said Colbeck, evenly. 'I applaud that.' He picked up his valise. 'The sergeant and I will take a cab to the police station and introduce ourselves.'

'Perhaps I should come with you.'

'That won't be necessary, Mr Quinnell.'

'But you're here at my behest.'

'We'll keep you fully informed of any developments, sir,' said Colbeck, anxious to shake him off. 'Come on, Victor. We have important work to do.'

After bidding farewell to Quinnell, they left him fuming quietly on the platform and headed for the exit. It was only when they were being driven into the city that Leeming asked the question that had been perplexing him.

'What exactly is the atmospheric railway?'

CHAPTER THREE

Maud Hope was a thin angular woman in her late forties with a ravaged prettiness. Plagued by arthritis in her knees and hip, she was often in pain and unable to do anything but the most simple domestic chores. When she heard the front door of their little house being unlocked, she was in the kitchen struggling to chop some onions. She thought at first that it might be the neighbour who popped in regularly to keep an eye on her. In fact, it was Dorcas. Maud was surprised to see her daughter and even more surprised that she was carrying a birdcage.

'What on earth have you got there, Dorcas?'

'It's Peter – Mr Heygate's canary. They said I could look after him.'

'Who did?'

'Well, it was Mr Woodford who asked,' gabbled Dorcas. 'He talked to a man who's something to do with the railway company. According to Mr Woodford, the man didn't want me to have Peter. He said the bird was railway property because the house belongs to them. But Mr Woodford spoke up for me and said how I'd fed him in the past, then the superintendent agreed that I should have him. They argued over it and I won in the end.'

'I'm not sure that I follow this,' said Maud, using the back of her hand to wipe away the tears that always streamed when she chopped onions. 'Are you talking about Mr Woodford the clerk?'

'Yes, Mother – he was kind to me.'

'I thought you didn't like him.'

'I don't. He looks at me in a funny way. But he was different today. He was friendly for once. Mr Woodford has taken over as stationmaster.'

'Your father won't like that. He's got no time for the man.'

'All I know is that he helped me and rescued Peter.' Setting the cage down on the table, Dorcas removed the cloth. The bird cocked its head to inspect its new home. 'He's so sweet, isn't he? I couldn't leave him in an empty house.'

Maud smiled indulgently. 'No, I suppose not.'

'I can't stop. I have to get back to the refreshment room. Mrs Rossiter can't manage on her own for long.'

'How has she taken the awful news?'

'She doesn't believe in it. She thinks that Mr Heygate is still alive.'

'But that's silly. He's dead. Everyone knows that.'

'Mrs Rossiter says it's not true. They made a mistake. It was someone else.'

'Well, she'll have to believe it one day,' said Maud,

laughing abruptly as the canary began to sing. 'He's a happy little fellow, isn't he?'

'Mr Heygate used to let him out of the cage. Peter would fly around the room then perch on his shoulder. He did it to me once.' She became anxious. 'Father *will* let me have him, won't he?'

'I'm sure that he will, dear. Where are you going to keep him?'

'The best place is in my room. I'll make sure he isn't a nuisance.' She picked up the cage. 'He eats hardly anything and only drinks water.'

'Leave him downstairs,' said her mother, amused by the bird's antics as it hopped about. 'Put him in the parlour where I can enjoy watching him. I wouldn't trust myself to carry that cage.'

'He can sit on the table,' said Dorcas, taking the cage out. She was back within seconds. 'I must go now.'

'Are you sure you feel well enough to go to work?' asked Maud, a hand on her shoulder. 'You were terribly shaken when you heard about Mr Heygate. He was such a good friend to you.'

'He was, Mother. Whenever I think about what happened, I want to burst into tears. But I can't let Mrs Rossiter down. She needs me.' About to leave, Dorcas paused at the door. 'Oh, there was one thing I meant to mention.'

'Yes?'

'It's something that Mr Woodford overheard.'

'And what was that, dear?'

'They've sent for a famous detective to come here from London.'

'Goodness!' exclaimed Maud.

'The superintendent didn't like the idea. He said that the police could solve the crime on their own. But the man from the railway company said that they needed this inspector from London. He's in charge from now on.' She scratched her head. 'I did hear his name. Now, what was it?' After a moment's cogitation, she snapped her fingers. 'Colbeck – that was it. His name is Inspector Colbeck.'

The police station was like the many others that they'd visited over the years. It was a nondescript building that comprised a reception area dominated by the duty sergeant's desk, a cluster of cells, a larder, a tiny kitchen and a sizeable room where the police could gather and rest. Two outside privies stood at the bottom of the bare garden. Superintendent Steel's office was in the largest of the upstairs rooms with a window that afforded him a good view of the street below. Clean and tidy, the office had shelves along two walls with books and documents stacked neatly along them. A fitful fire provided minimal warmth. On the wall hung a framed charcoal sketch of Steel in uniform. He'd given the visitors an unenthusiastic welcome and waved them to the two upright chairs, perching on the desk himself so that he occupied a position of strength. Sensing the man's resentment, Colbeck tried to mollify him.

'We're most grateful for your help, Superintendent,' he said. 'Though we've managed a measure of success over the years, it's not been entirely attributable to our own efforts. We've relied heavily on local police forces.'

'It's true,' confirmed Leeming. 'We'd have got nowhere in a murder investigation in Cardiff without the help of Superintendent Stockdale.'

'And the same goes for a case we dealt with earlier this year. Our enquiries took us to Manchester, where Inspector Boone gave us invaluable assistance. We always make a point of acknowledging such people,' stressed Colbeck, 'and giving them their share of the credit.'

Steel relaxed slightly. 'That's good to hear, Inspector,' he said. 'I must admit that it was galling to learn that my authority had been undermined. Mr Quinnell didn't even have the grace to discuss it with me beforehand. Your arrival was presented to me as a *fait accompli.*'

Leeming's brow furrowed. 'What's that?'

'Something already done and beyond alteration,' explained Colbeck.

'That's unfair.'

'It's also typical of Quinnell,' said Steel, bitterly. 'Be warned. He likes to throw his weight around and he's a man with influence.'

'He offered us accommodation in his own home,' said Colbeck, 'but I decided that that would not be in the best interests of the investigation.'

'You were quite right, sir,' said Leeming. 'I'd hate to have been forced to stare at him over breakfast every morning. He didn't like the look of me and he let me know it straight away. He made me feel like something nasty he'd stepped in.'

'Where will you stay, then?' asked Steel.

'We were hoping you could recommend somewhere,' said Colbeck. 'On the drive here, we passed a number of public houses.'

'At the last count, there were something like a hundred and twenty in all. At one end of the scale, we have pubs like the Pestle & Mortar in Guinea Street. I think we make more arrests there than almost everywhere else. There are some very squalid drinking establishments in the slums of St Mary Major's as well. The stink there is abominable.'

'What about the other end of the scale, Superintendent?'

'My choice would be the Acland Tavern in Sidwell Street.'

'Is that far away?'

'It's within easy walking distance of here and is an extension of High Street. You'll find it comfortable but it can get noisy if a function is being held. The last time I was there, it was for a banquet with almost a hundred guests. When drink flowed, the din became ear-shattering.'

'We live in London, sir,' said Leeming. 'It's pandemonium there.'

'I know. I served there as a young constable.'

'It sounds to me as if the Acland Tavern will be ideal,' decided Colbeck. 'Before we book rooms there, I'd like to know what action you've so far taken.'

'I had the debris cleared from the cathedral close and the remains taken away. Too many people were coming to goggle even though there was a tarpaulin over the man. It's rather taken the fun out of the events of Guy Fawkes Day. An inquest will be held in the coroner's court tomorrow.'

'Good,' said Colbeck, 'that should throw up a lot of information for us. And I'm glad that the formalities will be held in the appropriate place. The first inquest I attended was in the house where an old woman had been stabbed to death. She lay dead in the next room while neighbours were called in to give evidence. It was positively gruesome.'

'The inspector thinks that Mr Heygate was killed *before* the bonfire was lit,' said Leeming. 'By the time the flames got to him, he was already dead.'

'That's borne out by our findings,' said Steel. 'The cause of death was a blow to the head – several blows, in fact. The skull was smashed to a pulp. Frankly, I was astonished. Joel Heygate was a man who seemed to have no real enemies. He was an institution in Exeter.'

'So the cab driver told us.'

Colbeck stood up. 'We'll find our way to the Acland Tavern,' he said, resting his hat against his thigh. 'Before we do that, Superintendent, I have three simple questions to put to you. First, how many men do you have at your disposal?'

Steel pulled a face. 'I have far too few – less than forty altogether.'

'Second, have you ever led a murder investigation?'

'No, Inspector,' confessed the other, 'I haven't. We have a lot of crime here but it's largely confined to theft, disorder, drunkenness, fraud and prostitution. The last murder in Exeter was over fifteen years ago and that was before my time.'

Leeming was interested. 'Who was the victim?'

'It was a man named Bennett who worked for an insurance company. After visiting the Bonhay Fair, he fell in with some unsavoury characters in the Cattle Market Inn. Someone followed him home. He was later found floating in the river near Trews Weir.'

'Did they catch the killer?'

'Yes,' replied Steel, 'but the case against him rested on the word of an accomplice who turned Queen's evidence. The general feeling was that the accomplice was more of a villain than the man in the dock. Incredibly, the killer was found not guilty of murder but guilty of the lesser charge of larceny. Instead of being hanged, he was sentenced to fifteen years' transportation.'

Colbeck was impressed that he'd taken the trouble to look into details of the case. Steel struck him as an honest, straightforward, diligent man who took pride in his work and who was justifiably upset by the arrival of two detectives from Scotland Yard. Colbeck could see why Quinnell had described him as awkward. Steel was his own man and would not be browbeaten by others. If they could win his approval, he could be a useful ally.

For his part, Steel had been taken aback when he first met them. Leeming reminded him of the ruffians who glared at him from behind bars in his cells and Colbeck looked like anything but an experienced detective. Five minutes of talking to them, however, had convinced the superintendent that he should perhaps take them on trust. Colbeck was intelligent and incisive, while his sergeant was patently a man accustomed to the rough and tumble of policing. There was a mutual respect between the two and they seemed to complement each other. Some of Steel's reservations about them faded away.

'You said that there were three questions, Inspector,' he remembered. 'I fancy that I can guess the third one. Do we have any suspects?'

Colbeck smiled. 'You must be a mind-reader.'

'The answer is that we do. We have one in particular. He's a man well known to us and he's been arrested on previous occasions. Though he travels a great deal, he's been seen in the vicinity recently and that's always a worrying sign.'

'What makes you think he's capable of murder?'

'He has a violent temper and loses control of it when he's

drunk. He also nurses grudges and we know that he had a grudge against Heygate.'

'I thought you said that the stationmaster had no real enemies.'

'I was thinking of people in Exeter,' said Steel, 'and Bagsy Browne doesn't live here. He simply infects the city from time to time.'

'Why is he called Bagsy?' asked Leeming.

'Heaven knows – his real name is Bernard.'

'Tell us about this grudge he holds,' prompted Colbeck.

'It's rather more than a grudge, Inspector. They have troublesome passengers at St David's now and then but the stationmaster can usually handle them. Then Bagsy Browne rolled up roaring drunk one day and became obstreperous. When Heygate tried to eject him, Bagsy gave him a mouthful of abuse and broke some of the windows in the ticket office. He used foul language to female passengers then attacked one of the porters. Heygate was not standing for that,' said Steel, 'so he took matters into his own hands.'

'What did he do?'

'He knocked Bagsy out with the flat of a garden spade.'

'Good for him!' said Leeming.

'Needless to say,' Steel went on, 'Bagsy wanted him arrested for unprovoked assault. He was furious when I told him that Heygate was only acting in defence of his staff and of railway property. The stationmaster was a hero and Bagsy went off yet again to cool his heels in prison.'

'When did all this happen?'

'It was earlier this year, Sergeant. When he'd served his sentence, Bagsy went off somewhere, threatening that he'd be back one day and that he'd come looking for Joel Heygate.'

'Is that what you think may have happened?' asked Colbeck.

'Yes, Inspector – he got his revenge.'

With his shirt flapping and his breeches around his ankles, Bagsy Browne pumped away rhythmically between the thighs of a full-bodied woman with swarthy skin and long black hair. When he reached the height of his passion, he let out a piercing cry of triumph and simultaneously broke wind.

Adeline Goss lay back on the pillow and shook with mirth.

'You always do that, Bagsy,' she said.

'It's the beer,' he explained, reaching for the flagon on the floor beside them and taking a long swig. 'It makes me fart.'

She hugged him. 'Oh, it's so good to have you back again!'

'You're entitled to have a real man for once.'

Putting the flagon back on the floor, he pulled out of her and rolled over on to his back. The bed creaked under his weight. Browne was a big, barrel-chested man in his forties with a pockmarked face half-hidden beneath a black beard. His hair hung to his shoulders and there was hardly any part of his body that was not afforested. His naked companion was a middle-aged woman of generous dimensions with powder dabbed liberally over her cheeks and a beauty spot on her left breast. They were in one of the brothels in Rockfield Place. No money would change hands. Browne was there as a friend rather than a client. He'd once saved her from being badly beaten by a gypsy and she was eternally grateful to him.

'Did you miss me?' she asked, angling for a compliment.

'I always miss you, Ad.'

'Is that true?'

'You're my favourite girl.'

'Tell me why.'

'I just *showed* you why,' he said with a ripe chuckle.

She snuggled up to him. 'Where have you been all this time?'

'I've been here, there and everywhere.'

'Someone said they saw you at Honiton Fair.'

His shrug was non-committal. 'Maybe I was there, maybe not.'

'Don't you remember?'

'What's past is past, Ad. Forget it.'

'At least you got here in time for Guy Fawkes Night.'

'I wasn't going to miss that,' he said with a throaty laugh, 'and I wasn't going to miss you. You're the light of my life.'

'Then why don't you come here more often?'

'I've got things to do elsewhere.'

'Couldn't I go with you one time?'

'No, Ad – they're things I have to do on my own. Stop asking me questions,' he chided. 'Why not just enjoy me while I'm here?'

'I will,' she said, running her fingers through the matted hair on his chest.

'Good – I feel at home in your bed.'

'How long will you stay in Exeter?'

'Who knows?'

'Will it be a matter of days or weeks?'

'There's only one thing I'm sure of,' he said with a grin of satisfaction. 'I'm going to stay long enough for the stationmaster's funeral. If I had the chance, I'd piss on his coffin as they lower it into the grave.'

* * *

No sooner had Colbeck settled into his room at the Acland Tavern than a policeman came looking for him with a message. The inspector was summoned to the bishop's palace to meet Henry Phillpotts. He told Leeming where he was going and suggested that the sergeant used the hours before dinner by finding his way around Exeter. It was dark when Colbeck walked along High Street but there were plenty of people abroad. Since there was a lot of animated discussion, he surmised that the topic of conversation was the cruel death of Joel Heygate. In a city that had not witnessed a murder for so many years, it caused a sensation. When he reached the cathedral close, he found Steel waiting for him. The superintendent indicated the scene of the crime.

'The body was found right here,' he said.

'I'd like to view it before the inquest, if I may.'

'That can be arranged.'

'I take it that it was in a deplorable condition.'

'It was, Inspector. All bodily hair had been burnt off and the skin was black and shrivelled. Michael Heygate – the stationmaster's brother – was unable to say that it was definitely him.'

'Have there been any other reports of missing persons?'

'None that would tally,' said Steel.

'And can anyone account for Mr Heygate's disappearance?'

'No – it was highly uncharacteristic. The chances are that he is the murder victim but I want that established at the inquest before I fully accept it as fact.'

'That's very wise of you,' said Colbeck. 'Never rush to judgement.'

He looked up at the cathedral. In the gloom it seemed

quite menacing. Its west face was covered with an extraordinary array of sculpture but it was invisible now. The cathedral had dominated the city for centuries and its successive bishops had wielded immense power. There was no reason to suppose that Henry Phillpotts had surrendered one iota of it.

'I assume that you've been asked to present yourself to the bishop as well,' said Colbeck, turning to Steel.

'Indeed, I have.'

'What sort of a man is he?' There was obvious hesitation on the other's part. 'You can rely on me to be discreet, Superintendent.'

Steel weighed him up for a few moments then decided to trust him.

'Bishop Phillpotts has done such laudable things for this city,' he began.

'Go on.'

'He's given money for the restoration of the cathedral and the building of some churches. His philanthropy is remarkable. For instance, he gave ten thousand pounds to found a theological college here in the city.'

'I feel that there's a qualification coming.'

'There is. Mr Quinnell, as you discovered, is both arrogant and objectionable.'

'I couldn't have summed him up better.'

'Beside the bishop, however,' said Steel, bluntly, 'he looks like a saint.'

'Where on earth are they?' demanded the bishop, pacing the room. 'I sent for them ages ago. They should have been here by now.'

'I thought I heard the doorbell being rung only a moment ago,' said Barnes.

'Well, it's not before time. Go and meet them, Ralph. Acquaint them with my displeasure and bring them here.'

'Would you like me to remain?'

'Yes, I'd like your assessment of this detective from London. We've already taken Superintendent Steel's measure and found him wanting. Let's see if the Metropolitan Police employ worthier individuals.'

Barnes left the room and intercepted the visitors in the hall. He told them that the bishop was fretting over the delay then conducted them to the library. When they entered, the bishop had his back to them. He swung on his heel to confront them and struck a pose. After he'd been introduced to Colbeck, he offered the two men a seat then settled into the high-backed leather chair behind the ornate desk. Barnes was left to hover in the background.

'What time is the next train to London?' rasped Phillpotts, fixing Colbeck with a stare. 'Whenever it is, I suggest that you catch it.'

'That won't be possible, Bishop,' said Colbeck, smoothly. 'Sergeant Leeming and I will remain in Exeter until our work is done.'

'We don't need you, man.'

'That decision does not lie in your hands. We are here as a result of a direct appeal from the chairman of the South Devon Railway.'

Phillpotts snorted. 'Quinnell is an idiot.'

'That's something on which we can agree,' said Steel under his breath.

'Unfortunately, he's an idiot who has substantial power

56

and that makes him dangerous. I am responsible for the spiritual life of the diocese and it must take precedence over everything else.'

'I beg leave to doubt that,' said Colbeck.

'Damn your impertinence!'

'This crime is related to the railway and I will treat it as such.'

'When it has such religious significance? Open your eyes, Inspector. The murder was carried out in the cathedral close. There's an interpenetration of the sacred and the profane here.'

'That may be a coincidence, Bishop. There's a possibility that the victim was killed elsewhere and concealed beneath the bonfire because it was a convenient way of disposing of the body.'

'That's nonsense!'

'It's something we have to consider,' argued Steel.

'This outrage is far more to do with the Church than the railway. That's why we don't need anyone from Scotland Yard to poke his nose into our affairs. I suggest that you pack up and leave, Inspector.'

'I'm not answerable to you, Bishop,' said Colbeck, stoutly.

'The superintendent will agree with me. This is a local matter.'

'But it will test us to the limit,' conceded Steel. 'I've never handled a case of this complexity before, whereas the inspector is a renowned expert. It would be folly to scorn his assistance.'

Phillpotts recoiled as if from a blow. 'You dare to accuse me of folly?'

'I was thinking of myself, Bishop.'

Colbeck was grateful for the superintendent's support

but he was not sure if it was genuine or simply a means of annoying the bishop. Having been in charge of the police force for a decade, he reasoned, Steel would have had many battles with Henry Phillpotts and did not take kindly to being hauled before him like an errant schoolboy summoned to the headmaster's study for punishment.

'The superintendent has done exactly what I would have done,' said Colbeck, 'and deserves praise. He's removed the body, set up an inquest and – I see from the handbills on display – had "wanted" posters printed. The railway company is offering a handsome reward for information leading to the arrest of the person or persons who perpetrated this crime. In addition to that,' he went on, 'he's already identified a prime suspect.'

'Is this true?' asked the bishop, shifting his gaze to the superintendent.

'My men have been searching for the fellow all day,' replied Steel, 'and I've alerted other police stations in the county.'

'Who is this villain?'

'He's a rogue who goes by the name of Bagsy Browne.'

Phillpotts started. 'Isn't that the man caught urinating on my lawn?'

'He did rather more than urinate, Bishop,' recalled Barnes, uncomfortably.

'There – that proves my point. This murder was intended to ridicule me. Browne is an irredeemable rascal who spurns the very existence of God. What better way to taunt me than by slaughtering someone in the shadow of the cathedral?'

'You're forgetting who the victim is,' said Colbeck, pointedly. 'You are still alive, Bishop, but the stationmaster is not. *He* was the one who aroused the ire of this suspect – and we must bear in mind that he is only a suspect at this stage – so our concern should be for him. I discern nothing in this crime that relates directly to you or indeed to the Almighty.'

'I endorse that,' said Steel. 'If Bagsy Browne *was* the killer, it was a simple act of revenge. All that Guy Fawkes Night means to a man like that is an excuse to get horribly drunk and attack my officers. He's almost illiterate, Bishop. He's never heard of the Gunpowder Plot or the part it plays in our history.'

Phillpotts was adamant. 'The man was trying to get back at *me*.'

Rising to his feet and using the voice he'd trained to reach every corner of the cathedral, he treated them to a long diatribe against the evils of atheism as embodied in the suspect. Pretending to listen politely, Colbeck soon came to the view that Steel's verdict on the bishop had been correct. He posed a problem. Quinnell might be disagreeable but at least he was supporting the investigation. Henry Phillpotts not only wanted to control it himself, he was trying to send it off in the wrong direction altogether. The sermon only served to make Colbeck more determined to stay and solve the crime. As the booming voice kept assaulting his ear, he was simmering with quiet anger. The bishop was undoubtedly sincere and, as his extensive library showed, he was a cultured man. But he was also sanctimonious and supercilious, treating them like commoners dragged into the palace to be chastised by royalty. Retribution was needed. Colbeck felt that it would be a pleasure to prove to Phillpotts that he was wrong, misguided and absurdly self-absorbed. It gave the investigation a new edge.

CHAPTER FOUR

Old habits died hard. Though he'd finally retired from the London & North Western Railway after a lifetime's service to it, Caleb Andrews was unable to enjoy a more leisurely existence. He still woke early every morning and he still ended the day by drinking at the pub near Euston station that he'd frequented with other railwaymen for decades. Over foaming pints of beer, he loved to hear where his friends had been and what incidents had occurred in the course of their work. Known for his irascibility and forthrightness, Andrews had mellowed. He no longer argued for the sake of argument. Nor did he remind those who'd been on the footplate beside him of dire mistakes they'd made in their early days. He was a short, sinewy man with a fringe beard and a wealth of experience behind him. Among other railwaymen, he felt appreciated.

When he got home that night, there was a distinct lack of appreciation.

'What time do you call this, Father?' challenged Madeleine.

'I've no idea,' he said, swaying slightly.

'You said that you'd be home early.'

'I got talking to Dirk Sowerby and the time flew past.'

'You promised that you'd be home by nine o'clock,' she said.

'I'm sorry I'm late, Maddy. Why didn't you go to bed?'

'You forgot to take your key with you – that's why.'

'Oh,' he said, chortling. 'That was stupid of me.'

'It's no laughing matter. I should have left you out in the cold all night, sleeping on the doorstep. That would have taught you.'

He took off his hat and scarf. 'You'd never do that to me, Maddy,' he said, jocularly. 'You're my daughter. You'd never let your dear old father down.'

'Then don't tempt me.'

Her tone was stern but they both knew that her threat would never be put into action. Madeleine loved him too much. She was an attractive woman in her twenties with a vitality and sense of independence that had caught Colbeck's attention when they first met. Now that she was on the verge of marriage to him, she could not have been happier. After looking after her widowed father for so long, it would be a wrench to leave him but she felt that it was time to go. Her life would be transformed. Madeleine would be exchanging a small house in Camden for a large one in Westminster. Instead of having to make all the major decisions relating to the household economy, she'd have servants to whom she could delegate a range of tasks.

When she helped her father off with his coat, she could smell the beer on his breath. Madeleine didn't begrudge him his pleasures. He'd earned them.

'Have you had any word from the inspector?' he asked.

She clicked her tongue. 'Don't you think it's high time you started calling him Robert? In less than a month he's going to be your son-in-law.'

'I don't like to be too familiar.'

'That's ridiculous, Father,' she said. 'And the answer to your question is that I've had nothing beyond the letter he sent this morning. He must be in Exeter now.'

'Well, I hope he doesn't stay there too long, Maddy. I'll be leading you down the aisle at the end of the month. I don't want to reach the altar to be told that the bridegroom is still hunting a killer in Devon.'

'Robert will solve the crime in plenty of time – I hope so, anyway.'

He put a consoling arm around her and led her across to a chair. Lowering her into it, he sat opposite and loosened his collar. Andrews was almost bashful.

'There's something I must tell you, Maddy.'

'What is it?'

'There's a reason that I was later than usual.'

'Yes,' she said, 'you got drunk and lost track of the time.'

He stiffened. 'I'm never drunk,' he insisted. 'I simply get merry. That's very different.' He ran his tongue over dry lips. 'What I need to tell you is this. Before too long, I may have a new friend – a lady friend.'

She was surprised. 'Is it someone I know?'

'I don't think so. Binnie is Dirk Sowerby's aunt, you see. That's why I fell into conversation with him this evening. It turns out that she's admired me for years. Her husband was a guard on my train in the old days but he died of smallpox. Mrs Langton – Binnie, that is – has been alone ever since.'

'Have you seen much of her?'

'That's the odd thing, Maddy – I haven't. We barely know each other. But I've bumped into her a few times at Euston and we've exchanged a word or two. She's a handsome woman and you'd never guess she was almost my age.'

Madeleine was cautious. She had no objection in principle to her father having a female friend or, indeed, to his marrying again. But she had a protective instinct and reserved the right to approve of the woman in question. The fact that Mrs Langton was Sowerby's aunt was reassuring. She knew and liked Dirk Sowerby, her father's most recent fireman. What troubled her was the fact that there'd been apparently accidental meetings near Euston. If she spoke to her nephew, Binnie Langton could easily find out when Andrews was likely to be near the station. Had the meetings been contrived? Could it be that she was setting her cap at him? The thought was worrying.

'You've done this before, you know,' she said.

'What do you mean?'

'Well, you've claimed that this woman or that has a soft spot for you but nothing ever came of it.'

'This time it's different.'

'But you hardly know the lady.'

'I hardly knew your mother when I fell in love with her, Maddy, but I was determined to marry her one day and I did. I'm a lot older and wiser now. It's not something I've rushed into,' he went on. 'I just feel that I'm ready now.'

'Ready?'

'Yes – ready to take things a stage further. Dirk has invited me to tea on his day off and Binnie will be there as well. It'll be a chance to get to know her.'

'Then I'm all in favour of it,' said Madeleine, getting up to kiss him on the forehead. 'You must make new friends now that you're retired. I hope that Mrs Langton turns out to be one of them.'

Though she smiled lovingly at him, her doubts remained.

After an early breakfast at the Acland Tavern, they repaired to the morgue. The coroner admitted them and took them into the room where the corpse lay on a table under a shroud. The icily cold weather had delayed decomposition but the stench was in any case offset by the herbs that had been scattered to sweeten the atmosphere. When Colbeck gave a nod, the coroner drew back the shroud so that the whole cadaver was displayed. Leeming gulped in disgust. What remained of the body was hideously blackened, the face mutilated and the skull cracked wide open. It reminded him of a roast pig he'd once seen turning on a spit. Colbeck examined the body in more detail before turning to the coroner, a lugubrious man in his seventies with wispy white hair and a goatee beard.

'Thank you,' said Colbeck, indicating that the shroud could be drawn back into position. 'Were there any effects found?'

'Every stitch of clothing was consumed by the fire, Inspector.'

'I was thinking about a watch, a ring or some other item that might have helped to identify him. I know that a lot of heat would have been generated but they might have survived the blaze.'

'There was nothing at all on or beside him,' said the coroner. 'Mr Michael Heygate commented on it. He said that his brother would never have removed his wedding ring and that he'd possessed a large silver pocket watch.'

'The killer was also a thief, then,' suggested Leeming. 'He took anything of value before he hid the body under the bonfire.'

'That was a mistake,' said Colbeck. 'If we catch him with stolen goods, they'll give him away.' He looked at the coroner. 'Did you know Mr Heygate?'

'Everyone knew him,' replied the other. 'As it happened, I attended the inquest for his wife and daughter. They were killed on the railway line in Plymouth. It was a terrible ordeal for him but he bore up well. Mr Heygate had such dignity.'

'Tell us about his brother – assuming that this *is* the stationmaster's body.'

The coroner frowned. 'The less said about the brother, the better.'

'Why is that?'

'They were not close, Inspector, even though Michael lives not far away in Dawlish. They were like chalk and cheese. Joel Heygate was a delightful man and his brother, I fear, is not.'

'What's wrong with him?' asked Leeming.

'That's all I'm prepared to say, Sergeant.'

'Were there any other close relatives?'

'None at all, as far as I know.'

'So who would stand to inherit his worldly goods?'

'That would have to be his brother – undeservedly, in my opinion.'

'It was kind of you to let us in so early,' said Colbeck, 'and we're grateful that you did so. In a profession like yours, you must have become acquainted with a large number of families in the city.'

'Everyone who dies an unexplained death needs a coroner.'

'That's a cheerful thought!' murmured Leeming.

'We cater for rich and poor alike. Men, women and children of all ages and all faiths have lain on that slab. We've had two Negroes, an Arab and a Chinaman. One gets to see a complete cross section of humanity as a coroner. What we haven't had,' he continued, glancing down at the body, 'are murder victims. To my knowledge, this is the second this century.'

'I hope it's the last.'

'Does the name Bagsy Browne mean anything to you?' asked Colbeck.

'Oh, yes,' said the coroner with a flash of vehemence. 'He's well known in these parts. From time to time, his name is in the newspapers with details of his latest crime. He's a menace, Inspector. There are a lot of people in Exeter who'd prefer it if it was Bagsy Browne's body under this shroud.'

He was fast asleep when she came bursting into the room. Adeline shook him by the shoulder but she failed to rouse him. She resorted to more drastic methods. Lifting his head up with one hand, she used the other to slap his cheeks hard. When he still refused to wake up, she reached for a jug of water and poured it over his face. Bagsy Browne let out a yell and sat bolt upright in bed.

'Damnation!' he exclaimed. 'I dreamt that I was drowning.'

'You've got to wake up.'

He opened a bleary eye. 'Is that you, Ad? Come back to bed.'

'You must read this first,' she said, brandishing a newspaper. 'The police are looking for you. There's even a reward being offered.'

Coming fully awake in an instant, he snatched the newspaper from her.

'Where's the bit about me?'

'It's at the bottom of the page.'

Unable to read properly, he needed her help to decipher all the words. While the report terrified Adeline, it caused him no unease. Instead, he guffawed.

'It's not funny, Bagsy. What if they come here?'

'Nobody would dare to give me away.'

'The police might search the premises.'

'I thought you all paid them to look the other way.'

'Only the ones who'll take money,' she said, 'and there aren't many of those. The others even turn down the offer of free entertainment.'

He was appalled. 'You'd never give your body to a peeler, surely?'

'I wouldn't but there are those who would – and who do. Anyway, forget about them, Bagsy. We have to get you out of here somehow.'

'But I'm enjoying it here. Did you get that pork pie for my breakfast?'

She was amazed at his calm. 'Aren't you afraid that they'll find you?'

'No,' he said, blithely. 'The peelers are looking for Bagsy Browne, that ugly bugger with the long hair and the beard. When I get rid of the hair and shave off the beard, they won't know me from Adam. Before that, however,' he went on, grabbing her and pulling her on to the bed, 'I'd like to work up an appetite for that pork pie.' Pulling off her clothes, he tossed them on to the floor. 'This is my idea of a hearty breakfast.'

The inquest was held in the coroner's court and it was packed to capacity. Colbeck was seated between Leeming and Superintendent Steel, who was almost friendly towards the detectives now. He was also more confiding. Colbeck put it down to the fact that he and Steel had together weathered the howling storm that was the Bishop of Exeter. It was a bonding experience. Each man had been impressed by the way that the other had withstood the wild threats and imprecations without blenching. As they tried to solve the crime, they knew that they would forever be hampered and hectored by the Right Reverend Henry Phillpotts.

When the jury was sworn in, the coroner maintained an expression of professional inscrutability. He was commendably thorough, questioning almost all of Heygate's staff at the railway station as well as other people who'd claimed to have seen him on the eve of Guy Fawkes Day. Everyone told much the same story. The stationmaster had gone about his duties in the usual way, then returned to his house in the evening. They all praised his unblemished record of service. Colbeck had to give Gervase Quinnell credit for one thing. In order to allow his employees to attend the inquest, he'd brought in staff from other stations under his aegis to cover for them. Quinnell himself sat at the rear, watching with keen interest.

Most people managed to answer the questions put to them, albeit tentatively, but the effort was too much for Dorcas Hope. Being in front of such a large gathering unnerved her and memories of the stationmaster's kindness to her kept lapping at her mind. Overcome with emotion, she was unable to get any coherent words out and had to be helped sobbing out of the court. The most confident performance came from Lawrence Woodford. After singing his predecessor's praises, he gave a clear account of everything that Heygate had done on the fatal day and said that the stationmaster had talked about going to see a bird that evening.

The coroner was surprised. 'Going to see a bird in the *dark*?'

'It was a barn owl. Joel had more or less tamed it by taking it food. And yes,' he added, 'it was after nightfall but there was a moon. Besides, Joel would have taken a lantern with him.'

'Is there a lantern missing from the station?'

'Yes, there is.'

'Did he say where he'd find this owl?'

'He said nothing to me.'

Colbeck was interested by this new piece of information. Unlike the others, Woodford was measured and articulate. In fact, it occurred to Colbeck that he was rather too articulate, like an actor who'd memorised his lines perfectly. The man was not so much giving evidence as auditioning for the post of stationmaster.

Colbeck nudged Leeming. 'Find out more about this gentleman, Victor.'

'He's a cocky devil, sir.'

'He's also too ambitious for my liking.'

All the witnesses so far had accepted that the dead man was unquestionably Joel Heygate and the fact that the police search for him had been futile supported this view. The next person to face the coroner contradicted everyone else. Agnes Rossiter had put on her best clothes for the occasion, including the new hat with the ostrich feathers. She went on the attack at once.

'I think it's dreadful the way that the rest of you want to bury poor Mr Heygate when he's not yet dead. He's still very much alive,' she asserted, looking around defiantly. 'He's just gone astray, that's all.'

'Why do you think that, Mrs Rossiter?' asked the coroner.

'If anything had happened to him, I would know.'

'On what grounds do you make that claim?'

'Mr Heygate and I were . . . close friends.' The announcement caused a buzz of curiosity. 'We agreed to meet at the bonfire but he never turned up.'

'Isn't that because he lay dead beneath the blaze?'

'No, no, no!' she shouted. 'I don't believe that. It's cruel of you to try to *make* me believe that. I know he's alive. I sense it.'

'We need rather more proof than that, Mrs Rossiter.'

'Can't you take my word for it? I knew him better than anyone.'

'Then where is he?'

'Give him time and he'll come back.'

'Why did he go away in the first place?'

'Mr Heygate will explain that.'

'Let me ask you this, then. If *he* was not the murder victim,' said the coroner, patiently, 'can you suggest who was?'

'It was someone else.'

'But nobody else has been reported missing. Superintendent Steel will confirm that. When I question him in due course, he will tell you that he has a suspect in mind who swore that he'd kill the stationmaster. In short, there is someone in this city with a motive and means to commit this crime. All that he had to do was to create the opportunity. What do you say to that?'

Mrs Rossiter was incapable of speech. Puce with rage, she rose to her feet and emitted a high-pitched cry of anguish, pointing to the coroner as if he'd just betrayed her then turning her fury on the superintendent. She was shaking violently all over. As the cry soared to become the sustained screech of a wild animal, she suddenly fell silent, went limp and collapsed on the floor in a heap.

The inquest was adjourned while she was given medical attention.

The detectives took the opportunity to go outside for some fresh air. They could hear members of the railway staff talking excitedly about Mrs Rossiter.

'What was your opinion of the lady, Victor?' asked Colbeck.

'I thought she was raving mad, sir.'

'I felt sorry for her. She just can't acknowledge that her friend is dead. Not that I think their friendship was all that close,' he went on. 'When she made that claim, there were gasps of astonishment from people who knew her. From everything we've heard today, we have a very clear idea of the sort of person the stationmaster was. When he was not on duty, he liked nothing better than gardening and birdwatching, things that are done on one's own. Do you think that Mrs Rossiter would have any appeal for a man like that?'

'Frankly,' said Leeming, 'she would not. I don't wish to be unkind but I fancy that she'd scare most men away – me among them.'

'Who else caught your eye?'

'Mr Woodford was the only one who seemed to know what he was talking about, though he was far too full of himself for my money. The others were too tongue-tied for the most part, especially that young girl.'

'They might be more forthcoming if they were questioned in less daunting surroundings. They're still very shocked by what happened. The girl was Dorcas Hope, who works as a waitress under Mrs Rossiter. I'd like to know what she thinks of the manageress.'

'I think she'd be too frightened to tell you, sir.'

Steel came over to join them. 'The inquest is not without its drama, is it?'

'No,' said Colbeck. 'Have you been convinced yet that the victim simply has to be Mr Heygate?'

'I'm waiting for the coroner's verdict.'

'That hasn't stopped you searching for Bagsy Browne, though.'

'No,' replied Steel. 'If we find him and he's guilty, he'll be hanged. If he turns out to be innocent, we'll run him out of Exeter.'

'Is this rogue the only suspect?' wondered Leeming.

'I suppose that he is at the moment.'

'At times like this, the inspector always asks *cuo benny*.'

'Actually,' said Colbeck, 'it's *cui bono?* but I'm sure that the superintendent is familiar with the phrase. Who stands to gain? In the sense that it will assuage his lust for revenge, it will obviously advantage Browne. What about other possibilities?'

Steel pondered. 'I suppose that Mr Woodford will be a beneficiary,' he said at length. 'He's almost certain to be promoted to the position of stationmaster. Indeed, when he was giving evidence, he was acting as if the job was his already.'

'Do we know how he and Mr Heygate got on?'

'I understand that there'd been some tension between them. Not that you'd have guessed it from the way that Woodford behaved in there. He presented himself as Heygate's best friend.'

'Then why didn't he show more grief?' asked Leeming.

Colbeck pursed his lips. 'Why didn't he show *any* grief?'

'I still think that Bagsy Browne may be our man,' said Steel.

'But only if the victim really was the stationmaster. If it's someone else, Browne is in the clear. In any case,' continued Colbeck, thinking it through, 'he would have needed access to Mr Heygate. That was impossible during the day because there were so many people about. After work – if we accept the testimony of Mr Woodford – the stationmaster went in search of an owl. How would Browne have known where he was going?'

'He could have been lurking near the house and followed him.'

'Where would the murder have taken place?'

'At some lonely spot in the woods, I daresay.'

'Why was his head repeatedly battered when one blow would surely have killed him?'

'Ah,' said Steel, 'I can answer that. It's Bagsy's signature. He does nothing by half-measures. I'm amazed that he left the head on the shoulders.'

'Let's go back to that *cui bono*,' advised Leeming. 'I've just thought of someone else who stands to profit and that's his brother, Michael Heygate. According to the coroner, he's the only relative. And there seems to have been no love lost between the two brothers. What sort of man is Michael Heygate, Superintendent?'

'Make up your own mind, Sergeant,' said the other. 'The gentleman will be called as a witness when the inquest resumes.'

When they filed back into the room, there was no sign of Agnes Rossiter. She'd been given smelling salts to revive her, then was examined by a doctor. Although he could find nothing physically wrong with her, she was sent home for the day. The coroner's court quickly filled up and more evidence was taken. Eventually, it was the turn of Michael Heygate, younger brother of the deceased. He'd been sitting beside his wife throughout the inquest and she squeezed his arm in encouragement when he was called. His appearance caused a little consternation because there was such an obvious likeness to the stationmaster. Indeed, some people found the similarity so close that it stirred up their grief and they had to avert their gaze.

Heygate had his brother's bulk and even sported a walrus moustache but he had none of the stationmaster's good humour. He was terse and rather churlish. After identifying himself, he said that he'd seen his brother alive on 4th November.

'At what time would that be?' asked the coroner.

'It was early evening,' said Heygate. 'We stayed the night so that we could go to the bonfire next day. We made a point of seeing Joel.'

'How did he seem to you?'

'He was much as usual – calm and polite.'

'Did you see him at the station?'

'No – it was at his house.'

'How long were you there?'

Heygate shrugged. 'Not long – ten minutes, maybe.'

'Did you often see each other?'

'Of course – Joel was my brother.'

'Did he say where he was going on the evening in question?'

'Not to me, he didn't.'

'There was no mention of an owl?'

'No.'

'He didn't discuss his hobby with you?'

'No.'

'And you never saw him after that evening?'

'Not until I saw the dead body – if it really *is* him, that is.'

'You're not sure?'

'No.'

'Can you suggest the name of anyone who may have harboured a grudge against your brother?'

Heygate shook his head. 'Everyone liked him.'

'Did he ever talk about threats made against him?'

'No.'

'Tell us about the conversation you had with him that evening.'

'There's nothing much to tell.'

Heygate was laconic. As he recalled the meeting with his brother, however, he went out of his way to emphasise how close the two of them were. In view of what the coroner had told them, Colbeck found the claim unconvincing. He also wondered why, having come to Exeter with his wife, they didn't spend the night at the stationmaster's house. Michael

Heygate concluded his evidence, then returned to his seat. Colbeck noticed the way that his wife immediately seized his hands in a gesture of congratulation. It was as if he'd just come through an important test. Mrs Heygate was a stringy woman in her forties with a face that looked plain in repose but that took on a kind of vulgar attraction when lit by a smile. As the inquest continued, the couple held hands.

Next to be called was the man who actually discovered the body in the embers of the fire. He freely admitted that the sight had made him vomit on the spot. What he would never forget, he said, was the image of the man's boots, burnt to a cinder yet still clinging to the bottoms of his feet. He'd signalled to one of the policemen on duty and the alarm was raised. Superintendent Steel was the last person to be questioned, explaining the action he'd taken once the crime had been reported to him and how he'd later had the corpse moved from the cathedral close. There could be no doubt that an unlawful killing had taken place. He explained that they were following various lines of enquiry but that a prime suspect had been identified.

Though he seemed a trifle doddery, the coroner had missed no detail of the proceedings. His summing up of the evidence gathered was both lucid and comprehensive. Guided by him, the jury declared that the dead man had to be Joel Heygate and returned a verdict of unnatural death at the hands of one or more persons as yet unknown.

Colbeck left the room with Leeming and came out into a cold November day.

'What would you do if you'd been the killer, Victor?'

'I'd be hundreds of miles away by now, sir,' replied Leeming.

'I'm not sure that *I* would,' said Colbeck, meditatively. 'This crime was inspired by hatred. If I'd been the man who committed it, I think that I'd have come to the inquest in order to gloat.'

As Colbeck was speaking, somebody brushed past his shoulder. Bagsy Browne had emerged from the courthouse wearing a long coat, a greasy cap and a scarf that covered the lower part of his clean-shaven face. He melted into the crowd.

CHAPTER FIVE

Most people outside the courthouse had started to disperse but Gervase Quinnell held his ground in order to speak to Michael Heygate. He'd never met the stationmaster's brother before and he'd been struck by the physical resemblance between them. In character, however, there were clearly marked differences. Heygate and his wife had lingered in order to talk to the coroner. When they finally emerged, they saw that most people had now gone. One of the exceptions was Quinnell and he bore down on them with his features composed into a study in bereavement. He introduced himself with an air of condescension. Heygate, in turn, introduced his wife, Lavinia. Realising the man's position in the South Devon Railway, they were deferential towards him.

'Let me begin by offering my condolences,' said Quinnell. 'This is a tragedy, an absolute tragedy. It must have come as an appalling shock to you.'

'It did, sir,' agreed Heygate.

'Michael and I still haven't got used to the idea,' said Lavinia.

'The inquest has at least clarified the situation,' Quinnell pointed out. 'There was never a scintilla of doubt in my mind as to the identity of the victim. After all the evidence that was gathered today, even Mrs Rossiter must now admit that it was Joel Heygate.' He lowered his voice. 'By the way, I always got the impression that your brother preferred his own company. Is it true that he and Mrs Rossiter were close friends?'

'He never mentioned her to us,' said Heygate.

'Was she ever at the house when you called?'

'No, sir, she wasn't.'

'Then why should she claim to be rather more than a work colleague?'

'I've no idea.'

'I think that the occasion was too much for her. She was overwhelmed. The poor lady was clearly under great stress.'

'My brother-in-law was happily married, sir,' said Lavinia. 'He never looked at another woman while his wife was alive and I'm sure he didn't do so after her death. Joel was . . . not that sort of man.'

'That was my feeling,' said Quinnell, extracting his gold watch from a waistcoat pocket and glancing at it. 'I can't stay long. I have a meeting to attend fairly soon.' He put the watch away and buttoned up his coat. 'I just wanted to ask if you'd made any plans for the funeral.'

Heygate looked blank. 'We couldn't do that until we knew it was Joel.'

'No, of course, you couldn't.'

'And we don't know when the body will be released to us.'

'I can expedite that,' said Quinnell. 'There's no point in a post-mortem when the cause of death is so glaringly obvious. I'm sure that you'd like the funeral to be as soon as possible. I suggest that you talk to the undertaker about arrangements.' The couple exchanged a worried glance. 'No cost whatsoever will be incurred by you, incidentally. We – the railway company, I mean – will take care of any bills.'

Lavinia brightened. 'That's very kind of you, sir.'

'He was a valued employee. It's the least we can do.'

'Thank you, sir,' said Heygate, 'it's a load off our mind. We have very limited means. My wife and I were anxious about the costs incurred.'

Quinnell was grandiloquent. 'There's no need to be,' he said, raising a gloved palm. 'All will be taken care of, Mr Heygate – funeral and memorial service.'

'What memorial service?' asked Lavinia, mystified.

'We never thought about that,' admitted Heygate.

'That's because you don't know how important a person your brother was in Exeter,' said Quinnell. 'He was widely admired and had a legion of friends. His popularity went well beyond the city. We've had dozens of letters of condolence from visitors from other parts of the county. They all remember the cheerful welcome they got when they stepped on to the platform. A memorial service is a means of letting the wider community express its feelings.'

Heygate was dubious. 'Well . . . if you say so, Mr Quinnell,' he said, uneasily. 'Perhaps you can help us with something else,' he went on. 'As you may be aware, I'm Joel's next of kin. There are no other close relatives so he'll have left everything to me, I daresay.'

'That's a fair assumption, Mr Heygate.'

'Would it be possible to have some of the contents of the house now?'

'No, I'm afraid not.'

'But they'll be coming to us in due course.'

'That makes no difference.'

Lavinia was piqued. 'Why do we have to wait?'

'There are legal obligations to observe,' explained Quinnell. 'To begin with, I'm not even sure if he made a will. Knowing what a careful man he was, I'm almost certain that he did but, if not, he'll have died intestate. Complications can arise then.'

'What sort of complications?'

'You'll have to ask your brother's solicitor.'

Heygate was irritated. 'What's to stop us taking a few odds and ends now?'

'The house is the property of the South Devon Railway,' said Quinnell with quiet firmness, 'and you don't even have the right to cross the threshold as yet.'

'Why not? What harm can it do?'

'We have to follow the correct procedure.'

'But there are things that Joel promised to us,' said Lavinia, nudging her husband. 'Isn't that so, Michael?'

'Yes, it is.'

'So, by rights, they already belong to us.'

'You'll have to be patient, Mrs Heygate,' warned Quinnell. 'The law must take its course and it can't be rushed. Until then, nothing must leave the premises. If it had been my decision, that canary would still be there.'

'Do you mean Peter?'

'Yes, that was his name. I was only persuaded to let him

go when I feared that he might starve to death if left alone in the house.'

'He should have come to us,' said Heygate in annoyance.

'Yes,' added Lavinia. 'Peter is ours now.'

'Have you ever looked after the bird before?' asked Quinnell.

'Well, no, sir – to be honest, we haven't.'

'But we would have done if Joel had asked us,' affirmed Heygate.

'The person who *did* look after him while your brother was away,' said Quinnell, 'was the waitress who works in the refreshment room – Miss Hope. I'm assured by Mr Woodford that the canary has gone to a good home.'

'This is ridiculous,' said Heygate, hotly. 'A slip of a waitress is allowed to take something from the house but I'm given nothing even though everything there is mine.' He took a moment to control his temper. 'Can't we at least go into the house?'

'No, Mr Heygate, I'm afraid that you can't.'

'What's to stop me?'

'Inspector Colbeck wants everyone to be kept out of it.'

'Is he that detective from London?'

'Yes,' said Quinnell, 'I summoned him personally. He believes that the house may hold clues as to where your brother was going on the fatal night. Now that the inquest is over, he and Superintendent Steel will be conducting a thorough search of the property.'

The first thing that Colbeck noticed about the house was that it was also a shrine to the stationmaster's wife and daughter. Nothing that they ever had worn or owned had been thrown out. The daughter's room had been preserved exactly as it had been on the day of her death with toys, books and a doll's house in their usual place as if the girl was about to return at any moment. It was the same in the main bedroom where a whole wardrobe was given over to the wife's attire and where her possessions were on display everywhere. Joel Heygate had kept them alive in his heart. Agnes Rossiter's claim was demonstrably false. The idea that such a loving husband and father would let another woman take the place of a wife and daughter was ludicrous. In the privacy of his home, the stationmaster had all that he wanted.

Colbeck and Steel were systematic. They went from room to room, sifting through various items and comparing notes as they did so. There were a number of books about birds and some old copies of the *Railway Times* and of Herapath's *Railway Journal*. Of most interest was a series of letters, tied with a ribbon and kept in the drawer of a sideboard. As he read through them, Colbeck came to one that was signed by Michael Heygate. It had been dashed off when he was seething with anger and disappointment. Heygate was blaming his elder brother for not coming to his rescue when his business venture in Dawlish got into serious financial trouble.

'This confirms what we heard from the coroner,' said Colbeck, passing the letter to Steel. 'The two brothers were not exactly good friends.'

Steel read the missive. 'The language is rather intemperate,' he noted. 'I'm not sure that *I'd* remain friends with someone who hurled abuse at me like this.'

'Look at the date, Superintendent.'

'It was last May,' noted the other.

'That's six months ago,' said Colbeck. 'It may well be that they haven't even seen each other since then. Michael Heygate's letter comes close to breaking off all relations with his brother.'

'He gave a very different impression at the inquest.'

'I was watching his wife. She gave him a broad smile at one point. Her brother-in-law had been battered to death then burnt in a bonfire. What possible reason could she have to smile?'

Steel handed the letter back. 'That's very revealing, Inspector,' he said. 'It may be that Bagsy Browne is not a lone suspect, after all. Someone else had a strong motive as well. We know that Michael Heygate was in Exeter on the night that his brother was murdered. And we know – because he admitted it – that he actually met the stationmaster.'

'That puzzled me,' recalled Colbeck. 'He said that he and his wife had come to see the bonfire. Why come on the eve of Guy Fawkes Day instead of on the day itself? It's only a short train ride from Dawlish, isn't it?'

'It's a mere four stops away – Exeter St Thomas, Exminster, Starcross and then Dawlish. There was no reason to be here a day earlier.'

'Do you stay with family members when you're in their neck of the woods?'

'It's usually the main reason for the visit, Inspector.'

'So why didn't they spend the night under this roof?'

'The letter explains that.'

'It also makes it clear that Michael Heygate and his wife were very short of money. Did they stay with friends in Exeter or at an inn? If it's the latter, it raises the question of how they could afford it. Talking of money,' he went on, 'have you noticed anything about our search?'

'Yes,' said Steel, 'there's no cash whatsoever in the house – unless it's been carefully hidden, that is.'

'Presumably Mr Heygate would have had access to the station safe. Even so,' said Colbeck, thoughtfully, 'he'd need money for running expenses. You'd expect to find *some* ready cash on the premises.'

'Unless it was stolen,' conjectured Steel. 'Stolen to pay for a night or two at an inn, perhaps? Michael Heygate could afford it if he'd robbed his brother.'

Colbeck advised caution. 'We're getting ahead of ourselves, Superintendent. I think we need to question him – and his wife, for that matter – before we jump to any conclusions. What our search has uncovered is a rift between the two brothers. That, in itself, is enough to designate Michael Heygate as a possible suspect. But,' he added, 'we have to remember that there is another one.'

'Bagsy Browne remains the most likely culprit.'

'I was thinking of Lawrence Woodford,' said Colbeck. 'That's why I've asked Sergeant Leeming to take a closer look at the new stationmaster. Ambition can sometimes drive a man as hard as brotherly hatred – even harder in some cases.'

'I agree. It can gnaw at a man's soul.'

'Indeed, it can. By the way, I need to ask a favour of you.'

'What's that, Inspector?'

'Can you spare a man to stand guard on this house?'

'Is that necessary? Nobody is likely to come here.'

'You're overlooking something,' said Colbeck. 'According to the coroner, no effects were found on or near the deceased. When he went out that evening, Mr Heygate must have been carrying his key. Where is it?'

'The killer must have it,' said Steel.

'That's what I deduced. What if he stole it in order to use it?'

Dorcas Hope held the key in the palm of her hand and studied it with mingled pride and regret. She felt honoured that it had been entrusted to her but sad that she'd never be able to use it again. If, as expected, he was confirmed as the new stationmaster, Lawrence Woodford would move into the house in time and Dorcas would have no reason to go there. Her first impulse would be to return the key but that would involve explanations to the police and she wanted to avoid that. She was still jangled by her appearance at the inquest. Having to speak in front of all those people had shredded her nerves and sent her scuttling back home. She could simply not face the ordeal of returning to work that day. She needed time to recover. In the safety of her bedroom, she'd taken the key out from its hiding place under her bedroom carpet. It was a symbol of the friendship between her and Joel Heygate. He could have asked his cleaner, Mrs Penhallurick, to feed the canary when he was away but he'd chosen Dorcas instead. That meant a great deal to her.

After turning the key over a few times, she replaced it under the carpet and went downstairs. Her mood might have been sombre but Peter was in high spirits, chirping away and hopping nimbly around his cage. From time to time, he'd stop and hold his head to one side as he peered out through the bars. In the short time he'd been in the house, he'd provided Maud Hope with endless amusement.

Seated beside the table on which the cage stood, she looked up as her daughter entered the room.

'How are you feeling now, Dorcas?'

'I feel so sad and lonely. I'll never see Mr Heygate again.'

Maud sighed. 'None of us will.'

'Going to work won't be the same,' said Dorcas. 'It was such a pleasure to talk to him every day and I loved to peep through the window of the house to see Peter jumping about.'

'That's one thing you can still do,' said Maud. 'He's a lovely companion. It's such a big cage for a tiny bird like that. Your arm must have ached after you carried him all the way from the station.'

'It was rather heavy.'

'Will we be allowed to keep him?'

'I don't think anyone else would want Peter.'

'What about Mr Heygate's brother?'

'He wasn't really interested in pets, Mother. He used to keep a dog but he treated it so badly that it died. Mr Heygate told me about it. He was disgusted.'

'And so he should be. Peter can stay as long as he wishes.'

'Thank you.'

'He knows that he's among friends.' She looked at her daughter's anguished face. 'Will you be able to go back to work tomorrow?'

'I think I'll have to,' said Dorcas without enthusiasm. 'They only found someone to take over from me for one day. Mrs Rossiter and I will be needed in the refreshment room. If we're not there, Mr Woodford will want to know why.'

Lawrence Woodford didn't stay away from the station any longer than necessary. As soon as the inquest was over, he hurried back there to resume his duties and to relieve the man who'd temporarily replaced him. Within minutes, he was strutting up and down the platform and exuding a sense of ownership. Exeter St David's was now his.

Victor Leeming chose his moment. After checking the timetable, he waited until there was a sizeable gap before the arrival of the next train, then he called on Woodford in the stationmaster's office.

'I thought you spoke very well at the inquest, Mr Woodford,' he began.

'That's good of you to say so, Sergeant.'

'And I do admire the way you've kept this station running.'

'Someone had to maintain the high standards set by Joel.'

'Had you always yearned to be a stationmaster?'

'Yes,' replied Woodford. 'It's an ambition I've had for a long time. When the post here was advertised, I applied for it along with Joel Heygate but it was felt that I was too young at the time. The right decision was made,' he conceded. 'He was definitely the better man for the job and he proved it.'

Leeming was not persuaded that he was being entirely honest. Woodford was quick to praise the man whose job he'd taken over but he was not doing that job in the same spirit. Heygate, by all accounts, had won the respect and affection of the staff, whereas the new stationmaster – Leeming had watched him carefully – was much more dictatorial. He liked to exercise authority and he put people's backs up in the process. Though he kept the station running efficiently, Woodford didn't endear himself to those below him. Devastated by the death of a beloved stationmaster, they were visibly unhappy about the regime that had now been put into place.

'Tell me about the owl,' suggested Leeming.

'What owl is that, Sergeant?'

'The one you mentioned at the inquest.'

'Oh, that,' said Woodford, coming close to a sneer. 'Joel was always getting distracted by one bird or another. He had a thing about them. When he found an injured pigeon on the platform here, he nursed it for weeks before it was able to fly again. Then there was that canary of his, of course.'

'I want to hear about the owl.'

'I can't add anything to what I said earlier. He'd found it somewhere and sort of adopted it. I'm not sure that I would have bothered,' he went on with a half-laugh. 'I've got better things to do of an evening than go out in the cold looking for an owl.'

'What *were* you doing that evening?' asked Leeming, casually.

'I worked late here then called in at a pub for a drink.'

'Which pub would that be, Mr Woodford?'

The stationmaster became suspicious. 'Why do you ask?'

'I just wanted to know, that's all. The inspector and I are staying at the Acland Tavern, where they brew their own beer. I can't say that it's to my taste. If you can recommend another pub, I'd be grateful.'

'I always go to the Barnstaple Inn in Lower North Street.'

'Do they serve a good pint?'

'I like it and it's convenient. I live only a short distance away.'

Leeming looked around. 'You've got plenty of room here, I must say. My office at Scotland Yard is like a broom cupboard. This is much bigger and Mr Heygate obviously kept it very tidy.'

'That was his way, Sergeant, and it's mine as well.'

'In due course, I daresay, you'll take over the stationmaster's house.'

'There's no guarantee of that,' said Woodford. 'The post will have to be advertised. I'll apply for it, naturally, but there's bound to be competition.'

'But if you do get it – and I suspect you have an extremely good chance of doing so – then you'll be here on the premises, so to speak. What would you do with your other house?'

'Oh, we'd sell that. It's what Joel did when he took on the job and it's what my wife thinks we should do. Why pay for the overheads on one property when you can have another one rent-free? Joel made a tidy profit on his other house when he sold it,' he recalled. 'And he was never one to throw his money about. Most of it would have been salted away in a bank.'

Leeming's ears pricked up. 'So someone stands to inherit a fair amount?'

'Yes,' said Woodford, curling a lip. 'Unfortunately, that someone will be Michael Heygate. If he was *my* brother,' he went on rancorously, 'I wouldn't leave the bastard a single penny.'

As the train chugged south along the coastline, neither of them spared the scenic view a glance. Seated beside each other, Michael and Lavinia Heygate were far too preoccupied. She squeezed his arm in appreciation.

'You were wonderful at the inquest, Michael.'

'I enjoyed it,' he said, smugly.

'It was so different from the last time we were there.'

'Yes, I actually felt sorry for Joel then. It was horrible for him to lose Marion and young Olivia in that accident. I thought it might draw me and him closer – but it didn't. That inquest was gruelling.'

'What about this one?'

He grinned. 'I didn't feel sorry for him at all.'

'Neither did I,' she said. 'Everybody else was sitting there with sad faces and I was almost laughing inside. We've got what we want at last.'

'Yes, Lavinia – we can pay off our debts and have some pleasure out of life again. It's no more than we deserve,' he said. 'Joel should have helped us earlier. We have two children to support, whereas he was all alone. Yet he turned us down flat.'

She was harsh. 'I'll weep no tears for him.'

'All we have to do is to wear the right face at the funeral.'

'What about the memorial service Mr Quinnell talked about?'

'I'd forgotten that,' he said, 'and I'm against it. I don't want to sit there and listen to person after person saying kind things about Joel. He was no brother to me. He was an uncaring swine and I'm glad we got rid of him at last.'

Though he hadn't deigned to attend the inquest, Henry Phillpotts made sure that he had a pair of eyes and ears present. A full report of the event was written and handed to him. As he sat behind his desk in the library, he scrutinised the report. It caused him to suck his teeth and issue an occasional grunt of displeasure. As soon as he'd finished it, he set it aside, reached for a sheet of writing paper and took up his pen. His hand moved gracefully for a few minutes then he paused to read the letter before appending his signature. Picking up a little bell, he rang it a couple of times. Almost immediately, Ralph Barnes came in dutifully from the adjoining room.

'What can I do for you, Bishop?' he asked.

Phillpotts handed him the letter. 'Read that.'

The secretary did as he was told, noticing that the words were given more impact by the beautiful calligraphy. He put the missive on the desk.

'I can't fault it, Bishop,' he said. 'It's clear, concise and authoritative.'

'It should produce the desired result. I wish I'd written it earlier. It must be dispatched immediately,' said Phillpotts with polite malice. 'I'll stand for no more of it. Someone has to put salt on Inspector Colbeck's tail.'

'I lied about this beer,' said Leeming, quaffing his pint. 'I think it's very good.'

'You've earned it, Victor.'

'It's much better than the stuff they sell at the Barnstaple Inn.'

Colbeck smiled. 'Oh, you sampled that, did you?'

'Well, since I was there, I thought I might as well.'

It was evening and they'd adjourned to the Acland Tavern. Over restorative drinks, they were pooling the information they'd gathered. After interviewing Woodford, the sergeant had talked to other members of the station staff. He'd then made his way to the Barnstaple Inn in Lower North Street.

'There's never any harm in checking, sir,' he said.

'I'm very glad that you did.'

'The landlord knew Mr Woodford well because he goes in there a lot. But he wasn't there on the night before Guy Fawkes Day. Mr Woodford lied.'

'Was the landlord certain about that?'

'Yes, sir – he knows his regular customers.'

'Do you think that Woodford deliberately misled you?'

'I'm sure that he did, sir. But how did you get on at the house?'

'Oh, we discovered that someone else can tell barefaced lies. His name is Michael Heygate.'

Colbeck went on to discuss the search he'd made with the superintendent. The brother's letter had been significant and the absence of any cash was very worrying. Leeming agreed that it had been wise to leave a policeman on guard at the house.

'So,' he said, 'we have two additional suspects. Which one is the killer?'

'It's too early to tell, Victor,' replied Colbeck. 'One thing is certain. They'd never have acted together. Woodford was impelled by envy whereas the brother would have been activated by hatred. The question is whether or not his wife was party to the murder or even directly involved in it.'

'Mrs Heygate wouldn't be the first female killer we've arrested.'

'Superintendent Steel still favours Bagsy Browne.'

'That's not surprising, sir. He's a seasoned criminal whereas the others are not. I just wonder why the police haven't caught him yet.'

'From what I've heard, he's a slippery customer and he's as bold as brass. Well, you'd have to be to relieve yourself on the bishop's lawn.' Leeming chortled. 'Bishop

Phillpotts didn't find it very funny,' Colbeck went on. 'He'd like nothing better than to see Browne dangling from the gallows.'

Adeline Goss didn't even hear him come in. She was dozing on the bed that evening when she felt something brush across her face like a cobweb. When she tried to push it aside, she found herself holding the tassels of a beautiful silk shawl.

'Bagsy!' she cried, sitting up.

'I brought you a gift, Ad,' he said, letting go of the shawl.

She ran it between her fingers. 'It feels like real silk.'

'You deserve only the best, my love.'

'Thank you, Bagsy.' She put it around her shoulders but it was rather skimpy on her. 'How does it look?'

'Not as nice as I'd expected. The woman I stole it from was smaller than you. I'll choose a bigger target next time.' He sat on the bed and stole a kiss. 'It's my way of saying thank you, Ad. After what I've done, a lot of women would have turned me away in horror but you let me hide here. I'm grateful.'

'There's always a place for you here, Bagsy,' she said, seriously, 'whatever you've done. I don't care if you burn down the bleeding cathedral.'

He cackled merrily. 'Now there's a good idea . . .'

CHAPTER SIX

When she got to the stationmaster's house that morning, Dorcas was disturbed to find a uniformed policeman on guard outside it. It was a chilling reminder that its former occupant had died a hideous death. Now that she'd taken the canary into her own home, there was no point in peeping through the window for a glimpse of Peter. She was therefore glad to hurry past the house and walk along the platform. Because she'd left the inquest before Mrs Rossiter gave her evidence, she was quite unaware of the manageress's outburst and subsequent collapse. All that she knew was that Mrs Rossiter – in the face of damning evidence – was steadfastly refusing to believe that Joel Heygate was dead. At least, that had been the case when the two women were last together. As she entered the refreshment room, she discovered that the situation had altered dramatically. Agnes Rossiter had not only been compelled to accept the truth, she'd somehow promoted herself to the status of Heygate's widow. Standing behind the counter, she was wearing full mourning dress with a black lace hat and gloves. It was an incongruous sight. She looked as if she should be at home, weeping into a black-edged handkerchief, rather than moving teacups about. Dorcas was stunned by the extreme to which the woman had now gone.

'There you are at last, girl,' said Mrs Rossiter with a censorious sniff. 'I thought you'd never come. Mr Heygate would have disapproved.'

'But I'm earlier than usual, Mrs Rossiter.'

'That makes no difference. I *feel* as if you're late.'

'How long have you been here?'

'I came in over an hour ago. In deference to Mr Heygate's memory, I was prepared to put in extra time without hope of any reward. I'd like to think that you might do the same but that was too much to expect.'

Dorcas went over to her. 'Do you feel well, Mrs Rossiter?'

'What an absurd question! How can anyone feel well in the wake of a tragedy like the one I have to endure? I'm mourning a great man and a special friend.'

'Do you really think you should have come into work this morning?'

'It's my *duty*, Miss Hope. I had to come.'

'Have you spoken to Mr Woodford?'

'I'm only answerable to Mr Heygate and his precious memory,' said Mrs Rossiter, brusquely, 'so I suggest that you take off your coat and hat and get to work. Before too long, the next train will be due.'

Dorcas obeyed but she was very worried about Mrs Rossiter's state of mind and wondered what the new stationmaster would say when he saw the older woman behind the counter. A manageress in widow's weeds was not the most inspiring welcome for any customers entering the refreshment room. In the event, it was not Woodford who first appeared but Colbeck and Leeming. Having heard Mrs Rossiter's impassioned denial of Joel Heygate's death, they were astonished to find that she was now marking it as if she were the bereaved wife. Leeming gasped in amazement but Colbeck was anxious about the woman. With her flashing eyes and waving arms, she looked quite deranged.

'What may we get you, gentlemen?' she asked.

'Actually,' said Colbeck, 'I wanted a private word with Miss Hope. Sergeant Leeming and I have come from London to investigate the murder. My name is Inspector Colbeck, by the way. We were at the inquest yesterday when you seemed to think that the victim had been wrongly identified.'

'I sensed that it had,' said Mrs Rossiter, 'because we had such a bond between us. This morning, however, it was very different. The moment I opened my eyes, I knew that it had to be Joel – dear Mr Heygate – and I felt obliged to mourn him in the proper way.'

Dorcas was nervous. 'Why do you want to speak to me, Inspector?'

'I'd like to speak to you both in turn, Miss Hope, but I can't take you out of here together or nobody would be served refreshments.'

'You can't have my assistant,' complained the manageress. 'I need her.'

'All that you need is a willing pair of hands,' said Colbeck, 'and I'm sure that the sergeant will provide them.'

Leeming was aghast. 'You want me to act as *waitress*, sir?'

'Only for a short time, Victor – you'll cope admirably.'

'But I've never worked in a refreshment room before.'

'Mrs Rossiter will teach you all you need to know.'

'Yes,' she said, regarding him sternly, 'and the first thing you must do is to take off your coat and hat. There's a spare apron under the counter. You can put that on. Appearance is everything in here.'

'I can't see how this will solve a murder,' grumbled Leeming.

'You're solving a problem of keeping the refreshment room *open*,' Colbeck told him, 'and we're very grateful.'

He took Dorcas out and escorted her to the stationmaster's office. Quinnell had given him permission to use it whenever necessary and Woodford had been quick to agree. It was empty when they got there so they stepped out of the cold. Dorcas was fearful, eyes widening and stomach churning. She was glad when Colbeck doffed his hat. He looked less intimidating now. He offered her a chair then sat opposite her.

'There's no need to be afraid,' he soothed. 'You're not in any kind of trouble. It's just that you may be able to help us.'

'I said all I know at the inquest, sir – until it got too much for me, that is.'

'I felt that there were things you may have overlooked.'

Dorcas was confused. 'Were you there, sir?'

'Yes, we were.' He appraised her. 'You're the young lady we saw when we first arrived here, I fancy. You were carrying a large birdcage.'

'That was Mr Heygate's canary. His name is Peter. I used to look after him when Mr Heygate was away.' Her face clouded. 'I've done nothing wrong, have I, sir? Mr Woodford said I could have Peter. It's not against the law, is it?'

'Not at all,' said Colbeck with a smile. 'I'm only glad that the bird has gone to someone who'll care for him. When the superintendent and I searched the house yesterday, we found a couple of books on canaries.'

'Mr Heygate loved birds.'

'Yes, I'm told that he rescued an injured pigeon once and nursed it back to health. Is that true?'

'Oh, yes,' she said, gathering confidence, 'it was lying on the track. I was allowed to feed the pigeon sometimes. He kept it here in the back room. We called it Lucky because it almost got run over by a train.'

'It sounds to me as if it was lucky in finding people like you and Mr Heygate as well. You obviously have an affinity for birds.'

'What does that mean, sir?'

'You like them and they like you.'

'Well, yes, that's true. But Mr Heygate was the expert.'

'Did he ever mention a barn owl to you?'

'Oh, he did,' she replied, shedding her apprehension and talking with a degree of excitement. 'He stumbled on it by accident when he was out walking. He used to go and see it after dark and take it food. That was the best time, he said. The owl came to the shed most nights.'

'Do you happen to know where that shed was, Miss Hope?'

'No, sir, but it wasn't all that far away. Mr Heygate said that it only took him a quarter of an hour to get there.'

'According to Mr Woodford,' said Colbeck, 'he was going to see the owl on the night that he was . . . on the night that he disappeared. Did you know about that?'

'Yes, sir – Mr Heygate told me.'

'You were obviously a friend in whom he could confide.'

'He was a very nice man.'

'You must have gone into his house a number of times.'

'Yes – and not only to feed Peter. Mr Heygate invited me to tea on a Sunday once in a while. My parents were happy to let me go. They knew they could trust him.'

'Did you ever see any sign of money in the house?'

'Money?'

'Mr Heygate earned a good wage, yet we found no sign of money in the house and we searched hard. I wonder if he had a hiding place somewhere.'

'I'm sorry, Inspector. I wouldn't know about that.'

'Fair enough,' he said. 'Do you like working here, Miss Hope?'

She was hesitant. 'I used to like it.'

'What about now?'

'Things have changed. Mr Woodford is . . .' She needed time to find the right words. 'Well, he's very different and Mrs Rossiter is behaving strangely. She's nothing to do with Mr Heygate's family but she's pretending that she is. To be honest, sir, I was upset when I saw her dressed up like that.'

'I can imagine,' said Colbeck. 'What we need to establish is where exactly Mr Heygate was going that night when he set off to see this owl. You may not know. Is there anyone else who might?'

'No, sir – he was a very private man.'

'So we've discovered.'

'But there is *one* way to find out where he went.'

Colbeck's interest quickened. 'Is there?'

'Yes, sir,' she said. 'Mr Heygate kept a diary. He always made a note of where he'd seen certain birds. It was his hobby, you see.'

'We found no diary during our search and we were very thorough.'

'It ought to be there somewhere, sir. All you have to do is to look at the diary and it will tell you what you want to know.'

Victor Leeming had a well-earned reputation for handling a crisis and police work had given him plenty of practice. One thing he'd never done, however, was to handle a sudden influx of customers who poured out of a train and demanded refreshments before they continued their journey to Plymouth. Caught up in a whirl of non-stop activity, he could only marvel at the way that Mrs Rossiter took a stream of orders, accepted payment for them and set tea and food on the counter for Leeming to carry to respective tables. He was embarrassed to be wearing an apron and humiliated by being treated as a menial. The occasional tip did nothing to sweeten his temper. Passengers were given fair warning when the train was about to depart and they left in a solid group. Overwhelmed with relief, Leeming collapsed on to a chair.

'There's no time to sit down, Sergeant,' snapped the manageress. 'The tables need clearing and you can wash some of the crockery.'

He stood up wearily. 'Is it always like this?'

'No, we're usually much busier.'

He began to collect teacups and plates from the tables before stacking them on the counter. Mrs Rossiter, meanwhile, was boiling a fresh supply of water in readiness for the next invasion. When he heard the door open, Leeming feared another horde of passengers but it was only the stationmaster.

'Good God!' yelled Woodford, seeing the manageress for the first time that morning. 'What on earth do you think you're doing?'

'I'm remaining at my post out of loyalty to Mr Heygate,' she said, crisply.

'You can't work in here dressed like that.'

'I can and I will, Mr Woodford.'

'Think how it must look to our customers,' said the stationmaster. 'They want to eat and drink – not to take part in a funeral service.' He stared at Leeming's apron. 'And whatever are *you* doing, Sergeant?'

'It wasn't my idea,' said the other, disconsolately.

'Where's Miss Hope?'

'She's being interviewed by Inspector Colbeck.'

'Did I hear my name being taken in vain?' asked Colbeck, entering the room with Dorcas. 'I've brought your waitress back, Mrs Rossiter.'

She tossed her head. 'Not before time, if I may say so.'

'This is preposterous,' said Woodford, taking charge. 'I'm sorry, Mrs Rossiter, but I can't allow you to deal with the general public in mourning garb. You must either change into something more presentable or stay at home until you're ready to do so. I suggest that you leave at once.'

'I refuse to go,' she said, folding her arms.

'I'm giving you an order.'

'I prefer to obey my instincts.'

'If you don't do as you're told,' he warned, 'then you'll face dismissal.'

She was visibly shaken by the threat and Dorcas was utterly dismayed. Trying to relieve the tension, Colbeck stepped in with an emollient smile.

'There's no need for talk of dismissal,' he said. 'Mrs Rossiter is clearly an asset to this refreshment room. As it happens, I need to speak to her alone, so I'll borrow her if I may. I'm sure that Mrs Rossiter is as eager as the rest of us to move the investigation on to the next stage. Isn't that so?'

'Yes, it is, Inspector,' she confirmed.

'Very well,' said Woodford, 'but I'm not having any member of the staff dressed in mourning wear. When you've concluded your interview, Inspector, don't send her back in here.'

'Leave it to me,' suggested Colbeck. 'Mrs Rossiter and I have a lot to discuss. I'll certainly be touching on the subject of her appearance.' He indicated the door. 'Shall we go, Mrs Rossiter?'

She weighed up the situation carefully, looking first at the grim countenance of the stationmaster, then at Colbeck. After deliberation, she picked up her reticule, took her coat from its hook and walked towards the door.

Dorcas was alarmed. 'I can't manage in here on my own.'

'You won't have to,' said Colbeck. 'The sergeant will assist you.'

Leeming turned puce. 'Am I to be subservient to a *waitress*?'

'It could be worse, Victor.'

'That's impossible.'

'Think what Superintendent Tallis would say if he saw you in that apron.'

Edward Tallis sat behind his desk in a cloud of cigar smoke. Whenever he was under real pressure, he reached for a cigar in the mistaken belief that it helped his thought processes. In fact, it dulled his mind, shortened his breath, darkened his teeth and left him with an unpleasant taste in his mouth. Notwithstanding that, he enjoyed the act of smoking. It was one of the few luxuries that he allowed himself. Picking up the letter that lay on his desk, he read it for the fifth time. Each word was a sharp pinprick and the cumulative effect was painful. Tallis did not take criticism easily. When it was serious criticism, he was even less inclined to accept it and was adept at unloading it on to somebody else. Inhaling deeply, he then blew out more smoke to thicken the fug and ground his cigar into the ashtray with a vengeance. Tallis stood up, brushed the ash from his waistcoat and came to a decision. Minutes later, he left Scotland Yard.

'Were you aware that Mr Heygate kept a diary?' asked Colbeck.

'No,' she admitted, 'I wasn't.'

'Did you know where he kept his money?'

'It was none of my business, Inspector.'

'Did he ever mention an owl to you?'

'I don't believe that he did.'

'Mrs Rossiter,' he said, gently, 'you keep telling me how close you and he were but it's hardly borne out by the facts. You were never once invited into his house, were you?'

'That means nothing. We had an understanding.'

Colbeck was sympathetic. She was evidently under immense strain. To cope with the loss of someone for whom she had deep, if unrequited, feelings she'd convinced herself that their relationship was far closer than it had been. He was therefore handling her with tact. They were in the stationmaster's office and Agnes Rossiter was sitting beside the desk in Heygate's old seat. Encouraged by Colbeck, she talked about her life at the railway station. She'd taken over the position of manageress after the untimely death from cholera of her husband over a decade earlier. They had no children and it was an eternal regret of hers. To stave off despair, she'd eventually moved in with her unmarried sister but she clearly missed the company of a man.

'Mr Heygate knew my circumstances,' she recalled, 'and he showed me the greatest kindness. I never thought that I would get over the death of my husband but I did – thanks to him.' Her jaw tightened. 'The upsetting thing was that, when he lost his wife and daughter, Mr Heygate didn't let me offer the support I got from him.'

'He was doubtless grateful for the offer, Mrs Rossiter.'

'He just never talked about it. Don't you find that odd?'

'Each of us has his or her own way of dealing with setbacks,' said Colbeck, 'and there's no bigger setback than the loss of a loved one.'

'Yes,' she agreed, taking out a black-edged handkerchief to dab at her eyes. 'It's happened to me twice now and the anguish is unbearable.'

'That's all the more reason why you should take some time off. It's wrong for you to force yourself to work when you have so much on your mind. There's a clash here,' he pointed out. 'Mourning is a private matter while serving refreshments is a public one. You can't do both simultaneously.'

'I don't see why not.'

'Mr Woodford was quite right. Mourning dress is out of place.'

She was waspish. 'A fat lot he knows about mourning!' she said. 'He's a cold-hearted man, Inspector, and he showed Mr Heygate little compassion during his time of suffering. I dislike him intensely.'

'All the same, he is the acting stationmaster, so it's best not to antagonise him.'

'I won't be ordered out of my own refreshment room.'

'Then you should do as he advises,' said Colbeck, 'and wear something more appropriate. You don't want to get tea stains on that lovely dress, do you?'

She softened. 'It belonged to my mother. I inherited it.'

'Then save it for the funeral, Mrs Rossiter. It doesn't belong here.'

Mrs Rossiter studied him for a moment. He was quite unlike any policeman she'd met before and had a gentleness of manner that seemed at variance with the brutal world in which he was obliged to operate. Because Woodford had ordered her to change her apparel, she resolved not to do so. Colbeck had been more persuasive, arguing that she could not grieve properly while stuck behind a counter serving tea. She came to see how bizarre she must have looked.

'Go home,' he said, soothingly. 'I'll happily take you there in a cab.'

'Perhaps that might be wise,' she decided.

'Let them find someone else to run the refreshment room. Not that they'll do it half as well,' he added. 'Miss Hope was telling me how efficient you are.'

'Miss Hope is a good girl – a trifle slow, that's all.'

He stretched out an arm. 'Shall we go and find a cab, Mrs Rossiter?'

'Yes,' she said, taking his hand and rising to her feet. 'Have you ever lost someone you adored, Inspector?'

'I've lost several people who'd qualify under that description, alas. There was my mother, father and my younger brother, not to mention four grandparents. I'm no stranger to family funerals.'

'Are you married?'

'Not at the moment,' he replied, 'but our wedding is arranged for the end of this month. It's not the ideal time of the year but I'm blessed in having the ideal bride and that's wonderful compensation.'

'I hope that she never has to suffer what I've had to endure,' she said with sudden acrimony. 'Fate can be so cruel at times. It's happened to me twice now. I pray that your wife will be spared such unspeakable horror.'

It was no use. No matter how hard she tried, Madeleine Andrews could not concentrate on her work. Though she'd been standing at her easel for hours, she'd put very little on the canvas. It was Colbeck who'd spotted her artistic talent and who'd urged her to develop it. His encouragement was all the incentive that she needed. By dint of study and incessant practice, she produced paintings that were eventually good enough to be shown to a dealer and her first sale had been a joyous experience. Building on that early success, she'd managed to make a regular income of sorts from her brush. What had attracted the art dealer was her unusual choice of subject. Instead of painting a pretty landscape or a portrait, she took her inspiration from the railways. Locomotives were conjured on to the canvas with a mixture of love and growing expertise. She knew how to bring them alive. Her success was a source of continuous pleasure for her father, who boasted – correctly at times – that he'd been able to give her the benefit of his professional advice.

But she could not address her mind to the painting in hand that afternoon. All that she could think about was the wedding and the dress she'd wear to the event. It was years since she'd first met Robert Colbeck and, though their friendship deepened with each passing month, they seemed to get no closer to marriage. Then, when she least expected it, he proposed to her in the middle of the Birmingham Jewellery Quarter, where he'd bought the engagement ring she wore so proudly on her finger. The date was set, the church was booked, the invitations sent out and her wedding dress ordered. With so much to think about, Madeleine was mad even to imagine that she could work properly. Whenever she looked at her painting of a locomotive her father had once driven, the face of Colbeck smiled back at her from the easel. She was alternately aroused and dejected, lifted by the thought of the wedding day ahead and crestfallen at the prospect of some harm befalling her future husband. Danger always lurked in a murder investigation. She had to accept that.

The sound of approaching footsteps reminded her that she was not the only person in the house. Recognising her father's distinctive gait, she broke off and used a piece of cloth to wipe her brush dry. Caleb Andrews unlocked the door and stepped into the house. It was the day when he'd taken tea at Dirk Sowerby's. Among the guests was a lady in whom Andrews had taken more than a passing interest. Madeleine searched his face for a hint at the success or otherwise of the occasion but her father was unduly impassive.

'Well,' she asked, 'did you enjoy the visit?'

'It was pleasant enough, Maddy.'

'Is that all?'

'Dirk's wife makes a poor cup of tea.'

'Was Mrs Langton there?'

'Who?'

'The lady you were hoping to meet.'

'Yes, yes,' he said, off-handedly, 'I think she was there.'

'Can't you even remember? That was the whole point of going, wasn't it?'

'I forget, Maddy.'

She saw the telltale glint in his eye. 'You're teasing me, Father.'

'I'd never do that.'

'What happened?' she demanded. 'If you're expecting a meal this evening, you can stop playing games with me. How did you get on with Mrs Langton?'

His face was split by a grin. 'I got on very well,' he said, whisking off his cap. 'Binnie has invited me to her own home – and promised me a better cup of tea than I had today. Who knows where things will lead from there?'

'Am I invited to go with you?'

'We don't need a chaperone at our age, Maddy. That's the beauty of it. Binnie and I can do exactly as we please with nobody to stop us.'

Madeline felt a pang of unease. There could be trouble ahead.

It had been almost an hour before Leeming was rescued from his unsought role as an assistant waitress. In that time, three trains had come into the station and disgorged dozens of passengers in search of refreshment. Leeming had had no time to rest. While Dorcas handled the money and set up the various trays, he had been confined to the tedious job of carrying orders to the different tables. Even when the bulk of the customers departed, others drifted in to kill time over a cup of tea while they waited for a later train. It had seemed an age before Woodford was able to rustle up a young porter to replace the sergeant and assist Dorcas Hope.

Leeming had torn off his apron and flung it aside.

'It was demeaning, Inspector,' he said.

'Someone had to save the day, Victor, and you were the chosen man.'

'Why couldn't you have done it?'

'I was too busy interviewing Miss Hope and, later on, the manageress. In the latter case,' said Colbeck, 'I had to take the lady home in a cab because she was too unstable to travel alone. The woman is possessed by a fantasy.'

'So am I,' said Leeming. 'My fantasy is that I'm a sergeant in the Detective Department at Scotland Yard. Clearly, I'm not. I'm the lowest of the low, a drudge.'

'I'm serious about Mrs Rossiter. She needs medical help.'

'When the doctor's finished with her, please send him on to me. I need my head examining as well.'

Colbeck laughed. They were at the police station, having spent the afternoon dealing with bogus claims by people over-excited by the amount of money being offered for information. Two of them insisted that they'd seen a corpse being dumped on the bonfire the night before it was lit, a third remembered a dead body cunningly disguised as a guy, while a fourth maintained that he'd actually seen Joel

Heygate being murdered before being concealed under the heap of timber. Since he said that the victim had been stabbed to death, this last claimant was the easiest to unmask as a blatant liar. Had he read newspaper reports, he would have known that Heygate had, in fact, been bludgeoned. The detectives had quickly exposed the tissue of deceit and, after arresting and charging them, handed all four men over to a magistrate.

Having moaned about his stint in the refreshment room, Leeming turned his thoughts back to the investigation. His concern was the prime suspect.

'Do you think he's still in Exeter, sir?' asked Leeming.

'Are you talking about Bagsy Browne?'

'In his place, I'd make myself scarce.'

'I fancy that he's here. He doesn't want to miss the fun of the funeral.'

Leeming was startled. 'Fun!'

'That's how he'll see it, Victor. It'll be a celebration to him. If you loathe someone enough to murder them, you might well take pleasure out of seeing their remains lowered into the earth. That,' said Colbeck, 'might be our chance to catch the elusive Mr Browne.'

'Do we have to wait until the funeral?'

'We'll wait a lot longer if called upon to do so. That's assuming that Browne is our man, of course. I still think that we should keep Michael Heygate and Lawrence Woodford in mind. Patience is our watchword. We bide our time.'

'This case could drag on and on,' said Leeming, gloomily. 'I may not get to see my family again for weeks – and what about the wedding?'

'I try not to think about that, Victor.'

'Then you're very different from me, sir. When I was about to get married, it preyed on my mind for months beforehand. I could think of nothing else.'

'My only concern is to solve this crime.'

'But we've made no real progress so far.'

'I disagree,' said Colbeck. 'We've identified three possible suspects and the news about the diary has been in the nature of a breakthrough.'

'Except that we don't actually *have* the diary.'

'We know of its existence, that's the main thing.'

'Then why didn't you find it when you searched the house?' asked Leeming. 'My guess is that it was destroyed by the killer so it's gone for ever.'

'I remain more sanguine,' said Colbeck. 'It's highly unlikely that the killer knew that Heygate kept such a diary and the stationmaster would hardly carry it with him when he was going off on a nocturnal search for an owl. It's here somewhere and it may well hold the clue that leads to an arrest.'

'Then how do you find it?'

'It will turn up somehow.'

'I wish I had your confidence, sir,' said Leeming, dispiritedly. 'In every other investigation, I've always had the feeling that we're moving forwards. Here in Exeter, we seem to be treading water. I'm starting to hate the place.'

'Concentrate on its virtues, Victor.'

'I didn't know that it had any.'

'It has several, believe me, but the one that might recommend itself to you is its geographical position. As long as we're in this city, we're almost two hundred miles away from Superintendent Tallis.'

Leeming brightened. 'Now that *is* a bonus,' he said, chuckling. 'We don't have to put up with him yelling at us. The superintendent can't touch us here.'

When the train pulled into Exeter St David's station, the first person to step on to the platform was Edward Tallis. As a porter came towards him, he thrust his valise at the man and barked an order.

'Take me to a cab!'

CHAPTER SEVEN

Most people sought by the police would take refuge somewhere and make sure that they didn't venture out in daylight. Bagsy Browne was different. He took the view that nothing would keep him off the streets if he had a mind to go for a walk. Being hunted was a normal state of affairs for him. It never troubled his mind. Refusing to go to earth, he'd strolled around Exeter for most of the day, going into a series of pubs as he did so. Newspapers carried a description of him and he was, in any case, well known in the city, but nobody recognised him because he was clean-shaven and wearing smart clothing for once. Feeling immune from arrest, he became bolder. Instead of keeping to the shadows, he marched along High Street early that evening with his usual jauntiness. It proved to be a mistake. There was still enough light in the sky to illumine his features and one passer-by took a close look at him. The man was so certain that he knew him that he followed his quarry through a maze of streets. Unaware that he was being trailed, Browne suddenly veered off into an alleyway so that he could relieve himself against a wall. When he'd finished, he turned to find that his way was blocked by a thickset man in his fifties with a square chin.

'Hello, Bagsy,' he said.

'Sorry,' said Browne, gruffly, 'you've got the wrong man.'

'I'd know you anywhere.'

'You must be seeing things, my friend.'

'I can tell you by your stink.'

Bagsy's fists bunched. 'Say that again, you turd!'

'You don't remember me, do you?'

'Why should I?'

'Because I used to look after you,' said the man, taking a step closer. 'I've seen Bagsy Browne with his hair and his beard shaved off before – except that you had no name in prison, did you? We gave you a number instead.'

Bagsy glared at him. 'It's Wyatt, isn't it?' he said. 'I remember you now. You were one of those cruel bastards who baited me.'

'You only got what you asked for.'

'Get out of my way.'

'But we have so much to talk over, Bagsy,' said Wyatt, grinning. 'We shared such happy times in prison, didn't we?' He spat on the ground in disgust. 'If it had been left to me, we'd have locked you up and thrown away the key.'

'I won't ask you again,' cautioned Browne.

'Why don't we take a little walk? I'm sure that Superintendent Steel will be delighted to see an old acquaintance. In fact, he's so keen to meet you again that he put a notice about you in the newspaper.'

'I saw it.'

'Then why didn't you heed it?'

'Nobody stops me from doing what I want.'

'So you wanted to get caught – is that it?'

'No,' said Browne, lunging forward to grab him by the shoulders. 'I wanted the chance to pay you back for all the hours of torment you gave me in prison.' He punched Wyatt on the nose and blood spurted. 'It's not so easy when you haven't got those other mangy warders to help you, is it?'

Wyatt was enraged. Wiping the blood with the back of his hand, he fought back and landed some telling punches. Browne had to give ground for a moment. Gathering his strength, he began to trade blows with the prison warder. The result was a foregone conclusion. Strong and determined he might be, but Wyatt was up against a man seasoned by dozens of brawls. As the two of them grappled, Browne suddenly tripped him up and pushed him to the ground. Kicking him hard in the groin, he then grabbed his head and banged it repeatedly on the paving stone. Only when Wyatt began to beg for mercy did Browne relent.

He searched the man's pockets, took what money he could find and fled. Wyatt was left groaning in agony and regretting his decision to accost the former prisoner. Browne, meanwhile, made his way back to Rockfield Place and ran up the stairs to Adeline's room. When he opened the door, she was sitting in front of the mirror as she applied powder to her cheeks.

'There you are,' he said, tossing the stolen money on to the bed, 'I've brought you another gift, Ad.'

She was more concerned by his appearance. 'There's

blood on your coat,' she said, 'and a bruise on your face. Have you been fighting?'

He sniggered. 'No – I was just teaching someone a lesson.'

The unwelcome arrival of Edward Tallis had astounded Colbeck and sown instant terror into the heart of Leeming. They had been discussing the case over a drink in the bar at the Acland Tavern when the superintendent popped up like a jack-in-the-box. Charging across to them, he leant menacingly over their table.

'I was told that I'd find you here,' he snarled.

'Good evening, sir,' said Colbeck, recovering his poise. 'You must have had a long and tiring journey. May we offer you a drink?'

'No, Inspector, but you can offer me an explanation.'

'For what, dare I ask?'

'For this,' said Tallis, taking a letter from his pocket and flinging it down on the table. 'Read it.'

Colbeck picked it up. 'It appears to be from the Bishop of Exeter.'

'Indeed, it is, and he's a very angry bishop. He's demanding that I remove you and Leeming from this investigation and take you back to London.'

'That would suit me, sir,' Leeming piped up.

'Your wishes are irrelevant.'

'We don't want to outstay our welcome.'

'You'll obey orders and do as you're told. To begin with, the pair of you can offer an abject apology to the bishop.'

'Why should we do that, sir?' asked Colbeck, finishing the letter. 'He has a colourful turn of phrase, I grant you, but I see nothing here that would make me behave any differently

120

towards him. He's been rude, high-handed and extremely unhelpful. The sergeant will bear me out on that score.'

'I will,' said Leeming. 'What does the letter say?'

Colbeck handed it to him. 'I think you should read it, Victor.'

'Yes,' added Tallis, lowering himself into an empty chair. 'And while you're doing so, remind yourself of the position that the bishop occupies here. He has far more power than the mayor and more influence than anyone in the county. Crucially, Bishop Phillpotts has the ear of Archbishop Sumner. Do you want to bring the wrath of Lambeth Palace down upon us? Is that the intention – to provoke the Archbishop of Canterbury?'

'The only provocation of which I'm aware is in that letter, sir.'

Leeming was shocked by what he'd read. 'I never knew that a man of the cloth could be so harsh,' he said, returning the letter to Tallis. 'I'm surprised he didn't write that in blood rather than ink. Did you see what he called you, Inspector?'

Colbeck smiled. 'Yes, I did. Apparently, I'm a boorish disrespectful oaf.' He looked at Tallis. 'You've called me far worse than that in the past, sir.'

'This situation has got to be retrieved,' asserted Tallis.

'Yes,' agreed Leeming. 'We make our apology and go home.'

'Be silent, man! We need no inane interjections.'

'Nobody wants us here, sir.'

'Especially the killer,' said Colbeck, 'but I'm not going to oblige him by quitting the field. As for the bishop's letter, sir, I'm sorry that it aroused your ire so much that you came all the way to Devon. Had you met Bishop Phillpotts, you might not have been quite so eager to enter his fiefdom. I advise you to reserve judgement until you've come eye to eye with the right reverend gentleman.'

Tallis eyed him malevolently. 'Do I detect a note of sarcasm?'

'Nothing could be further from the truth, sir.'

'You must consider how to make amends for your behaviour.'

'The best way to do that is to solve the crime,' argued Colbeck, 'and we've more chance of doing that if Bishop Phillpotts is kept on a leash.'

'Kept on a leash?' howled Tallis, close to apoplexy. 'We're talking about a senior figure in the Anglican Church. He's entitled to deference. You can't operate freely in Exeter without his blessing.'

Colbeck indicated the letter. 'He seems more inclined to curse than bless.'

'We'll make an appointment to see him tomorrow – both of us.'

'I'll be happy to accompany you to the bishop's palace. While we're doing that, the sergeant can take the train to Dawlish.'

'Why should I do that, sir?' asked Leeming.

'I want you to interview Michael Heygate and his wife. He's the brother of the deceased,' he explained to Tallis, 'and he may turn out to be a suspect as well.'

'Then why not arrest him so that he can be interrogated?'

'We lack the evidence to do that, sir. If he knows that we harbour suspicions about him, he'll become defensive and uncooperative. Victor will sound him out.'

'Do you have any other suspects?'

'We have two at the moment,' said Colbeck, 'but

Superintendent Steel favours one over the other. He's a local villain named Browne and he's made threats about killing the stationmaster in the past.'

'Is the fellow in custody?'

'He's managed to evade us so far. But he's still in Exeter.'

'How do you know that?'

'We were at the police station earlier when a prison warder staggered in, covered in blood. He recognised Browne as having served sentences in prison and sought to apprehend him. He got a broken nose and a lot of bruises for his pains. Bagsy Browne is still here somewhere,' said Colbeck, 'and he won't be taken easily.'

'Hasn't a search for this individual been launched?'

'Of course, sir, but the police force has limited numbers.'

'What manner of man is their superintendent?'

'He's a fine policeman, hampered by lack of resources. He objected to our presence at first, but I think he's come to accept that we could be useful.'

'Yes,' muttered Leeming, 'even if all we do is to serve tea in the station refreshment room.' He raised his voice. 'Superintendent Steel ought to see that letter, sir. I gather that he's had a lot of difficulty with the bishop over the years.'

'Yet he's held his own,' said Colbeck. 'I admire him for doing that.'

'Where exactly was the murder committed?' asked Tallis.

'We're not entirely certain, sir, but a missing diary may give us a clue.'

'To whose diary are you referring?'

'The stationmaster's, sir,' replied Colbeck. 'It transpires that Joel Heygate had a passion for birds.'

* * *

Peter had brought some welcome pleasure into the household. He not only cheered Maud Hope up, he acted as a distraction. There were times when she was able to forget that she was in pain. The canary was a tuneful companion but she didn't mind that. He filled the room with sweetness and song. However, not even Peter was able to divert her now. As she sat beside his cage in the armchair, she didn't even notice that he was there. Dorcas was late coming home. That disturbed her. Her daughter was a sensitive young woman who'd been profoundly rocked by the death of her one real friend at the railway station. Maud had told her to stay away from work until she felt better but Dorcas was driven by a keen sense of loyalty. Against her parent's wishes, therefore, she'd gone to the refreshment room that morning and should have returned an hour ago. Since her husband was also late, Maud was left alone to fear for her daughter's safety.

When she finally heard the front door being unlocked, she almost swooned with relief. If it was Nathaniel Hope, at least he'd be able to comfort her and go out in search of Dorcas. Maud would not have to suffer alone. She made an effort to get to her feet but the arthritis bit sharply into her hip and forced her to sit back down again. The pain made her head swim. Her hip was still throbbing when Dorcas came into the room. Maud let out a cry of gratitude.

'Thank heavens!' she exclaimed.

'Are you all right, Mother?' asked Dorcas, going to her.

'I was frightened that something had happened to you.'

'Mr Woodford made me work late because I was in charge of the refreshment room. I had to count up all the money and put it away in the safe.'

Maud was impressed. 'You were in *charge?*'

'Yes, I never thought I'd cope but I did somehow.'

'What about Mrs Rossiter?'

Dorcas sighed. 'She had to go home, Mother. She was . . . unwell.'

She told Maud about the way in which the manageress had dressed and behaved that morning and how Woodford had refused to let her continue serving refreshments. Dorcas also explained that Inspector Colbeck had questioned both her and Mrs Rossiter.

'Why did he want to talk to you?' asked Maud, anxiously.

'He thought that I might be able to help.'

'But you know nothing whatsoever about the murder.'

'I knew Mr Heygate. In fact, I think I knew him better than anybody at the station. That's why he trusted Peter with me. How is he?' she went on, crouching down to peer into the cage. 'Hello, Peter, have you missed me?' The bird chirped a reply. 'There you are – he understands what I said.'

'He's been good company for me all day.'

'Did you feed him and change his water?'

'Yes, yes,' said Maud. 'I spoilt him good and proper.'

Dorcas took off her hat and coat. 'Thank you, Mother.' She went into the passageway to hang them up on a peg. 'I feel so weary,' she said, coming back into the parlour. 'I've been on my feet all day.'

'What about tomorrow?'

'What about it?'

'Will you be the manageress again or will Mrs Rossiter be back?'

'Oh, I don't think there's any chance of seeing her for a while. She's not very well at all. According to Mr Woodford, the inspector wants her to see a doctor. He said that he'd look into it.'

'What business is it of the inspector's?'

'He took pity on her,' said Dorcas. 'Inspector Colbeck is a very kind man and not at all like the policemen on duty in the streets. Because he could see how nervous I was, he treated me very gently. I'm sure that he was gentle with Mrs Rossiter as well.' She flopped into a chair. 'I wish I could say the same about Mr Woodford.'

'Was he unkind to her?'

'Yes, he spoke very harshly to Mrs Rossiter. He seemed to forget all the good service she'd given over the years and threatened to dismiss her on the spot.'

'That's dreadful!' exclaimed Maud.

'Luckily, Inspector Colbeck came to her rescue. Afterwards, he persuaded her to go home and took her there in a cab.'

'It sounds to me as if Agnes Rossiter is really ill.'

'She is, Mother, but it's not like an ordinary disease.'

'What do you mean?'

'I heard the inspector discussing it with Sergeant Leeming. He said that Mrs Rossiter was so overcome by grief that it had affected her mind.'

Illumined by dozens of candles, the cathedral was at its most beautiful and imposing, its ancient walls and soaring columns acting as an echo chamber for the choir. When she let herself in that evening, the rehearsal was at its height, well-trained voices merging in perfect harmony and rising up to heaven with mellifluous adoration. Agnes Rossiter was in no mood to join in the praise of a God who'd signally failed her. The loss of her first husband had been a shattering experience but the death of Joel Heygate was somehow even more devastating. She'd known happiness with her husband and could look back on years of pleasure. Fond memories could console her. Such memories of Heygate didn't exist. What the stationmaster had represented was the promise of a better life for her, an enrichment of her world, a redemption. Instead of sharing a dull and arid existence with her sister, she would have been a married woman again with all the position and sense of fulfilment that it brought. Yet it was not to be. Her last chance of true happiness had been snatched away. She felt utterly betrayed.

She might be in God's house but she no longer felt either welcome or respectful there. Indeed, the whole edifice seemed to her to be a huge architectural mistake, dedicated to a supreme being who didn't exist or, if he did, had a brutal streak. She had felt the full impact of that brutality, a helpless victim who'd had all hope and ambition squeezed out of her life by a malign act. It was infuriating. As her rage mounted inside her, she suddenly gathered up the skirts of her black dress and ran down the nave, screaming at the top of her voice. The choir were still singing as she raced past them, ran up the altar steps and made for the crucifix, snatching it up and brandishing it like the standard of a defeated army.

It was minutes before they could overpower her.

When they were shown into the library at the bishop's palace next morning, Colbeck was surprised how timid Edward Tallis appeared. Ordinarily, he was fearless, having seen action during his army career and having confronted armed criminals many times. Yet here he was, looking round tentatively like a small child who has stumbled into a strange room. Colbeck knew that the superintendent was a devout man but had never expected him to be quite so reverential in the presence of a bishop. He suspected that Tallis's attitude might change when he actually met Henry Phillpotts. He also suspected that they were deliberately being kept waiting. It gave Colbeck the opportunity to take a closer look at the bookshelves, filled to capacity with leather-bound tomes and a veritable treasure trove of smaller volumes. He was interested to see so many collections of poetry tucked away among the endless religious studies. Milton occupied pride of place on one shelf.

Without warning, the door opened and the bishop sailed in with his secretary trotting at his heels. Phillpotts made for the chair behind his desk.

'I'm sorry for the delay,' he said without a trace of apology in his voice, 'but I had to speak to the choirmaster. Apparently, we had a madwoman in the cathedral yesterday, daring to grab the crucifix from the altar. The police had to be called to remove her. For an act of such wanton sacrilege, she needs locking up in perpetuity.'

'I beg to differ, Bishop,' said Colbeck. 'As it happens, I know the lady and was told about the incident by Superintendent Steel. Her name is Mrs Agnes Rossiter and she deserves compassion rather than condemnation. When you're apprised of the full details, you may reach the same conclusion. However,' he went on, indicating his companion, 'you haven't met Superintendent Tallis yet, have you?'

Introductions were made and they all sat down. Tallis perched on the edge of his chair, wishing that he could have a cigar to settle his nerves. Colbeck was completely at ease. Ralph Barnes sat at the side of the desk, interested to view the encounter. The bishop pretended to peruse a document in front of him before setting it aside and looking up. He gave Tallis a thin-lipped smile of disdain.

'I take it that you've come to rid us of Inspector Colbeck and his assistant,' he said. 'Please make your apology then take the pair of them away from Exeter.'

'If one of my detectives has inadvertently upset you, Bishop,' said Tallis with deference, 'then I apologise on his behalf. What I will not do, however, is to withdraw him from the investigation.'

Phillpotts bridled. 'Didn't you read my letter?'

'I read it several times.'

'Then why is there any prevarication?'

'My detectives were engaged by the South Devon Railway and it only lies within the power of Mr Quinnell to dispense with their services.'

'Quinnell doesn't understand the implications of this crime,' said the bishop, fussily. 'It was committed as a direct affront to me by a man who has already behaved atrociously by fouling my lawn in broad daylight.'

'The bishop is alluding to Bagsy Browne,' explained Colbeck.

Phillpotts glowered. 'Browne is an incorrigible heathen.'

'From what I hear,' said Tallis, 'he's a very violent man. When a prison warder tried to arrest him last night, Browne beat the fellow to a pulp.'

'He must be caught, tried and hanged.'

'I accept that he must be caught and tried,' said Colbeck, 'but he should only face execution if he turns out to be the stationmaster's killer.'

'We *know* he's the killer. Isn't it blindingly obvious?'

'Not to me, Bishop.'

'I, too, would need more evidence,' said Tallis. 'When we heard about the attack on the warder last evening, the inspector made an interesting point.'

'It made me look at Browne in a slightly different way,' said Colbeck, taking his cue. 'If he really was a ruthless killer, why didn't he murder the prison warder? After all, he had every reason to loathe the man. Yet he let him off with a beating. It may be that Browne is not the wild animal you portray him as, Bishop.'

'He's been a thorn in my flesh for years,' said Phillpotts, scowling. 'Isn't that true, Ralph?'

'Yes,' replied the secretary, dutifully.

'List a few of his outrages.'

Barnes winced. 'There are so many,' he said, 'that I don't know where to start. I suppose one of the worst examples of his loutish behaviour was during the procession held through the streets last Christmas when there was snow on the ground. Browne dislodged the bishop's mitre with a snowball. Then there was wilful damage to church property in Teignmouth,' he went on, 'and – most reprehensible of all in my opinion – he was caught half-naked with a loose woman on consecrated ground. They had to be prised apart.'

'These crimes were all personal attacks on *me*,' declared the bishop.

'They're thoroughly shameful,' said Tallis, 'I agree. But they're not of the same order as the killing and burning of the stationmaster.'

'You're not listening to me, man – there's a *pattern* here.'

The bishop treated them to another sermon, emphasising the importance of the Church and the villainy of those who mocked and subverted it. In trying to grind Tallis into submission, however, he was achieving just the opposite. Colbeck could see the superintendent's hackles slowly rising. Tallis might have verged on the obsequious at the start but he was rapidly losing respect from the bishop. As the holy tirade grew louder, Tallis brought it to a premature close by interrupting it with a shout of protest.

'That's enough, Bishop Phillpotts!' he said, standing up. 'You've convinced me that I was right to send Inspector Colbeck and Sergeant Leeming here and would never dream of withdrawing them at your behest.'

'Do you dare to oppose my will?' blustered Phillpotts.

'I've come to see the situation in a new light.'

'This is a local crime that should be solved locally without interference from people who know nothing of Exeter and my position within this county.'

'Actually,' said Barnes, piously, 'it's a much wider area than merely Devon. The diocese extends from the borders of Somerset and Dorset to the Isles of Scilly in Cornwall. Bishop Phillpotts has the care of an untold number of souls.'

'That's irrelevant,' said Tallis.

The bishop sat up indignantly. 'It's a measure of my importance.'

'I acknowledge that, Bishop, but I challenge your self-appointed right to send my officers packing. They are well versed in the art of detection and will remain here until the case is solved.'

Colbeck rose to his feet. 'It's in everyone's interest that the killer is caught and brought to justice,' he said, smoothly, 'and the fewer handicaps we have to face, the sooner we can achieve that result. In short, Bishop, instead of trying to steer the investigation in the wrong direction altogether, I suggest that you simply let us get on with our job. We have no desire to remain in Exeter a minute longer than necessary.'

'I couldn't have put it better, Inspector,' said Tallis.

'This is insufferable,' said Phillpotts, cheeks reddening. 'I find your attitude both insolent and disgraceful. I will be writing to the commissioner at Scotland Yard to voice my displeasure.'

'You have every right to do so, Bishop.'

'This matter will not end here.'

'It will only end when we have the killer in custody,' said Colbeck.

Phillpotts turned to his secretary. 'Show these gentlemen out.'

'Yes, Bishop,' said Barnes, moving to the door.

After an exchange of muted farewells, the visitors went out. When they left the building, Tallis was able to let his true feelings show. Taking out the bishop's letter, he waved it in the air.

'This is not Holy Writ,' he said.

'The bishop evidently thinks that it is, sir.'

'He has all the attributes of a tyrant.'

In that respect, Colbeck mused, Tallis and the bishop were very similar: men of power who hated to have their authority questioned and who sought to quash any sign of what they felt was opposition. While Phillpotts operated in a spiritual sphere, Tallis was restricted to the temporal and both of them followed a policy of aggressive and unequivocal dictatorship. What Colbeck had witnessed in the library was, in microcosm, a skirmish between Church and State. Tallis had been the victor.

'The fellow is not fit to hold his bishopric,' he said, thrusting the letter back in his pocket. 'He should be shunted into instant retirement.'

'He probably feels the same way about us, sir,' said Colbeck, 'and is writing to the commissioner at this very moment to have us summarily dismissed.'

'He's nothing but a sanctimonious bully.'

'Leave him to us, sir. He's not your problem any longer. Now that you've put him in his place – your forthrightness, may I say, was exemplary – you can return to London to supervise the policing of the capital.'

'Oh, I'm not stirring from here now.'

'But the sergeant and I can manage on our own.'

'Not if you have to withstand sniping from the bishop,' said Tallis, seriously. 'You need me to keep him at bay. Besides, an extra pair of hands is always useful in an investigation and this case is one of such unimaginable horror that I wish to make my contribution to it. I'm staying to see it through.'

Colbeck's heart sank.

Madeleine could not keep away from it. Now that the wedding was imminent, she took every opportunity she could to walk past the place where the ceremony would be held. St Pancras New Church had been built over thirty years earlier and, like the rival Camden Chapel, looked more like a Greek temple than a traditional Anglican church. It stood on Euston Road and was intended to serve the population in the southern part of the parish. As she made her daily visit that morning, Madeleine looked up in awe at the spacious Ionic portico that ran the length of the western facade. Spearing the sky was a magnificent tower that enjoyed a view over the whole of Camden Town and its neighbouring parishes. She could scarcely believe that she'd be married to Robert Colbeck in such an imposing edifice and she recalled how nervous she'd been when they attended services there together to hear the banns being read. It would not be long before they were stepping out of the church as man and wife.

It made her reflect on the immense changes Colbeck had brought about in her life. As a rule, someone of her modest upbringing could never aspire to befriend – let alone to marry – a person from a distinctly higher class. Before he joined the police force, Colbeck had been a barrister, a well-educated man who'd inherited a large house and a clutch of servants. In social and intellectual terms, the gap between them had been wide, yet it had narrowed dramatically over the years. Quick to learn and keen to study, she'd borrowed countless books from Colbeck's library. Then there was her skill as an artist. Under his tutelage, it had developed and blossomed, giving her immense pride. Madeleine had never been short of confidence but the fact that she could command an income of sorts was a huge fillip. What had really bonded her and Colbeck together, however, was her readiness to join in his investigative work when required. Though she lacked his insight and deductive powers, Madeleine had nevertheless been able to offer significant help at times and hoped to render it again, especially when she could do so as Mrs Colbeck.

Tearing herself away from the church, she walked slowly home, luxuriating in thoughts of her wedding day and of the blissful married life that would follow it. When she let herself into the house, she was still dreaming fondly of the future. Caleb Andrews brought her out of her reverie.

'This came while you were out, Maddy,' he said, giving her a letter.

'It's from Robert!' she exclaimed, opening it at once.

Andrews stuck out his chest. 'If he needs any assistance in Exeter,' he said, 'tell him that I'll be happy to join him there – even if it means travelling on Brunel's railway. I may not be a trained detective but I've got great experience of the world. That must count for something.' He saw the distress on her face. 'What's the matter? Has something happened?'

'Robert sends his apologies,' she said, her lower lip trembling. 'It seems that his case is going to take much longer than he anticipated.' She looked hopelessly at her father. 'What if it's not solved by the time of the wedding?'

CHAPTER EIGHT

Though still unhappy about the continued absence from his family, Victor Leeming boarded the train that morning with a measure of interest because the journey would take him past a number of pumping stations used in an experiment in powering a train by atmospheric pressure. Leeming still didn't quite understand what exactly it had involved but his curiosity had been aroused. He wanted to know more. In places like Starcross, however, the abandoned pumping station was a sad reminder of the failed atmospheric railway. What Leeming would remember most clearly of the small seaport were the turrets of nearby Powderham Castle, its extensive grounds stocked with deer, shrubberies, plantations, lawns and pleasure grounds, all of it bronzed by the glow of autumn sunshine. Its Belvedere Tower soared above all else and looked down on the River Exe as it flowed between broad banks to join the sea. For someone who led an urban existence and who saw nothing but bricks and mortar in a normal day, the view was breathtaking. Leeming wished that he'd been able to bring his wife and children away from the grimy streets of London to this delightful watering place. It spoke of a healthier, quieter, better way of life.

He had to remind himself that he was there to work and not to enjoy the scenery and the fresh air. Dawlish was equally picturesque, a village situated on the shore of the English Channel and well established as a seaside resort. The train chugged along with the sea on its left and he noted the beach huts, baths and other amenities built for visitors. Leeming was glad that the tide was out, exposing the gentle curve of the bay and an array of jagged rocks. At high tide – he'd been warned by Colbeck – the sea would frequently splash over the railway tracks and slap against the side of the locomotive and its carriages. It was an experience that he was more than willing to miss. Trains were uncomfortable enough in his opinion without being lashed by angry waves. As he stepped on to the platform, he was greeted by a cold wind that blew in off the sea and threatened to dislodge his top hat.

While he took his bearings, he looked up at the red sandstone cliffs looming over the village and adding a sense of grandeur. After taking directions, Leeming ventured out of the station. Even at that time of year, Dawlish itself was so endearingly pretty that he longed to bring his family there one day. Long hours of work and a modest income meant that such holidays were rarities for him. He still savoured a trip he'd once made to Brighton with tickets provided by a grateful railway company for whom he and Colbeck had worked. His children talked fondly of their magical time on the beach. Though on a much smaller scale, Dawlish would provide them with similarly vibrant memories. He looked forward to describing the place to them when he returned to London. The village was bisected by a brook that meandered its way towards the sea with a flotilla of ducks and the occasional swan gliding on its bubbling waters. Dawlish looked serene, unrushed and parochial. Gulls wheeled, dived and perched on rooftops. The salty tang of the sea was bracing.

It was easy to find the address he sought. He walked past a row of houses and shops that ran alongside the brook. Several of the properties offered accommodation and there was an inn and a chapel to satisfy the competing needs of the populace. Leeming arrived at a tiny shop that looked irredeemably closed. Blinds had been drawn down over the window and a sign announced that business had been suspended. Michael and Lavinia Heygate lived with their two children at the rear of the premises. After ringing the bell, Leeming had to wait some time before the door was eventually opened. Heygate was unwelcoming.

'We're closed,' he said.

'I came to see *you*, Mr Heygate. My name is Detective Sergeant Leeming. I've been sent from Scotland Yard to investigate the murder of your brother.'

Heygate was insulted. 'Why come here? I had nothing to do with it.'

'I'd just like to discuss a few things with you, sir.'

'It's not a convenient time.'

'Really?' said Leeming, looking him in the eye. 'Are you telling me that you're too busy to help in the search for your brother's killer? The shop is closed and your business no longer exists. What is it that's of such importance that it takes precedence over the death of your closest blood relation?'

Heygate had the grace to look slightly shamefaced. After considering what could be the awkward consequences of turning his visitor away, he decided to let him in. He stood aside so that Leeming could step into the passageway. It led to a parlour at the back of the property. Lavinia was seated beside the fire. Rising to her feet, she was introduced to Leeming and hid her displeasure behind a forced smile. Like her husband, she was in mourning attire but there was little sense of actual mourning. Both of them were plainly irritated at the notion of having to answer questions about the stationmaster.

Heygate gestured towards the chairs and they all sat down around the fire.

'I watched you at the inquest, Mr Heygate,' Leeming began. 'I was interested to hear that you'd spoken to your brother on the day of his death.'

'It was only for a short time,' said Heygate.

'Why were you in Exeter at that time?'

'I explained that. We came for the celebrations.'

'But that was on November 5th, the following day,' Leeming pointed out. 'Why come twenty-four hours earlier?'

'We wanted to enjoy the atmosphere that builds up beforehand.'

'I believe that you have two children.'

'That's right,' said Lavinia. 'We have two sons, one of twelve and one of ten.'

'Then why didn't you take them with you, Mrs Heygate?

140

Our information is that the day is really intended for the young of Exeter. I'm sure that your children would have loved the occasion.'

'We chose to leave them in Dawlish.'

'Was there any reason for doing that?'

'It's a private matter,' said Heygate. 'They stayed here with friends.'

'While you and your wife spent the night at an inn, I presume.' When he got no answer, Leeming changed his tack. 'What sort of a mood was your brother in when you met him?'

'Joel was . . . rather testy.'

'At the inquest, you said he was calm and polite.'

'That wasn't entirely true. He was short with us.'

'He mentioned an owl to you.'

'That's right, Sergeant.'

'Did he say where he'd found it?'

'No,' replied Heygate. 'It was in an old shed somewhere. That's all we know.'

'He was always going off to look at birds,' said Lavinia with a slight edge. 'In fact, he was more interested in them than he was in us. It was unnatural, Sergeant. What sort of man cares more for birds than for human beings?'

'Now, now, Lavinia,' warned Heygate. 'Let's not speak ill of the dead. Joel may have had some strange ways but he was my brother. And there was a time when we were much closer.'

'Why did you drift apart, sir?' asked Leeming.

'He let us down.'

'Could you be more specific?'

'Well,' said Heygate, trading an uneasy glance with his

141

wife, 'he refused to help me in a time of need. That's what I'd have done in his place. I've always had a generous nature. Joel wasn't like me. When I needed some money to put into the business, he turned me away. It was very hurtful.'

'What did you sell in the shop?'

'It was fishing tackle. There was a steady demand for it but we never had enough stock to give all our customers what they wanted. All that I needed was some extra capital, then I could have rented a storeroom nearby and maintained a large stock. As it was,' said Heygate, sullenly, 'we had to turn custom away and it went to a shop in Teignmouth instead. Their profit was our loss.'

'And you blame your brother for that, do you?'

'Of course – it was his fault.'

In Leeming's estimation, both man and wife would be adept at shifting the blame for any failures on to something else. Neither was ready to take responsibility for the collapse of their business and their inability to raise finance from elsewhere. The stationmaster was the scapegoat for their lack of success.

'Did your brother ever lend you money in the past?' asked Leeming.

'As a matter of fact, he did,' admitted Heygate. 'It helped to set up the business in the first place.'

'And did you repay the loan in due course?'

'That's immaterial.'

'I don't think so, sir. If I'd given money to a relative of mine, I'd think twice about giving him a second loan when he hadn't repaid the first one. Was that the situation with your brother?'

Heygate was roused. 'I thought you came here to talk

about Joel's death,' he said, seething with resentment, 'and not about our financial affairs. He and I had our differences – I'm not disguising that. But I mourn him nevertheless and I ask you to respect our feelings.'

'My husband and I have been distracted by grief,' said Lavinia, pulling a handkerchief from her sleeve as if about to stem tears. 'Please bear that in mind.'

'I will, Mrs Heygate,' promised Leeming, 'and I'm sorry to intrude at such a time. But the more we learn about the character of your brother-in-law, the more helpful it is to us. Everyone speaks highly of him and yet he was the victim of a despicable crime. Can either of you suggest who committed it?'

'No, we can't,' said Heygate.

'Did he never confide that he had enemies?'

'It was something we never discussed, Sergeant.'

'Did he seem at all afraid on that last occasion when you saw him?'

'Joel was never afraid.'

'He was a brave man,' added Lavinia. 'I'll say that for him. He loved his job at the station and wouldn't let anyone cause trouble there. Isn't that true, Michael?'

'Yes, it is,' confirmed her husband. 'Joel would tackle anybody.'

'That's the impression we've been getting,' said Leeming.

After a few more questions, Leeming apologised again for disturbing them. He then asked them to get in touch with him and Colbeck if they remembered anything – even the slightest detail – that might be of relevance to the investigation. So eager were they to get rid of him that they both accompanied him to the front door. Heygate opened it and ushered the visitor into the street.

'I did some fishing as a lad,' recalled Leeming.

'It's a very popular hobby,' said Heygate. 'That's why I opened the shop.'

'I'm sorry that it faltered, sir.'

'We prefer to forget about that . . . Goodbye, Sergeant.'

'Goodbye, sir, and goodbye, Mrs Heygate.' About to turn away, Leeming paused. 'Oh, there is one thing I meant to ask. Have you lived in Devon for long?'

'We've both spent all our lives here,' said Heygate. 'I was born in Exeter and my wife hails from Starcross. It's not far away.'

'I know. I came past it on my way here. In fact,' said Leeming, 'perhaps you can help me. According to Inspector Colbeck, Starcross was one of the places where they tried to run trains by atmospheric pressure.'

'That's right. Joel was very excited about it at the time. He was upset when the experiment was abandoned. What did you wish to know, Sergeant?'

Leeming smiled hopefully. 'How exactly did it *work*?'

Agnes Rossiter was in a pitiable condition. Still dressed like a grieving widow, she sat in the corner of the room and stared blankly ahead of her through red-rimmed eyes. Colbeck had called at the little cottage and been admitted by Frances Impey, the unmarried sister. Frances was older, paler and thinner with plain features and watery eyes. Lacking any confidence, she was in a state of continual embarrassment as if forever apologising for her very existence. As he glanced around the cluttered parlour with its fading wallpaper, its sparse furniture, its insipid paintings, its threadbare carpet,

144

its potted plant, its stuffed fox and its vague smell of damp, Colbeck felt that it was the ideal habitat for the spinster. It was a place into which she could withdraw from life surrounded only by what was old, worn and familiar.

'She's been like this all morning,' said Frances, hands fluttering like a pair of giant butterflies. 'Agnes won't eat a thing. I made her a nourishing broth but she refused to touch it.'

'Did she get any sleep?' asked Colbeck.

'No, Inspector, she sat up all night in that chair. I don't know what's got into my sister. Is it true that she created a scene at the cathedral?'

'There was an incident of sorts,' he said, trying to play down its significance. 'Mrs Rossiter is clearly unable to control her emotions.'

'It frightens me.'

'I daresay that it does, Miss Impey.'

'It's so unlike Agnes, you see. She always has so much to say for herself.'

'I've taken the liberty of asking for a medical opinion,' said Colbeck, raising a hand when he saw the panic in her face. 'Have no fear about the cost. I spoke to Mr Quinnell and told him of your sister's sterling service. In view of that, the railway company has offered to pay the bills for any treatment.'

The word alarmed her. 'Treatment? What sort of treatment?'

'That depends on Dr Swift's advice.'

'Agnes has never been this ill before. She couldn't afford to be.'

'Tell me how it started,' said Colbeck. 'How did your

sister seem when she came home after hearing about Mr Heygate's death?'

'She was as white as a sheet, Inspector. It was even worse than when her dear husband died – God rest his soul! Agnes wept for hours on end.'

'Were she and the stationmaster close friends?'

'Oh, yes, she thought the world of him.'

'Did Mr Heygate ever visit her here?'

'Lord, no,' said Frances, drawing back defensively. 'I don't have any gentlemen under my roof – except for the vicar, of course, but he's different. Agnes would never have brought Mr Heygate into my house. That was understood when she first moved in with me. She would have seen him elsewhere.'

'Yet they don't appear to have spent any time together outside working hours.'

'I think you're wrong there, Inspector. Agnes would go out of an evening now and then and it was always to see Mr Heygate.'

'Is that what she told you?'

'It was the truth. We kept no secrets from each other.'

Colbeck preferred to rely on the testimony of others. The stationmaster had never spent an evening alone with Mrs Rossiter. She'd invented a fantasy courtship and persuaded a gullible sister to believe in it. Now that Heygate had died, her fantasy had crumbled and her unrealistic hopes of a second marriage had perished. She was forced to confront a bleak future without a dream of escape to sustain her. As a result, something inside her had snapped.

Looking at her now, it was difficult to imagine her running wildly down the nave of the cathedral, but Colbeck had no reason to doubt the report he'd been given by the police. The manageress had gone from one extreme to another. After her dramatic and uncontrolled action, she'd now lapsed into a wounded silence. Sitting opposite her, Colbeck tried to break it.

'Good morning, Mrs Rossiter,' he said, softly. 'How are you today?'

There was no reply. She didn't even seem to notice that he was there.

'It's Inspector Colbeck,' he went on. 'You remember me.'

'It's no use,' said Frances. 'I couldn't get a word out of her myself. She just sits there and broods.' She held her sister's hands. 'It's the inspector, Agnes, the kind man who brought you home in a cab. He'd like to talk to you.' There was no response at all. 'There you are,' said Frances, giving up, 'I told you that it was hopeless.'

'So it would seem.'

She let go of her sister's hands. 'What will happen to her?'

'That will depend on the diagnosis.'

'I don't mean her illness,' said Frances. 'Though I don't know the full details, Agnes did something terrible in the cathedral. The police brought her home. We've never been in trouble before, Inspector. We're good, law-abiding people.'

'I'm sure that you are, Miss Impey.'

'Will my sister have to go to prison?'

'Oh, I don't think there's any danger of that,' said Colbeck, soothingly. 'Mrs Rossiter caused a stir but there was no actual damage. Superintendent Steel is a humane and understanding man. He's not inclined to press charges.'

'What about the bishop?'

Colbeck grimaced. 'He may take a different view, alas.'

The doorbell rang. 'Ah, that will be Dr Swift, I suspect. May I let him in?'

'Please do so.'

Colbeck went to the front door and opened it to admit Dr Morton Swift. After introductions, Swift removed his hat and scrutinised the patient. Frances described her sister's symptoms and was slavishly deferential. Colbeck, meanwhile, sized up the newcomer. Swift was a tall, suave individual in his early forties with a searching gaze. He was not the family doctor but had been recommended by Superintendent Steel as the man best qualified to deal with a hysterical woman. He was calm, experienced and reassuring. Like Colbeck, he paid considerable attention to the quality of his apparel.

'I'd like to speak to Mrs Rossiter alone,' decided Swift.

'But she won't talk to anyone, Doctor,' said Frances.

'Why don't you and I step into the next room?' suggested Colbeck as he shepherded her to the door. 'Dr Swift doesn't want us in the way.'

'Oh, well . . . I suppose not.'

With a fearful glance at her sister, Frances went into the kitchen. Colbeck went after her, relieved that Mrs Rossiter was getting the medical attention that she obviously needed. Dr Swift had an excellent reputation. After his examination, he would be able to prescribe the appropriate treatment.

'An owl, a canary, a missing diary, a bonfire, an angry bishop, a well-known thug on the loose, a crazed female in a revolting display of blasphemy – this is the most bizarre case in which I've ever been involved,' said Tallis. 'One is bound to wonder what comes next.'

'I'm grateful that you came all this way to take charge of

the investigation, Superintendent,' said Quinnell.

'I'm here at the behest of Bishop Phillpotts.'

'Have you met him yet?'

'I had that displeasure,' said Tallis, scowling. 'It was an abrasive encounter. I came in the spirit of obedience and, if truth be told, left in something of a temper.'

Quinnell smiled. 'The bishop has that effect on me as well.'

They were in the stationmaster's house. Keen to see everything for himself, Tallis had asked to be shown around the station. Happy to oblige, Quinnell took him on a short tour and they ended up in the dwelling once inhabited by Joel Heygate.

'When someone in authority criticises my officers,' explained Tallis, 'I wish to know why. That's why I'm here.'

'Well, I have no criticism of them,' said Quinnell. 'Inspector Colbeck imparts confidence somehow. This case is too complex for the local police. We needed help from Scotland Yard.'

'Bishop Phillpotts thinks otherwise.'

'What does he know about solving a murder?'

'I had the feeling that he considers himself to be an expert on everything under the sun. One has to respect his position, of course,' said Tallis, 'but there are limits even to my instinctive reverence for a prelate.'

'Say no more, Superintendent. We've all had tussles with him.'

He was about to expand on the theme when he was interrupted by the arrival of Lawrence Woodford, who stepped into the house and tipped his hat to Quinnell.

'Good morning, sir,' he said, politely. 'I noticed you earlier but was too busy supervising trains to attend to you both. If there's anything at all I can do, you only have to ask.'

'Thank you, Woodford,' said Quinnell. 'This is Superintendent Tallis from Scotland Yard, by the way. He's now in charge of the investigation.'

'Oh, I see.' He tipped his hat to Tallis. 'You're most welcome, sir. Joel Heygate was a friend as well as a colleague. His killer must be caught.'

'He will be,' said Tallis, resolutely.

'I've taken over Joel's duties because I know how important it is to keep the station operating as smoothly as usual. A murder is a bad advertisement for any railway company. We have to reassure the public that it's not affected the quality of our service.'

'Quite right,' said Quinnell. 'You're a good man, Woodford.'

'I'm only doing what Joel would have wanted me to do, sir.'

'The reputation of the South Devon Railway has been besmirched. That's why I turned to Superintendent Tallis and his detectives. We want this crime solved and our good name restored.'

'I'm ready to lend any assistance that I can,' said Woodford.

'Yes, I'm sure.' Quinnell turned away. 'That will be all.'

'Then I'll get back to my duties, sir.'

After a covetous glance around the room, Woodford went out.

'He seems a capable man,' observed Tallis.

'Yes, he's very capable, albeit a little too ingratiating for my taste. I like our staff to get on with their jobs instead of expecting a round of applause for doing so. Heygate was an ideal stationmaster,' said Quinnell. 'He was industrious, efficient and calm under stress. He didn't feel the need to be obsequious.'

'Then he'll be a very difficult man to replace.'

'We'll cast our net wide, Superintendent. First, however, we must concentrate all our efforts on catching the fiend responsible for the murder. I know that Inspector Colbeck is hoping for a quick resolution.'

'Only because he's getting married at the end of the month.'

'Indeed? Then his urgency is understandable.'

'The wedding is irrelevant.'

Quinnell chuckled. 'It's not irrelevant to him,' he said, 'or, indeed, to his bride. They will have looked forward to the great day for months. I know that's what my wife and I did. It must have been the same for you, Superintendent.'

Tallis glowered. 'I was never tempted to marry, Mr Quinnell.'

'You've remained a bachelor all this time?'

'And will do so to my dying day,' said Tallis with emphasis. 'Fighting crime is too important a task to take lightly. I allow no distractions into my life. As for the inspector, he knows that this investigation takes precedence over everything else. While he's here in Exeter, Colbeck must not even think about his wedding.'

It was both strange and exasperating. Madeleine Andrews could conjure any number of locomotives on to her canvas and give them startling verisimilitude. When it came to figurative art, however, she tended to flounder. She knew every last detail of Colbeck's face and had always wanted to paint his portrait but it was beyond her talents. Standing at her easel after her latest attempt to bring him to life before her, she had to accept defeat yet again. The portrait was a disaster.

'Thank you, Maddy,' said her father, coming up behind her. 'I didn't know that you were painting a picture of me.'

'It's not you, Father.'

He stared at it intently for a moment. 'No, no,' he went on, 'I can see that now I've taken a closer look. It's Dirk Sowerby, isn't it?'

She was offended. 'Why on earth should I paint a portrait of him?'

'That's what I asked myself. Dirk is no fit subject for an artist.'

'It's supposed to be Robert.' He burst out laughing. 'It's not *that* bad.'

'It's not that good either, Maddy. I think you should stick to painting locomotives – as long as they're ones that run on the LNWR. I'm not having my daughter painting anything that belongs to another railway company.' He put his face close to the canvas. 'There *is* a faint resemblance, I suppose.'

'You should have been able to see at once who it was.'

'I'm sorry. I just couldn't do that.'

'It's not your fault,' she said, sadly. 'I have to accept that I simply don't have the skill to be a portrait artist. That's why I never put people into my paintings. If I want a portrait of Robert, someone else will have to paint it.'

Andrews was dressed to go out for his morning walk. He regretted mocking her attempt at portraiture because he knew what had impelled her to pick up her brush. She was missing Colbeck so much that she'd tried to create an image of him.

'He'll be back before long, Maddy,' he said, kissing her on the temple.

'His letter said that the murder wouldn't be easy to solve. What if the investigation carries on for a few weeks?'

'Then I'll go down to Exeter and drag him back for the wedding.'

'Robert hates to abandon a case before he's brought the culprit to justice.'

'Marrying my daughter comes before anything else.'

'It doesn't stop me from fretting,' she confessed. 'I've waited for years to become Mrs Colbeck. I'm terrified that something will happen at the last minute to ruin the arrangements.'

'Take heart, Maddy. It's not like you to be down.'

'Robert takes his work so seriously.'

'And so he should do,' said Andrews. 'I was the same. There's no point in doing a job if you don't put all your energy into it. Anyway,' he added, 'I'm on my way out. Why not come with me for a walk?'

'I'd much rather stay here, Father.'

'Brooding will get you nowhere.'

'I'll be fine – off you go.'

'Goodbye,' he said, cheerfully. 'And there's no need to worry about the arrangements being ruined. Since the church has been booked for a wedding, we simply replace the pair of you with another happy couple.'

She was baffled. 'What are you talking about?'

'I'll give you one guess.'

Opening the door, he let himself out with a cackle of amusement. When Madeleine realised that he'd been talking about himself and Mrs Langton, she was shaken. Her father

153

hardly knew the woman yet he was already thinking of marriage. Madeleine had a sneaking suspicion that Mrs Langton's mind was also inclined in that direction. It gave her something else to worry about. Returning to her easel, she looked at her portrait and sighed with disappointment. She reached for a damp cloth and wiped Colbeck decisively off the canvas.

They were in the tiny kitchen for a long time. Colbeck could think of many better companions with whom to be cooped up than Frances Impey but he had no choice. She was tense, lacklustre and a poor conversationalist. All that she did was to bleat about her sister's condition. Colbeck kept his ears open to pick up the sounds that came from the parlour. Incredibly, Dr Swift had somehow got Mrs Rossiter talking. What she was saying Colbeck was unable to make out but he could hear her getting increasingly expressive. Desperate to listen at the door, Frances felt unable to do so. She was positively writhing with anxiety.

'What are they saying, Inspector?' she asked.

'I'm not sure, Miss Impey.'

'How ever did the doctor get Agnes to talk?'

'It's a secret I'd like to learn.'

'We've been in here for ages. How much longer must we wait?'

Dr Swift answered the question by opening the door and inviting them in. Frances immediately went to embrace her sister who was now on her feet. While she still looked far from well, Mrs Rossiter had more colour in her cheeks and some animation in her eyes. Frances led her sister into the kitchen to question her in private.

Colbeck was quick to exploit their absence.

'What's your diagnosis, Doctor?' he asked.

'Mrs Rossiter has had a profound shock,' replied the other, solemnly. 'It's destroyed some of the certainties in her life.'

'You achieved a miracle in getting her to talk.'

'Once she got started, the problem was to stop her.'

'Did you ask her about the incident at the cathedral?'

'Yes,' said Swift, 'and she wasn't in the least repentant. In fact, she said she'd do exactly the same if she were given the chance. That was worrying. Her mind has been unbalanced by the loss of a dear friend. I've seen it happen before many times. She's exhibiting far more than natural grief at the death of a loved one.'

'Yet she and the stationmaster were not close,' said Colbeck. 'They merely worked together. They were never bosom friends.'

'Mrs Rossiter *believes* that they were, Inspector, and therein lies the problem. She's in the grip of an obsession.'

'Is it possible to break that obsession?'

'I can prescribe medication that might help to calm her down but there's no cure for a mania. That's what we have here. Though I began my career as a general practitioner,' he went on, 'my main interest is in psychiatry and I spend much of my time at the County Asylum. That's the work that really interests me. I've treated several manic patients. Some have recovered enough to warrant release while others remain in the custody of the medical staff indefinitely.'

Colbeck glanced towards the kitchen and lowered his voice so that he wouldn't be overheard by the two women. He could imagine how shattering a blow it would be for Frances Impey if her sister were taken away from her. Colbeck was not at all sure that she could cope with the stigma of having her sister confined because of a mental disorder. For both their sakes, he hoped that this last resort would somehow be avoidable. Yet he had to accept the doctor's expert opinion.

'Does Mrs Rossiter belong in a lunatic asylum?' he asked.

'Let me put it this way,' said Swift, adjusting his cravat. 'That extraordinary outburst in the cathedral was prompted by her obsession. It has left her with a hatred of religion and what she perceives as its specious benefits. She feels utterly betrayed by God, hence her act of defiance. If the lady has another hysterical episode of that order,' he stressed, 'I'd have no hesitation in signing the certificate to commit her to the County Asylum.'

CHAPTER NINE

When he met them over luncheon, Tallis was not impressed with the way that his detectives had spent the morning. Expecting signs of visible progress, he was very disappointed. He did not mince his words.

'Let me get this straight,' he said, glaring first at Colbeck then at Leeming, 'the sum total of your endeavours is as follows. The inspector wasted his time with a mad old lady while you, Sergeant, seem to have gone to Dawlish for the sole purpose of discovering how the atmospheric railway worked.'

'That's unfair, sir,' said Leeming, hotly. 'I only mentioned that in passing. My interview with Mr and Mrs Heygate did yield a result.'

'I fail to see it.'

'The pair of them must definitely be considered as suspects.'

'You knew that before you went to their home.'

'I had to confirm our suspicions,' argued Leeming. 'They fell out with the stationmaster because he'd refused to advance them money for the second time. There was no sense of gratitude for the loan he'd already given them. Without that, they'd never have been able to set up in business in the first place.'

'Resentment does not make them killers.'

'It could do, sir.'

'I agree,' said Colbeck, coming to his rescue. 'What Victor learnt was that they had a strong motive to murder Joel Heygate. They'd not only wreak their revenge, they'd inherit more than enough from him to buy their way out of their financial difficulties. And there are unanswered questions to consider,' he went on. 'Why did Mr and Mrs Heygate come to Exeter a day earlier than they need have done? Why did they leave their children at home when the celebrations were aimed at the youth of the city? I'm sure that Victor would never have dreamt of depriving his children of such a treat.'

'I certainly wouldn't,' said Leeming. 'They love bonfires.'

'Finally, where did they stay on the fateful night?'

'They must have lodged with friends,' said Tallis, dismissively.

'Then why didn't they say so?'

'Who knows?'

'I'd be surprised if they *had* any friends,' said Leeming. 'They're an unlovable couple, sir. In fact, I think that's another reason why their shop failed. I can't believe that customers enjoyed dealing with them.'

'In that case,' decided Tallis, 'they must have stayed at an inn.'

'When they're so short of money?'

'Damn it, man! They must have stayed *somewhere*.'

'Not necessarily,' Colbeck put in. 'It's conceivable that they committed the murder on the night before Guy Fawkes Day, concealed the body under the bonfire then took the train back to Dawlish.'

'The sergeant should have pressed them for details.'

'That would have given the game away, Superintendent,' said Leeming. 'They'd have realised that they were suspects and clammed up completely.'

'Perhaps *I* should have a word with them.'

'Oh, I don't think that would be a good idea,' said Colbeck, firmly.

He sat back so that the waiter could remove his plate. Letting Tallis loose on their suspects was something that Colbeck was determined to avoid. Both he and Leeming were searching for ways to get rid of the superintendent altogether. With the best of intentions, Tallis nevertheless managed to impede an investigation. When he'd once joined them in Yorkshire to take charge of a case involving suicide and murder, he'd been hopelessly ineffective and unwittingly obstructive. It was only when Tallis had returned to London that they'd been able to move the investigation forward.

'Let's turn to you,' said Tallis, eyeing Colbeck. 'Why did you spend a whole morning at the home of a raving lunatic?'

'That's an unkind description of the lady, sir.'

'What else would you call her? When someone runs amok in a cathedral, then she's clearly of unsound mind and should be locked away.'

'Mrs Rossiter is an important person in this investigation,' insisted Colbeck. 'She worked alongside Mr Heygate for many years and was able to supply some useful information. Common decency compels us to assist her in her hour of need. Mr Quinnell accepted that she'd been a good servant of the railway company and offered to pay for any medical attention.'

'The fact remains that you learnt nothing of value this morning.'

'Yes I did, sir. I learnt that Mrs Rossiter and her sister live in straitened circumstances and I discovered that Dr Swift has an excellent tailor.'

'You're being flippant.'

'I came to understand the lady's position more clearly,' said Colbeck, 'and, as a result, extend her much more sympathy than you are able to summon up at present. Doesn't it tell us something about the stationmaster's character that he could inspire such devotion in a woman?'

'She was the victim of romantic folly.'

'We've all been guilty of that at some time in our lives,' volunteered Leeming.

'Oh no, we haven't,' growled Tallis, reaching for his glass. 'Passion of that nature is always dangerous. It can distort the mind – as in this case.' After taking a sip of his wine, he announced his decision. 'Michael Heygate and his wife must be looked at more closely,' he said. 'We can soon establish if they stayed at an inn here on that particular night. I'll get the local police to make enquiries. We might as well get them to do something.'

'That's unjust, sir,' said Colbeck. 'Superintendent Steel and his men have been willing and cooperative. You must take their limitations into account. It's not easy policing a city over which the bishop holds such sway.'

Tallis gave a nod of assent. 'The man is a confounded nuisance.'

'Then why did you take his complaints so seriously?' asked Leeming.

'Yes,' said Colbeck, 'why didn't you simply send a reply to the effect that you had every confidence in us? That would have saved you a long journey and you'd have been spared a bruising interview with Bishop Phillpotts.'

'I didn't realise at the time that the fellow would be so unpleasant and domineering,' said Tallis. 'I've stayed here because my leadership is needed.'

'It's also needed in London, sir. In fact, the need there is far greater. A case like this comes along once in a blue moon in Exeter, whereas the capital is plagued by serious crime. That's where you should be.' Colbeck nudged Leeming. 'Don't you agree, Victor?'

'I do,' said Leeming, enthusiastically. 'Why not leave everything to us, Superintendent? We can manage on our own. Go back to Scotland Yard.'

'Don't you dare tell me what to do!' said Tallis, flaring up. 'As for managing on your own, how can you question a suspect properly when all that you do is discuss the atmospheric railway with him?'

'I was interested to know how it worked.'

'I'm more interested to know how *you* work, Leeming.'

'I'll make a point of speaking to Michael Heygate myself,' said Colbeck.

'You should have done that in the first place,' snarled Tallis, 'instead of bothering with a woman who's obviously taken leave of her senses. So far, you have three suspects. The police are still combing Exeter to find the most likely

161

one and the other suspect is acting as stationmaster. In fact,' he continued, 'I met Mr Woodford this morning and I have to say that he did not strike me as a potential killer.'

'I'm not sure that he'd have the strength or the nerve,' said Leeming.

'Neither do I,' agreed Colbeck. 'I can't see him battering anyone to death. But I think that Mr Woodford is more than capable of hiring someone else to do the deed.'

Dorcas Hope's career as a manageress was brief. As soon as it was evident that Agnes Rossiter would be away for some time, the former manager of the refreshment room at Newton Abbot station was brought out of retirement. Dorcas was relegated once more to the role of assistant. Timothy Vesey was a short, compact man in his sixties with a gnarled face and a slight stutter. He was much less talkative and self-important than Mrs Rossiter and Dorcas liked him. They worked well together. Woodford made sure that there were no problems. As he stepped into the room for the fourth time that day, he called out to Vesey while keeping his eyes on Dorcas, who was bending over a table as she wiped it clean.

'Is everything under control in here?' he asked.

'Yes, it is,' replied Vesey.

'The next train is due in eight minutes.'

'It will find us in a state of complete r-r-readiness, Mr Woodford.'

'I expect no less.'

'Is there any news about Mrs Rossiter?' wondered Dorcas.

'There's none that I'm aware of, Miss Hope.'

'I heard a rumour that she'd run wild in the cathedral.'

'Don't listen to tittle-tattle,' advised Woodford. 'It's always wrong.'

'They say the police had to take her away.'

He drew himself up. 'What did I just tell you?' he warned. 'I won't have my staff passing on idle gossip. Mrs Rossiter is unable to perform her duties here. That's all you need to know.'

Dorcas was cowed. 'Yes, Mr Woodford.'

'Perhaps you'd care to step outside for a minute.'

'I'm sorry. I won't even mention the rumour again.'

'I'd like to speak to you on another matter,' he said, opening the door and taking her on to the platform. 'There was no need for Mr Vesey to hear this.' He stood very close to Dorcas. 'What did Inspector Colbeck say to you?'

'He asked me a few questions, that was all.'

'What sort of questions?'

'Well,' she said, 'he wanted to know everything I could tell him about Mr Heygate. He was very interested to hear that I was looking after Peter. That was thanks to you, Mr Woodford. I don't think that Mr Quinnell would have let me have the canary if you hadn't spoken up for me.'

'You were the best person to take charge of Peter.'

'He's become one of the family. Mother dotes on him.'

He moved even closer to her. 'What else did the inspector ask you?'

'He wondered if I knew where Mr Heygate kept his money.'

'Any income from the ticket office and the refreshment room goes straight into the safe at the end of each day. You should know that.'

'He was talking about Mr Heygate's own money,' said

163

Dorcas. 'When they searched the house, they couldn't find a penny, yet he must have had some cash to buy food and so on. I think it's odd that there was nothing at all there.'

'It may be in a hiding place,' he ventured.

'The search was very thorough, according to the inspector. He gave me a couple of books on how to look after canaries. Mother's been reading them.'

'Forget canaries,' said Woodford, impatiently. 'Did they find anything of real interest in the house?'

'I don't know. They were simply vexed at what they *didn't* find.'

'The money, you mean?'

'Yes, Mr Woodford – and the diary.'

He became wary. 'What diary was that?'

'The one I told the inspector about,' she explained. 'It was really to do with his birdwatching, you see. Mr Heygate used to keep a note of all the species that he saw and where he'd found them. You can understand why the inspector wished that he'd found the diary. It might have told him where Mr Heygate went that night in order to see that owl.' Woodford seemed distracted. 'Did you hear what I said?'

'Yes, yes,' he said, abruptly. 'That diary could be important.'

'Yet it wasn't anywhere in the house.'

'Or if it was, it was carefully hidden.' He rubbed a hand across his chin and seemed to forget that she was there. After a minute, he noticed her again. 'Back to work, Miss Hope,' he ordered. 'You're going to be very busy before too long.'

'Yes, Mr Woodford,' she said, relieved to get away.

While she went back into the refreshment room, he

sauntered down the platform towards the stationmaster's house. He studied it with fresh interest and was about to get closer when a uniformed policeman came into view. The house was still being guarded. Woodford gave the policeman a friendly wave but his emotions were in turmoil. He suddenly felt under threat.

When yet another summons came from the bishop's palace, Superintendent Steel was irritated. He had far too much to do to dance attendance on the bishop. After toying with the idea of ignoring the letter, he elected to obey the request in the end but made a point of arriving late. Predictably, it infuriated the bishop.

'I don't like to be kept waiting,' he rasped from his chair in the library.

'I had something more important to do, Bishop.'

'Nothing is more important than what I have to say. I want that woman hauled before a magistrate at once and sent to prison.'

'I think you're being unnecessarily vindictive,' said the other.

'Don't you realise what she did, man?'

'My officers gave me a full report.'

'She defiled the house of God and, by implication, challenged my authority.'

'When she entered the cathedral,' said the superintendent, 'I don't believe the lady had you in mind at all. It was an impulsive act by a desperate woman.'

'It was also a calculated attack on me,' declared the bishop, 'and it comes on the back of a murder that was an orchestrated assault on my position in the city.'

'I'm sorry, Bishop, but I fail to see that.'

'There are far too many things you fail to see, Superintendent. Blindness in a police officer is a grave shortcoming.'

'Lack of compassion in a bishop is an even graver one.'

Bishop Phillpotts could not believe what he'd just heard. His eyes were aflame, his cheeks scarlet and his whole body shaking. They were alone in the library and he'd been sitting behind his desk. His visitor's retort made him leap to his feet.

'Do you have the audacity to accuse me of such a fault?'

'It was not an accusation,' said Steel, striking a conciliatory note. 'It was an observation. I respectfully submit that your attitude towards Mrs Rossiter falls short of Christian forbearance. The woman is patently unwell. She needs help and understanding.'

'Punishment is what she needs,' said the bishop. 'It must be a harsh and visible punishment to deter others. Charges must be brought against her.'

'Inspector Colbeck felt that that would be unkind.'

'He's not the person who suffered a gross public insult.'

'And neither were you, Bishop,' said Steel. 'Mrs Rossiter didn't know what she was doing. For some reason, she lost all inhibition. We should strive to forgive her for what was clearly uncharacteristic impetuosity.'

'Heavens above, man!' exclaimed the bishop. 'She grabbed the crucifix.'

'It was a foolish gesture.'

'It was a denial of the very existence of the Almighty.'

'As such, it's to be condemned,' said Steel, 'but I still don't believe it deserves imprisonment. Inspector Colbeck concurs. He's arranged for her to be examined by Dr Swift. If she is to be incarcerated, it will be in the County Asylum.' The bishop seemed partially soothed. 'May I return to my duties now, please?'

'No, Superintendent, you may not.'

'We have a killer to find.'

'That's the other matter I wished to discuss. Browne must be arrested.'

'He's proving elusive.'

'Then you need more men to search for him,' said the bishop. 'To that end, I urge you to call in the troops from Topsham Barracks.'

'Oh, no,' said Steel, holding up both palms. 'That would be quite wrong. You seem to forget that relations between the police and the military are strained at the best of times. We need to stay well apart. Besides,' he continued, 'it's not simply a question of having more men. The best way to track down Bagsy Browne is to seek good intelligence. That's why Mr Quinnell has increased the amount of money on offer for information leading to his arrest.'

'Has any information been forthcoming so far?'

Steel was uncomfortable. 'We've had none that's entirely reliable.'

'And we both know why,' said the bishop. 'Whenever he's here, Browne terrorises this city. People won't help you because they're afraid of the consequences. They want the reassurance of seeing army uniforms on our streets.'

'It would be a disastrous step to take.'

'We need protection, Superintendent. I, in particular, demand it.'

'Why so?'

'Browne committed that murder out of spite against me. And he's still *here*,' said the bishop, waving an arm to take in the whole of Exeter. 'If he's got away with murder once, he may feel able to do so again – and I may well be his target.'

Steel mastered a surge of hope that such an eventuality might occur.

'That's absurd, Bishop,' he said, reasonably. 'There's no evidence at all to suggest that the killing of Joel Heygate is in any way directed at you. Bagsy Browne is a deep-dyed villain who acts out of malice rather than because he has a hatred of the Church. Of one thing you can rest assured – you are completely safe.'

'Then why don't I *feel* safe in this city?'

Steel saw a chance to get rid of him. 'Why not withdraw to Torquay?' he counselled. 'There'd be no sense of danger there, Bishop. You can return to Exeter when we've got Bagsy Browne in custody.'

The bishop struck a pose. 'I don't run away from danger,' he boasted. 'I stay to confront it and take positive action. I give you this warning. Catch this vile recreant in the next few days or . . .' he paused for effect '. . . or I will contact the army myself.'

After scanning the newspaper with growing annoyance, Bagsy Browne scrunched it up and tossed it on the floor. Adeline Goss retrieved it. They were in her room and he was lolling discontentedly on the bed.

'Why did you do that, Bagsy?' she asked, smoothing the paper so that it could be read again. 'Did something in there upset you?'

'I'm upset because something *wasn't* in the paper.'

'What were you expecting?'

'I wanted details of Heygate's funeral.'

'That may not be for days yet.'

'I can't stay in Exeter for ever, Ad.'

'Where will you go?'

'I need to find somewhere warm for the winter.'

She sat beside him. 'It's very snug in here,' she said, stroking his arm. 'I keep the fire burning day and night.'

'You certainly keep *my* fire burning,' he said with a crude snigger.

'That's what I'll always do, Bagsy.' She saw a headline in the newspaper. 'They're still looking for you.'

'So?'

'Maybe it wasn't such a good idea to attack that prison officer.'

'It was him who attacked *me*, Ad. I had to defend myself. Also, I had a score to settle with Bob Wyatt. He made my life a misery in prison. I got my own back in the end,' he said, triumphantly. 'I always do. Anyone who crosses Bagsy Browne will wish that they hadn't.'

'Don't go to that funeral,' she implored.

'Nothing would keep me away. I loathed that stationmaster.'

'You'd be taking too big a risk, Bagsy.'

'Stop worrying. I know what I'm doing.'

She grasped his shoulder. 'I'd hate to lose you, I really would.'

'Then I'll make sure you don't, Ad,' he said, pulling her on to the bed. Before he could lift her skirt, they heard a dog barking furiously.

Bagsy sat up. 'That sounds like trouble.'

* * *

There was a shifting population in Rockfield Place. It consisted largely of petty criminals, whores, drunkards and unemployed men. Respect for the law was not widespread. Precautions had therefore been taken against any visit by the police. A guard dog had been trained to bark at the sight of a police uniform. His warning had saved a number of fugitives from arrest. Whole families there might have been desperately short of food but the dog, a flea-bitten cur, was always well fed. He earned everything he ate. Four policemen had come purposefully into Rockfield Place. They grabbed the first woman they could find, a scrawny prostitute with missing teeth.

'We're looking for Adeline Goss,' said the sergeant.

'I can give you a better time in bed than her,' she bragged, 'and I charge less. Come on up to my room and I'll prove it.'

'Where is she?'

'I'll tell you later.'

He shook her violently and she screeched in protest. When she tried to break away, he held her tight. The dog snapped at his legs and he kicked it away. Under threat of arrest, the woman finally capitulated. She pointed a greasy finger.

'Ad has the top room up there,' she said.

They were off in a flash. Shoving her aside, the four policemen ran to the house in question and banged on the door. It was opened by a girl with ragged clothes and bare feet. Before she could ask what they wanted, they rushed past her and thundered up the stairs to the top floor. When they burst into her room, Adeline was sitting at the table, eating a biscuit and reading the newspaper. She feigned surprise.

'Where have *you* all come from?' she asked, one

provocative hand on her hip. 'No matter – I've been starved of business lately. You can take it in turns.'

'We're looking for Bagsy Browne,' said the sergeant.

'Well, he's not here. Take a look if you don't believe me.'

It took them less than a minute to search the room. They looked in every possible hiding place and peered under the bed. Adeline was unruffled.

'I think an apology is in order,' she said. 'Don't you?'

'You should apologise for harbouring a killer,' said the sergeant. 'You've had Bagsy Browne up here, haven't you?'

She was pugnacious. 'Who says so?'

'We have a witness who saw you together. Where's Bagsy now?'

'I've never heard of him.'

'We've got no time to play games,' he said, turning to the others. 'She's under arrest. Take her in for questioning.'

Adeline squawked in protest but she could not fight off the two strong men who took an arm apiece and carried her out of the room. After a last look around, the sergeant went out and slammed the door behind him. It was an hour before Bagsy Browne moved the concealed panel in the ceiling and lowered himself down.

It was early evening when they met Superintendent Steel at the Acland Tavern. Colbeck and Leeming were far more at ease than they had been over luncheon with Tallis. Steel had accepted them and they, in turn, had recognised his true merit. They could converse as friends and fellow policemen. When they heard about the bishop's threat of bringing in the army, the detectives were dismayed.

'The only time that soldiers are of use is when a riot has

to be quelled,' said Colbeck, 'and even then I'd think twice about deploying them. We're searching for one man, not trying to subdue an entire city.'

'Bishop Phillpotts is afraid that he may be the next victim,' said Steel.

'That's ridiculous.'

'He believes that everything that's happened is aimed at him.'

'Then perhaps he should be examined by Dr Swift,' suggested Colbeck. 'He specialises in people with delusions. Incidentally,' he continued, 'I must thank you for passing on Dr Swift's name. The way that he handled Mrs Rossiter was admirable. He's the sort of man in whom one can have complete faith.'

'I've heard nothing but good about Dr Swift. That's why I recommended him. As for the bishop,' continued Steel, 'we all have our cross to bear, I fancy. When I met Superintendent Tallis, I sensed that he could be just as objectionable as Bishop Phillpotts. Am I right?'

'He can be trying at times,' conceded Colbeck.

'He's a monster,' said Leeming. 'He enjoys finding fault with us and always gets in our way. I wish that he'd go back to London and stop harassing us. We work so much better on our own. Let's not talk about the superintendent,' he went on. 'It upsets my stomach. I wanted to ask you about Dawlish. Is there much crime there?'

'Not as a rule,' replied Steel. 'Why do you want to know?'

'The place appealed to me somehow. I could see myself living there with my family. It wouldn't be too difficult to police. I could grow to like that.'

'No you couldn't,' said Colbeck with a laugh. 'You

wouldn't last five minutes there, Victor. You'd be bored to death by it. You thrive on action and I don't think that a quiet Devonshire coastal resort will provide you with much of that. Isn't that so, Superintendent?'

'Nothing much happens in Dawlish,' said Steel. 'Nothing, that is, of interest to the police. Rowdy behaviour at the pub is all you'd have to contend with, Sergeant, and some very occasional larceny.'

'You're forgetting Michael Heygate,' Leeming reminded him. 'Dawlish could well have a killer lurking in its midst.'

'I stand by my earlier judgement. Bagsy Browne is our man.'

'I'm not ruling out Woodford,' said Colbeck. 'We could all be wrong, of course,' he admitted. 'It may be that none of our three suspects is guilty. The culprit could be someone else entirely.'

'I don't think so, Inspector. My money is on Bagsy.'

'Are you any nearer to catching him?'

'We believe that we are,' said Steel, confidently. 'Earlier today my men arrested a prostitute by the name of Adeline Goss. She lives in Rockfield Place and that's infested with them. We received information that she knew Bagsy Browne and had recently been seen with him. That's why I authorised the raid.'

'What happened?'

'Her room was searched but there was no sign of him.'

'How reliable is your informant?'

'He's very reliable, as a rule,' explained Steel, 'because he needs the money. He's an Irishman named Finbar Mulleady and he got fed up with eating prison food. So he mended his ways and became an informant instead. We've been paying for his drink these last couple of years.'

'Did you get anything out of the woman?' asked Leeming.

Steel grinned. 'Yes, we got the vilest abuse I've ever heard.'

'I take it that she even denied knowing Browne.'

'They're old friends. Several people have confirmed that.'

'Are you certain of securing a conviction?' asked Colbeck.

'There's no doubt about that. Mulleady is prepared to swear on oath that he saw them together in Rockfield Place, so she'll be convicted of harbouring a wanted man. And once Adeline Goss is imprisoned, we have the perfect bait for Bagsy.'

'Do you think he'd try to rescue her?'

'I'm sure of it, Inspector. It's the kind of perverted gallantry I'd expect of him. Catch his woman and we have a good chance of catching him.'

Colbeck was sceptical. 'It may not be as simple as that.'

'We have the trump card,' said Steel. 'We have Mulleady. His eyesight may get blurred after a few pints of beer but he knows what he saw. Bagsy and the woman are lovers. Because she aided him, he won't desert her now. Once we've caught him,' he added with a complacent smile, 'we can prosecute Bagsy for the murder and Mulleady can collect a very large reward.'

A wet and blustery night kept most people at home but one man had been lured out. Impervious to the weather, he floated gently along the canal. Finbar Mulleady would be unable to claim anything now.

CHAPTER TEN

Caleb Andrews was deadly serious about his new friendship and it was disturbing. Madeleine had never known him take such care with his appearance. He was not due to visit Binnie Langton's house until the afternoon, yet he was all spruced up in his best suit and kept stopping in front of a mirror to comb his hair and stroke his beard. Someone who jokingly criticised Colbeck for his vanity was now leaving himself open to a similar charge. Madeleine worried that her father had been far too quick to bestow his affections on a woman he knew too little about.

'Perhaps I should come with you,' she said.

'What would be the point of that?'

'I'd like to meet Mrs Langton.'

'All in good time, Maddy,' he said. 'I want to enjoy the pleasure of being alone with her for once. That's how we can really become acquainted.'

'Things are moving too fast.'

'They have to at our age. We're not like you and Inspector Colbeck. Both of you are young enough to take your time. We don't have years to spare.'

It was a sobering reminder of her long courtship. Madeleine had always known that she'd marry Colbeck one day but she'd been kept waiting far longer than she'd anticipated. Indeed, the delay was so protracted that her father – though talked out of it by Madeleine – had toyed with the notion of asking if Colbeck really did intend to lead her to the altar. His daughter was an attractive woman with many admirers. If one man was keeping her waiting, Andrews argued, perhaps it was time she looked elsewhere. Madeleine had disagreed. Her love for Colbeck was far too deep for her even to entertain the idea of befriending another man, but it hadn't stopped her from wondering if and when they could at last set the date for their wedding.

'I've done this before, remember,' said Andrews, back in front of the mirror again. 'I know how to choose a wife. Your mother was the light of my life, Maddy. I couldn't wish for a better wife. I'm not pretending that Binnie could match her in any way but . . . I feel the need for female company. Is that such a crime?'

'No, Father, it isn't.'

'I hoped that you'd be happy for me.'

'I would be if I knew more about the lady.'

'I like her – that's all you need to know.'

'And is she just as fond of you?'

He chortled. 'I think it's safe to say that.'

'Have you told her about me?' asked Madeleine.

'What a silly question! Of course I've told her about you.

She wanted to know everything about me and she was very excited when I told her that the famous Railway Detective was going to be my son-in-law.' He took her gently by the shoulders. 'Try to stop worrying, Maddy. I'm not some lovesick young man with his head in the clouds.'

'I just don't want you to make a decision you'll later regret.'

'I haven't made *any* decision yet.'

'Then why are you dressed as if you're going to church?'

He stood back and spread his arms. 'I want to make a good impression,' he said. 'Think of all those years when I came home with the filth and stink of the railways on me. That's all in the past, Maddy. I'm going to be well groomed and smartly dressed from now on – just like a certain person I could mention.'

Madeleine smiled. 'You could never look as elegant as Robert.'

'I couldn't afford it, for a start.'

'But you do look nice, Father. I hope that Mrs Langton appreciates you.'

'There's no doubt about that,' he said with another chortle. 'Binnie is full of appreciation. She's going to make a cake for me. Apparently, she's a very good cook.'

'What time will I expect you back?'

'I haven't gone yet.'

'I need to know when to prepare dinner.'

'I'm sorry, Maddy, I can't say when I'll be back. I'm only invited for tea but, if things develop in the way I hope, I may stay a lot longer. Expect me when you see me. That's my advice.'

Madeleine's anxiety was intensified.

Preoccupied as he was with the search for a killer, Colbeck never forgot that he was due to get married at the end of the month. Whenever he passed a church or caught a glimpse of the cathedral, he felt a surge of pleasure. In the weeks leading up to the event, it would have been far more convenient for him to be working in London, but crime popped up in all parts of the railway network and he would travel anywhere to grapple with it. Morning started with breakfast at the Acland Tavern. Mercifully, Tallis was late getting up, so Colbeck and Leeming were able to enjoy the meal without his invasive presence. They also had the opportunity to discuss domestic concerns.

'I miss Estelle and the children so much,' said Leeming.

'You could always keep in touch by letter.'

'It's not the same as seeing them in the flesh, sir. Well, it must be the same for you and Miss Andrews.'

'It is,' said Colbeck, resignedly. 'I'd love Madeleine to be here with me but that's wholly impractical.'

'I know the feeling. When I went to Dawlish yesterday, I had this sudden desire to show it to my family. I could just imagine stepping off the train and giving them their first look at that lovely beach. Then they could feed the ducks on the brook.' He pulled a face. 'There are no beaches where we live and there isn't a duck for miles.' He munched a piece of toast. 'It makes you think, though, doesn't it?'

'Think about what?'

'Well, marriage and the happiness it can bring. There's nothing to compare with it. I'm blessed in my wife and, from what you told me about the stationmaster's house, it's obvious that he was happily married as well.' He took a noisy sip of tea. 'I wouldn't say the same about his brother. Michael Heygate and his wife were together but you'd never say they were contented with each other. They both seemed miserable and it wasn't because they were in mourning.'

'Marriage affects people in different ways, Victor,' said Colbeck. 'You and Estelle have set a good example. Others are not so fortunate in their choices.'

'You certainly are, sir. Miss Andrews will make an excellent wife.'

'No question about that. I like to think that I may be a worthy husband.'

'It's something you have to work at,' said Leeming, sagely. 'But I wish you both well. Estelle was delighted that you'd invited us to the wedding. It's not often she has an excuse to dress up in her finery.' He took another bite of toast. 'Have you changed your decision about the superintendent?'

'No, I haven't. He'd be embarrassed if we sent him an invitation and it would certainly be declined. In his company, it's safer to pretend that the wedding is not actually happening. That reduces the risk of friction.'

Leeming rolled his eyes. 'There's always friction when he's around.' He choked on his toast as he saw Tallis enter the room. Colbeck patted him on the back to help him clear his throat. 'Talk of the devil! Here he is.'

They manufactured a smile apiece to greet Tallis. Annoyed that they'd started without him, he sat in the vacant seat at the table.

'Why didn't one of you call me?' he demanded.

'We felt that you needed your sleep, sir,' said Colbeck.

'I'm always up at the crack of dawn in London.'

'Country air can be very soporific.'

'What does that mean?' asked Leeming.

'It encourages you to sleep, Victor.'

'I never need any encouragement to do that, sir.'

'I'm here now,' said Tallis, 'that's the main thing. We can discuss our plans for the day.' He broke off when the waiter arrived to take his order. As soon as the man withdrew, Tallis became businesslike. 'We need to split up so that we can maximise our effectiveness.'

'Are you going back to London, then?' asked Leeming, hopefully.

'Not until this case is solved. Now, you were talking about an interview with Michael Heygate, were you not, Inspector?'

'Yes, sir,' said Colbeck.

'Leave him to me. I'll set off for Dawlish this morning.'

'Take note of the pumping stations,' said Leeming.

Tallis glared. 'If you mention the atmospheric railway once more, Leeming,' he warned, 'I won't be responsible for my actions.'

'In theory, it's such an interesting concept.'

'In practice, you can be such an imbecile at times.'

Leeming was hurt. 'That's a bit harsh, sir.'

'It's also untrue,' said Colbeck, touching his arm. 'The sergeant and I will stay here. I need to have a talk with Mr Woodford and Victor is going for a walk.'

'Am I, Inspector – where to?'

'I've been thinking over what the stationmaster told Miss Hope. The old shed in which he found that owl was only a quarter of an hour's walk away. It may be possible to locate it. Walk for fifteen minutes in every direction and keep your eyes peeled.' He could see that Tallis was nursing doubts. 'Mr Heygate must have had a lamp with him when he went out that night and one is missing from the station. If the sergeant could possibly find that, we'd have a valuable clue.'

'I remain to be convinced,' said Tallis.

'It's an avenue worth exploring. We have to press on as hard as we can, sir, especially in view of the latest threat from Bishop Phillpotts.'

'What's the wretched fellow been up to now?'

'He's talking about bringing in soldiers from Topsham.'

'That will muddy the waters completely,' complained Tallis. 'Nobody has more respect for the army than I do but there's a time and place for them. We can't do our jobs properly if we keep bumping into a battalion of soldiers.'

'The bishop felt that they could assist in the search for this man, Browne.'

'He should leave crime detection to those trained to do it. Browne is our prime suspect but I'm not persuaded that he definitely committed the murder. I need more evidence and I won't get that with the army tramping through the streets of Exeter. That's the best way to frighten Browne off,' said Tallis, 'and we need to keep him in the city to have any chance of catching the rogue.'

'Superintendent Steel has ensured that he'll stay a while,' said Colbeck.

'Really – how has he done that?'

'He's arrested a woman who has allegedly been harbouring Browne. A police informant saw them together and will swear as much in court. The superintendent believes that the arrest will flush Browne out of hiding to attempt a rescue.'

'That sounds promising,' said Tallis. 'My regret is that it comes from the initiative of the local police and not from either of you.' He looked meaningfully from one to the other. 'An informant is involved, you say? Will he be a credible witness in court?'

'Oh, yes,' said Colbeck. 'We're told he's very reliable.'

He was floating face down when they found him. They had to use a pole to haul him to the side of the canal. Two burly policemen dragged him ashore and stood back as water cascaded off him. Though his trousers were sodden, they could see ugly bloodstains down one leg. As the superintendent looked on, one of the policemen turned the corpse over. Steel needed only a cursory glance to identify him.

'It's Finbar Mulleady,' he said.

Frances Impey was close to despair. Dr Swift had broken the news as gently as he could but it had still had the impact of a cannonball. Her sister had a mental disorder. If it expressed itself in violence again, it might be necessary to send her to Devon County Asylum. The very thought of the place made Frances shudder. Built in nearby Exminster over ten years earlier, it was a tall, forbidding, uncompromising brick edifice with six radiating arms and the appearance of a prison for those of unsound mind. A number of horror stories had leaked out of the asylum and they'd scared Frances stiff. Even though he'd assured her that the rumours were arrant nonsense, Dr Swift was unable to allay her fears. If her sister went into the place, Frances was afraid that she might never come out again and that she herself would therefore be left to bear the stigma alone.

There had been an improvement and it was something to which she could cling. Agnes Rossiter looked better. Thanks to a sedative prescribed by the doctor, she'd slept well and awoken in a more amenable mood. Frances was able to have a proper conversation with her. Over breakfast, her sister seemed quite normal. Ignoring advice to the contrary, Mrs Rossiter insisted on wearing mourning dress once more but she'd apparently stopped brooding on the stationmaster's death. At one point, she even talked about going back to work.

'I'm not sure that that will be possible, Agnes.'

'Why not, may I ask?'

'Dr Swift said that you were not ready yet.'

Mrs Rossiter frowned. 'Was he that gentleman who called yesterday?'

'Yes,' said Frances. 'He was here with Inspector Colbeck.'

'I remember now. They were both so well dressed. I like smartness in a man.' She smiled proudly. 'Joel was very smart.'

'Finish your breakfast, dear. It's so good to see you eating again.'

'Have I been a burden to you, Frances?'

'No, no – you're my sister.'

'I'd hate to be a burden to anybody. I've always been so independent.'

Frances kissed her. 'You're no trouble at all, Agnes.'

When the meal was over, Frances cleared away the plates and did the washing-up in the sink. Such had been the improvement in her sister's behaviour that she dared to hope for a complete recovery. She was drying her hands on a towel when Mrs Rossiter came into the kitchen wearing her hat, coat and gloves.

'What on earth are you doing?' she cried.

'I'm going out, Frances.'

'But the doctor said that you were to stay indoors.'

'He can't stop me going for a walk,' asserted Mrs Rossiter. 'I need some fresh air and exercise. I can't stay here all day.'

Frances took off her apron. 'I'll come with you.'

'I'd like that.'

'Where shall we go?'

'I want to see Joel.'

'But he's dead. His body will be at the undertaker's by now.'

'That's where I want to go,' said Mrs Rossiter, simply. 'It's my right. I need to pay my respects. I have to see him for one last time. Don't you understand?'

Colbeck arrived at the station as the Plymouth train was departing. Having consulted the timetable, he knew that there would be a gap of twenty minutes before Lawrence Woodford would be called upon to despatch another train to its destination. He took the stationmaster into the refreshment room, chose a table in the corner and ordered two cups of tea.

'How are you finding your new role, Mr Woodford?' he asked.

'Well, it's not entirely new,' replied the other. 'I deputised for Joel when his wife and daughter died, so I learnt the ropes then.'

'You've shown remarkable flair.'

'It's kind of you to say so, Inspector.'

'Do you live nearby?'

'We have a house not far from the cathedral.'

'And what does Mrs Woodford think of what is, in essence, your promotion?'

'My wife is very proud of me. Her regret, of course, is that I've only become stationmaster temporarily because Joel was battered to death by a thug.. We'd much rather that he'd been spared such a grisly fate.'

'How much did you see of him on a daily basis?'

'Not a great deal,' said Woodford. 'I was locked away in my office most of the day while Joel was on patrol out here. But we exchanged friendly banter when we had the chance.'

Colbeck didn't believe him for a second. In his opinion, Woodford was not a man who'd indulge in friendly banter with anyone. He was too abrupt and officious and would be much more likely to enforce rules than to make a humorous remark to a colleague. Nor was Colbeck fooled by the man's claim to be close to his predecessor. Woodford was too well defended to let anyone get too close to him and there was a prickly side to him that would keep others away. Dorcas arrived with the tea on a tray.

'Is there any word of Mrs Rossiter?' she asked, putting the cups on the table.

'She was seen by a doctor yesterday,' replied Colbeck. 'He advised rest.'

'When will she be coming back to work?'

'I can't answer that, Miss Hope.'

'Don't bother us now,' said Woodford with a hostile glance. 'The Inspector and I are trying to have a conversation.'

Dorcas backed away. 'I'm sorry, Mr Woodford. Do excuse me.'

'That young lady works hard,' observed Colbeck as she moved away.

'She has to be kept in her place.'

'People work best when given encouragement. That's

what I always find.' He studied Woodford. 'If you live near the cathedral, you must have been well placed to attend the bonfire celebrations.'

'They had no interest for us and – as we have no children – there was no reason to take part in them. Things get out of hand too easily, Inspector. Drink is taken and tempers flare up. I abhor violence of all kinds,' said Woodford, 'even if it's in fun. My wife and I steer well clear of the cathedral precinct on Guy Fawkes Day.'

'Mr Heygate intended to go, I believe.'

'Joel had a childish streak in him at times.'

'People of all ages enjoy a bonfire,' said Colbeck. 'Did your predecessor ever discuss his birdwatching with you?'

'No, Inspector, it's not something that appeals to me.'

'So you've no idea where he went?'

Woodford scratched his chin. 'He did once mention the Exminster marshes to me,' he recalled. 'Joel said that he'd seen a variety of species there.'

'How far away would that be?'

'Oh, it's over three miles south of the city.'

'So it couldn't have been the place he went on the night he was killed He'd hardly walk that distance in the dark. Exminster is an unlikely destination.'

'It most certainly was. Joel went . . .' He turned as if about to point in one direction but thought better of it. 'He must have gone somewhere else'

'Was it a cold night on November 4th?'

'It's always cold at this time of year.'

Colbeck put milk into his tea and stirred it. 'Do you have any hobbies?' he asked, casually.

'My work doesn't allow me much leisure time.'

'I have the same problem, Mr Woodford.'

'My wife and I do go for a walk on Sunday after church. It's become a sort of tradition. The weather has to be really bad to deter us.'

'Regular exercise is good for us. It's probably the reason you look so healthy.'

'Yes,' said Woodford, adding milk and sugar to his tea. 'It's one thing where I had the advantage over Joel. He put on weight after the tragedy involving his wife and daughter. One can't blame him for that. Food was his consolation.'

'Did he ever mention a diary to you?'

'Not that I can remember.'

'He seems to have kept one.'

'It's the first I've heard of it,' said Woodford, checking to making sure that Dorcas didn't hear him. 'What was in the diary, Inspector?'

'We don't know until we find it. But it might be of significant help.'

'Maybe the killer destroyed it for that reason.'

'I doubt if he knew that it even existed.'

'Isn't it squirrelled away in the house somewhere?'

'We couldn't find it. Just in case it is there,' said Colbeck, 'I asked for a policeman to guard the house. If the killer finds out about the diary, he may well come looking for it. We need to find it first.'

'I wish you well in your search.' It was Woodford's turn to sound casual. 'I take it that Bagsy Browne is the only suspect.'

'Yes, he is,' said Colbeck, easily. 'Superintendent Steel is convinced of his guilt. Mr Browne is a man with a fearsome reputation, I gather.'

'I was here the day he caused a rumpus. He fought like

an animal until Joel knocked him out. When he came to, he vowed to get even with Joel one day.' He breathed in sharply. 'Unfortunately, he kept his promise.'

The caterwauling made it impossible for Superintendent Steel to concentrate on his work. He was just about to investigate the ear-splitting noise when the custody sergeant came into his office.

'It's that woman, sir,' he said. 'She won't shut up till she's spoken to you.'

'Then I'd better see what she wants.'

'What she wants is a gag over that foul mouth of hers.'

'Yes, she does have a colourful vocabulary.'

They went downstairs together. When they reached her cell, Adeline Goss was still yelling at the top of her voice. At the sight of Steel, she quietened down. He nodded to the sergeant who unlocked the door of the cell.

'What seems to be the problem?' asked Steel, confronting her.

'I want to know what's going on,' she demanded.

'You're under arrest, Miss Goss. I'd have thought that was obvious.'

'They said I'd go before a magistrate this morning.'

'And you will do in due course. But there's been a development.'

She squinted at him. 'What's happened?'

'Bagsy Browne has disrupted our plans,' said Steel. 'You remember him, don't you?' She looked blank. 'Everyone knows you're his friend. Why deny it?'

'I've had nothing to do with anyone of that name.'

'Would you swear that on the Holy Bible?'

'Yes!' she shouted. 'Who is this Bagsy Browne?'

'He's the man you were seen with by a witness, Miss Goss.'

'What bleeding witness?'

'He's someone who knows you both by sight. His name is Mulleady.'

'Finbar Mulleady!' she said with derision. 'Don't believe a word that drunken Irish scoundrel tells you. The only thing Mulleady ever sees is how much is in his tankard. He'll tell you any damn thing you want if you buy his beer.'

'As it happens,' explained Steel, 'Mulleady's not in a position to tell us anything at the moment. His dead body was pulled out of the canal this morning.' She cackled with delight. 'There's nothing to laugh about. It's one more crime to chalk up to the man you've never heard about – Bagsy Browne. He obviously got wind of the fact that Mulleady was going to bear witness against the pair of you. That's *two* murders we'll hang him for – and you'll be his accessory to one of them.'

Adeline was silenced at last. Fear and disbelief seized her. Her mind was racing madly as the cell door was slammed shut in her face and locked.

Michael Heygate and his wife were surprised when Tallis turned up on their doorstep. Since he was now in charge of the investigation, however, they felt that he'd come to give them a report on its progress. Tallis didn't disillusion them. He was there to question them without appearing to do so. Invited into the parlour, he sat by the fire and refused the offer of refreshment.

'Sergeant Leeming came to see us yesterday,' said Heygate.

'So I understand. Like me, he found Dawlish a charming place.'

'It's not been all that charming for us,' muttered Lavinia. 'But our prospects have suddenly improved,' she added with a whisper of a smile. 'When the sergeant heard that I came from Starcross, all he wanted to talk about was the—'

'Yes, yes,' said Tallis, cutting her off. 'I'm all too aware of that. What I came to tell you is that the net is closing in on the killer.'

'Have you identified him, then?' asked Heygate.

'We believe so.'

'What's his name?'

'Bernard Browne – though I understand that he's known as Bagsy.'

'Yes, we've met him,' said Lavinia before she could stop herself. After collecting a stern look from her husband, she gave a nervous laugh. 'We don't really know the man, but someone called Bagsy came into the shop once.'

'Oh?' said Tallis, interested. 'What did he want?'

'He bought a fishing rod,' said Heygate, indicating to his wife that she should hold her tongue. 'It was a long time ago. I'd forgotten all about him.'

'He *bought* a fishing rod?' Tallis was astonished. 'Everything I've heard about this villain suggests that he'd be more likely to *steal* one.'

'He paid us the full price.'

'If he came here, he must have seen your name above the shop.'

'That's true.'

'Did he connect you with the stationmaster at Exeter St David's?'

'I doubt it.'

'Well, it's not all that common a name.'

'He was just one customer of many when we had such things,' said Heygate, evasively. 'If my wife hadn't remembered his name, I wouldn't have done so.'

'I'm very glad that Mrs Heygate did so.'

Tallis gave her a nod of congratulation but she was squirming with discomfort. A link had been made between two of the murder suspects. That fact alone made Tallis feel that his journey hadn't been in vain. He began to wonder if Heygate had either employed Browne to commit the crime, or assisted him in doing so. It could be a fruitful area to explore. He tried to dispel their obvious disquiet.

'There's no guarantee that Browne *is* guilty,' he stressed. 'He just happened to be in the vicinity and has a long criminal record. We suspect that he was there on the night of November 4th – but, then, so were you.'

'That's right, Superintendent,' said Heygate.

'My sergeant thought it odd that you didn't bring your children.'

'They preferred to stay here with school friends.'

'Yet the celebrations in Exeter would have been much more spectacular.'

Heygate was stony-faced. 'It was their choice.'

'So *you* must also have stayed with friends.'

'Yes, we did.'

'Was it for the one night or for two?'

'It was just for the one night, Superintendent. My wife and I stayed for most of the celebrations, then caught a late train back here. Little did we know at that time, mind you, what they would find when the bonfire burnt itself out.'

'Quite so, quite so – you have my deepest sympathy.'

'It came like a thunderbolt,' said Lavinia, finding her voice at last and contriving a look of grief. 'Michael and I are still stunned.'

'Yes,' added her husband. 'We've been very grateful to Mr Quinnell. He's been immensely helpful. In fact, we received a letter from him this morning to say that the funeral will be next Monday. The railway company will bear the cost.'

'That's very noble of them.'

'All the arrangements will be taken care of. Mr Quinnell was anxious to relieve us of that and he's also talking about a memorial service – though I feel that might be going too far.' A sly look came into his eye. 'How soon after the funeral will my brother's will be read, do you think?'

'Oh, I can't say, Mr Heygate. Legal wheels grind very slowly.'

'Will it be a matter of weeks?'

'You'd have to ask the solicitor concerned.'

'Is there any means of speeding up the process?'

'I wish that there were,' said Tallis with a chuckle. 'Solicitors are like snails. They never rush. But you'll get your inheritance in the fullness of time,' he went on. 'I hear that you're the only close relative. My advice is to forget about the will for the time being. You have to brace yourself for the funeral before that. It's going to be a harrowing experience for both of you.'

'Yes, it is,' they said in unison.

Victor Leeming paced himself. He worked on the theory that the stationmaster would have walked more slowly in the dark. Even so, he reasoned, Heygate might have gone a fair distance. He strode in a westerly direction, taking note of all

192

the buildings he passed. There was no shortage of sheds. In fact, he counted over a dozen before he'd gone more than a couple of hundred yards. Housing then began to thin out, separated by patches of open ground. Trees abounded. It was a natural habitat for birds. When he stopped to check his watch, Leeming saw that he'd been walking for the best part of a quarter of an hour. He was at the fullest extent of his range. Yet he could see a cottage in the middle distance and there was an old shed at the bottom of its garden. Perhaps the stationmaster had moved faster than he thought. The shed was clearly worth investigation.

Lengthening his stride, he pressed on, pausing from time to time to peer into a clump of bushes. But there was no trace of the missing lamp. The closer he got to the shed, the more dilapidated it looked, with holes in the roof large enough for birds to get in easily. Leeming's hopes rose. If it was the old shed mentioned by the stationmaster, then – in all probability – it was the place where Heygate had been ambushed and killed. He walked around it and searched the ground but there were no bloodstains visible and no sign of a struggle having taken place. Leeming was undaunted. He somehow felt that he'd found the murder scene. The shed was unlocked. Pulling the door open, he fully expected to see some clue relating to the crime. Instead he was forced back in alarm as a large black cat came out of the shadows to snarl angrily at him before darting off between his legs.

Frances Impey was both amazed and relieved at the difference in her sister. Agnes Rossiter had shaken off her gloom and seemed her old self. But for her black attire, nobody would have known that she was in mourning. Mindful of what had happened at the cathedral, Frances tried to guide her sister away from it but the latter insisted on walking through the precinct. There was no repeat of her earlier outburst. In fact, Mrs Rossiter glanced apologetically towards the cathedral as if keen to make amends. Her sister found that heartening. It was a clear indication of recovery.

The undertaker's premises were in the High Street and Frances implored her sister not to go there, arguing that it would upset her too much.

'It's my duty, Frances,' she said, calmly. 'Joel would never forgive me.'

'Mr Heygate was badly burnt. The body will be in a terrible condition.'

'I don't care. It's him – that's all that matters.'

'You don't belong here,' said her sister with concern. 'Let's go home, Agnes. *Please* – let me take you home.'

Mrs Rossiter ignored the plea and turned into the High Street. When she reached the undertaker's premises, she rang the bell. All that Frances could do was to stand a few yards away in trepidation. The undertaker opened the door, listened to Mrs Rossiter's request and politely refused to let her in. There was a brief argument but the man was firm. He would not admit her to view the remains of Joel Heygate. Stepping back, he closed the door. Mrs Rossiter gave a shrug of acceptance and rejoined her sister.

'I told you that they wouldn't let you in,' said Frances.

'They have to,' insisted Mrs Rossiter, looking down at the ground. 'It's my right. Nobody is going to keep me away from Joel.'

'What are you searching for?'

'I won't be turned away like that. I'll fight back.'

Seeing what she was after, Mrs Rossiter bent down and picked up a large stone. Before her sister could stop her, she hurled it at the window with all force. As the glass shattered, the undertaker's name painted on it was split into a thousand shards. Mrs Rossiter had not finished. Scrambling through the window and cutting herself in the process, she pushed aside the black drapes and stepped into the building.

'I'm coming, Joel!' she yelled. 'I'm coming!'

CHAPTER ELEVEN

By prior arrangement, Colbeck met Leeming at noon at the railway station so that they could exchange information. Since a train had recently left, they were able to sit in the empty waiting room. Colbeck described his interview with Woodford and felt that the man had been shifty. The stationmaster had done nothing to remove his name from the list of suspects. Leeming then took over, explaining that he'd walked in all directions but to no avail.

'I found far too many old sheds, sir,' he moaned. 'How do I know which was the one we're after? It certainly wasn't the first one I looked in, I know that. There was this vicious black cat in there. He'd frighten away any birds.'

'Black cats are supposed to bring good luck, Victor.'

'This one didn't. Given the chance, he'd have scratched my eyes out.'

'All we know is that Heygate must have been killed

somewhere between here and the place he was going to that night. He could have been ambushed anywhere along the way.'

'What if he was marched into the city and *then* murdered?'

'That seems unlikely,' said Colbeck. 'The place was teeming with people. Excitement about the event had been building for days. The likelihood is that he was battered to death in some quiet location, then smuggled into the precinct at night and hidden underneath the bonfire. It's a pity you didn't find that lamp.'

'The killer must have taken it with him, sir.'

'Not if he had a body to carry. He might have used a cart, of course, but the lamp was the property of the railway. It has the name painted on it, as you can see.' He gestured towards the large metal lamp beside the door. 'That might have caught someone's eye. I know it was dark but there are street lamps aplenty. The killer may have thought it was too risky to be seen with railway property. Any policeman who saw it would assume that it was stolen.'

'Well,' said Leeming, 'I didn't find the lamp and I didn't see the owl.'

'That's not surprising, Victor. Owls are nocturnal.'

'I hope you're not going to send me out after dark, sir.'

Colbeck grinned. 'Wouldn't you like to go birdwatching at night?'

'No, I wouldn't.'

'Then I'll spare you the ordeal.'

'Our job would be so much easier if we found that missing diary.'

'Woodford claimed that he didn't know it existed, but I had a sneaky feeling that he was lying. And yes, that diary could well be a godsend. Perhaps we should ask Peter where Heygate used to keep it.'

'Who's Peter?'

'He's the canary that Miss Hope is looking after.'

'I'd forgotten him.'

'Heygate and Peter were inseparable. The owl and the canary,' said Colbeck with a smile. 'It's like one of Aesop's fables, isn't it?'

'I remember learning about those at school.'

'Owls are usually regarded as birds of ill omen.'

'Mr Heygate should have taken heed of that.'

People were drifting into the waiting room now because the next train was due very shortly. They broke off their conversation and stepped outside on to the platform. Woodford walked past and tipped his hat to them. He was clearly relishing his elevation to a position of power. Leeming looked towards the stationmaster's house and saw the policeman standing outside it.

'Do we really need to have it guarded day and night, Inspector?'

'I suppose not, Victor,' said Colbeck. 'I was being over-cautious in asking for protection. If the killer came in search of the diary – and we don't even know that he's aware of its existence – he's not going to find it there. Superintendent Steel and I looked in every nook and cranny. I'll tell him to stand his man down.'

'Talking of superintendents,' said Leeming, 'how can we convince ours that he's needed in London?'

'I wish I knew.'

'I get so nervous when I have him looking over our shoulders.'

'Blame the bishop. It was his letter that brought Mr Tallis here. If he wants to do something really useful,' said Colbeck, 'he can persuade Bishop Phillpotts not to call in the army. Their presence would be a hindrance to us.'

He looked up as a train appeared in the distance, puffing smoke into the air and rattling along at a slowly diminishing speed. It eventually reached the station and drew up to a halt in front of them. Passengers waited to board the train while several people on it alighted. Tallis was amongst them.

'Ah,' he said, walking over to them, 'I'm glad that you're both here.'

'What did you think of Dawlish, sir?' asked Leeming.

'I found it quite enchanting.'

'Did you remember to look out for those pumping stations?'

Tallis bared his teeth. 'Be warned, Leeming. If you so much as mention the atmospheric railway once more in my presence, you'll be walking the beat in Whitechapel for the rest of your police career. Well,' he said, 'do either of you have good news to report?'

'I'm afraid that we don't, sir,' said Colbeck, 'but it's not for want of trying.'

'No,' said Leeming, bitterly. 'I've seen enough old sheds to last me a lifetime. And don't ever tell me that a black cat brings luck.'

'What are you on about?' demanded Tallis.

'It's nothing, sir. Tell us your news.'

'I learnt something that you failed to learn, Sergeant. It turns out that Michael Heygate actually knows our chief suspect, Mr Browne. He said that Browne had bought a fishing rod from them but I have doubts about that.

200

The point is,' said Tallis, beaming in triumph, 'that I've established a link between two of our suspects. In short, they could have been working together.'

'That's an interesting possibility, sir,' said Colbeck. 'Michael Heygate might draw back from actually killing his brother but he could have engaged Browne to do so. It's worth recalling that he knew the stationmaster would be going out that night and could easily have followed him.'

'What about Mrs Heygate?' asked Leeming. 'I fancy that she might have a poisonous tongue when upset but I can't see her involved in a murder.'

'She'd condone anything her husband did. She's under his thumb.'

'I noticed that, sir.'

'You must also have noticed that she's far from grief-stricken.'

'That was apparent at the inquest, sir,' said Colbeck. 'She was far more concerned with her husband's performance as a witness than with her brother-in-law's fate. Mrs Heygate can't wait to reap the benefits from his death.'

'Neither can her husband,' said Tallis. 'He asked when the will would be read. It never occurred to him that it might be an indelicate question. The funeral is on Monday, incidentally. Mr Quinnell is responsible for the arrangements.'

'That gives us the weekend to solve the crime,' said Colbeck. 'Otherwise the bishop is going to flood the city with troops. Thanks to you, sir,' he added, 'we have a new line of enquiry. We must look for further evidence of collusion between Heygate and Bagsy Browne. Your trip to Dawlish has paid dividends.'

'The first step is to apprehend Browne,' said Tallis, crisply. 'As soon as we do that, we can end this investigation and return to London.'

Bagsy Browne spent the morning considering his options. The one thing that never crossed his mind was the idea of vanishing from Exeter altogether. Being hunted gave him a thrill. He loved dodging the police. It would be time to move on before long but he couldn't do so while Adeline was in custody. She was both friend and lover. Moreover, she'd provided a safe haven for him. When arrested by the police, she hadn't given him away. Adeline had remained fiercely loyal. The very least that Browne could do was to show his gratitude. He was sitting in the back row of the church as he pondered. They wouldn't search for him there. In any case, he'd adopted a new disguise. Wearing baggy old clothes and a greasy cap, he'd made himself look much older by hobbling along on a walking stick. In the event that he was recognised, it would be a useful weapon, though he also carried a dagger under his coat.

When he'd made his decision, Browne looked around to make sure that he was unobserved. Two other people were in the church, both of them knelt in prayer. He sidled across to the exit. Secured to the wall beside the door was a collecting box. It was the work of seconds to prise it open with the dagger and grab its contents. As he walked slowly along the street with the aid of the stick, the coins jingled in his pocket. Two policemen passed him on patrol but neither took any notice of the old man. He carried on until he reached the police station, a building with which he was only too familiar. Propping himself against a wall nearby, he waited patiently and smoked a pipe while doing so. It was over an hour before he saw what he wanted. A policeman was bringing out a prisoner, released after a night in custody. After issuing a stern warning to him, the policeman pushed the man away and went back inside the building.

Browne ambled across to intercept the man, who seemed only half-awake.

'Drunk and disorderly?' he asked.

The man tottered. 'I can't remember.'

'There's a woman locked up in there.'

'Is there?'

'You know there is,' said Browne. 'Tell me which cell she's in and there may be money in it for you.' The man's face lit up. 'There – that jogged your memory, didn't it? I thought it would. Where is she?'

Adeline Goss was no stranger to police cells. She'd first been arrested for soliciting when she was only fifteen. After a night behind bars, she'd been let off with a fine. During a spell plying her trade in Totnes, she'd come to an arrangement with the custody sergeant, offering him her professional services in return for being released with no more than a caution. That would never happen in Exeter. Superintendent Steel was a man of integrity and moral probity. He'd stamp on any sign of corruption.

She felt cold, frightened and alone. Arrest for being a prostitute had happened too many times to hold any fear for her. But she was being held in relation to a vastly more serious offence now. The prospect of the gallows had been raised. It made her wonder if she'd been wise to offer Bagsy Browne refuge. He was an inveterate villain and had done some terrible things but she preferred not to know what they were. It was safer to remain ignorant of what he did. This time, it seemed, he'd gone too far and she was implicated. It was devastating. And yet he'd brought such joy into her life for the last week or so. He'd brought laughter and love and plenty of money into her squalid little room in Rockfield Place. That needed to be remembered.

When she'd been arrested, Browne had escaped but only because she had a hiding place for him. What would he do now? Would he flee the city? He'd obviously stayed long enough to take his revenge on a man who'd betrayed them to the police. What was his next step? On balance, she felt, he'd take to the road. She had to be realistic. Browne had talked of moving on and given no hint that he might take her with him. He was a free spirit. An ageing prostitute would be a handicap to him. Adeline had been abandoned. Nobody would help. The tears ran down both cheeks in rivulets. She was doomed.

Then something spun through the bars of the window and landed with a chink on the floor. She bent down to retrieve a small coin and held it in her palm.

'Bagsy!' she said to herself, and her heart lifted.

When the detectives called at Steel's office, they were surprised by the news.

'There's been another murder?' asked Colbeck.

'Yes,' said Steel. 'We fished the body out of the canal.'

'Who was the victim this time?'

'That informant I told you about – Finbar Mulleady. And

at least we know for certain who the killer is this time.'

'Do we?' said Leeming. 'Who is he?'

'It's our old friend, Bagsy Browne.'

'Do you have any proof of that, sir?'

'Look at the evidence, Sergeant,' said Steel. 'Mulleady provides intelligence that leads to the arrest of Bagsy's doxy, Adeline Goss. There's nothing Bagsy hates more than what he sees as treachery. He silenced Mulleady for ever.'

'But how did Browne know that this man was an informer?' asked Colbeck.

'We have a criminal underworld here as you do in London, Inspector. Ours is much smaller but it operates by the same rules. Mulleady was once part of it, hence his usefulness to us. He heard things on the grapevine.'

'Yes,' said Leeming. 'There's a grapevine in London as well. How it works I don't know but word travels like wildfire. You can arrest a man in secret but, an hour later, every criminal in the city is aware of it.'

'Somebody tipped Bagsy off,' said Steel.

'How was the Irishman killed?'

'We think he was stabbed to death. His trousers were soaked with blood. I had the body taken away for a post-mortem. We'll know the full details later.'

'You said that he was fished out of the canal,' noted Colbeck.

'Mulleady was probably on his way back to his lair. That's where he lives, you see, in a half-derelict barge. Everyone knows that,' said Steel. 'I'm sure that Bagsy did. All that he had to do was to follow Mulleady home from the pub.'

'Browne is a natural suspect, Superintendent, but there must be others. Men who betray people to the police usually have short lives. I daresay that many in your criminal fraternity would have been happy to see Mulleady dead.'

'It's too big a coincidence. The woman is arrested and the man who made that arrest possible is promptly killed. There's a direct connection there.'

Leeming readily agreed but Colbeck was more cautious in allotting the blame. They were still trying to assimilate one surprise when Steel sprang another on them.

'My men had to arrest Mrs Rossiter again,' he told them.

'Oh dear!' said Colbeck. 'She didn't go into the cathedral again, did she?'

'No, Inspector, her target this time was the undertaker's.'

'Do you mean the one where the stationmaster's body is kept?'

'She insisted on viewing it.'

Leeming was horrified. 'Doesn't she realise the state it's in?'

'That's irrelevant, Victor,' said Colbeck, sorrowfully. 'Dr Swift diagnosed her illness. She's in the grip of an obsession and it won't slacken its hold. Mrs Rossiter believes that she would have married Heygate. She's driven by a mania.'

'What exactly did she do, Superintendent?'

'She lost all control,' said Steel. 'When they wouldn't let her in, she smashed the window with a stone and clambered into the premises. She cut both hands on the splinters of glass and tore her dress. By the time my men got to her, she was howling like a she-wolf and trying to fight her way into the room where the body was kept. You can imagine the sort of crowd that she drew.'

'What about her sister?' asked Colbeck. 'Was she there as well?'

'Miss Impey fainted on the spot and had to be revived with smelling salts.'

'It looks as if we missed all the fun,' said Leeming with a chuckle. 'While I was having a long and boring walk, there was high drama at the undertaker's.'

'It's not a subject for amusement, Victor.'

'All the same, sir, I'd like to have been there.'

'I wish you had been,' said Steel. 'You could have restrained her earlier.'

'Where is the poor woman now, Superintendent?' asked Colbeck.

'She's on her way to the County Asylum in Exminster. I'm always sad to see someone carted off there but it's the best place for her. Dr Swift agreed. As soon as he heard what had happened, he signed the committal papers for her.' He sat back in his chair with a wry smile. 'You must wish you had never come anywhere near the city, Inspector. Since you've been here, you've had a whole series of problems cropping up. It's hardly the best way for you to prepare for your wedding.'

'I sometimes forget that it's even happening.'

'It must happen,' said Leeming. 'My wife and I have an invitation.'

'My sympathy goes out to your bride,' said Steel. 'As long as you're here, the young lady must be tormented by anxiety.'

'Yes,' said Colbeck, pursing his lips. 'I fear that you may be right.'

* * *

Madeleine gave her father a farewell kiss and watched him strolling along the street. He was off to take tea with Binnie Langton, and his daughter wished that she could feel happier about it. Closing the door, she came back into the house and moved over to her easel, placed near the window to catch the best of the light. A half-finished locomotive stood on the canvas before her, its massive bulk partly obscured by wisps of steam. Madeleine had no urge to pick up her brush. Her mind was on her father's impending meeting with a woman who had inexplicably transformed his life. She told herself that Binnie Langton was probably a kind, respectable, pleasant and considerate person who would make an ideal companion for Caleb Andrews. Yet the worries lingered that he might be walking into some kind of trap.

She scolded herself for having such negative thoughts. Madeleine felt that she should put her father's needs first. She'd been flustered by his glib talk of marriage but even he couldn't be thinking of so serious a commitment yet. There was plenty of time for her to meet the woman and make a fair assessment of her. Nothing would be done without her approval. Though her father was the nominal head of the household, he always deferred to her advice. That being the case, her apprehension was ill-founded. All that he was doing was having a cup of tea and a piece of cake with a new friend. There was nothing sinister or troubling in that.

Madeleine picked up her brush and worked with peace of mind at last.

The house was on the other side of Camden and very much like the dwelling that Andrews had left. He stood at the window of the house next door and used it as a mirror in which to inspect his appearance. After a few adjustments to his dress, he was ready for the big occasion. Binnie Langton opened the door the moment he knocked on it, giving him a gushing welcome and helping him off with his overcoat. She was a fleshy woman with a large bosom and a spreading midriff that was barely kept in check by her corset. It was her face that had entranced Andrews. She had a chubby handsomeness and a winning sparkle in her eyes.

'It's so good of you to come, Caleb,' she cooed.

'I've been looking forward to it,' he said, inhaling her perfume. 'Did you keep your promise about the cake?'

'Oh, I've made a lot more for you than a cake.'

'Then I'm very glad I came.'

'You must stay just as long as you wish.'

'Thank you, Binnie.'

Her hand brushed his arm and made it tingle. He'd been in the house less than a minute yet he already felt at home. The prospect of spending a whole afternoon with such a delectable creature was almost intoxicating. As she led him into the parlour, Andrews gave a giggle of pleasure. It died in his throat. Waiting to meet him was a middle-aged woman with a slender figure and a narrow face.

'This is Ivy,' said Binnie, putting her hand on the woman's shoulder. 'She's my sister and she's being dying to meet you.'

Ivy Young extended her hand. 'How do you do, Mr Andrews?'

He was speechless.

Edward Tallis had been reluctant to meet the bishop for the second time but he accepted the necessity of doing so.

Someone had to persuade him not to resort to calling on the soldiers at Topsham Barracks. He had unhappy memories of the militia being summoned in London to control disorder. Accidents always happened. Innocent people were usually hurt or even killed. It was true that the army would not be there to police a riot but their presence would be disruptive and likely to incite violence. The very sight of a soldier's uniform somehow inflamed some people. They simply had to protest against the occupation of their city.

On the way to the bishop's palace, he rehearsed his arguments. He had even more time to do so when he got there because the bishop kept him waiting for a long time. When he was finally admitted to the library by Ralph Barnes, his annoyance was not assuaged by Bishop Phillpott's greeting.

'Good afternoon,' said Phillpotts. 'I can only spare you twenty minutes.'

'I expected more time than that.'

'Then your expectations will be dashed.'

'Bishop Phillpotts has another appointment,' explained Barnes. 'Do sit down, sir.'

Tallis sat in front of the desk. 'I've come about the soldiers.'

'I'm glad that someone agrees with me,' said Phillpotts. 'I had thought to leave it a few days but I'm minded to summon them immediately.'

'I strongly oppose the plan, Bishop Phillpotts.'

'Oh – I assumed that you'd come to endorse it.'

'Let me state my case,' said Tallis, 'and I do so as an army man who had almost thirty years' service in uniform. I rose to the rank of major and was proud to have such authority. But I always sought to use it wisely.'

Bishop Phillpotts was cantankerous. 'I don't have time

to listen to your military reminiscences, fascinating though they doubtless are. You are an interloper in this city and should bear that in mind. I know what's best for Exeter.'

'Do you wish to provoke chaos?'

'I wish to ensure the capture of this unconscionable rascal named Browne and the only way to do that is to employ more men in the search. They can go from house to house until they find out where he's hiding.'

'The police *know* where he'd taken refuge, Bishop. They raided the place and arrested his accomplice.'

The bishop was peevish. 'Why wasn't I told?'

'You just have been.'

'Is the villain in custody as well?'

'No,' said Tallis, 'he's still at liberty, but Superintendent Steel is confident that his accomplice will act as bait. In other words, his capture is imminent.'

'I see,' said the bishop, ruminating.

'Call in the troops and you'll upset everything – not least the police force. The last time you sent word to Topsham Barracks, I'm told, the soldiers caused mayhem here and engaged in a free fight with the police.'

'I refuse to accept the blame for that,' declared Phillpotts.

'The bishop acted correctly in an emergency,' said Barnes.

'Yet it seems as if another emergency was created. Let me be frank,' said Tallis, leaning forward. 'Policemen are unpopular. That's a fact of life. Soldiers are even more unpopular if they're seen taking over the streets of a city like this. Why stoke up civil resentment? It's foolhardy. I beg you to reconsider.'

The bishop had a silent conversation with his secretary before replying.

'Your argument is reasonable,' he confessed. 'It's right to point out the possible consequences. But I haven't made the decision lightly. In one day, I submit, the soldiers will find the stone under which this reptile named Browne is hiding. They can then withdraw to their barracks. As an army man, you should surely endorse the use of trained soldiers.'

'It's a question of circumstances, Bishop. This is not the place for them.'

Phillpotts had another wordless exchange with his secretary. For all his submissiveness, Barnes was clearly exerting some influence and making the bishop pause for thought. Phillpotts offered a concession.

'Very well,' he resumed, turning back to Tallis. 'I'll revoke my earlier decision to summon them instantly – or, indeed, in a few days. I grant you a week in which to capture this odious individual. But I insist on police protection. Tell that to Superintendent Steel. Browne clearly has a personal animus against me. So does someone else, it appears. An unhinged female ran wild in the cathedral and mocked my authority. I've had to warn the cathedral staff to be on the lookout for her.'

'The lady in question will never repeat that outrage, Bishop.'

'I can't be certain of that.'

'Yes, you can,' said Tallis. 'Mrs Rossiter has been arrested by the police a second time. My information is that she's now confined in the lunatic asylum.'

Exminster station had been opened five years earlier and still had a sense of newness about it. The train took Colbeck on the short journey there. He had his first look at the County Asylum through the window of his carriage. It rose above all the buildings around it with an arresting bulk and solidity. He felt sorry for anyone detained inside it and reserved special compassion for Agnes Rossiter. A week ago, she'd been a conscientious employee of the South Devon Railway with a secret passion for Joel Heygate. As a result of his death, she'd now been committed to a lunatic asylum.

'How long will you keep her here, Dr Swift?'

'It's far too early to put a timescale on it.'

'Was she violent when she was brought here?'

'Yes,' said Swift, 'she fought every inch of the way. I had to sedate her. You must have heard what happened at the undertaker's.'

'Superintendent Steel gave me a vivid description.'

'I had no alternative. She had to be brought here for her own safety.'

'I agree,' said Colbeck.

They were in Swift's office, a room that was excessively tidy and that smelt faintly of disinfectant. Bookshelves ran along two of the walls, laden with files. On the desk was a small pile of books. Colbeck noticed that one of them had been written by Morton Swift. It was placed so that any visitors would see it and was another instance of his vanity.

'What will happen to Mrs Rossiter now?' asked Colbeck.

'She'll be given time to adapt to her new situation. We keep inmates to a set routine, Inspector. That's very important.'

'Will you be in charge of her case?'

'Initially,' said Swift, 'but I may have to hand her over to someone else before long. We have a capacity of eight hundred beds here, most of which are filled. I can't give personal attention to each inmate.'

'I understand that,' said Colbeck. 'Is it possible for me to see her?'

Swift was adamant. 'I'm sorry, but I can't allow that,' he said. 'I've given her a strong drug and she's probably asleep by now. In any case, she needs to be left in our charge for some time before we even discuss the possibility of visitors. The outside world doesn't exist for her at the moment.'

'What about her mourning attire?'

'That's been taken from her. She's dressed in the same way as the rest of our inmates. We don't let them wear their own clothing in here, Inspector.'

Colbeck was disappointed. He'd wanted to see Mrs Rossiter for himself but accepted that it was impractical. Swift was more qualified to assess her needs. The inspector just wished that he could feel more sanguine about her prospects. The doctor's manner was professionally comforting and his office was impressive. On the way to it, however, Colbeck had seen burly male nurses manhandling one of the inmates and he heard a series of female screams and wails from other parts of the building. The asylum was not the quietest place in which a disturbed person could recover. It was a clamorous prison for the insane and incurable.

'I appreciate your concern, Inspector,' said Swift, 'but your sympathy might be directed elsewhere. Agnes Rossiter is in our care now. The person who really deserves some attention is her sister, Miss Impey. What occurred today must have been unbearable for her – it's hardly surprising that she fainted. If you could spare a moment to look in on her, you might be able to offer welcome reassurance.'

'I intended to do just that,' said Colbeck, getting to his

feet. 'Thank you, Dr Swift. It was good of you to see me so promptly.'

Swift stood up. 'You're bound to be interested in her case,' he said. 'After all, she's a hapless victim of the crime you're here to investigate. Her derangement was caused by the ghastly murder of Mr Heygate. May I ask,' he went on as he led Colbeck to the door, 'if you've made any progress so far?'

'We believe so, Dr Swift. We have a prime suspect and every hope of snaring him very soon. It may even be that he's committed a second murder in the city.'

'Dear God!'

'It's very unfortunate,' said Colbeck, sighing, 'because it will give further ammunition to the bishop.'

'Oh – what has Bishop Phillpotts been up to now?'

'He's insisting that we bring in troops from Topsham to assist the search for our main suspect. This latest development will only intensify that urge. I've asked my superior, Superintendent Tallis, to do all he can to dissuade him but my fear is that the bishop is far too inflexible.'

'Have you met the bishop?'

'I've had two encounters with him.'

'Go on.'

'They were less than enjoyable.'

'Yes,' admitted Swift, 'he can be spiky at times but he's unfairly maligned, in my view. I know what a philanthropic gentleman he can be.'

'Oh?'

'This may look like a house of detention, Inspector, but we try to make it as pleasant as possible. You'll have noticed all the paintings in the corridors. They bring colour and a note of domesticity into the asylum. There are several others in public rooms and all of them were donated by Bishop Phillpotts.'

'That's uncommonly generous of him.'

'His interest in the asylum did not end there. When it was opened in 1845, the first thing he did was to appoint a chaplain from his own staff. Canon Smalley is still here and does splendid work. He has a gift for calming unruly patients. He just sits there holding their hands and *listens*. That's all that some of them need,' he said. 'They want someone to listen to them.'

'I clearly need to revise my opinion of the bishop,' said Colbeck.

'He's a good man at heart.'

'I never doubted his sincerity.'

'Next time you meet him, try to be more tolerant of his idiosyncrasies.'

'Thank you for your advice. I can see that I misjudged him.'

'He's been a friend to this asylum from the start.'

'Then I can see why you feel so grateful.'

'It's more than simple gratitude, Inspector. It's closer to veneration. The bishop was instrumental in furthering my own career.'

Colbeck was curious. 'In what way did he do that?'

'Out of his own pocket, he gave me a bursary that allowed me to take time off in order to do some vital research. The fruit of that research,' he said, crossing to the desk to pick up the copy of his book, 'is contained in here. That's why it's dedicated to Henry Phillpotts, Bishop of Exeter.' He opened the book and showed the dedication to Colbeck. 'Be sure to look at the paintings in the corridor as you leave. They're an important visual stimulus for our inmates. In his own way,' concluded Swift, 'Bishop Phillpotts is a holy psychiatrist.'

CHAPTER TWELVE

After the warning he'd given her, Madeleine Andrews had expected that her father might not return home until well into the evening. She was therefore amazed when he came back in little over an hour from the time when he'd left the house. There was a secondary surprise for her. The first time he'd taken tea with Binnie Langton, he'd come back in a state of euphoria. Andrews was more guarded this time. There was no smile hovering and no nostalgic glint. Madeleine was intrigued.

'Did you have a nice time?' she asked, helping him off with his coat.

'Yes.'

'And did Mrs Langton make you a cake?'

'She made all manner of things.'

'Why are you back here so early?'

Handing her his cap, he slumped into a chair. 'I'd had enough, Maddy.'

'I thought you'd spend hours with Mrs Langton.'

'So did I,' he said, wistfully, 'and I would have done so if Binnie and I had been alone. But her sister was there – Mrs Young – and that changed everything.'

She hung coat and cap on a peg. 'I don't understand, Father.'

'Ivy Young came to look me over and to see if I was sound in mind and limb. I tell you, Maddy, I felt as if I was an old bull in a market, being poked and prodded by a farmer who wasn't sure if I was worth spending money on. It was dreadful. Mrs Young did everything but ask me my weight.'

'Why didn't Mrs Langton stop her?'

'You can't stop a woman like Ivy Young. When she gets up a head of steam, she has as much traction power as one of the locomotives I used to drive. I wasn't questioned – I was interrogated.'

'Oh dear!' said Madeleine, sitting down opposite him. 'That must have been very unpleasant for you.'

'The really unpleasant thing is that she was obviously there because Binnie had invited her. She wanted her sister to check me over. I suppose it's a good sign in some ways,' he went on. 'It shows that her interest in me is serious. But it was really uncomfortable at the time.'

'Was Mrs Young anything like her sister?'

'No, she was much slimmer and – if I'm honest – a bit more intelligent than Binnie. She lost her own husband years ago and was very supportive to Binnie when she was in the same position. Ivy Young is an attractive woman,' he said, 'and she dresses very well. I'm surprised that she hasn't married again. She must have many admirers. On the other hand, they would have been frightened away if she'd treated them the way that she treated me this afternoon.'

Madeleine was at once sympathetic and relieved. Though she was sorry that her father had not enjoyed the event as much as he'd hoped, she was secretly glad that his whirlwind romance had slowed to a more reasonable speed. It would give him time to appraise the situation in a more objective frame of mind. While he might still have strong feelings about Binnie Langton, they might be tempered by the fact that marriage to her would encumber him with an over-inquisitive sister-in-law.

'How do things stand with you and Mrs Langton?' she asked, tentatively.

'That's the trouble, Maddy – I don't really know.'

'But you still like her, I assume.'

'Yes, I like her very much but I just had to get out of there.'

'What do you think her sister will say about you?'

'I've no idea. I hope that she doesn't advise Binnie to have nothing more to do with me. She could see how fond we were of each other – and still are. I'd love to see Binnie again but I'm not sure that I could sit through another ordeal like that.'

'Why not invite her here, Father?'

He was doubtful. 'I'll think about it.'

'It would give me the chance to meet Mrs Langton.'

'What if she turns up with her sister?'

'You make it clear that the invitation is only for her,' said Madeleine. 'Does she know where you live?'

'She knows every single thing about me,' he protested. 'Her sister made sure of that. Where did I live? What church did I attend? Who were my friends? How would I manage now that I was retired? Did I have anything put by?'

'She sounds as if she was terribly nosy.'

'That's how it felt at the time, Maddy. On the walk back home, however, I tried to see it from her point of view. She only wants to protect Binnie. After all, there are some men who might try to take advantage of a handsome widow.'

She was outraged on his behalf. 'Nobody could suspect *you* of ever doing that, Father,' she said. 'Mrs Langton must realise that. In any case, Dirk Sowerby would have spoken up for you. She couldn't possibly have any qualms about you.'

'And I have no qualms about Binnie – only about her sister.'

After some thought, she offered her counsel. 'Take plenty of time to mull it over. If you want to see Mrs Langton again, invite her here for tea.'

'I will, Maddy.' He gave a self-deprecating laugh. 'This is ridiculous. I owe you an apology. A man of my age shouldn't be in a situation like this, boring his daughter with silly nonsense about his private life. *You're* the one who needs the attention. You have a wedding at the end of the month, yet you don't even know if there'll be a bridegroom able to get there in time. Have you had any word from him?'

'Not since his last letter.'

'Then it's high time he wrote another one. If he doesn't do so very soon, I'll send Binnie's sister down to Exeter to interrogate him. That will shake up the famous Inspector Colbeck.'

Sunday morning found all three of them attending a service at the cathedral. The bishop was there, seated in state, but it was one of the canons who officiated. Tallis found it inspiring

to take communion in such a beautiful and imposing place. It added resonance to the whole exercise. Closing his eyes, Colbeck kept imagining Madeleine and himself standing before the altar on their wedding day. Leeming was grateful that he'd taken the precaution of sitting on the other side of the inspector so that there was a buffer between the superintendent and him. Even so, proximity to Tallis was still unnerving. Since he wasn't at all engaged by the long, abstruse and high-minded sermon, Leeming let his mind drift to his family and thought of them settling into their pew in the more modest setting of the parish church. They – like him – would be praying earnestly for his early return to London.

When the three of them left the cathedral, Tallis excused himself and went off in the hope of having a brief word with Henry Phillpotts. Colbeck had told him about the bishop's philanthropy with regard to the Devon County Asylum and Tallis had been duly impressed. It helped to adjust his opinion of the man quite radically. Colbeck and Leeming were left standing near the spot where the charred body of Joel Heygate had been found. As the rest of the congregation strolled past them on their way home, the detectives reviewed the state of the investigation.

'Something is missing,' said Colbeck.

'Yes,' agreed Leeming, mournfully, 'it's Estelle and the children.'

'I'm talking about this case, Victor.'

'I know, sir, and what's really missing is an arrest.'

'We've had one arrest,' Colbeck reminded him, 'and the woman is still languishing in a cell. But I was referring to something else.'

'There's no need to do that. We know who the killer was. We know that he has a link to Michael Heygate. And – most certainly of all – we know that Bagsy Browne committed a second murder.'

'That's not a proven fact.'

'Who else would want to have killed that Irishman?'

'Quite a few people if the fellow was working for the police,' said Colbeck. 'The post-mortem might give us some clues but I still think it's far too early to condemn Browne. And just because he and Michael Heygate once met, it doesn't mean that they were in league with each other.'

'What are you saying, Inspector?' asked Leeming. 'That neither of them is guilty and that Lawrence Woodford is responsible for one or both murders?'

'Woodford remains a suspect in only the first case, Victor. No, what is missing is the chain on which we can hang all the disparate elements of this investigation. We have plenty of bits and pieces but no connecting link. I believe that our most reliable witnesses are the owl and the canary. Unfortunately,' said Colbeck, 'neither is able to offer his evidence in a court of law.'

'What must we do next?'

'First of all, we should call on the superintendent and see if he has any news for us. After that, a visit to Miss Dorcas Hope will be in order.'

'Why is that, Inspector?'

'She's minding the canary. Miss Hope is also a sensitive young lady with, I suspect, a caring nature. If I confide details of Mrs Rossiter's plight, I'm sure that she'll wish to offer the sister some support. Miss Impey will have been poleaxed by what happened.'

'At least the manageress didn't save her performance for the funeral,' said Leeming, jocularly. 'It could have been very embarrassing if she'd turned up there and tried to stop them lowering the coffin into the grave.'

'She'll be in the asylum for some time. I'm hoping that Dr Swift and his staff will be able to bring about some sort of recovery but I very much doubt if she'll ever be able to work at the railway station again. Mrs Rossiter will for ever associate it with Joel Heygate.'

'Can she ever be completely cured?'

'We must pray for that outcome, Victor,' said Colbeck. 'To be candid, I found the place faintly disturbing. Being surrounded by so many other people with mental disorders is hardly the ideal environment. She's only one patient out of hundreds, of course, so can hardly expect much individual attention.'

'Asylums are awful places,' said Leeming. 'You only have to look at them. If she wasn't mad when she went in there, she soon will be.'

'That's too harsh a judgement. I have more faith in Dr Swift.'

Breaking into a walk, they went out of the cathedral precinct, discussing the case and its profound consequences on the city. On their journey, they saw only one policeman on duty, an indication of the lack of resources available to Steel.

'How are they going to catch Browne with so few men?' asked Leeming.

'The idea is that he'll be coaxed out of hiding.'

'That's absurd, sir.'

'Why?'

'What sort of man would risk his life to rescue a woman like that?'

'Strange as it may seem,' said Colbeck, 'the age of chivalry is not dead. Bagsy Browne may well feel that he has an obligation to his friend. Most people in his predicament would have fled some time ago. My guess is that Browne hasn't done that. I've never met the fellow but I'll wager that he's still somewhere in the area.'

Since it was too dangerous to stay in Rockfield Place, he had to find another refuge. It was not a problem for Bagsy Browne. He found a boat that was under repair and moored in the estuary near Topsham. It was cold, cramped and shorn of any comforts but it was a safe hiding place. As he sat in the tiny cabin, he smoked his pipe and studied the rough diagram he'd sketched on a piece of paper. Based on memories of his time spent in custody there, it was a floor plan of the police station and showed him how many locked doors there would be between Adeline's cell and the main exit. Getting inside the place was relatively easy. Escaping with someone else in tow was more of a challenge. But it was one he was prepared to accept.

The element of surprise was critical. On a Sunday, he knew, there were fewer policemen on duty in the streets and at the police station. If he could time his attack, he might be able to achieve what at first looked impossible. Adeline would know that he was coming for her. The coin he'd tossed into her cell had been a promise that had to be honoured. She'd be ready. There was no doubting that. After poring over the diagram, he worked out his plan in detail. He would wait until the city was shrouded in evening shadows before he made his move. Darkness would aid their flight. They would spend her first night of freedom in the boat. It would soon be time for Bagsy to quit Exeter altogether, but not until he'd been able to watch the funeral of Joel Heygate and gloat with satisfaction. Where he would go, he was not entirely sure, but one detail had already been decided upon. He would leave alone.

Having rescued Adeline, he'd have discharged his duty to her. From then on, she could fend for herself. That was the way it was. Bagsy Browne had an inflexible rule. He always travelled alone.

When they entered the superintendent's office, Steel was studying a report with a frown of disappointment. Putting it aside, he gave them a welcome and there was an exchange of pleasantries. Each of the visitors gave his impression of the service at the cathedral. Colbeck was complimentary, while Leeming admitted that the experience had been overwhelming. Steel gave a sardonic smile.

'At least you were spared a sermon by Bishop Phillpotts,' he said. 'He's been known to go on for an hour.'

'Is that all?' asked Colbeck.

'The first time I saw him in full flow, he was not so much justifying the word of God as impersonating him.'

'Superintendent Tallis does that at times,' moaned Leeming. 'It's as if he's handing down the Ten Commandments to us. But while we're here, sir, perhaps you can settle an argument.'

'What sort of argument?' said Steel.

'Well, it's more of a professional disagreement than anything else. I think that Bagsy Browne committed two murders, with the possible assistance of Michael Heygate

225

in the case of the first. Inspector Colbeck is unconvinced. Which one of us would you support?'

'I'd have to say that – at first – I agreed with you, Sergeant.'

'There you are,' said Leeming, savouring his victory. 'For once, I'm right.'

'We're still in the realms of hypothesis,' cautioned Colbeck.

'No,' said Steel, 'we are not.'

'There's been a development?'

'Yes – and it's a very significant one, Inspector.' He held up the report he'd been reading. 'This is from the post-mortem on Finbar Mulleady.'

'He's that Irishman killed by Browne,' noted Leeming.

'I'm afraid that you're wrong, Sergeant. He may not have been killed by anyone. The wound which stained his trousers with blood was caused by a broken flagon of beer in his pocket. There was no sign of violence upon him. According to this,' he went on, passing the report to Colbeck, 'the most likely cause of death was drowning after he'd fallen into the canal. He went lurching along the towpath while blind drunk, tripped and hit the ground hard. The flagon in his pocket was smashed to pieces and he rolled into the freezing water.'

'Browne could have pushed him into the canal,' maintained Leeming.

'That possibility can be eliminated,' said Steel. 'A witness came forward to say that he saw Mulleady staggering along the towpath. It was a clear night and there was no sign of anybody else. That's not surprising because it was extremely cold. The witness also lives in a barge, apparently, and is used to seeing Mulleady tottering home every night.'

226

'In other words,' said Colbeck, reading the report. 'Browne is innocent.'

'Only innocent of the death of Mulleady – I was far too hasty in ascribing it to him. Bagsy Browne is still wanted for the murder of the stationmaster.'

Leeming was chastened. 'What if he didn't kill Joel Heygate either?'

'I have no doubts on that score,' said Steel.

'And I have no doubt that the brother was somehow involved.'

'What do *you* think, Inspector?'

Colbeck was mischievous. 'There is another question we might ask,' he said with a twinkle. 'What if the body under the bonfire was not that of the stationmaster? After all, it was virtually impossible to identify. We've been operating almost entirely on circumstantial evidence. Could it be that Joel Heygate was the killer and that the corpse was merely a decoy while he disappeared from the scene?'

Leeming shuddered. 'If that's true, we'll be here for months!'

'I didn't say it was true, Victor. In fact, it's highly unlikely. I'm merely repeating what I said to you earlier. Something is missing. There's a vital piece of evidence that may bring together all the information so far gathered and give it clarity.' He put the report on the desk. 'Let's talk to Peter.'

'A canary is not going to be able to help us, sir.'

'You never know,' said Colbeck. 'Stranger things have happened.'

To the delight of Dorcas Hope and her mother, Peter hopped about in his cage and chirped happily. He was clearly contented in his new home and had provided a lot of comfort for Maud during the long stretches when she was alone. There had been only one scare. When Dorcas had opened the cage door so that she could reach in and clean the base of droppings, the canary had escaped and flown around the room. But it was only a tour of inspection. Once he'd taken his bearings, Peter flew back down and went back to his perch in the cage. It meant that it was safe to let him fly around in the house. There was no danger of losing him.

Dorcas loved Sundays. It was her one day away from the hurly-burly of the refreshment room. After going to church, she could spend precious time with her family, now enlarged to include a canary. While she missed the manageress, she'd quickly grown to like Mrs Rossiter's deputy. Timothy Vesey was much less critical of her and more ready to praise her work. Passengers who recognised him from his long stint at Newton Abbot station were all pleased to see him. A day in Vesey's company was much less tiring than one under the erstwhile manageress.

'I tried to read one of those books on canaries,' said Maud. 'All that detail was a bit confusing. I didn't realise that canaries were a type of finch.' She peered into the cage beside her. 'And to think you've come all the way from the Canaries.'

'Actually,' corrected Dorcas, 'that's not true. I remember Mr Heygate telling me that Peter came from Madeira.'

'Isn't that one of the Canary Islands?'

'I don't think so, Mother.'

'I never was much good at geography.'

'I'd so love to visit Madeira, but there's no hope of that

happening. The farthest I've ever been in my life was to Cornwall with you and Father.'

Maud was resigned. 'Travelling abroad is not for the likes of us.' When there was a knock on the front door, she sat up. 'Who can that be?'

'I'll go and see.'

Dorcas left the parlour and opened the front door. Maud could hear a man's voice. After a short discussion, Dorcas came back with Colbeck and Leeming. Maud felt a little intimidated to have two detectives in the small confines of the parlour. She apologised for not getting up but her hip was causing her pain if she moved. The visitors sat down and Leeming stared at the canary.

'He's a colourful little chap, isn't he?'

'Yes,' said Dorcas. 'He's given us so much pleasure.'

'Mr Heygate obviously cared for him,' said Colbeck. 'That cage is far bigger than it needs to be for such a small bird. He has plenty of room to fly around.' He became serious. 'We're really here to talk about Mrs Rossiter.'

'How is she, Inspector?'

'She's not at all well, Miss Hope. In fact, for reasons we needn't go into now, she's been taken to the County Asylum.' The women were horrified. 'It was on the advice of Dr Swift.'

Dorcas gasped. 'Does that mean that Mrs Rossiter is . . . insane?'

'It means that she's in need of some help.'

'How long will she be in there?'

'Nobody can say, Miss Hope.'

'This is terrible news,' said Maud. 'In some ways, the asylum is worse than going to prison. Even if they let her out, you'd never look at her the same way again. Mental patients are so . . .'

'I think that the word you're after is "unpredictable", Mrs Hope,' said Colbeck as he saw her struggling. 'But some conditions are curable and patients go on to lead perfectly ordinary lives. However,' he went on, 'we really came to talk about Mrs Rossiter's sister. As you can imagine, the news will have shocked her deeply. Unlike your colleague in the refreshment room, she's not the most robust lady.'

'No,' said Dorcas. 'Miss Impey is a very shy and private person.'

'I wondered if you might find time to visit her.'

'Yes, yes, I'll be glad to, Inspector.'

'At a time like this, she needs a friend.'

'I'll make a point of going there later today.'

'Thank you, Miss Hope.'

Leeming was still eyeing the canary. 'If only he could talk,' he said. 'He must know where that missing diary is.' Peter chirped at him. 'I think he's trying to tell us.'

'The diary is not in the house,' said Colbeck, 'we know that.'

'That's what I told Mr Woodford,' said Dorcas. 'It was after you explained that you'd seen no trace of it when you searched the house.'

'Yet he claimed to know nothing about the diary.'

'I certainly mentioned it to him, Inspector.'

'I'm obliged to you for the information.'

'By the way, the house is no longer guarded by a policeman.'

'That was my doing,' explained Colbeck. 'In case the killer knew of that diary's existence and came looking for it, I wanted the house protected. Since there's been no sign of anyone on the prowl, we decided to bring guard duty to an end. A policeman is a valuable asset. There's no point in keeping one at the railway station when he can be far more use in the city.'

Dorcas blushed. 'While we're talking about the house,' she said, guiltily, 'there's something I must confess.'

'Go on,' urged her mother. 'Tell the truth. Nobody will blame you.'

'The thing is that I still have a spare key to the house. Mr Heygate gave it to me so that I could feed Peter when he was away. There were two other keys – his and the one belonging to his cleaner, Mrs Penhallurick.' She opened a drawer in the sideboard and took a key out. 'This is the third one,' she continued, handing it over to Colbeck. 'I didn't mean to keep it so long.'

'Thank you,' he said, 'but there's no call for worry. It's a tribute to you that Mr Heygate entrusted the key to you – as well as his canary, of course. His own key was not on the body when it was found under the bonfire, so the police had to gain access by using the one belonging to his cleaner. I'll pass this on to Superintendent Steel. Let me ask you once again,' he added. 'Are you quite certain you told Mr Woodford about the diary?'

'Yes, Inspector,' replied Dorcas. 'He was very interested in the news.'

Lawrence Woodford waited until there was a lull in activity then he strolled nonchalantly along the platform to the stationmaster's house. The key had been put into the safe and it had been easy for him to get access to it. Making sure that nobody was watching, he let himself into the house and looked around with the air of the commander of a besieging army that finally brings the walls of a city down. This was his new domain. He was in at last. Woodford shook off his feeling of triumph and got to work. Convinced that the diary was there somewhere, he began a frantic search.

Being locked up always brought out an aggressive streak in Adeline Goss. When a policeman brought her food, she was combative.

'You can't keep me locked up,' she asserted.

'We can do as we wish.'

'You've got no reason to hold me.'

'Yes, we have, Adeline,' he said. 'You were seen with Bagsy.'

'In the course of a week,' she argued, 'I could be seen by a number of men. It doesn't mean that I'm hiding them. When they've had their money's worth, most of them are only too glad to run straight home to their wives.'

'Bagsy Browne is more than a friend of yours.'

'So – is friendship against the law now?'

'You've been harbouring a killer.'

'I don't harbour anyone. I simply give them an hour's pleasure.'

'And you take money for it,' he pointed out. 'That's illegal.'

'It's also common sense. I put a price on my womanhood.'

'Eat your food and shut your mouth.'

'I can't eat this pigswill!' she yelled.

'Then save it for Bagsy.'

He locked the door of her cell and walked away. Adeline sat down on the bare wooden board that served as a bed. It was attached to the wall by two chains and could be lifted up to give her marginally more room in the cell. Using a wooden spoon, she tasted a first morsel of the stew she'd been handed. It made her retch. Spitting it out, she threw the bowl at the door. Needing reassurance, she took out the coin tossed into the cell by Bagsy. It was a message. He'd not forgotten her or the service she'd rendered him. Somehow – sooner or later – he'd come for her.

She lay on her back on the bed and let out a full-blooded laugh.

Superintendent Steel had seen enough of Tallis to realise that he could never work under him. Colbeck and Leeming carried their authority lightly but Tallis thrust it at people. Even in a casual conversation, he had to exert control. Steel was reminded of the man's status with every syllable he spoke. It was dusk and Tallis had called at the superintendent's office. After discussing the case in exhaustive detail with his detectives, he wanted to see the report of the post-mortem on Finbar Mulleady and be kept abreast of the very latest news. It was an effort for Steel to remain polite.

'I can add nothing to what Inspector Colbeck will have told you, sir,' he said.

Tallis finished reading the report. 'This must have come as a relief to you.'

'As a matter of fact, it came as something of a setback.'

'I fail to see why.'

'I'd made the elementary mistake of solving a crime without having all the details at my fingertips. Browne is on the run. Mulleady sees him with Adeline Goss and reports to us. We arrest her but not Browne. Mulleady is killed by

233

Browne in an act of revenge. It was too cut and dried,' he said. 'I should have known better.'

'In your place, I'd be glad.'

'I don't see any reason for gladness.'

'Did you really want a *second* murder in the area?'

'No, sir, it's the one crime that's thankfully rare.'

'Think what would have happened,' said Tallis, handing over the report. 'If you'd had two unsolved murders on your hands, the press would have been baying at your heels and the Watch Committee would be calling you in to explain yourself.'

'I've had plenty of trouble from both quarters, believe me.'

'People will expect instant solutions. It's unrealistic.'

On his feet, Tallis seemed to fill the room. It was like having both Colbeck and Leeming there together. While he couldn't wait for his visitor to go, Steel was unable to think of a way to get rid of him.

'What's your opinion of Michael Heygate?' asked Tallis.

'He's involved in this whole business somehow – and I don't just mean as beneficiary. I still can't understand why he and his wife spent the night of November 4th in Exeter. Incidentally, they stayed at the Crown Inn,' said Steel. 'Further to your suggestion, my men checked all the hotels.'

'Is the Crown Inn an expensive hostelry?'

'It's reasonably expensive, sir.'

'How could they afford it when they are manifestly short of money?' asked Tallis. 'And why did they tell me they stayed with friends? I don't like being lied to.'

'Then you shouldn't have joined the police force, sir. We must hear more lies than anyone else in creation.' Tallis actually grinned. 'However, I'm holding you up. I'm sure that you have much more important things to do.'

'Nothing is more important than solving this case,' said Tallis, settling into a chair. 'Let's review the evidence so far. Colbeck insists that something is missing and he's almost invariably right. Let's see if – between us – we can't tease out some new evidence about this fellow Browne. Where do you suppose he could be?'

Wearing his disguise as an old man, Bagsy Browne bided his time. He stayed close enough to the building to keep it under surveillance but far enough away not to arouse suspicion. Light was slowly seeping out of a sullen sky. No policemen were on patrol nearby and few people were walking past. Since Adeline would not be able to outrun any pursuit, he'd taken the precaution of stealing a horse and cart. They waited in an alleyway at the rear of the police station. When he judged the time ripe, Browne hobbled off with the aid of his stout walking stick. Once inside the building, he was confronted by the duty sergeant, a middle-aged man with side whiskers.

'Can I help you, sir?' asked the policeman.

'I've come to report a crime.'

'Oh?'

'Two lads have just robbed a woman in the street.'

'Was she hurt?'

'Yes,' said Browne. 'She's lying on the pavement. I tried to stop them but I'm too old to fight any more. Come with me and I'll show you where the woman is.'

Browne stood back so that the sergeant could pass him. As soon as the man had his back to him, Browne struck him hard across the back of his head, sending him to the floor, then administered two more crushing blows to knock him unconscious. Grabbing a bunch of keys from their peg, Browne quickly opened a door that led to a passageway and a second one that led to the cells. He then ran along to the cell at the end and tried various keys in the lock.

Adeline was overjoyed. 'Bagsy!'

'We have to move fast.'

'I knew you wouldn't let me down.'

'One good turn deserves another.' He found the right key and the door opened. 'Off we go, Ad. I've got transport waiting for you.'

They rushed down the corridor and out of the cell block. But the escape plan suddenly faltered. Having finished his discussion upstairs, Tallis had come down and found the duty sergeant on the floor. Realising that there was an escape bid, Tallis stood up and filled the doorway.

'Out of the way!' ordered Browne, brandishing his stick.

'Give that to me,' retorted Tallis.

'I did warn you.'

He began to belabour Tallis who stood there bravely and took most of the blows on his arms. Eventually, he managed to grab the stick and wrench it from Browne's grasp. The latter was infuriated. Pulling out his dagger, he threatened Tallis with it but the superintendent stayed his ground. The commotion had brought Steel out of his office and roused a policeman in the back room. Both came to investigate. Desperate to get away, Browne dived at Tallis and thrust the dagger into his arm. All resistance vanished. With a cry of pain, Tallis clutched the wound, allowing Browne to push him out of the way so that he and Adeline could step over the body of the duty sergeant and run out of the building. The policeman went after them but he was too slow. Before he could get close to them, they'd clambered on to the cart and driven away at speed through the streets of Exeter.

Steel, meanwhile, tried to revive the fallen man and was relieved when the duty sergeant began to regain consciousness. Turning his attention to Tallis, he helped him to stem the bleeding from the wound. Steel was penitent. He'd set a trap for Browne but had failed to catch him. He'd not only lost a prisoner and had one of his men knocked out in the process, he'd contrived to have the Scotland Yard detective in charge of the investigation stabbed.

'Damn you, Bagsy Browne!' he swore. 'I'll get you for this.'

CHAPTER THIRTEEN

Frances Impey was close to despair. She'd lived alone before and was quite capable of looking after herself but the situation was very different now. Her sister had been incarcerated in the County Asylum. It was humiliating. When Agnes Rossiter had scandalised everyone in the cathedral by her antics at the altar, Frances hadn't been there to witness it and was therefore unaware of the full horror of the spectacle. Her sister's second act of madness had occurred when Frances was standing beside her. One moment they were walking serenely through the city, the next her sister was smashing a window with a stone and climbing through it. All that Frances could remember was passing out on the cobbles. When the smelling salts brought her round again, her sister was howling piteously in the grip of two policemen. Such memories would haunt Frances for ever. It had been a shock to see her beloved sister taken off to Exminster but, in truth, Frances knew that she could never look after her at home.

She was far too afraid to venture out to church that morning. While she wanted to pray for her sister's recovery, she feared the pointed fingers and the murmured comments from other members of the congregation. There was no hiding the disgrace. Everyone would know by now. Even those who offered sympathy would be treating her with more caution, as if she might somehow infect them with her sister's mental disorder. Limited as it had been, her social life was virtually extinct. Frances would henceforth be the source of whisperers.

As she sat in the kitchen with a cup of tea untouched beside her, she brooded on the future. Though dismayed at the dramatic change in her own life, her thoughts were largely centred on her sister. How long would she be detained? Would she ever be let out? If so, what sort of condition would she be in? In the past, Agnes Rossiter had been the wage-earner and the more forceful character. She would be neither if she was released from the asylum. Who would even consider employing a woman with her medical history? What sort of life would the two sisters lead? The problem was that the madness had a public dimension. Its effects had been seen in the cathedral and outside the undertaker's. It was the stuff of general discussion now. Frances could see only one mode of survival. If her sister was finally discharged, they would have to move out of Exeter. But the asylum cast a very long shadow.

Would they ever be able to outrun it?

Frances was still deep in thought when there was a knock on the door. It startled her. Who could possibly want to visit a house of shame? At first, she tried to ignore the caller, but a second and third knock showed that the person knew she was inside. Plucking up her courage, she went to the front door, opened it a few inches and peered nervously through the gap.

'Hello, Miss Impey,' said Dorcas, smiling gently. 'How are you?'

'Oh, it's you, Miss Hope.' She opened the door wider to check that nobody else was there. 'You're on your own, I see.'

'I just came to offer help.'

Frances was suspicious. 'What sort of help?'

'Well, you may want someone to do the shopping for you or help with jobs around the house. I know that Mrs Rossiter did so much when she was here. You may find it difficult to manage on your own.'

'Yes, I might.'

'You know where I live. All you have to do is to ask.'

'Thank you, Miss Hope. That's very kind of you.'

'I have to work at the refreshment room, of course,' said Dorcas, 'but I do have some free time each day. I must say that we miss your sister at the railway station. Mrs Rossiter was such an efficient manageress.'

'Agnes was efficient at everything she did – unlike me.'

'It may be that you just feel the need for company.'

'At the moment, to be honest, I just wish to be alone.'

'I can understand that. I won't bother you any longer.'

'It was so kind of you to call.'

'I'll come again when you've . . . settled down.'

'I suppose they're all talking about Agnes,' said Frances, meekly.

'Mrs Rossiter was in our prayers in church this morning.

241

However,' said Dorcas, 'I don't wish to intrude. I've made my offer and I hope that you'll take advantage of it. I owe a lot to Mrs Rossiter. She taught me everything.'

With a smile of farewell, Dorcas withdrew and walked away. Frances closed the door and went back to the kitchen. She had a friend. She was not quite so isolated, after all. The visit had been brief but it had brought immense reassurance. She was touched by the sincerity of the offer of help. Dorcas Hope would help her through the nightmare that lay ahead. She had someone to whom she could turn. Though it was now stone cold, Frances was at last able to drink her cup of tea.

The wound had needed several stitches and his blood had soaked the sleeves of his shirt and frock coat. The encounter with Browne had also shaken Tallis up. He was sitting in a chair in his room at the tavern. The doctor had just left but Colbeck and Leeming were bending over him in concern. Neither of them had ever believed he would feel so sorry for Tallis. He was pale, drawn and somehow reduced in size. One of his arms was heavily bandaged and supported by a sling. Their sympathy was edged with admiration. It was clear that Tallis had shown great courage in taking on Browne. He was wearing a dressing gown now, but they'd seen the ugly bruises on both arms when he'd been attended by the doctor. Tallis obviously felt embarrassed to be a patient. He shooed them back with a nod of his head.

'You don't need to stand over me,' he said. 'You'd be more use joining in the search for the villain who did this to me.'

'Superintendent Steel has already organised a manhunt,

sir,' said Colbeck. 'All off-duty policemen have been recalled to take part in it.'

'I wish that more of them had been there at the police station.'

'Browne must have known that numbers would have been depleted.'

'What news of the duty sergeant?'

'According to the superintendent, there's no permanent damage but the man has a bad headache. Browne must have felled him with his walking stick.'

Tallis felt a stab of pain. 'Don't mention that stick to me, Inspector.'

'It was lucky that you happened to be there, sir,' said Leeming.

'I don't *feel* lucky, I can tell you.'

'But you were able to delay the escape. That will have helped.'

'Nevertheless, they managed to get away.'

'They won't get far, sir. There must be dozens of witnesses who saw a horse and cart careering through the streets. And where will they hide?' asked Leeming. 'They can hardly go back to the woman's room in Rockfield Place.'

Tallis's familiar growl resurfaced. 'Leeming.'

'Yes, sir?'

'Oblige me by holding that irritating appendage known as your tongue. At a time like this, I don't need your mindless speculation.'

'Victor was making a reasonable point, sir,' said Colbeck in support of his friend, 'but I can see that you need to be left alone to rest.'

'I do feel weak,' admitted the other.

'Then we'll disappear. Our rooms are only down the passageway. If you need us this evening, you only have to call.'

'Thank you, Colbeck,' said Tallis. 'All that I need at the moment is peace and quiet. Tomorrow, I'll be fit enough to take up the reins of this investigation once again. Next time I meet Browne, he won't get away so easily.'

'Oh, I don't think you should tackle him again, sir,' said Leeming.

'Your opinion is redundant.'

'I happen to share it,' said Colbeck, becoming more assertive. 'You heard what the doctor advised, sir. He was talking about days of bed rest. I don't think that's necessary for someone as resilient as you but it's clear that you shouldn't continue to take charge of the case when you must be in constant pain and discomfort.'

'My arm *is* on fire,' conceded Tallis, touching it gingerly with his other hand. 'It's almost as if the dagger is still in there.'

'That settles it. Tomorrow morning, I'll put you on a train back to London so that you can return home and rest in more comfortable surroundings. Since you won't be able to carry any luggage,' said Colbeck with a sly wink at Leeming, 'the sergeant will accompany you and make sure that you are not jostled in the course of your journey. I daresay that you'd like your own doctor to examine the wound. He's far and away the best person to give you advice about convalescence.'

'I'm not an invalid, man. I need no convalescence.'

It was a half-hearted protest. Tallis knew that Colbeck was right and that it would be an effort for him to remain in Exeter. While he hated having to quit the field, he was confident that the Railway Detective would ultimately bring the case to a satisfactory conclusion. For his part, Leeming was delighted that Colbeck had devised a way to get him back to London where – if only for a short time – he could see his family. In a sense, Colbeck had killed two birds with one stone. He was getting rid of Tallis and doing his sergeant a favour at the same time. The inspector would be able to control the investigation more effectively with his superior out of the way and he would soon be rejoined by someone refreshed by a visit to his wife and children.

'We'll leave you alone now, sir,' said Colbeck.

'Thank you,' said Tallis, wearily.

'Don't worry, sir,' Leeming put in. 'I'll get you safely back to London.'

'Please do so in total silence.'

'Yes, yes, I'll be as quiet as the grave.' He opened the door. 'Goodbye, sir.'

'Wait a moment,' said Tallis, adjusting the sling on his arm. 'Before you go, could one of you do me a favour?'

'I'll be happy to do so,' offered Colbeck.

'Then you can light me a cigar.'

The mood had changed in the little house in Camden. Since tea with the two ladies, Caleb Andrews had lost some of the wind from his sails. He was not moping but he was markedly less enthusiastic about his friendship with Binnie Langton. Meeting her sister had suddenly applied a brake to a relationship that he had planned to pursue at speed until now. Ivy Young was a troubling new factor in the equation.

Madeleine found it distracting to have her father sitting in the parlour while she was trying to paint. Instead of his usual jovial patter, all that he was contributing was a vague sense of discontent. He didn't even feel able to take his daily walk.

'The weather is brighter today,' she observed.

'I hadn't noticed.'

'The sun is out. It's a good time for a stroll.'

'Are you trying to get rid of me, Maddy?'

'Frankly, I am,' she said. 'Fresh air will do you good. There's no point in simply brooding in here.'

'It's only what *you've* been doing,' he argued. 'Ever since he left, you've done nothing but think about my future son-in-law.'

'But they've mostly been happy thoughts about the wedding.'

'Mine were happy thoughts until Mrs Young turned up.'

'She really upset you, didn't she?'

'Yes, Maddy. Everything has been turned upside down.'

'When are you going to invite Mrs Langton to tea?'

'I'm having second thoughts about that.'

'It's only polite to ask her here,' said Madeleine. 'It's a way of thanking her for her hospitality – and you'll see her on her own this time.'

Andrews cheered up. 'That will be good.'

Before he could say why, they were diverted by the sound of a cab rattling down the street and slowing to a halt outside the door. Madeleine moved quickly. In the hope that it might be Colbeck, she put down her brush, wiped her hands on a cloth and scuttled to the door. Flinging it open, she saw Leeming descending from the cab.

'Oh,' she said, saddened, 'it's you, Sergeant.'

'I was asked by the inspector to deliver this,' said

Leeming, giving her a letter. 'It will explain why I'm in such a rush. Superintendent Tallis and I caught the early train from Exeter and I have to return there this afternoon. Before then, I'm keen to snatch a little time with my family.'

'Then I won't hold you up. Thank you so much for this,' she went on, holding up the letter. 'Please give Robert my love.'

'I will,' said Leeming as he climbed back into the cab. 'He'll be very glad to receive it because it won't have been a pleasant day for him.'

'Oh – why is that?'

'At this very moment, Inspector Colbeck is attending a funeral.'

He signalled to the driver and the cab drew away from the kerb.

The funeral of Joel Heygate was a sombre affair. While he had few close relatives, he'd acquired a wide extended family of friends. Those who were able to get off work had joined the throng at St Olave's Church in Fore Street. It was the place where Heygate had been christened, then married, so his life had come full circle. The little Saxon church was really no more than a chapel, so many of those there would be unable to get inside for the funeral service itself. They would have to wait until the proceedings came out into the churchyard. Having arrived early, Colbeck was able to have a chat with Steel, who had shed his uniform for once and was wearing apparel more suited to the occasion. They watched black-clad mourners filing into the church.

'I suppose that St Olave's is an appropriate place for

Heygate to end up,' said Steel. 'It's named after St Olaf, an eleventh-century king of Norway who was martyred in battle. There are those who'd call the stationmaster something of a martyr.'

'It's a very pretty piece of architecture.'

'You wouldn't have been able to say that twenty odd years ago, Inspector. St Olave's was almost derelict then. So were a number of other churches. Thanks to the initiative of the then recently appointed Bishop Phillpotts, some twelve of them were repaired and restored.'

'That's another good thing in his favour, then.'

'He later formed a diocesan society to promote the further building and enlargement of churches. Oh, yes,' said Steel, 'he was full of energy in those days. Unfortunately, he still is.'

'Some of his energy is misdirected, that's all,' said Colbeck, tolerantly. He looked around. 'Do you expect Browne to put in an appearance?'

'He wouldn't dare turn up.'

'Don't you believe in the compulsion to return to the scene of the crime?'

'Bagsy will be miles away by now. In his shoes, I know that I would be.'

'He's clearly a remarkable man who doesn't think like you and me. Which of us would have had the gall and the bravado to rescue a prisoner from custody?'

'Neither of us, Inspector – we've got too much sense.'

'It's the reason that we wouldn't even conceive of the idea of attending the funeral of a man we'd killed. Mr Browne may find the temptation irresistible.'

'If he does, my men will be on the lookout for him.'

'I hope you've warned them how dangerous he can be.'

'They heard what happened to the duty sergeant yesterday. While we're on the subject,' Steel went on, 'how is Superintendent Tallis?'

'He's probably safely back in London by now.'

Colbeck told him how he'd persuaded Tallis to leave the city in the company of Victor Leeming. While he'd been struck by the superintendent's bravery in confronting Browne, Steel was glad that he was no longer there to hinder the inquiry. Colbeck would have a free hand and that was a positive improvement. Tallis was at his best behind a desk, delegating work to others and demanding quick results. He was too slow and lumbering to work on location as a detective.

'Mr Woodford has remained on duty at the station,' said Steel, 'but he's kindly released some of his staff to come here. I'm not quite sure what that tells us about him.'

'He's the stationmaster now and he wants everyone to know it. If he *was* involved in the murder,' said Colbeck, 'he might have been lured here if only for the perverse pleasure of seeing his old enemy laid to rest. But I suspect that he'd see the wisdom of staying away. He's a shrewd and cunning man.'

'Will he be installed as Heygate's successor, do you think?'

'He seems to have appointed himself already.'

'The post will be advertised. The final decision will lie with Mr Quinnell.'

'We'll have to wait until the service is over before we can speak to him. Mr Quinnell was among the first to arrive because he's in charge of the arrangements.'

'Only a man of his influence could have got the funeral

arranged in such a short time,' said Steel. 'I'm told that another one had to be postponed to make way for Heygate. Think of the upset that must have caused another grieving family. Let's go on in while we can,' he added, leading the way. 'I asked them to reserve seats for us near the back.'

'Thank you,' said Colbeck. 'That showed foresight.'

'I want to see every moment of the ceremony, Inspector – just in case Bagsy Browne does sneak in at some point.'

'Thanks to Mr Tallis, we have a very good description of the man.'

'Yet his disguise fooled the duty sergeant. That's worrying.'

'Would you like to place a small wager?'

'As long as it really *is* small,' said Steel. 'I'm certain that Bagsy won't show his ugly face at the funeral. You think otherwise, I believe.'

'It's a feeling I have,' said Colbeck, 'and I'll back it with money.'

'Then I'll wager a sovereign that I'm right.'

'I accept the bet.'

'You're very prodigal with your money, Inspector.'

'Not at all,' said Colbeck with a confident grin. 'To save time, you might as well hand over the sovereign now. Browne will be here. He *has* to be.'

Adeline Goss had been thrilled at the risk that Browne had taken on her behalf. The escape had been exciting and wholly successful. After reaching the suburbs, they'd abandoned the horse and cart and made their way in the gathering gloom to the boat. Early next morning, they'd been bold enough to slip back into the city. They collected everything of value from Adeline's room before most people had even woken up.

Her things had been temporarily stowed away in the boat. By afternoon they were back in Exeter. She was disguised as a washerwoman with a basket of laundry over her arm and a floppy hat covering most of her face.

'Don't do it, Bagsy!' she pleaded. 'There's no need.'

'There's every need, Ad. I want to spit on his coffin.'

'It's too dangerous.'

'Heygate was my enemy. I'm entitled to my moment of triumph.'

'What if you're caught?'

Browne sniggered. 'They had their chance to catch me yesterday,' he boasted, 'and they failed. I'm like a cat, Ad. I've got nine lives.'

'You used one of them up yesterday.'

'Is that a complaint?' he asked, slipping an arm around her waist.

'No,' she replied with a laugh. 'I loved every second of it.'

'I always pay my dues, whether it's to a friend or an enemy. It's my code.'

'You could be putting a noose around your neck, Bagsy.'

'There's no chance of that,' he scoffed. 'Those Scotland Yard detectives will think I took to my heels and ran away. They'd never expect me to stay in Exeter and neither would Superintendent Steel.' He cackled. 'I'd love to have seen his face when he saw that your cell was empty.'

'Thank God you came for me – the food in there was like horse shit.'

'We'll have a proper meal this evening, a sort of celebration.'

'What are we celebrating?'

'I'll tell you later,' he said. 'I don't want to be late for the

251

funeral. Heygate will be wishing he'd never upset me now –
what's left of him, anyway.'

He marched off, singing happily to himself.

In one respect, Joel Heygate was fortunate. The South
Devon Railway gave him the sort of funeral that he could
never have afforded and which was hopelessly beyond the
means of his brother. No expense had been spared. Preceded
by a mute, the coffin arrived in a glass-sided hearse drawn
by black horses with black plumes. It was carried with great
solemnity into the church by six men in mourning garb. The
crowd assembled outside watched it all with hearts weighed
down with fond memories of a man they'd never see again.
The manner of his death gave the whole event an added
poignancy.

Colbeck was grateful for the way that the railway company
had honoured its former stationmaster. Quinnell was only
one of a number of its directors there. The inspector had
seen far too many paupers' funerals where the deceased was
treated with little more respect than an animal carcass and
where the proceedings were almost indecently perfunctory.
Heygate had taken care to avoid such a fate. When they'd
searched his house, they found a record of the instalments
he'd paid over the years into a funeral club, ensuring that he
would be buried in a proper Christian manner. In the event,
his foresight had been unnecessary. His employers had taken
charge.

There were no women inside the church, though some
had gathered outside. Colbeck wondered what sort of a
scene Agnes Rossiter might have created if she'd stormed
in during the service. Thankfully, she was miles away and

probably unaware of what was going on at St Olave's. Seated near the back, Colbeck was able to keep an eye on Michael Heygate, the chief mourner and – though he didn't realise it – a suspect in the investigation. To his credit, he seemed genuinely moved when the coffin was carried in and produced a black-edged handkerchief. Colbeck could not decide if he was seeing the natural bereavement of a brother or the delayed remorse of a killer. Lavinia Heygate was elsewhere. Colbeck suspected that she was more likely to be anticipating a much-needed inheritance than weeping for a dead brother-in-law.

The funeral oration was appropriately comforting and filled with praise for the deceased. It was given by a vicar who'd known and liked Heygate for many years and who was able to call on his memories of the stationmaster. He even found a moment to mention the canary. When the service was over, they moved out into the small churchyard for the interment, joined by those who'd been unable to get inside the building. Colbeck lingered on the fringes this time, anxious to have freedom of movement so that he could study the faces of those present. Most were bent in respect, eyes down and mouths tight-lipped. The majority of people wore funeral attire but there were a number of bystanders who'd simply come in their normal apparel. One of them was a chunky man in the simple garb of a gravedigger, his cheeks darkened by smudges of dirt and his hands filthy. He was holding his cap and kept his chin on his chest. What made Colbeck notice him was that he inched himself nearer and nearer to the grave, slowly burrowing his way through the mass of bodies.

When the burial was at last over, people began to disperse

in small groups. Colbeck waited to take a closer look at the man who'd interested him. Before he could do so, however, he was spotted by Gervase Quinnell.

'Good afternoon, Inspector,' he said. 'I'm sorry we meet on such a sad day.'

'I must congratulate you on the arrangements for the funeral. They've done something to alleviate the general sadness.'

'I wanted everyone to know that we prized his years of service.'

'Nobody was left in any doubt about that.'

Taking him by the arm, Quinnell moved him aside. 'Is it true what I hear about Superintendent Tallis?'

'Yes,' said Colbeck, 'he's returned to London to nurse his wound.'

'Browne's effrontery knows no bounds.'

'Some would account it daring rather than effrontery, Mr Quinnell. I'm sure that Browne himself would. Nothing seems to daunt him.'

'I think we should increase the amount of the reward again.'

'That's not the answer, sir,' said Colbeck. 'If anyone had the information we need, they'd have come forward by now. As it is, the one person who did tell us something of use has drowned himself by accident. He fell into the canal in a stupor. Superintendent Steel had a report from one of the more disreputable pubs that Finbar Mulleady spent the whole evening pouring beer down his throat and boasting that he was about to come into a very large amount of money. In other words,' he concluded, 'he'd have claimed your reward.'

'If Browne had been caught, this man would have deserved it.'

'But he hasn't been caught as yet.'

'He can't elude you indefinitely, Inspector Colbeck.'

'No, he can't, and his time at liberty is fast running out.'

While talking to Quinnell, he'd been keeping one eye on the individual who looked like a gravedigger. He was talking to the two men who were leaning on their spades as they waited to fill in the grave. Colbeck saw them him pick up a handful of earth and toss it on to the coffin then spit after it.

'Excuse me, sir,' he said to Quinnell.

'But I have several things to ask you, Inspector.'

'They'll have to wait.'

'You can't just dash off. It's most unseemly.'

'I think I've just seen Bagsy Browne, sir.'

Quinnell gaped in disbelief. 'You've seen that villain *here*?'

'I believe so.'

Colbeck turned back to the grave but the man had now vanished. Pushing his way through the last of those still in the churchyard, he hurried across to the two gravediggers who were now shovelling more earth on to the coffin.

'What happened to the man who was talking to you just now?'

One of them shrugged. 'He just left, sir.'

'Where did he go?'

'Don't ask us. We've never seen him before.'

Colbeck scoured the churchyard but the man seemed to have disappeared. He chided himself for not cornering him earlier when the crowd would have prevented his escape. All that he was left with was the nagging suspicion that he'd just let Bagsy Browne get away right under his nose. Colbeck was still searching when Steel joined him among the headstones.

'Far be it from me to sound mercenary, Inspector,' he

said, 'but I have to remind you of a small wager that we made.'

'I remember it well – you owe me a sovereign.'

'Bagsy Browne never came anywhere near the funeral.'

'Oh yes he did,' said Colbeck, ruefully. 'And he got away before I could arrest him. On second thoughts,' he went on, 'it would be unfair to take any money from you. I won the bet but lost the putative killer. That being so, I'd like you to accept this by way of apology.' Taking a sovereign from his waistcoat pocket, he gave it to Steel. 'Be warned, Superintendent. I shall win it back before too long.'

It was evening before Michael Heygate was able to escape from the dozens of people who wanted to offer their condolences and tell him anecdotes about his brother. He repaired to a room at the Crown Inn where his wife was awaiting him. Lavinia had stayed away from the funeral in its entirety, pleading unbearable grief over the loss of a much-loved brother-in-law. Since most people didn't know her, they accepted the excuse and offered their sympathy by way of her husband. When she let him into the room, there was little indication of sorrow on her part. Seizing her husband's hands, she gave him a welcoming kiss on the cheek.

'Well?' she asked.

'It's over.'

'You look exhausted.'

'It was harrowing,' he confessed. 'In spite of all the bad things that happened between us, Joel was my only sibling. We grew up together as boys and liked each other in those days. It was only later that we drifted apart.'

'Were there many people there?'

'Half the city seemed to have turned out. There'll be even more if we hold a memorial service.' He put his top hat aside. 'I can't say that I'm looking forward to that. I'm going to have to wear a sad face again.'

She helped him off with his frock coat. 'You need a rest, Michael.'

'Thank heaven we didn't have to pay for the funeral!' he said. 'It must have cost a fortune. The railway company did him proud.'

'Forget your brother,' she said. 'It's time to think about us.'

He lowered himself on to a chair. 'I know, Lavinia.'

'Was Joel's solicitor there?'

'Yes, he was.'

'Did you manage to speak to him?'

'I made a point of doing so.'

'And?' she pressed. 'What did he say?'

'Mr Lyman mumbled something about the law of probate and said that he'd be in touch with us in the fullness of time.'

Lavinia was annoyed. 'Didn't he tell you *anything*?'

'It wasn't the time and the place.'

'I thought you'd at least get some sort of hint out of him,' she said. 'We need to know about the bequest, Michael. Your brother was comfortably off. When he sold his house, he made a pretty penny and, when he lost his wife and child, the railway company set up a fund for him. Because everyone was shocked by the tragedy, money poured in from everywhere.'

'Five pounds of it was ours,' he said ruefully. 'We had to contribute.'

'Joel was always so careful with money.'

'He had nothing to spend it on, Lavinia.'

'Then why didn't he give some of it to us?' she said, waspishly. 'I think that you should tackle his solicitor again tomorrow.'

'We don't want to appear too money-grubbing.'

'You're his brother, Michael. You're entitled to it.'

'Yes, I am,' he said, relishing the thought. 'I did my duty at the funeral and I'm ready to reap the reward. Now that it's over, I don't feel any regret and even less guilt. Joel got what he deserved. When I go to that memorial service, the expression on my face will be grim but I'll be laughing triumphantly inside.'

It had been a gruelling day for Dorcas Hope. Though she'd tried to concentrate on her work, her mind was at the funeral. She'd seen passengers arrive in mourning wear to attend the event, then watched some of them leave late in the afternoon. Dorcas was slow, distracted and clumsy. At one point, she even broke a cup. Timothy Vesey, the new manager, made allowances for her but Woodford was less understanding. He'd been jumpy all day and Dorcas had put it down to his own sense of bereavement. It had not affected the sharpness of his tongue. When he saw Dorcas making mistakes in the refreshment room, he was as critical as Mrs Rossiter.

'Be more careful, girl,' he snapped as she dropped a tray.

'I'm sorry, Mr Woodford.'

'Pick it up again.'

'Yes, yes, I will.'

'And try to keep your mind on what you're doing. That's why we pay you.'

She retrieved the tray and took it apologetically to the counter. Woodford had made frequent visits to them throughout the day and found a reason to castigate her each time. His final comment was the most hurtful.

'You're in a world of your own,' he said with asperity. 'At this rate, you'll end up in the County Asylum with Mrs Rossiter.'

The wounding remark had brought tears to her eyes but she'd soldiered on. At the end of the working day, Dorcas more or less ran home, anxious to get away from the station and its association with a man she'd loved. Where his successor was sarcastic, he'd been more forgiving. Where Woodford used his authority like a stick with which to beat people, the old stationmaster had simply led by example. Dark days lay ahead for Dorcas. She'd lost the two colleagues who'd been fixtures in her life – Agnes Rossiter and Joel Heygate. Eager to get to work when she was under their aegis, she now went with great reluctance.

Arriving home, she was surprised that there was no chirpy greeting from Peter. The canary welcomed everyone to the house, yet it was eerily silent now. Dorcas went into the parlour where her mother was in her accustomed place beside the cage. She saw why there'd been no greeting from the canary. Peter's cage was covered in a black cloth. Maud Hope was subdued.

'He's been quiet all day,' she explained. 'He knows about the funeral.'

CHAPTER FOURTEEN

Victor Leeming had an unusual experience. He could never bring himself to like rail travel – and he'd already endured one long train journey that day – but the return trip to Exeter had a bonus for him. He shared a carriage with an elderly couple on their way to Teignmouth and discovered that they had an interest in the concept of the atmospheric railway. Leeming was in his element, speaking with the airy confidence of someone who knows only a little more than his listeners and undeterred by the fact that he had a very unsure grasp of the technicalities involved. He told them about his recent visit to Starcross, one of the places where the experiment had been tried out.

'Robert Stephenson called it a rope of air,' he said, knowledgeably, 'and it was, in essence, a very clever idea. Apart from anything else, it might have saved money and reduced the amount of smoke that locomotives generate.

Alas,' he went on, quoting Colbeck, 'it must be put down as one of Mr Brunel's rare failures.'

The elderly couple had been pleasant companions, unlike the man who'd sat beside him on the journey to London. Arm in a sling, Tallis had been as friendly as a wounded bear and as talkative as a deaf mute. Leeming had only been able to stand the sheer boredom of it all by thinking of the brief reunion he'd have with his wife and children. That insulated him against the superintendent's tetchiness. An hour with his family had revived him. He returned to Devon with his energy restored.

Knowing his time of arrival, Colbeck was waiting to greet him at the station.

'Welcome back, Victor,' he said, shaking his hand. 'How was your journey?'

'There were two of them, sir, and as different as black and white. The trip to London was as enjoyable as having my teeth pulled out one by one.'

Colbeck laughed. 'Mr Tallis was in a churlish mood when he left.'

'The journey here went much more quickly because I was actually allowed to talk this time. It was a welcome novelty.'

'Did you deliver my letter?'

'Miss Andrews was pleased to receive it and sends you her love.'

'How were Estelle and the children?'

'They gave me a marvellous welcome,' recalled Leeming with a broad grin. 'Fatherhood is the most wonderful gift – as you'll soon discover.'

'Don't get ahead of yourself,' warned Colbeck. 'There's the small matter of the wedding to come first.'

'Estelle showed me the dress she's been making for it.'

'Then you hold a distinct advantage over me. I'm not allowed to see the bridal dress beforehand.'

'Miss Andrews will look beautiful whatever she wears, sir.'

Colbeck smiled. 'You don't need to tell me that, I assure you.'

He was delighted to find Leeming in such a positive frame of mind and was amused to hear that he'd set himself up as an expert on the atmospheric railway. On the cab ride into the city, he brought him up to date with events in Exeter. Leeming was astounded at one piece of information.

'Bagsy Browne was *there*?'

'As large as life,' said Colbeck. 'I'd put money on it. As a matter of fact, I did just that but I couldn't collect my winnings because the sighting hadn't been verified by Superintendent Steel. I could *smell* that Browne was there.'

'He was taking an unnecessary risk.'

'His whole criminal career has been a compendium of unnecessary risks, Victor. That's what animates the man. It isn't enough for him to evade the law. He has to taunt us with his devilry time and again.'

'Superintendent Tallis deserved a medal for standing up to him.'

'We've never doubted his bravery. He was a military hero, after all. It's his other qualities that are more questionable.'

'Browne did us a big favour by getting rid of him for us.'

'I hope you didn't say that to him on the train journey.'

'I wasn't allowed to open my mouth, sir. Every time I cleared my throat, I got a cold stare. Anyone would think that *I'd* been the man to stab him.' He looked remorseful.

'Though there have been occasions, I must confess, when I have dallied with the idea of causing him pain.'

Colbeck lowered his voice. 'We're equally guilty on that score, Victor.'

Instead of heading for their tavern, the cab turned down a side street.

'Where are we going, sir?' asked Leeming.

'I thought that we'd pay a call on Woodford,' said Colbeck. 'You've seen Michael Heygate in his domestic setting and taken his measure. I think it's time to see if Woodford was egged on by a Lady Macbeth.'

'Who's she?'

'A character from Shakespeare – she incites her husband to murder.'

'Is that what Lavinia Heygate did?'

'It's not beyond the bounds of possibility.'

'What about Mrs Woodford?'

'I'll be interested to find out,' said Colbeck.

It was difficult to copulate in the limited space of the cabin but Browne and Adeline eventually managed it. Flushed with drink and high on emotion, they held a joint celebration for her escape and his valedictory encounter with Joel Heygate. From her point of view, however, the event was tinged with sadness. It was all over. Now that he'd seen his enemy lowered six feet into the ground, there was nothing to keep Browne in Exeter. He was ready to move on. She recognised the signs.

'When will I see you again, Bagsy?' she asked, snuggling up to him.

'I haven't gone yet.'

'It won't be long before you do. I can sense it.'

He squeezed her. 'There's no fooling you, is there, Ad?'

'I've a mind to head for Plymouth,' she said. 'The police will be looking for me, so I can't stay here. I've a cousin in Plymouth who'll take me in. If I dye my hair and change my name, nobody will know the difference.'

'I will. Be sure to give me your cousin's address before you go.'

'What about you, Bagsy?'

'North Devon is starting to call me,' he said. 'It must be years since I've seen Barnstaple. I might give it the privilege of my presence for a while.'

'You're a true rolling stone.'

'That's why I gather no moss, Ad.'

'I don't know,' she teased, running a hand through the matted hair on his bare chest. 'What do you call this, then?'

'That's my animal fur.' He gave an involuntary shiver. 'It's getting colder. Let's put our clothes on. If I stay like this any longer, my sweat will turn to ice.'

She looked around. 'There are better places to spend our last night together.'

'It was all I could find, Ad.'

'I'm not complaining. It's got the two things I enjoy most – plenty of brandy and plenty of Bagsy Browne.'

He embraced her with a guffaw then reached for his shirt. Even when they were dressed, it was still cold. He came to a decision.

'There's plenty of spare wood along the bank,' he said, 'and there are bits of the boat we can use as well. Let's have a fire to warm us both up, shall we? I daresay that it will put us in the mood for another celebration, don't you?'

* * *

265

The idea that Lawrence Woodford's wife might be a latter-day Lady Macbeth was shattered the moment they met her. She was a small, skinny, nervous mouse of a woman totally devoid of any character or spirit. When the detectives called at the house, she hustled the children upstairs and stayed there for safety. Woodford invited the visitors into a parlour bare of ornament and smelling of the fish the family had eaten earlier that evening. Tellingly, the master of the house was still wearing his stationmaster's uniform, clear proof that he remained on duty even at home and supervised the comings and goings of his family as if following a timetable.

'We're sorry to disturb you at this hour,' said Colbeck, 'but I wanted to congratulate you on your devotion to duty. It was so important to have a strong presence at the railway station on this day above all others.'

'Thank you, Inspector.'

'Let me add my congratulation as well,' said Leeming. 'It must have been a very difficult decision for you to make.'

'It was,' said Woodford. 'I'd have preferred to go to the funeral, naturally, but something told me that Joel would have wanted me to take control at the station instead. I plan to visit his grave in due course to take my leave of him.' He glanced at Colbeck. 'Were you there?'

Colbeck explained that he'd attended the funeral but that Leeming had taken their injured superior back to London. Woodford remembered seeing the pair of them boarding the train and had been curious about Tallis's sling. When he heard that the wound had been inflicted by Browne, he was livid.

'That man is a menace,' he declared.

'He does appear to be,' said Colbeck.

'First of all, he murders Joel, then he rescues his mistress from custody and stabs your superintendent in the process. Mr Tallis might have been killed.'

'I don't think that's true, sir.'

'Browne had nothing to lose.'

'I've been reflecting on that,' said Colbeck. 'If he'd wanted to kill Mr Tallis then he could easily have done so. One thrust of the dagger into the heart would have been sufficient. But he deliberately stabbed him in the arm to disable him. It may be that Browne is not the desperate killer we all take him for.'

Woodford looked stunned. 'Are you saying that he *didn't* murder Joel?'

'I require more evidence.'

'How much more evidence do you need, Inspector? Bagsy Browne is the bane of our police force. He's been in and out of prison for years. Heavens!' exclaimed Woodford, 'it wasn't long ago that he beat up one of the warders and left him in a pool of blood. If that isn't evidence of this man's murderous intent, what is?'

'He didn't *kill* the warder, sir,' said Leeming, 'yet he had the chance to do it.'

'That's two victims he spared,' added Colbeck.

'If you knew Browne as well as we do,' said Woodford with growing vexation, 'you'd realise that he was capable of anything. He once threw a firework at the bishop and relieved himself on the lawn in full view of his palace.'

'That sounds more like horseplay than proof of homicidal leanings.'

'If you don't believe me, talk to Superintendent Steel. He has no doubt at all that Joel was battered to death by

Bagsy Browne. He'd threatened to kill Joel and carried out that threat. You don't need to be a detective from Scotland Yard to see the facts that are staring you in the face.'

'Thank you for your advice on the art of detection,' said Colbeck, ironically. 'We'll bear your words in mind. They'll provide useful guidance to us. Let me come to the question that really prompted this visit,' he continued. 'When I mentioned the existence of Mr Heygate's diary, you denied all knowledge of it.'

'That's true. I had no idea that he kept a diary.'

'May I suggest you think again, sir?'

'I've no need to do so, Inspector.'

'Then perhaps you'll explain to us why you claimed never to have heard about the diary when, in fact, Miss Hope had told you about it earlier?'

For a second, Woodford was caught off balance. He recovered swiftly.

'Miss Hope is mistaken.'

'She remembers the talk she had with you very well.'

'The girl is imagining things.'

'She strikes me as very level-headed for her age.'

'Who are you going to believe, Inspector?' challenged Woodford, jabbing a finger at him. 'Do you believe a clumsy waitress who can barely remember what day of the week it is, or do you believe a man whose integrity has earned him the right to take charge of the entire station? It's her word against mine.'

'Indeed, it is,' said Colbeck, smoothly. 'There's just one problem.'

'What's that?'

'I don't believe that Dorcas Hope could tell a lie if she tried.' He rose to his feet. 'Come on, Sergeant,' he said. 'We stayed long enough. I think we've learnt what we came for, don't you?'

'It's no fun being a waitress,' said Leeming. 'I should know. I tried it. I have a lot of respect for Miss Hope. She's a good, honest, hard-working young lady.'

Woodford was fuming. 'I'll show you both out.'

Back in the street, the detectives put on their top hats and strode towards their tavern. Colbeck was content but Leeming was critical for once.

'You showed your hand too soon, sir,' he said. 'Now that he knows we have suspicions about him, he'll be far more careful.'

'I thought it was time to prod him into life.'

'You did that, well and truly.'

'Did you notice how eager he was to convince us that Browne was the killer? What did you gather from that, Victor?'

'I don't know which of them murdered the stationmaster, sir, but it was obvious that they couldn't possibly have done it together. Was he blaming it all on Browne to save his own skin?'

'It's more than likely.'

'You really shook him when you asked about that diary.'

'I know,' said Colbeck. 'I must remember to get to the station early tomorrow morning. The first thing Woodford will do is to browbeat Miss Hope into changing her story. He'll try to get her to swear that she didn't mention the diary.'

'What do you think she'll do?'

'She'll do what she always does, Victor – she'll tell the truth.'

'But it's in his power to dismiss her.'

'That's why I need to be there to remind him of something,' said Colbeck. 'It's in Mr Quinnell's power to dismiss Woodford.'

As they walked on through the darkness, Leeming was pensive.

'Did you think that his wife was like Lady Macbeth, sir?'

'No, I didn't.'

'Somehow I couldn't see her inciting anyone to murder.'

'Look at it another way,' suggested Colbeck, 'and you'll see how unlikely a female monster she is. If Lady Macbeth had been like Mrs Woodford, then Scotland would still be ruled by King Duncan.'

An excellent meal had left Bishop Phillpotts contemplative. Sipping his port, he looked across the table at his secretary. Barnes, as ever, was attentive.

'Under other circumstances, I might have liked the man,' said Phillpotts.

'To whom are you referring, Bishop?'

'I am talking about Superintendent Tallis.'

'Ah, I see.'

'He's a man of principle and a good Christian.'

'Then he should have shown more respect for your position,' said Barnes. 'It's the same with Inspector Colbeck. What is it that entitles detectives to overlook the simple rules of hierarchy? There's a bumptious quality about them that I abhor.'

'Both men spoke their mind. I admired them for that.'

'Yet they treated your advice with flagrant disregard.'

'They'll come to see its innate wisdom,' said Phillpotts. 'At least, the inspector will come to do so. The superintendent, I hear, has withdrawn to London with a nasty wound in his arm. One is bound to look up to any man who is ready to tackle a ruffian like Browne. I'm the first to admit that I'd never do it. That's why we have a policeman on guard outside. He's protecting me against attack from Browne.'

'Surely, even he would never come here to the palace, Bishop.'

'Remember what happened on my lawn. I'll never forget the sight of those bare buttocks as they delivered their coarse message to us. Browne is little more than a beast. He should be shot on sight like any wild animal.'

'Your anger is natural,' said Barnes, 'but you are, in reality, as anxious as any of us that the fellow faces the due process of law. To shoot him dead would be to let him escape a proper punishment. He needs to be arraigned in public, convicted and sent to the gallows.'

Phillpotts smiled. 'Trust you to think like a lawyer.'

'I used to be one, Bishop – centuries ago.'

'Have we been here that long, Ralph?'

They traded a dry laugh then fell into a comfortable silence, sipping their port by the light of the silver candelabra and looking back on the events of the last week or so. There was much that troubled Bishop Phillpotts. He singled out one element of his disquiet.

'I wonder if I should have attended the funeral,' he said, moodily.

'You made the right decision when you stayed away.'

'Do you think so, Ralph?'

'You hardly knew the stationmaster because you rarely travel by train.'

'That is so,' said Phillpotts, 'but I wonder if it was expected that I would be there. Mr Quinnell clearly believed that I should be. He sent a letter to that effect.'

'Mr Quinnell doesn't understand the jeopardy you're in, Bishop,' said the secretary. 'As long as Browne is on the loose, it's too dangerous for you to go abroad. Had you been at St Olave's, you'd have presented a tempting target and Browne would not be discouraged by the fact that you'd be inside a church. No, on balance, your decision was right and proper.'

Phillpotts nodded, glad that he'd been given an excellent excuse for staying away from the proceedings. Personal safety was involved. There would be a time when he could show his admiration for Joel Heygate by taking a memorial service in his honour. Since it would be weeks away, there'd be no danger of an assassination attempt on him. While he'd taken a dislike to Colbeck, he expected him to have caught Browne before too long and have him locked away. It would therefore be safe for the bishop to move freely about the city. As a gesture, he might even offer the cathedral as the venue for the memorial service. It was his home territory. In there, he was supreme.

As he envisioned himself standing in the pulpit at the cathedral, another image came into his mind. It was that of a woman, screaming her way down the nave, racing past the choir and committing an act of utter blasphemy at the altar.

'Mrs Rossiter should be restrained,' he asserted.

'The lady has been, Bishop.'

'She should remain in the County Asylum in perpetuity.'

'No,' said Barnes, firmly. 'That's a fate we should wish on nobody. Think of the conditions there. It will be a daily ordeal for her.'

The bishop was sobered. While he wanted retribution, he had expected it to take place in a court of law. When he considered her future properly, the fact that Agnes Rossiter was being treated as a lunatic aroused his sympathy. He pitied anyone sent to the asylum. People of unsound mind could not be held accountable for their actions. He believed that they deserved forgiveness.

'Poor woman!' he said, finishing his port with a gulp. 'We must pray for her recovery and we must mention her name to the asylum chaplain.'

'I'll make a point of writing to him, Bishop.'

'Canon Smalley may be able to offer her some comfort.'

Canon Smalley was a cadaverous man of middle height and years. Assigned to the asylum when it first opened, he'd soon felt that the role of chaplain was his mission in life and implored the bishop to make it a permanent appointment. Everyone trusted him and he moved freely about the establishment. Unlike those of the asylum staff, his methods never included restraint or the sudden administration of pain. What he offered to the patients was time, understanding and compassion. When someone was first admitted, Smalley always took the trouble to see them as soon as possible so that he could assess their needs and see how he could best meet them. The patient on whom he now called was Agnes Rossiter.

She was locked in a room with bare white walls and no furniture apart from a bed and a chair. A gas lamp illumined the scene and gave off a faint whiff. Dressed in the standard asylum garb, she was sitting on the uncarpeted floor with a faraway look in her eye. His arrival disturbed her and she tried to get up.

'No, no,' he said, with a gentle hand on her shoulder, 'stay where you are, Mrs Rossiter. I'll come down to you.' He lowered himself to the floor. 'My name is Canon Smalley and I'm the chaplain here.'

'I don't believe in God,' she said, belligerently.

'A lot of people say that when they first come here and even the most devout of us sometimes question His existence. But that's not what I came to talk to you about, Mrs Rossiter. I'm here to help. I'm here to listen to what you have to say.'

The softness of his voice and the kindness of his manner were soothing. He was not at all like the male nurse who marched her to the room and locked her in it. While the nurse had treated her like a prisoner, Canon Smalley was treating her like a human being and giving her a mild sense of dignity.

'They wouldn't let me go to the funeral,' she said.

'I'm sorry to hear that.'

'It was my right.'

'Why do you think that, Mrs Rossiter?'

'We'd planned to marry one day,' she insisted. 'Before too long, I'd have been Mrs Heygate, living with the most wonderful husband in the world.'

'I knew the stationmaster at St David's. He was indeed a splendid man.'

'It was a joy to work beside him.'

'Tell me why,' invited Smalley, patting her arm. 'Tell me why it gave you so much pleasure to work with him. And there's no need to hurry, Mrs Rossiter. I'll listen for as long as you wish. That's what friends should do.'

Disguise was an important component in Browne's continued freedom from arrest. His ability to change his appearance had saved him time and again. As soon as light began to filter into the cabin, he got up, collected a bowl of water from the estuary so that he could wash and shave, then donned his latest outfit. Adeline laughed in approval.

'You look a proper gentleman from top to toe, Bagsy,' she said. 'Where did you get hold of the frock coat and top hat?'

'They fell into my hands, Ad.'

'In other words, you stole them.'

'I borrowed them for just such a day as this.'

In fact, he'd purloined the clothes from the room of one of her neighbours in Rockfield Place. As he was coming down the stairs in the wake of Adeline's arrest, he heard the telltale grunts of a client thrusting away inside the woman he'd hired for an hour. Browne had eased open the door, seen that both of them were too busy to notice him and grabbed the man's discarded clothing and shoes. They were rather tight on him but he was prepared to stand the discomfort.

Adeline had also disguised herself. By cleaning the powder from her face, she'd added a decade to her age but no longer looked like a whore. Her hair was pinned up so that it could disappear under her hat and her coat was buttoned up to the neck. To Browne's eye, she seemed almost wholesome. The belongings she needed were packed into a valise. Everything else had been burnt on their fire.

'I can manage on my own, you know,' she said.

'I wouldn't dream of letting you go alone, Ad. I'll see you off.'

'Thank you, Bagsy. I'd appreciate that.'

'Everyone will take us for a gentleman and his servant,' he said.

'They wouldn't have done that if they'd seen us celebrating last night,' she said with a crude laugh. 'The owner of this boat will have a shock when he sees that we burnt the doors and shutters to keep warm.'

'It was a very special night, Ad.'

'I hope we have others like it.'

He wouldn't be drawn into making a commitment. Instead he offered his arm.

'Right,' he said, 'let's get you on the train to Plymouth, shall we?'

Woodford was hovering like a bird of prey. The moment that Dorcas turned up for work that morning, he pounced on her, taking her by the elbow and guiding her into the gap beside the waiting room.

'I need to have a word with you, young lady,' he said.

She was frightened by his intensity. 'What have I done, Mr Woodford?'

'You told a lie about me.'

'I'd never do that.'

'According to Inspector Colbeck, you said that you'd mentioned Mr Heygate's diary to me whereas you did nothing of the kind, did you?'

'Yes, I did.'

'No, you didn't.'

'But I did, Mr Woodford. You wanted to know what the inspector had been asking me and I told you that . . .'

Her voice petered out in fear when she saw the look he was giving her. Though she was limited in many ways, Dorcas had a good memory. She knew what she'd told Woodford and she couldn't understand why he was denying it. Patently, it was a matter of importance to him. He stressed the fact by seizing her shoulder.

'You'll have to apologise to the inspector for making a mistake,' he said.

'Why should I do that?'

'It's what I'm telling you to do, Miss Hope.'

'You're hurting me.'

'Do you like working here?'

'Well, yes, I do. It's my job.'

'If you wish to keep that job, do as you're told.'

She was scandalised. 'I can't tell a lie to Inspector Colbeck.'

'You'll do whatever I say,' he warned, tightening his grip and making her squeak in pain. 'Do you understand?'

'Mr Heygate never made me tell a lie,' she said.

He grinned. 'Mr Heygate is dead. I'm the stationmaster now.' He released her but applied more pressure with a threat. 'If you don't do as you're told, Miss Hope, I'll see that the canary is taken away from you.' Dorcas let out a gasp. 'I thought that might make you change your mind.'

'Am I interrupting anything?' asked Colbeck, spotting the pair of them. 'Good morning, Miss Hope,' he added, touching his hat. 'I'm sad to say that you have the look of a young lady who's being bullied.'

'That's nonsense,' said Woodford with a dismissive

chuckle. 'I was just giving Miss Hope some instructions.'

'Did they relate to a diary, by any chance?'

'Yes, they did,' said Dorcas.

'No, they didn't,' countered Woodford, shooting her a glance.

'I had a feeling that this might happen,' said Colbeck. 'That's why Sergeant Leeming and I decided to come along and establish the full truth of the situation. Victor,' he went on, turning to his companion. 'Why don't you take Miss Hope to the refreshment room so that she can begin work?'

'Yes, sir,' said Leeming.

'There's a train due very soon, so she'll be needed. Oh, and you might ask her once again if she ever mentioned that diary to Mr Woodford.'

'I will, Inspector.'

'The girl was mistaken,' said the stationmaster as Leeming led her away. 'She'd have told you so.'

'What threat did you use to coerce her into dishonesty?'

'I used no threat at all.'

'Your stance was very menacing when we came along and Miss Hope was palpably scared.' Colbeck met his eye. 'Let me issue a threat of my own,' he said. 'If that young lady is harassed in any way or even dismissed from her job, I'll report you directly to Mr Quinnell. Is that clear? Leave her alone, Mr Woodford. If you value your position as the stationmaster here, you can stop bullying your staff and learn to tell the truth.'

'All right,' confessed Woodford, giving ground with reluctance, 'I'd forgotten that Miss Hope had mentioned the diary to me. It was an honest mistake. I've had so much else to think about since I took over Mr Heygate's duties. It must have slipped my mind.' He looked up at the station clock.

'The London train will be here in a minute. You'll have to excuse me, Inspector.'

Colbeck stood aside to let him pass. 'Off you go, sir.'

Straightening his shoulders, Woodford strode along the platform to greet the incoming train. Colbeck was left to look along the line of waiting passengers. Two of them caught his attention. A well-dressed man was escorting a middle-aged woman in the modest attire of a domestic servant. What interested Colbeck was the man's gait. He was sure that he'd seen that walk somewhere before. The train was heard before it was actually seen. When it finally steamed into sight, it was belching out smoke and assaulting the eardrums of those in the station. The locomotive eventually squealed to a halt amid clouds of steam. Carriage doors opened and passengers alighted, their places quickly taken by those clambering aboard for the next stage of the journey.

Colbeck kept his eye on the couple he'd noticed earlier. Lifting his hat, the man gave the woman a kiss then held the door open so that she could board the train. Woodford was at his most officious, urging late arrivals to hurry up, then warning everyone still on the platform to stand clear. When he gave the signal for departure, the engine burst into life and flexed its muscles. The train slowly pulled out of the station on its way south. Colbeck strolled across to the man who'd sparked his interest, making sure that he kept between him and the exit.

'Good morning,' he said, cheerily. 'It's Mr Browne, isn't it?'

'I'm sorry,' said the other, unperturbed. 'My name is Jenkins.'

'I remember seeing you yesterday at Mr Heygate's funeral. You were wearing a very different disguise then.'

'I've no idea what you're talking about.'

'Then perhaps you'd like to accompany me to the police station where we can sort the matter out,' suggested Colbeck. 'Superintendent Steel will be delighted to see you, I'm sure.'

Bagsy Browne tensed. 'Who *are* you?'

'My name is Inspector Colbeck of Scotland Yard.'

'Then it's time you bought yourself some spectacles, Inspector, because your eyesight has failed you. I'm not the man you think I am.'

'Yes you are, Bagsy,' said Colbeck. 'You gave yourself away.' He pointed to Browne's ankles. 'No gentleman would wear trousers that are too short or tie his cravat the wrong way. As for your shoes, they appear to be covered in mud. I can't believe that any servant would let you leave the house in that condition.'

Browne's eyes were flicking in every direction as he looked for a means of escape. It was clear that he couldn't bluff his way past Colbeck. He fingered the dagger hidden under his coat.

'Is that the weapon with which you stabbed Superintendent Tallis?' asked Colbeck, extending a hand. 'Give it to me, Mr Browne. You're under arrest.'

'Stay back!' yelled Browne, pulling out the dagger.

'You can't kill both of us, sir.'

'There's only one of you.'

'No, there isn't. The gentleman who just came out of the refreshment room is my colleague, Sergeant Leeming. Over here, Victor!' called Colbeck. 'Come and meet Mr Browne.'

Leeming ran over to them. 'Is this him, sir?'

'Yes, it is. He's either Bagsy Browne or a man with the most inept tailor. That dagger would indicate the former.'

Colbeck took a step forward and Browne flashed the weapon at him. Leeming was waiting for the opportunity to leap on the man they'd been chasing for so long. A small crowd watched from the safety of the waiting room. Woodford had retreated into the ticket office out of fear. Colbeck and Leeming edged slowly forward, each of them stepping back out of range when Browne jabbed the dagger at them. Seeing that he could never leave by means of the exit, Browne decided to trust in the speed of his legs. After a last thrust at the detectives, he jumped down on to the track and began to run at full pelt in the direction just taken by the train.

The detectives went after him. Shedding their coats and tossing away their hats, they leapt on to the track and sprinted after Browne. Colbeck was the fitter and more athletic of the two and opened up an immediate gap, leaving the sergeant puffing gamely in the rear. Browne was fast but Colbeck's long, loping stride allowed him to gain ground on the fugitive. It was only a matter of time before he caught up with him. Realising that, Browne started to panic. There was another problem. He'd flung away his top hat but the tight-fitting clothes remained a handicap, restricting his movement and biting into his legs and body. His heart was pounding, his lungs were on fire and the first trickle of sweat ran down his collar.

Conscious that Colbeck was right behind him, he tried to produce a surge of speed but his legs wouldn't obey. When he glanced over his shoulder, he saw that he'd been caught. A couple of yards behind him, Colbeck suddenly hurled himself forward in a dive and tackled him around the thighs, sending Browne crashing to the ground and knocking his head on the iron rail. Stunned by the impact, he lost his grip on the dagger and it rolled out of reach. Colbeck got to his feet, took Browne by the collar and hauled him to his feet. Blood dribbled from a gash on the man's forehead. He was far too dazed to offer any resistance.

When Leeming came running up, he was panting hard and his brow was sleek with perspiration. Colbeck handed the prisoner over to him.

'There you are, Victor,' he said. 'Clean him up and take him way.'

'Your trousers are torn, sir,' observed Leeming.

Colbeck looked down at the bad tear in one leg and the dirt on both knees.

'I blame Mr Browne for that,' he said, bitterly. 'Before they hang him, I'll send him a bill from my tailor. These trousers weren't made for diving on a railway line. Why didn't this fool have the sense to surrender?'

CHAPTER FIFTEEN

The news that Bagsy Browne had finally been captured was quickly disseminated throughout the city. It was the main topic of discussion in the pubs, shops and streets of Exeter. Henry Phillpotts was in the library in the bishop's palace when he was told. He was delighted. At a stroke, the threat of attack he perceived as looming over him was swept away, allowing his vengeful streak to come to the fore.

'The man should be hanged, drawn and quartered!' he decreed.

'That punishment was used for treason,' Barnes pointed out, 'and, in my opinion, it was unnecessarily barbaric. When the body was quartered, the four parts were sent to separate corners of the kingdom by way of a warning.'

'It's the fate that Browne deserves.'

'Happily, it's no longer on the statute book. Do you really wish the public to be treated to the grisly sight of a man being hanged until he's on the point of expiry then cut down so that he can be sliced open and have his intestines drawn out? What purpose is served by such a hideous spectacle, Bishop?'

'It would bring me satisfaction.'

'It's nothing short of butchery.'

'And what about Browne's butchery?' retorted Phillpotts. 'Have you so soon forgotten what he did to the stationmaster? He battered him to death, then burnt the body to provide amusement to the public. I may sound vindictive but I believe that we should reward cruelty with judicial cruelty.'

'We must agree to differ on that score.'

'The Old Testament teaches us to demand an eye for an eye.'

'I've no wish to take issue with such a learned theologian as you,' said Barnes. 'That would be foolhardy and presumptuous. I simply feel that we should let the law take its course. You're still too inflamed by the outrages that Browne directed at you to take an objective view.'

Phillpotts took several deep breaths before speaking. 'Then it's just as well that I have you to introduce a note of reason,' he said, calming down. 'I owe you my thanks. I'm getting old, Ralph. My stock of forgiveness has run low. In its place is this venomous impulse to inflict far more pain than I myself have suffered.' His voice hardened. 'But I still wish to watch Browne hang.'

'That's a popular sentiment in the city.'

'It's a pity that Inspector Colbeck won't be here to witness it. He, after all, is the hero of the hour. If reports are correct, he pursued the villain for over a hundred yards, then jumped on him even though Browne was armed with a dagger.'

'He showed exceptional courage, Bishop.'

'He needs to be told how much we appreciate what he did.'

'You wish to send him a letter?'

'I'll draft it immediately. I took Colbeck for yet another stubborn and single-minded policeman but he's redeemed himself in my eyes. He had the wit to recognise Browne and the nerve to challenge him.' Sitting at his desk, he reached for his quill pen and dipped it in the inkwell. 'Now, then . . . how shall I phrase it?'

'Before you commit pen to paper,' warned Barnes, 'there's something you should know. There's a rumour going round that Inspector Colbeck is still not entirely persuaded that Browne is the man who killed Mr Heygate.'

'Of course he is!' exploded Phillpotts. 'It's as plain as the nose on my face. Whatever is the inspector thinking? He goes to all the trouble of catching a brutal killer then has doubts about his guilt? It's monstrous!'

'That's why I suggest you should hold fire, Bishop.'

'Who does he think *did* commit the murder?'

'I've no idea. I merely passed on a rumour that may or may not be correct.'

Phillpotts put the pen aside. 'I'll delay my letter until I know the truth of it,' he said. 'I'm certainly not going to congratulate a man who thinks that Browne is innocent of the murder. How can he be so blind?'

'We may be maligning him unfairly,' said Barnes. 'Perhaps we should give him the benefit of the doubt. Inspector Colbeck won't even have had time to question the prisoner. He may even be able to wrest a full confession out of him.' Phillpotts laughed mirthlessly. 'Given what we know of

Browne, I accept that it may be next to impossible.'

'Browne is a seasoned liar. He'll confess nothing.'

'He's up against a worthy adversary, Bishop. In my estimation, Inspector Colbeck is a very astute man. Didn't Mr Tallis tell us on Sunday that the inspector used to be a barrister?'

'I believe that he did.'

'Then he'll know how to cross-examine the prisoner.'

They were taking no chances. Since Browne had rescued a prisoner from a police cell, extra precautions were put in place at the police station. Every door was locked and the man himself was handcuffed. He was interviewed in a bare room with a barred window. Policemen were on sentry duty outside the building. Before he could question the prisoner, Colbeck had returned to the Acland Tavern, glad that he'd had the foresight to bring a change of trousers with him. He would never have consented to question any suspect while wearing a pair of torn trousers, especially if both knees had been scuffed. As a courtesy, he permitted Superintendent Steel to take part in the interview. Arms folded, Leeming stood in front of the door to prevent any dash for freedom. While he was glad that Browne was at last in custody, he wished that he'd made the arrest. A tussle with an armed man was meat and drink to him.

Browne was seated on an upright chair with the wound on his head bandaged. Colbeck and Steel sat opposite him but the prisoner only had eyes for the inspector. It was a blow to Browne's pride that he'd been captured and he bristled with resentment at Colbeck. Even though his hands were manacled behind his back, he looked as if he was about to launch an attack on him at any moment.

Colbeck was droll. 'You've been rather busy, Mr Browne,' he began. 'A long list of crimes can be laid at your door.'

'I'm innocent of every one of them.'

'Do you deny assaulting a man by the name of Wyatt?'

'Yes.'

'He was a prison warder known to you.'

'Then he deserved what happened to him.'

'He recognised you in the street,' said Steel.

'A lot of people do. I'm a handsome man.'

'Yet you still deny the attack?'

'I was defending myself against a violent assault.'

'You were being sought by the police,' Colbeck reminded him.

Browne's face was motionless. 'Was I?'

'Every newspaper carried details of the search.'

'I never read newspapers, Inspector. They're full of lies.'

'You must have known that the police were after you.'

'They're *always* after me. They've got nothing better to do.'

'Whenever you come to this city,' said Steel, rancorously, 'you leave a trail of wreckage behind you. Last time, it was confined to theft and disorder. This time, the crimes are far more serious.'

'Wyatt beat me black and blue in prison. Why not arrest him?'

'We're not talking about Mr Wyatt.'

'You should do, Superintendent. You don't know half of what goes on behind those prison walls. They flog you if you so much as fart.'

'Let's turn to another charge,' said Colbeck. 'On Sunday

287

evening, you came in here and knocked the duty sergeant unconscious before rescuing a woman by the name of Adeline Goss. In the course of your escape, you wounded Superintendent Tallis of Scotland Yard.'

'He was in our way.'

'You came in here prepared to use a weapon.'

'I told him to stand aside.'

'It was a case of attempted murder,' said Steel.

'No,' returned Browne, vehemently. 'I gave him a prod, that's all. If I'd wanted to kill him, I'd have cut his throat from ear to ear.'

'At the very least,' said Colbeck, 'you face a charge of malicious wounding. That's in addition to the other crimes you committed while you were here.'

'A friend of mine was in trouble. I helped her.'

'She was harbouring a wanted man. That's illegal.'

'She committed no crime. Since I've been in Exeter, I've seen Ad for less than five minutes. Someone saw us together and claimed I was hiding in her room. Did your men find me there, Superintendent?' he challenged. 'No – of course, they didn't because I was never in Rockfield Place. Ad was wrongly arrested.'

'She was your accomplice, Mr Browne.'

'I always work alone.'

'Then why did you put her on the train this morning?'

'That wasn't Ad,' said Browne, blithely. 'It was a woman I spent the night with. She never told me her name.'

'I believe it was Adeline Goss,' said Colbeck, 'but we'll soon know the truth of it. After Sergeant Leeming dragged you off here, I took the trouble to speak to the clerk in the ticket office. When I described your appearance, he remembered selling you a single ticket to Plymouth. I promptly sent a telegraph with enough detail for them to identify the lady in question. I asked that she be detained at Plymouth station and brought back here immediately. We'll put her in the next cell to you,' he went on with a disarming smile, 'then you can discover the name of the person with whom you admit you spent the night. You can exchange fond reminiscences.'

Bagsy Browne shifted uncomfortably on his chair.

The train journey from Exeter to Plymouth was just over fifty miles, taking the passengers past some of the most glorious sights in the county. It was almost as if the line had been constructed specifically to display uninterrupted scenic beauty. Adeline Goss saw little of it and cared even less about it. Her mind was on the new life on which she'd just embarked. She'd be a different woman with a different name in a different town. There was a surface excitement but it was underscored by the disappointment of parting with Bagsy Browne. He was not the only man in the world – she'd very soon find others – but he was the most special. None of the others had ever indulged her so much or taken such risks on her behalf. Yet he'd now vanished and she might never see him again. It was depressing.

After a series of stops along the way, the train eventually reached its final destination and groaned to a halt in Plymouth station. Telling herself that she had to make the best of her new situation, she gathered up her belongings and stepped on to the station with a sense of purpose. Then she saw police uniforms converging on her.

* * *

Questioning Bagsy Browne was like trying to hold a bar of wet soap in hands already covered in oil. He was slippery and adroit. Colbeck had never met anyone so skilled in the art of evasion and barefaced dishonesty. Leeming had the urge to knock some truth out of Browne and regretted that raw violence was not a permissible means of interrogation. Steel had crossed swords with the man on many previous occasions and had never got the better of him. Every time he asked a question, it was hit back hard at him like a cricket ball that was impossible to catch. All that he got for his trouble were burning palms and mounting frustration. In the end, he let Colbeck do all the talking and simply watched from the boundary.

'Let's turn to the murder of Joel Heygate,' said Colbeck.

Browne sniggered. 'I was in favour of it.'

'Did it give you any satisfaction?'

'I enjoyed reading the details of it.'

'Yet you told us earlier that you never read the newspapers.'

'I made an exception for Heygate. I loathed the man.'

'Why is that?'

'We had a disagreement at the station.'

'You were roaring drunk, from what I've heard.'

'A man is entitled to his pleasures, Inspector. What are yours?'

'My chief pleasure,' said Colbeck, easily, 'is catching malefactors and making them pay the full price for their crimes. In the case of murder that invariably means a walk to the gallows.' He stared deep into Browne's eyes. 'Do you fear that walk?'

'No,' replied Browne, cheekily. 'Why should I?'

'It's a walk you're destined to make,' said Leeming.

'You can't hang me for bashing a peeler on the head. Nor for drawing a little blood from a detective's arm. I know the law, Sergeant. Rescuing a friend from a police cell is naughty but it won't put my head in a noose.'

'You killed the stationmaster.'

Browne was offended. 'Who told you that?'

'All the evidence picks out you as the culprit,' said Colbeck, 'and your subsequent crimes identify you as a dangerous and aggressive man.'

'I didn't kill Heygate!' shouted Browne, squirming on the chair. 'I'd *like* to have done, I'll admit that. There's lots of other people I'd like to have wiped off the face of this earth as well. But *wanting* to do something and doing it are two separate things. In the case of Heygate, someone got there before me.'

'What were you doing on the night of November 4th?'

'Mind your own bleeding business!'

'We believe that you met and killed Joel Heygate.'

'That's a lie!' howled Browne.

'Then tell us what you *were* doing at that time.'

'It's private.'

'You don't *have* privacy any more,' interjected Steel.

'Look, I never went near Heygate, I swear it.'

'You vowed to get even with him some day.'

'And I would've done, if I'd had the chance. I detested him.'

'In other words,' said Colbeck, 'you admit you're capable of murder.'

'Every man is capable of murder, Inspector, and most women. Steal a baby off a parent and you'll see what I mean.'

'Take your mind back to November 4th.'

'Why? That's history now. It's so much piss down the sewer.'

'You laid in wait to ambush the stationmaster.'

'No!' exclaimed Browne.

'You battered him to death with a blunt instrument, then – with or without the aid of an accomplice – you carried his body to the cathedral precinct and concealed it beneath the bonfire.' Browne bellowed a protest, fiercely indignant at the charges levelled against him. 'Why don't you break the habit of a wasted lifetime and tell the truth for once? You killed Joel Heygate and you can't deny it.'

Colbeck's accusation had Browne seething with denial and ready to express it in the most forceful way. Sticking his head down, he suddenly dived off his chair and tried to smash the inspector's nose. Because of his sharp reflexes, Colbeck moved his head out of the way just in time but he was knocked from his chair and fell to the ground. Leeming, meanwhile, grappled with the prisoner and subdued him with some heavy punches to the body and head. Dumping him back in his chair, he stood behind Browne and held him firmly by the shoulders. Resuming his own chair, Colbeck spoke with equanimity.

'That's one more charge to add to the list, Mr Browne,' he said, 'but it pales beside the main one.' He narrowed his lids. 'Why did you kill Mr Heygate?'

'I didn't.'

'We don't believe you.'

'Then here's something you *can* believe.'

With a surge of anger, Browne tried to spit in his face but Colbeck dodged the phlegm by shifting his head smartly to the side. The inspector remained cool.

'Let's start all over again, shall we?' he suggested.

* * *

It had been a day of mixed emotions for Dorcas Hope. Pounced on by Woodford, she'd felt a sensation of naked fear that was alleviated by Colbeck's intervention. Leeming had soothed her, then she'd experienced alarm and excitement when, with her nose pressed to the window of the refreshment room, she'd seen the detectives confront an armed man on the platform and send him haring off along the railway track. On hearing that Joel Heygate's killer had been caught, she was overcome with joy and relief at the turn of events. Every time Woodford popped his head into the room, however, Dorcas felt a lurching unease, but he never actually spoke to her or repeated his earlier threat. He merely regarded her with malevolence.

What helped her to withstand the new stationmaster's mute hostility was the reassuring friendship of Timothy Vesey. He was kind and supportive and she found his slight stutter endearing. It only seemed to affect two letters of the alphabet.

'You've worked very well t-t-t-today, Miss Hope.'

'Thank you, Mr Vesey.'

'I daresay you're still worried about Mrs R-R-R-Rossiter.'

'Yes,' she said. 'I think about her a lot.'

'I can never be as efficient as her in this r-r-r-refreshment r-r-r-room. You'll have t-t-t-to make allowances for me.'

'There's no need for me to do that. You're so experienced.'

'I hoped I'd r-r-r-retired from this job.'

'It was very good of you to take over from Mrs Rossiter.'

'How is she?' he asked. 'Have you heard any news?'

'No, Mr Vesey, I haven't.'

'I had a friend who went into the asylum. It was years before they let him out.'

'What was wrong with him?'

'He kept seeing strange visions all the t-t-t-time.'

'That's not what Mrs Rossiter does,' said Dorcas. 'Father says that she was shocked by Mr Heygate's death and it turned her brain. He thinks she's in the right place now. They'll know how to look after her.'

'I spent a long time with Agnes Rossiter,' said Canon Smalley. 'It's a sad case.'

'They're all sad cases in here,' remarked Swift. 'But it's no part of my job to feel sorry for them. I leave that to you.'

'Christian love can sometimes do what medicine is unable to do.'

'Between us, we can offer both, Canon Smalley.'

'Mrs Rossiter talked endlessly about the stationmaster.'

'I know. I heard the tale from her myself. What she fails to understand is that the stationmaster would never have talked in the same way about her. In his view, she was merely someone with whom he worked. It's only in the febrile recesses of her mind that she decided she is effectively his widow.'

Dr Morton Swift enjoyed his occasional meetings with Canon Smalley. While he retained complete control over the treatment of those confined in the asylum, Swift was always ready to listen to the man who had dedicated his life to providing pastoral care. They'd both had successes in the past. Thanks to him, some of Swift's patients had been nursed back to health to a point where it was safe to release them. Canon Smalley's triumphs could not be measured in terms of numbers who left the asylum. His achievements were related to the relief of anguish and the building of trust. Of the canon's many skills, none was valued more highly by Swift than his ability to quell the fire inside violent patients. It was a skill that was in constant demand.

'Another new case is being admitted today,' said Swift, opening a file on his desk. 'The young lady's name is Esther Leete.'

'I'll make a point of talking to her before the day is out.'

'That's not possible, I'm afraid. Miss Leete is deaf and dumb. She's been subject to fits of violence, so has come into our hands. Treat her with care.'

'I'll do so, Dr Swift.'

'Thank you.'

'First, however, I promised to call on Mrs Rossiter again.'

'Don't mention Mr Heygate's funeral,' advised Swift. 'It's best that she knows nothing of what's happening in the outside world.'

Agnes Rossiter had no idea where she was or what she was doing there. She missed her sister, her friends and her job. Most of all, she missed the freedom to do what she wanted. She needed to mourn the man she adored, to attend his funeral and to place flowers on his grave. Yet she couldn't even leave her room until it was unlocked. She couldn't eat, drink, wash or relieve herself until she was told. Her own clothing had been taken from her and she had been put into a coarse shift and a rough woollen dressing gown. They'd stolen her identity and turned her into something she neither liked nor recognised as herself. It was demeaning. But there was one thing they could never take from her and that was the memory of Joel Heygate. As long as she held on to that, she had a bulwark against the multiple indignities of the asylum. He was her comfort and salvation. She would tell that to Canon Smalley.

Although he'd joked about putting them in adjoining cells, Colbeck made sure that Bagsy Browne and Adeline Goss never even saw each other. While the former was locked up, the latter was interviewed by Colbeck and Steel. There was no need for handcuffs and Leeming was not required to stand in front of the door. He'd been sent by the inspector on another errand. Unaware that Browne was in custody, Adeline was careful to say nothing to incriminate him.

'We believe that you were harbouring a man named Bernard Browne,' said Colbeck. 'How long did he stay with you in Rockfield Place?'

'He didn't stay with me,' she replied.

'Then why did he feel the need to rescue you from a police cell?'

'It's the sort of thing Bagsy would do for an old friend.'

'So, until then, you'd spent no time together?'

'That's right.'

'What about the last couple of days? Where did you spend those?'

'I was on my own.'

'You're lying, Adeline,' said Steel, 'as you always do when we haul you in here. You haven't got an honest bone in your body. Don't take us for fools. Even Bagsy wouldn't go to all the trouble of getting you out of here, only to abandon you to your own devices.'

'Yet that's what he did.'

'We don't believe you.'

'After you left here, then,' resumed Colbeck, 'you and Browne parted company. Have you seen him since?'

'No,' she said. 'I've seen neither hide nor hair of him.'

'Then how to do you explain the fact that he saw you off on the train this morning? It's how we caught you, Miss Goss. We learnt that Browne bought you a single ticket to Plymouth. I sent a telegraph there.'

'Well?' pressed Steel as she fell silent. 'Are you going to deny it? Or are you going to claim that it was Bagsy's twin brother?'

She looked anxious. 'Where is he?'

'It doesn't matter.'

'You're trying to trick me,' she said with an accusatory glare.

'We're trying to discover to what extent you were his accomplice,' said Colbeck, taking over once again. 'As things stand, it looks as if you've been hand in glove with him from the time he first came to Exeter. That may be a very unfair judgement on you. For your sake, Miss Goss, I sincerely hope that it is. Cast your mind back, if you will, to the night of November 4th. Did you spend it with Browne?'

'No!' she affirmed.

'Did you see him at all that day?'

'No, I didn't.'

'You seem very sure of that.'

'I know who I sleep with, Inspector.'

'In other words,' he said, 'you can't provide him with an alibi.'

She grinned slyly. 'You're trying to trick me again, aren't you?'

'It was a simple question,' said Colbeck. 'All we wish to

know is whether or not you spent the night before Guy Fawkes Day with your old friend, Browne.'

'I've told you,' she snapped, 'I bleeding well didn't.'

'Do you have any idea where he was that night?'

'No, I don't.'

'Would you swear to that in court?' asked Steel.

'I'll yell it from the bleeding rooftops, if you like.'

'That won't be necessary, Adeline.'

'We believe you,' said Colbeck. 'It's the only thing you've said so far that we *do* believe, mind you, and it may save your neck.'

Adeline was disturbed. 'What do you mean?'

'How long have you known Mr Browne?'

'Tell me what you mean about my neck,' she demanded.

'Calm down, Miss Goss.'

'You can't make threats like that against me. I'm a whore, that's all I am. My mother was a whore and I was brought up in the trade. I'm good at it, though I say so myself. Arrest me for that, if you like,' she said, spiritedly, 'but don't start accusing me of anything else.' She stood up. 'What's going on?'

'Sit down, Adeline,' said Steel.

'I won't be blamed for something I didn't do.'

'Sit down or you'll have to be restrained.'

After a silent battle of wills, she eventually gave in and resumed her seat.

'Let me tell you why we have such an interest in you,' said Colbeck, 'and I advise you to listen carefully. Bernard Browne is in custody, charged with a number of offences, some related to you. He has also been charged with the murder of Joel Heygate and we wish to know if you were party to it.'

Adeline paled. 'No, I wasn't,' she said, genuinely scared for the first time. 'I had nothing to do with it and neither did Bagsy.'

'Then what was he doing at Mr Heygate's funeral?'

'I didn't know he was there.'

'The only reason he'd take such a risk is that he wanted to gloat over the burial of the man he'd battered to death.'

'It couldn't have been Bagsy,' she argued. 'It just couldn't.'

'He has no alibi for the night before Guy Fawkes Day.'

'He wasn't even in Exeter.'

'Then why didn't he say that?'

'You've got the wrong man, Inspector. Bagsy is no saint, I admit, but there are some things he'd never do. Murder is one of them.'

'He's going to hang, Adeline,' said Steel. 'Why don't you save your own skin and confess that you know he killed the stationmaster? You don't want us to think that you were an accessory, do you?'

Adeline quailed. She was trapped.

Bagsy Browne paced up and down the tiny cell like a caged animal. When a policeman came to taunt him, he was driven back by a torrent of bad language. Browne's predicament was frightening. He'd been arrested for a whole host of crimes, some of which carried long prison sentences. But it was the charge of murder that rattled him. There was no prison sentence for that – only an appointment with the hangman. What really rankled was the fact that Adeline might be inveigled into giving evidence against him. If she talked about his burning hatred for Joel Heygate and his determination to attend the funeral, she would be inadvertently helping to condemn him. He needed to school her, to rehearse all the answers she was to give to the police. But he had no chance to get anywhere near her. They would be working on Adeline in another part of the building. In any other circumstances, Browne would be fearless. When a meeting with the public executioner was a likely outcome, however, he discovered that he was only human, after all.

On his second trip to Dawlish, Leeming was struck afresh by its enchantment. Even on a dull autumn afternoon, its beach, its brook and its encircling hills were things of wonder. Far less appealing were the people on whom he'd come to call. Michael and Lavinia Heygate were even less welcoming than on his first visit but they invited him in and offered him refreshment. Ensconced in front of their fire, he drank a cup of tea and nibbled at a biscuit as he listened to Heygate's description of the funeral.

'It was an ordeal,' said Heygate. 'Frankly, I don't know how I got through it. I kept remembering all the good times that Joel and I had shared – before we came to a parting of the ways.'

'That's what I wanted to ask about, sir,' said Leeming. 'If you and your brother didn't speak to each other any more, why did you call at his house on the evening before Guy Fawkes Day?'

'We went as a courtesy.'

'Yet you told me that he was testy with you.'

'Michael made the effort to bury their differences,' said Lavinia, 'but Joel was as frosty as ever.'

Heygate nodded. 'We were both wounded by his attitude.'

They were still dressed in black but they were no longer using sepulchral voices and pretending that they were racked by grief. Leeming was aware of a muted note of victory and a deep satisfaction.

'Tell me about the evening of November 4th,' he invited.

'We've already discussed it with you and with Superintendent Tallis,' said Heygate. 'There's nothing we can add.'

'Oh, I think there is, sir. Remind me where you stayed that night. It was with friends, I gather.'

'That's right.'

'You didn't stay at an inn, by any chance?'

'Why pay for an inn when you can enjoy the hospitality of friends?'

'We can't afford to stay at an inn,' added Lavinia. 'At least, we couldn't then. Things will be different in the future.'

'Is that what you told Superintendent Tallis?'

'Yes,' replied Heygate. 'We don't understand why he sent you back here.'

'It wasn't him who sent me, sir. He's not even in Exeter. I'm sure you'll be distressed to hear that he's back in London, nursing a wound inflicted by one of your former customers – this man named Bagsy Browne.' They were both startled. 'Don't worry. We have the villain in custody. Inspector Colbeck and I arrested him at the railway station this morning. Apart from his many other crimes, he'll be charged with the murder of your brother. Since we feel that he may have an accomplice,' he went on, regarding each of them in turn, 'we'll be looking closely at anyone who's been in touch with him recently.'

'Well, you can exclude us,' said Heygate, nervously. 'It's a long time since we've seen Bagsy. My wife will tell you.'

'Yes, yes,' she said. 'It was a very long time ago.'

301

Leeming smiled. 'We'll have to ask him exactly when it was.'

'Don't accept the word of a rogue like that,' warned Heygate.

'You were ready to accept the money of a rogue, sir. You obviously made no distinction between good and bad customers.'

'Business was slack, Sergeant. We couldn't turn anyone away.'

'I see.' Leeming swallowed the last of the biscuit and washed it down with some tea. 'What did you think of Superintendent Tallis?'

'We were touched that the man in charge of the investigation took the trouble to keep us informed of its progress. It was very considerate of him.'

'Yes, he can be considerate. He's also very observant. He takes nothing on trust, you see. When you told him you'd stayed with friends in Exeter that night, he asked Superintendent Steel to deploy his men as detectives. And they made an interesting discovery that rather contradicts what you claimed. It seems,' said Leeming, putting his cup on a side table, 'that a Mr and Mrs Michael Heygate spent the night in question at the Crown Inn.' He smiled benignly at them. 'What do you both say to that?'

They were speechless, each looking desperately to the other for help.

At the end of her working day, Dorcas tried to slip away without being seen by Woodford but he was waiting to waylay her. Though he didn't say anything, his eyes were full of menace. She read the message that they held for her. While he was in the city, Colbeck might be able to protect her but the inspector would leave before long. She would then be at the mercy of the new stationmaster and could expect no quarter.

Cowed into silence, she trotted all the way home and arrived there with her heart beating like a drum. The first thing that greeted her was the chirping of the canary and she brightened immediately. Dorcas went into the parlour and saw her mother, struggling to put a hand into the cage so that she could clean it. Peter watched from the comfort of his perch and kept up a cheerful commentary.

'No, no, Mother,' said Dorcas. 'Leave that to me. You shouldn't try to do that when you must be in pain.'

'It has given me a few twinges,' admitted Maud, withdrawing her hand and lowering herself gently into her chair. 'Here – take this cloth, Dorcas.'

'Wait a moment.'

Dorcas first removed her hat and coat. After hanging them up, she took the cloth from her mother and examined the cage. The base was covered in seeds and droppings. Peter cocked his head to one side and peered quizzically at her.

'There's a way of doing this properly,' she said, going to the cage. 'Now that it's safe to let Peter out, he can fly around the room.'

The canary seemed to hear her and seized his chance of freedom, hopping on to the open door then flying out into the room and up to the picture rail. From that eminence, he looked down and regaled them with full-throated song. Dorcas lifted the cage up at a slight angle.

'Mr Heygate had this specially made,' she explained. 'He wanted it very large and with this thick base in it.'

Maud was worried. 'What are you trying to do?'

'He told me once that the whole base is hinged so that it

opens out. That way, you can get inside the cage to give it a good clean.'

'Wait for your father. It's far too heavy for you to handle.'

'I can manage, I promise you.'

Tilting it at a sharper angle, Dorcas felt for the clips that held the base to the back edge of the cage. She pulled hard and the base flapped down like a trapdoor, spilling the items hidden away beneath it. Dorcas and Maud looked at the things which had just tumbled on to the table. They were absolutely mesmerised.

CHAPTER SIXTEEN

Madeleine Andrews could see that her father was deeply troubled. While he still talked fondly of Binnie Langton, there was none of his earlier boyish enthusiasm at the rediscovery of love. He now spoke with the caution of a middle-aged man who was weighing up all the possibilities before he made a major decision. When she visited her aunt that evening, Madeleine persuaded him to go with her. Wrapped up warmly against the chill wind, they strolled along side by side. The walk gave them an opportunity to discuss the situation.

'Are you going to invite her for tea?' she asked.

'I don't know, Maddy.'

'Do you *want* to invite her?'

'Part of me wants to,' he said, 'but another part is holding me back somehow.'

'You're still thinking about her sister, aren't you?'

'Yes, I am.'

'Mrs Langton will be expecting some kind of response,' said Madeleine. 'You went to her house for tea. The least she's entitled to is a letter of thanks and I daresay she'll want to know why you stayed such a short time.'

'I can hardly tell her that I was scared of her sister.'

'Then you must invent a polite excuse.'

They paused at a kerb and waited for two cabs and a cart to roll past before crossing the road. Once on the opposite pavement, Andrews spied a possible means of escape.

'It may all be over, Maddy,' he said, hopefully. 'I don't think that Mrs Young took to me. Why should she? She probably told her sister that there was no future in our friendship and that the best thing Binnie could do was to let me go.'

'I don't think she'd say that at all,' argued Madeleine, hurt by the suggestion that her father was unworthy of the woman for whom he cared. 'You'd be a very presentable suitor to any unattached lady of that age. Besides, Mrs Langton clearly has no objection to you. She wouldn't be put off by a few words of criticism.'

'That's true.'

'You should have more faith in the friendship.'

'If only two of us were involved,' said Andrews, gloomily, 'then I would. But there are three of us involved now – Binnie, me and her sister.'

'You can't count, Father. The correct number is four and it includes me.'

He looked surprised. 'Yes, I suppose it does.'

'Not that you'd ever take my advice,' she added.

'I hang on your every word, Maddy,' he said, laughing.

'But you're right. I have been in too much of a rush. I should have introduced you to Binnie earlier. Whenever we've been together, she's always asked after you and about the wedding.'

'On one thing I must put my foot down,' said Madeleine, firmly. 'Mrs Langton will not be invited. It's a small affair with family and friends. Invitations have already been sent out. There's no room for anyone else.'

'That's fair enough.'

'Robert wouldn't be happy about it, I know.'

'It's a pity he didn't come to Binnie's house with me,' said Andrews. 'I could have done with police protection when I was set on by Mrs Young.'

'She sounds like a real harridan.'

'Well, she didn't look it, Maddy. That's the odd thing. She was a very striking woman. In many ways, she's a more interesting person than Binnie. But for the sharp tongue, Ivy Young would be a catch for any man.'

Madeleine stopped and turned to face him. She took him by the shoulders.

'Be honest, Father,' she advised. 'What would you really *like* to do?'

'I'd like to go back to my job on the railway.'

She blinked. 'Why ever do you say that?'

'When I was driving up and down the country all day long, I had no time for silly thoughts about women. I acted my age, Maddy. I was happy. It's not the same any more,' he confessed. 'I'm cut adrift. That's why I was so pleased when Binnie crossed my path. Everything seemed so wonderful at first.'

'I'm sorry that her sister has blighted everything.'

'She made me look at Binnie in a different way and it

sort of changed my mind. Oh, I don't know what to do,' he moaned, shaking his head. 'If you want the truth, right now I'd like to be hundreds of miles away from here.'

Colbeck was both astounded and elated. On the table in the parlour was a pile of banknotes that had been hidden under the false base in the birdcage. Of far more interest to him, however, was the diary belonging to Joel Heygate. Its hiding place had at last been found.

'I always said that the canary knew his secret,' said Colbeck. 'This device is better than a safe because nobody would dream of looking there.'

'We only found it by accident,' said Dorcas, meekly.

'That's why we sent for you at once, Inspector,' said Maud.

Colbeck picked up the diary. 'You did the right thing, Mrs Hope,' he said. 'This may give us vital clues that will help to solve the murder.'

She was puzzled. 'But you've already solved it, haven't you? I thought that you'd caught the man responsible.'

'We have someone in custody but he's being very tight-lipped about what actually happened on the night that Mr Heygate was killed. This diary may at least tell us *where* the murder occurred and throw up a lot of other valuable information.'

'What about the money?' asked Dorcas.

'It shows you what a frugal man Mr Heygate must have been. At a glance, I'd say that we have at least two hundred pounds. Having so little to spend his money on, he took the sensible decision to save it.'

'What will happen to it, Inspector?'

'First of all,' said Colbeck, 'I'll count it in your presence and give you a receipt for the amount. I'd like to say that you could keep it, because you certainly deserve to do so, but it must be handed over to Mr Heygate's solicitor. It will then be bequeathed to the person or persons nominated in the will.'

'That will be his brother, even though Mr Heygate didn't really like him.'

'We shall see, Miss Hope. In a sense, the cash is immaterial. This diary is worth much more than two hundred pounds. I'll study it with the greatest interest.'

Dorcas smiled. 'Will there be any mention of me in it?'

'I daresay there will be. You looked after Peter for him.'

The canary cheeped in response and fluttered about in the cage.

'He always does that when he hears his name,' noted Maud.

'Birds are more intelligent than we think, Mrs Hope,' said Colbeck.

'What about Mrs Rossiter?' asked Dorcas.

'I expect to see her name in the diary.'

'I didn't mean that, Inspector. I wondered if you had any news of her.'

'It's too early for that,' replied Colbeck. 'When I went to the asylum, Dr Swift told me that she needed time to adjust to her new surroundings. But she won't be without a friend in there. He sang the praises of the chaplain and said that he had a gift for helping people like Mrs Rossiter.'

'Her sister is terribly upset.'

'Have you been to see her?'

'Yes, I did. After you suggested it, I went as soon as I

could. Miss Impey feels lost and alone. It's her house but Mrs Rossiter more or less ran it. Now that she's gone, her sister doesn't know how to cope. She's afraid to step outside the door.'

'We must invite her here,' said Maud, sympathetically. 'Miss Impey ought to know that there are some of us who don't judge her sister harshly.'

'That would be a comfort to her, Mrs Hope,' said Colbeck. 'In time, I trust, more reassuring news about Mrs Rossiter will come out of the asylum. I was very heartened by what I heard about the chaplain there. He'll surely take pity on her.'

It was evening before Canon Smalley found the time to visit the new arrival. His daily round had taken him all over the asylum, offering whatever help and solace he could. As on the previous occasion, he spent a long while with Agnes Rossiter, listening to her complaints and holding her hands. There were marginal improvements. She was no longer so agitated and her rage against the Church and the god it served seemed to have abated somewhat. But she was still under the illusion that she and Joel Heygate had been destined to marry and still ranted on about her rights as his beloved. When he left her, Smalley had promised to visit her on the following day. She thanked him profusely and had squeezed his hands in gratitude.

As evening wore on, his interest shifted to Esther Leete. He had some idea what to expect because Dr Swift had shown him her file. She'd been admitted to the deaf and dumb asylum two years ago at the age of fifteen. The diagnosis had been one of melancholia at puberty. Throughout her stay, she'd been depressed. Suddenly, she'd become violent and the staff were unable to control her. Swift's diagnosis was that she was in the grip of a mania. Unable either to speak or to hear, Esther Leete presented special problems. When he called on her, Canon Smalley saw what they were. She was being held in a locked room with a burly female nurse standing over her. Seated on the bed, the girl was strapped into a straitjacket.

Smalley disapproved. 'Does she have to wear that?'

'It's what Dr Swift ordered,' said the nurse.

'Can't you release her so that I can talk to her?'

'She won't understand a word of what you say, Canon Smalley. Besides, my orders are to keep her restrained. When she was free, she smashed a glass and tried to cut her wrists.'

'Dear me!' he exclaimed. 'What pain she must be in to be driven to such an extreme.' He approached the patient and smiled at her. 'Hello, Miss Leete.'

'I'd advise you not to get too close,' warned the nurse.

'She's not frightened of me. I pose no threat.'

'She's dangerous.'

'What about her parents?'

'They were unable to look after her. When her father died, she became very depressed. That's when she was taken into care.'

Smalley sat on the edge of the bed, barely a yard from the patient; Esther was studying him with glinting eyes. If her face had not been so contorted, she would have been a beautiful young woman. Smalley felt that it was cruel that she had to suffer twin disabilities. Normal life was impossible for her. She had to rely on the patience and assistance of others. Esther looked at his cassock and seemed to understand what it betokened. It did nothing to comfort her. Twisting her features into a grimace, she leapt to her feet and began to make a muffled noise of protest. The nurse grabbed her before she could kick out at her visitor.

'There you are, Canon Smalley,' she said. 'I did tell you.'

He got up calmly. 'I'll be back,' he said. 'She obviously needs me.'

The diary was a revelation. It covered a period of almost two years and was rich in detail. When Colbeck examined it back in his room at the Acland Tavern, Leeming sat beside him. It took them a little time to decipher some of the abbreviations used. Once they'd done that, it was possible to read the diary like a novel, albeit one with a limited number of characters and a repetitive plot.

'So much for the brother's claim that he hardly ever saw Heygate,' said Colbeck, looking at another entry. 'This is the seventh time in a row that he called on the stationmaster. And instead of *asking* for money, he demanded it. And look,' he went on, turning a page and tapping it with a finger, 'here's another reference. This time it's his sister-in-law who comes in search of a loan.'

'She'd have been put up to it by that snake of a husband.'

'They really seem to have persecuted the stationmaster.'

Leeming was sarcastic. 'It's funny that they never mentioned *that*, isn't it?'

'They're almost as dishonest as Bagsy Browne.'

'I disagree, sir. They're *more* dishonest. Browne doesn't try to hide the fact that he's a criminal. In fact he revels in it, whereas Heygate and his wife try to pass themselves off as decent people badly treated by someone who should have helped them. At least I caught them out telling one lie.'

'Yes, they didn't spend that night with friends but at the Crown Inn.'

'You should have seen the expression on their faces when I challenged them about it,' said Leeming with a chuckle. 'They turned bright red.'

'What was their explanation, Victor?'

'Heygate claimed that the landlord of the inn *was* the friend they'd talked about and that he let them stay there for nothing.'

'One lie follows another,' said Colbeck. 'Nevertheless, it will do no harm for you to go to the Crown Inn and test the claim. But that can wait. The diary takes priority. Most of the entries refer to birds. I hadn't realised that there were so many different species in Devon. He's listed dozens and dozens. Ah,' he went on, 'there's a mention of Lawrence Woodford here.'

'What sort of bird is he, sir?'

'I think he's some sort of vulture. No sooner was the stationmaster dead than he swooped down on the carcass.'

'I dislike the man. What does it say about him?'

'It just says "First warning to Woodford", with no details of what the warning was about.' Colbeck flipped over the pages. 'He's mentioned in dispatches again and this time we know why. "Second warning – bottle confiscated." It looks as if the new stationmaster was caught drinking on duty.'

'It's no wonder Woodford didn't like him.'

'He should have been grateful, Victor. People have been dismissed for less. It's only because Mr Heygate didn't make an official complaint to the company that Woodford held on to his job.'

'And now he's strutting about like the cock of the walk.'

'Yes, Victor. It's because Joel Heygate is dead. Woodford is safe.'

'So he had a very strong motive to murder him.'

Colbeck continued to flick through the diary. There were several mentions of Dorcas Hope by a man who clearly saw her as his closest friend. Agnes Rossiter, however, earned only one fleeting reference. Colbeck eventually reached the place where he'd first started and that was at the final entry. It was the day on which Heygate had been murdered. The entry was brief – 'Visit owl.' It meant nothing to the detectives. There were three earlier references to the bird but the only indication of its whereabouts was in the first one – 'Barn owl near M.V.' Colbeck was disappointed. The diary had taught them a lot about certain people but, on the most important point of all, it had let them down.

'We must talk to Miss Hope,' decided Colbeck.

'Will she be able to help us, sir?'

'She knows the city far better than we do, Victor. I'm sure she'll be able to hazard a guess at what these initials stand for.'

'It could be the name of a person rather than a place.'

'That's very true.'

'I've just thought,' said Leeming with a short laugh. 'This diary really belongs to Michael Heygate. Do you think he'll enjoy reading it?'

'Not if it's used against him in a court of law,' said Colbeck.

'There's no real evidence there to convict him, sir. Besides, we already know who the killer was. He's in custody and

314

his name is Bagsy Browne. Did you send that telegraph to Superintendent Tallis?'

'It would have reached Scotland Yard this afternoon. I know that Mr Tallis was advised to rest but he'll have gone straight to his office and carried on working.'

'He'll be pleased that we finally caught the culprit.'

'He'll be pleased that we caught the man who stabbed him,' said Colbeck, 'but I'm still not sure that we're holding the one who murdered the stationmaster.'

Leeming was incredulous. 'It *has* to be Bagsy Browne, sir.'

'Does it?'

'He has a record of violence.'

'Yet he's always stopped short of murder in the past.'

'He and that woman were in this together.'

'Then why does he refuse to tell us where he was on the fateful night and why does Adeline Goss swear that he wasn't with her? Browne has raised untruthfulness to the level of an art and he practises it like a master. There's no doubt that he's guilty of several crimes,' said Colbeck, 'but I maintain that the murder is not one of them.'

Leeming was bewildered. 'If it wasn't Browne who killed the stationmaster, then who on earth did?'

Colbeck tapped the diary.

'The answer lies somewhere in here, Victor.'

Ivy Young watched from a vantage point further along the street. She had a good view of the house and was impressed by its size and state of repair. Caleb Andrews obviously knew how to look after a property. It was almost an hour before the front door opened and she realised that her vigil was about to deliver what she'd hoped. Madeleine emerged with a basket over her arm and headed in the direction of the market. Evidently, she'd be gone for some time. Ivy didn't waste a second of it. Scampering across the street, she walked up to the house and knocked on the front door. After a few seconds, it was opened by Andrews. His jaw dropped.

'Hello, Caleb,' she said, sweetly. 'May I call you that? I feel that we're on first-name terms now. Forgive me for surprising you like this but I've got something important to tell you.'

'What is it?' he gulped.

'I can't possibly talk on the doorstep. May I come in?'

'I was just about to go out, Mrs Young.'

'You can call me Ivy.' She glanced down at his feet. 'And I don't think you can be going out when you still have your slippers on. Let me in. I won't stay long.'

Andrews was helpless. Before he could prevent her, she'd eased him aside and stepped into the house. When he closed the front door, she was looking around the parlour. She crossed to the easel and reached for the cloth covering the painting.

'No,' he said, rushing across to intercept her. 'Don't touch that. My daughter hates anyone to see her work before it's finished. Maddy would be livid.'

'There's no need why she should ever know. Let me take a peek.'

'I'm afraid that I can't, Mrs Young.'

She beamed at him. 'I do have a Christian name, you know.'

Andrews was nonplussed. She was so different from the woman he'd met earlier. Instead of the beaky and inquisitive sister, he was now looking at a handsome woman in her finery who was speaking in a low and confiding manner. The warm smile never left her face.

'We need to talk,' she said, sitting down.

'Do we?'

'I came about Binnie.'

'Oh, I see.'

He sat down opposite her, embarrassed to be caught in his slippers and grateful that he was wearing a collar and tie. Andrews felt invaded.

'I know how much you like Binnie,' said her sister. 'She's very fond of you and I can see why. You're a fine upstanding man, Caleb. What you need to know about Binnie is that she can be headstrong. She makes up her mind too quickly and that always leads to tears in the end. It's happened before, you see.'

'What has, Mrs Young? . . . Ivy, that is.'

'I'm talking about her sudden passion for a gentleman. It flares up at the start but it soon burns itself out. The one before you lasted only three weeks.'

'I didn't realise that.'

'There are lots of things you don't realise, I'm afraid. Take your visit to her the other afternoon. What did you think of the food?'

'It was delicious. Binnie is a good cook.'

'That's what she'd like you to believe,' said Ivy, 'but, in fact, she hates cooking and has never baked a cake in her life. Everything you ate at the house was my doing. I made it all for her.'

'Why did you do that?'

'My sister wanted to impress you.'

'She certainly did that.'

317

'Binnie said that you liked your food.'

'I do. I've been spoilt. Maddy – my daughter – is a wonderful cook.'

'I'm sure, she is,' said Ivy, letting her gaze travel around the room before alighting on the easel. 'She's a wonderful cook, a gifted artist and she's going to marry a detective whose name is always in the newspapers. You must be very proud of her, Caleb.'

'Oh, I am. I couldn't wish for a better daughter.'

'The house will be terribly empty when she's gone.'

'She's promised to visit whenever she can.'

'It's not the same as having someone to share your life with,' she said, moving her gaze back to him. 'Companionship is so important to people of our age. I daresay you thought that Binnie would give it to you, but her interest would soon flag. She's not like me, Caleb. Once I make my choice, I stand by it.'

His collar suddenly felt very tight and sweat broke out under his armpits. He was in his own home and yet he felt obscurely under threat. Andrews didn't know how much of what she was saying was true or why she felt obliged to say it. In her earlier hawkish mood, Ivy Young was intimidating. Now that she'd gone to the other extreme, she was even more overwhelming.

'Were you thinking of inviting Binnie here to have tea?' she asked.

'Yes, I was,' he admitted.

'Don't do it, Caleb. The closer you get to my sister, the more upset you'll be when she lets you down. Leave her be for a while.'

'But she'll think it's very rude of me to neglect her.'

'Put yourself first. She'll soon move on to the next one.'

He was dejected. 'How many others have there been?'

'You'd be too distressed to know,' she said, getting up. 'I must leave you in peace. I just wanted to pass on a friendly warning.'

'Thank you – thank you, Ivy.'

'Ease yourself gently away from my sister.'

He got to his feet. 'I'll do as you say.'

'I knew that you would.' Broadening her smile into a grin, she placed a hand on his arm and put her face close to his. 'Just because the friendship between you and Binnie is more or less finished,' she went on, taking a slip of paper from her pocket and handing it to him, 'there's no reason why you and I shouldn't keep in touch, is there? That's my address. Let's meet again very soon, shall we?'

Andrews showed her out. When he shut the door, he not only locked and bolted it, he moved a chair up against it to bolster his defence. Then he went swiftly upstairs and put on a pair of shoes.

'I'm sorry,' said Steel, 'but I can't help you, Inspector.'

'Can't you even hazard a guess?' asked Colbeck.

'No, I can't. I don't know the name of every property in Exeter and, in any case, this may not even be a property.'

'I thought it might be someone's name,' said Leeming.

'That, too, is possible.'

Their first call that morning had been on Superintendent Steel. They told him about the money concealed in the birdcage and showed him the stationmaster's diary. He was intrigued by the information about Michael Heygate and Lawrence Woodford. However, Steel was less taken with

Colbeck's claim that Bagsy Browne might not have been the killer, after all.

'With all due respect, Inspector,' he said, 'you are profoundly wrong.'

'Victor agrees with you,' said Colbeck. 'He believes I should have my head examined by Dr Swift.'

'I wouldn't go that far, sir,' said Leeming. 'I just think we've got the right man. Why bother to look for someone else? Michael Heygate may have been a rotten brother and Woodford may have been drinking on duty but that doesn't make them capable of battering a man to death. Browne is our man. I'd bet on it.'

'I wouldn't want to relieve you of your money.'

'I'll be happy to relieve you of more of yours, Inspector,' said Steel with a grin. 'Are you ready to wager another sovereign that Bagsy Browne is innocent of the murder?'

'No,' said Colbeck. 'I'm ready to wager five whole pounds.'

'In that case, I accept the bet.'

'And I'm the witness,' said Leeming.

Colbeck looked at Steel. 'How did Browne spend the night?'

'He never stopped protesting his innocence,' said Steel. 'We're taking him before a magistrate this morning so that we can get him remanded in prison. I want him where he can't possibly escape or collude with Adeline Goss.'

'But she's in a separate cell,' said Leeming.

'Bagsy would have found a way to communicate with her. We arrested him and another man some years ago and put them in cells that were fifteen yards apart. They sent messages to each other by tapping on the pipe that ran through all of the cells. It's the reason I had it lagged.' He turned to Colbeck. 'What about Adeline? Do you think she was Bagsy's accomplice?'

'She couldn't have been his accomplice in a murder he didn't commit,' said Colbeck, wryly. 'And if it turns out that he *is* guilty of it, I still don't think Miss Goss was involved. She loves Browne. The only way she could do that is to turn a blind eye to the things he does. She'd never condone murder.'

'I'm inclined to agree with you there.'

'What happens now, Inspector?' asked Leeming.

'We'll need to pay a visit to Joel Heygate's solicitor. I believe that his name is Mr Lyman of Lyman, Cole & Harmer. The money found in the birdcage must be handed over to him. So should the diary, by rights,' Colbeck said, 'but we need to hang on to that because it contains crucial evidence.'

'It doesn't absolve Bagsy of the murder,' said Steel.

'And it doesn't implicate him in it either.'

'What about Michael Heygate and Woodford? If Bagsy is innocent – and I don't accept that for a second – should we bring them in for questioning?'

'No, Superintendent, there's no need. The arrest of Browne will give them the feeling that the case is solved. If one of them was somehow involved in the death, they'll think they're quite safe now. They'll be off guard. Come on, Victor,' said Colbeck, 'we need to hand over this money. You can then pay a visit to the Crown Inn and find out just how friendly the landlord was with Mr Heygate's brother. Meanwhile, I'll have a chat with our unpaid assistant.'

'Who is that, sir?'

'A helpful young lady named Dorcas Hope.'

She knew that he'd be waiting for her to renew his pressure on her. Before she got anywhere near the refreshment room, Woodford descended on her. The difference this time was that he was actually pleasant to Dorcas.

'Good morning, Miss Hope,' he said.

'Good morning, Mr Woodford.'

'It's good to see you so punctual.'

'Mr Heygate taught me that,' she said.

'Is there any news of Mrs Rossiter?'

'I've heard none – though I did speak to Miss Impey, her sister. She's very distressed, as you can imagine. She thinks everyone is talking about her.'

'Well, she's quite wrong there,' said Woodford. 'Bagsy Browne is the person who's keeping all the tongues wagging and not Mrs Rossiter. She's been forgotten. All that people are talking about is the hanging.'

'*I'm* not talking about it, I assure you. I can't bear the thought of it.'

'It's what that devil deserves, Miss Hope.'

'Why can't they just lock him away for good?'

He broke off to answer a question from a passenger. It gave Dorcas a momentary break and allowed her to wonder why the stationmaster's manner towards her had changed so radically. Having bullied her before, he was making an effort to be kind to her. She could not understand why.

'I'm sorry about that,' he said as the passenger walked away. 'The reason I asked about Mrs Rossiter is this. Much as I sympathise with her plight, I can't see a time when she'd ever be ready to return to her old job here. The passengers wouldn't like it. They've all heard the tales about her. In other words,' he went on, 'we may be looking for a new manager or even a manageress.' He smiled knowingly at her. 'Mr Vesey has agreed to stay on until the end of the year but he's not getting any younger and will have to be replaced. He feels that *you* may be ready to take over.'

She was thrilled. 'That's so kind of him!'

'You suffer from the opposite handicap, of course,' he said. 'While he's rather old, you're rather young. Without Mrs Rossiter to look after you, there could be some harassment from certain quarters. The way to obviate that is to have a man working under you as a waiter. His presence will offer you protection against any unwanted attentions.' He smiled again. 'I take it that you'd be interested in the post.'

'Oh, yes, Mr Woodford. I've always enjoyed working here.'

'Leave it to me.'

'Thank you.'

'Before you go,' he said, touching her arm as she tried to move away, 'I just wanted a word about that diary again. I quite forgot that you mentioned it to me. I'm sorry for the confusion. You were right to tell the truth, Miss Hope.'

'I've been brought up to speak honestly at all times. But I expect you haven't heard what's happened, have you?' she said with excitement. 'The diary has been found. It was hidden in the bottom of Peter's birdcage.'

He was rocked. 'Where is the diary now?' he demanded.

'I gave it to Inspector Colbeck.'

Woodford looked so ill that she thought he was about to faint.

* * *

When she got back from the market, Madeleine was surprised that she could not open the front door of the house with her latchkey. She rapped with her knuckles and heard something being moved away before the bolt was drawn. The door opened and her father's head emerged to look up and down the street.

'Has she gone?' he asked.

'Who are you talking about?'

'Mrs Young has been here. She frightened the life out of me.'

'Let me come in then you can tell me all about it.'

He stood aside so that Madeleine could enter the house. She took the basket into the kitchen and left it there while she removed her coat and hat. When they'd been hung up, she confronted her father.

'What was Mrs Young doing here?' she asked.

'That's the trouble, Maddy. I don't really know.'

'When did she arrive?'

'It was the moment you left the house. I have a horrible feeling that she was waiting outside for the chance to catch me alone. That gave me a shiver.'

'Sit down and tell me all about it.'

They sat beside each other and Andrews gave her a garbled account of what had happened. It was clear that he still hadn't understood the full import of what had occurred. Madeleine, by contrast, seized on the salient point.

'She's after you, Father,' she said.

'How can that be? I'm Binnie's friend, not hers.'

'She's trying to prise you away from her sister. Why else should she give you her address? Mrs Young wants you to enter into a conspiracy with her.'

He was appalled. 'I'd never do that. I like Binnie too much.'

'From what I can gather,' she said, 'Mrs Young likes *you* too much. I think she's jealous of her sister and wants to take you away from her. As for coming here without an invitation, that's unforgivable.'

'She pretended that she was doing me a favour.'

'Did you believe everything she told you?'

'I did and I didn't, Maddy,' he replied. 'I did at first because she was so convincing. After she'd gone, however, I got to thinking about all the things she claimed. She said that Binnie chased after men, then cast them aside when she lost interest in them. That doesn't sound like the Binnie Langton I know. She's a respectable woman, Maddy. I wouldn't have looked at her twice if she hadn't been.'

'What about the tea you had at her house?'

'Binnie baked everything. I'm certain of it.'

'Then why did her sister lie to you?'

'I don't know. I suppose she wanted me to think well of her.'

'And do you?'

'No,' he said. 'As soon as she left, I barricaded myself in.' Madeleine burst out laughing. He was hurt. 'What's so funny?'

'I can't leave you alone for a minute, Father,' she teased. 'Most men in your position would be flattered if one woman took an interest in them. You've got two sisters fighting tooth and nail over you.'

'There's nothing to laugh about, Maddy. It was very unpleasant.'

'I'm sure it was,' she said with a consoling arm around

him, 'and I didn't mean to poke fun. How has it left you feeling about Mrs Langton?'

'To be honest, I'm not very keen to see her again.'

'What about her sister?'

'I'd run a mile if she turned up here again.'

'Then the solution is obvious,' said Madeleine. 'You must write Mrs Langton a letter to thank her for the invitation to tea and tell her that you're going away for some time.'

'But I'm not, Maddy. I'm staying here.'

'No, you're not. We both deserve a short holiday.'

'Where would we go?'

'I know just the place,' she said with growing conviction. 'You heard what Robert said in the letter I had this morning. They've made an arrest but he still has doubts about the man's guilt and expects the case to drag on a little longer. That means I'll continue to fret about him if I stay here and your knees will continue to knock at the thought of a second visit from Mrs Young.'

'Heaven forbid!'

'We can take the train to Exeter and solve both of our problems.'

'But that would mean travelling on the Great Western Railway,' he said with disgust. 'Do you really expect me to do that, Maddy?'

'Would you rather be caught in your slippers again by Mrs Young?'

It took him only a few seconds to weigh up the alternatives.

'I'll write that letter to Binnie at once,' he said, 'then we can pack our bags and catch the next train to Exeter.'

CHAPTER SEVENTEEN

Colbeck's visit to the solicitor had been enlightening. Having handed over the money found in the birdcage, he went off to the station with a quiet smile playing around his lips. The first person he saw was Lawrence Woodford but the man studiously avoided him. Since the refreshment room was quite busy, he had to wait until it was emptied by the arrival of the next train. He was then able to take Dorcas Hope aside. She was anxious to know what he'd discovered. He told her that the diary was largely devoted to the listing of birds and said nothing to her about the references to Woodford and Michael Heygate. She made a confession.

'I was very tempted to read it myself,' she said, 'but Mother told me that the diary was private property and I had no right to look into it. That's why I called on you, Inspector.'

'You did the right thing.'

'Has it been of any help?'

'Oh yes, it's given us a fascinating insight into the running of this station. As I foresaw,' said Colbeck, 'Mr Heygate thought very highly of you.' She blushed. 'Your name was mentioned a number of times.'

'That's nice to know.'

'I can't tell you how grateful I am to you for finding the diary.'

'It was pure chance,' she admitted. 'As soon as I saw it, I thought it might be useful to you. That's why I couldn't understand Mr Woodford's reaction.'

Colbeck was alert. 'Has he been threatening you again?'

'Not at all – he's been very pleasant to me. He even said that I might be the manageress here one day. But when I told him that the diary had been found, he looked quite ill. I don't know why.'

'I'll talk to him about it,' said Colbeck, thoughtfully. 'First, however, I need your help. Mr Heygate wrote that he discovered that barn owl "near M.V." Have you any idea what those initials represent, Miss Hope?'

'No, I don't,' she said after consideration.

'Is it a place he visited or a person he knew?'

'I can't say, Inspector.'

'Well, will you please think about it?'

'Yes, yes, I will. "M.V." could stand for Mr Vesey, who's taken over as manager here, but I really don't believe those initials have anything to do with him. He lives in Newton Abbot and the owl certainly wouldn't be there.'

'Let it lie at the back of your mind,' he suggested. 'Something may trigger a memory. If it does, then you must make contact with us at once.'

'I understand. While you're here,' she said, 'is there

anything you can tell me about Mrs Rossiter? I worry so much about her and Miss Impey.'

'As far as I know, she's being well looked after.'

'Is there any chance of visiting her?'

'I'll try to find out for you.'

'I'm free on Sundays,' she said. 'Do you think I should offer to take her sister with me? In some ways, Miss Impey is rather frail. I wouldn't want her to get upset.'

'That's very considerate of you,' said Colbeck. 'It's perhaps better to wait until Miss Impey is ready to go there of her own volition. You've already offered to help her. If she feels she needs your support when she goes to the asylum, I'm sure that she'll ask for it.'

Dorcas frowned. 'What sort of treatment is Mrs Rossiter getting?'

'Why do you ask that?'

'You hear such frightening stories about the asylum,' she said, worriedly. 'There's talk of patients being put in a straitjacket, or plunged into a cold bath, or locked up all the time in the dark. You don't know what to believe.'

'Dr Swift will prescribe the appropriate treatment,' he said, 'and I doubt very much if it will involve any of the things you've just mentioned. Rumours of that kind are usually misleading. Mrs Rossiter is being cared for, Miss Hope. Her recovery is in hand. And don't forget what I told you about the chaplain,' he added with a note of reassurance. 'He'll provide Mrs Rossiter with healing of a different kind.'

'How is the poor creature?' asked Bishop Phillpotts.

'Mrs Rossiter is like all the patients when they first come

here,' replied Canon Smalley. 'She's utterly bewildered. Until one gets used to it, this can be a rather frightening environment.'

'That's unavoidable. It is, after all, a place of detention.'

'And it's run on the twin principles of hard work and strict discipline. I've no objection to the hard work. It keeps the patients occupied and gives them a sense of achievement. Where discipline is concerned, mind you, I do sometimes feel that it's taken to extreme and inhumane limits.'

'That's outside your remit, Canon Smalley.'

'I've had to accept that.'

'Dr Swift knows what he's doing.'

'I mean no criticism of him, Bishop.'

Henry Phillpotts was not often subject to remorse but his conscience could be pricked on occasion. Having written to the chaplain to draw Agnes Rossiter to his attention, he felt that he had not done enough to atone for his earlier condemnation of the woman. As a result, he decided to pay an unheralded visit to the asylum. He and Canon Smalley were talking in the little room that the chaplain used as his office. There was a crucifix on the wall and a Holy Bible on the desk beside a pile of religious tracts. In stark contrast to the luxury of the bishop's palace, the room had a decidedly Spartan feel to it.

'I'm full of admiration for the work you do here,' said the bishop.

'I don't think of it as work. It's something I was called to do and I was happy to answer the call. I share my life with people in desperate need of my help.'

'Yet it does cut you off from the outside world.'

Smalley smiled. 'That's a cause for celebration rather than regret.'

'You've missed all the excitement of a murder investigation.'

'It's not been very exciting for Agnes Rossiter, I'm afraid. She's been one of the victims of the crime. She talks of it incessantly.'

'Then you may be able to cheer her up,' said the other. 'Inform her that the killer has been arrested and will go to trial. His name is Browne and he had the gross impertinence to threaten me in an indirect way. For some unknown reason, Inspector Colbeck, who is now in charge of the case, casts doubt on Browne's guilt, yet it's incontestable. He murdered the stationmaster elsewhere, then hid the body under the bonfire in the cathedral precincts as a brazen taunt at me.'

'I'll pass on the news to Mrs Rossiter.'

'Do that. Has she shown any sign of contrition?'

'Not as yet, Bishop.'

'There's been no apology for her antics in the cathedral?'

'Her belief in the existence of God has been seriously undermined.'

'Then it must be restored,' said Bishop Phillpotts. 'It's an important factor in her recovery. Don't you agree?'

'I do,' said Smalley, 'but it's something that will take time and patience. I'll do whatever I can for Mrs Rossiter, but please bear in mind that I have many others in need of my help. There's another recent arrival here, for instance, who's in dire straits. In addition to her other problems, the girl is deaf and dumb.'

'What dreadful handicaps to suffer!'

'There are others here with equally bad disabilities. Mrs Rossiter, on the other hand, is a relatively healthy woman. It's only her mental health that causes alarm.'

'Nevertheless,' said Bishop Phillpotts, meaningfully, 'I wish you to keep a particular eye on her. You'll oblige me by doing so.'

'I'll obey your instruction, Bishop.' He gestured towards the door. 'If you're ready to leave, I'll walk with you to the main exit.'

'Thank you. I'd like to take a closer look at the paintings.'

They left the room and ambled along the corridor so that the bishop could study some of the paintings he'd donated to the asylum. They consisted very largely of landscapes and seascapes, designed to please and soothe. There was no hint of violence or drama in any of the art. When they reached the end of the corridor, they turned at a right angle into another longer one. Bishop Phillpotts immediately stopped to examine a painting of Dawlish, but Smalley's attention was fixed on the three people walking towards him. One of them was Dr Swift and the other was a nurse. Between them was the slim figure of Esther Leete, no longer restrained in a straitjacket and no longer exuding a sense of danger. As she gazed around, her face had a bewildered loveliness. Canon Smalley was amazed at the transformation.

Colbeck had to delay his conversation with Woodford until three trains had come and gone. The platform at St David's was awash with people for what seemed like an age. When the last train had departed and the passengers had vanished, Colbeck saw the stationmaster trying to sneak off into the ticket office. He quickly intercepted him.

'Good morning, Mr Woodford,' he said.

'Oh,' replied the other, uneasily, 'good morning to you, Inspector.'

'I wondered if I might have a word.'

'I am rather busy at the moment.'

'This won't take long,' said Colbeck. 'It concerns the diary.'

'I'm told that it's been found.'

'And I've been told that you were unhappy at the news.'

Woodford scowled. 'Someone has been telling tales again, has she?'

'Is it true?'

'It's nonsense, Inspector. Why should I be unhappy about anything that helps you in your investigation? I was pleasantly shocked, that's all. Miss Hope has obviously misinterpreted my reaction.'

'You do leave yourself open to misinterpretation at times,' said Colbeck, archly. 'What do you suppose is in the diary?'

'I have no idea and no real interest.'

'Not even when it contains information about you?'

Woodford's scowl darkened. 'What sort of information?'

'It's not entirely to your credit, sir.'

'Don't pay too much heed to what Joel wrote. He was always trying to find fault with me. I put it down to the fact that I applied for the job at the same time as him and he resented the competition. Take anything he says with a pinch of salt, Inspector.'

'I thought you claimed that you were good friends.'

'We were – but we also had our differences.'

'Tell me about them, Mr Woodford.'

'I don't want to bother you with trivialities.'

'I wouldn't describe the retention of your post here as a triviality,' said Colbeck, 'because that's what was entailed. For reasons I need hardly recall, it was more than possible for Mr Heygate to have you dismissed. The diary makes that crystal clear. He spared you that fate.'

'Joel is dead,' said Woodford, testily. 'Let his diary die with him.'

'How can I ignore the diary when it will lead us to his killer?'

'You already *have* the killer – it's Bagsy Browne.'

'That's a matter of opinion.'

'I know what mine is.'

'Then you share it with almost everyone else, sir.'

'Bagsy swore revenge,' insisted Woodford, 'and there were lots of witnesses. Surely Joel recorded the incident in his diary, didn't he?'

'Oh, yes,' said Colbeck. 'Browne's threat is mentioned in detail.'

'Isn't that good enough for you?'

'Unfortunately,' said Colbeck, 'it isn't. Bagsy Browne seems to have been easily provoked into issuing grim warnings. Mr Heygate was one of a large group of people in the city who got one. Anybody who upset Browne had his fist waved in their face. Yet not one of them – and I've been through police records – was murdered by him. The worst any of them suffered was a beating.'

'That's what he meant to give Joel and he went too far.'

'It's a possible explanation, I grant you, but it's an incorrect one. Answer me two questions. First, how did Browne know that the stationmaster would be out after dark on that night? Secondly,' Colbeck went on, 'if he did murder Mr Heygate, why not leave the body where it fell, instead of taking it to the site of the bonfire? That would have involved risk. It would have been far easier simply to walk away.'

'Bagsy was trying to dispose of the body altogether.'

'That's the general belief. I happen to disagree with it. However,' he said, 'let me return to the appearance of Lawrence Woodford in the diary.'

'It only happened once,' said Woodford, quickly. 'The second time he caught me with the bottle, I was actually off duty and what I do in my own time is of no concern to anyone else.'

'You're forbidden to bring alcohol on to the premises.'

'It was an honest mistake.'

'Like your denial of the fact that you were told about Mr Heygate's diary?'

Woodford's annoyance made him snarl. 'I bought the whisky for a friend. Joel happened to see it.'

'That's not what it says in the diary.'

'Damn the diary, Inspector!'

'I'm sad to say that it's the diary that damns *you*, sir.'

Woodford was rescued from further discomfort by the approach of another train. Mumbling an excuse, he went off to welcome it. Colbeck was about to go into the refreshment room for a cup of tea when he saw Leeming coming towards him. He waited until the sergeant was within a few paces.

'Well met, Victor. May I offer you refreshment?'

'Yes, please,' said Leeming.

'Have you been to the Crown Inn?'

'Yes, sir, and there was a surprise in store for me.'

'Don't tell me that the landlord is a friend of Michael Heygate.'

'He's not a friend, exactly. In fact, he doesn't even like the man. But he did let Heygate and his wife stay there at his expense on the night before Guy Fawkes Day.'

Colbeck gaped. 'Why did he do that?'

'He was hoping that they'd buy the pub off him, sir.'

Michael and Lavinia Heygate sat side by side at the table with a pad in front of them. On it was a series of financial calculations. They'd discarded their mourning attire and put on their normal clothing. Behind closed doors, they were safe from criticism. Having had three separate visits from a detective, they reasoned, it was unlikely that they'd have a fourth. The death of Joel Heygate didn't impinge on their minds. Their sole concern was with its consequences for them.

'How much do you think we'll get?' she asked.

'It's difficult to put a figure on it, Lavinia.'

'We know that he had a healthy bank account and also kept a lot of money at home. Then there are the contents of the house. They should fetch a good sum.'

'I think we'll have enough,' said Heygate, looking at the figures before him. 'I know it's a bad time to sell but, even at a conservative estimate, we should get a fair amount for the shop. The house agent has already had enquiries.'

'I can't wait to get away from here.'

'We've rather exhausted all that Dawlish can offer, haven't we?'

'We failed, Michael,' she said, bitterly. 'We started a business and it lost money. Everyone here knows that. You can tell from the looks they give you.'

'The business wouldn't have failed if Joel had given us the money to tide us over. We just didn't have the stock to meet the demand. And you didn't help by cutting our prices like that.'

'I thought it would help.'

'It only helped to move the business closer to collapse. Then there was that foolish mistake with Bagsy Browne,' he recalled. 'Trust him to come in here when he saw you were on your own.'

She was defensive. 'He wanted a fishing rod and I sold him one.'

'The only fishing he ever does is with his hand – it goes into people's pockets and steals from them. He didn't want the rod, Lavinia. All he was after was the chance to make a quick profit. So what did he do?'

'There's no need to keep on about it,' she said, petulantly.

'He comes in here, turns on what passes for his charm and he haggles until you lower the price of that rod by several pounds.'

'He paid in cash, Michael,' she said, nastily. 'We needed it.'

'What did Bagsy do then?' he asked, sarcastically. 'Did he go fishing?'

'You know quite well that he didn't.'

'He went straight across the road to the pub, scrounged a drink out of a complete stranger then sold the rod for a lot more than he paid for it. I was teased about it for weeks.'

'And you're still blaming me for it.'

'I'm sorry,' he said, slipping an arm around her, 'but it does rankle. Let's learn from our mistakes,' he went on, sounding more optimistic. 'When we take over the Crown, we must have strict rules – no free drinks and no haggling over the price. And if anyone causes the slightest amount of trouble, out he goes.'

'The landlord said there was very little rowdiness there.'

'It's one of the things that appeals to me. Success is entirely in our own hands, Lavinia. We must be more businesslike. You've seen the accounts for the last three years. The Crown has been making a decent profit. If we invest some of the money we inherit from Joel,' he said, 'we can increase that profit.'

'I just want to be where there's more *life*, Michael. This place is lowering. You see the same old faces day after day. Exeter is a city. Things happen there.'

'Yes – like the murder of my brother.'

'That was a stroke of good fortune for us.'

'I know. We must exploit it to the hilt.'

'I don't follow.'

'It will still be fresh in people's minds, Lavinia. We can use that to our advantage. The landlord said that the Crown will come with a lot of goodwill. It has plenty of regular customers. I think we can increase their number by making the most of the fact that we're members of Joel's family. It will arouse sympathy,' he said. 'It will create even more goodwill. We can use Joel in an even more effective way.'

'Can we?'

'I think so. We both know how popular he was.'

'So?'

'We change the name of the inn.'

She was taken aback. 'Can we do that, Michael?'

'When the place is ours, we can do what we like.'

'What will the new name be?'

He kissed her on the cheek. 'The Stationmaster.'

Having promised Dorcas Hope that he'd find out about the possibility of visiting, Colbeck took the train to Exminster.

He was interested to learn how Agnes Rossiter had settled in and to discover if she'd been told about the arrest of a man believed to be the stationmaster's killer. Leeming went with him and shuddered as they entered the County Asylum.

'I don't like the feel of this place, sir,' he confided.

'We can walk out at any time, Victor. The patients don't have that option.'

'I'd hate to end up in somewhere like this.'

'They don't all end up here,' said Colbeck. 'Dr Swift told me that several people respond to treatment and are allowed to return home to their families. It's only those with incurable conditions who remain here until they die.'

'Do you think that Mrs Rossiter will be one of them?'

'I wish I knew the answer to that question.'

Since Dr Swift was not available to see them, they were introduced instead to Canon Smalley. Colbeck was delighted to meet him and he, in turn, was pleased to meet a man whose name he'd heard many times. He invited them into his office.

'It's my day for visitors,' he said.

'I hope that's not a complaint, Canon Smalley,' said Colbeck.

'Far from it, Inspector. I spend my whole life visiting others. It's a pleasant change to have someone calling on me. You come on the heels of the bishop.'

Having heard the disparaging comments made about him by Colbeck and Tallis, Leeming was tempted to feign surprise that they'd let the bishop out of the asylum but the sight of the crucifix on the wall made him hold his peace.

'What was he doing here?' asked Colbeck.

'The same as you, I suspect,' replied Smalley. 'He asked after Mrs Rossiter.'

'Has he taken a special interest in the case?'

'Yes, Inspector – she's aroused his compassion.'

'Then I applaud him. The lady needs all the sympathy she can get.'

'I can't muster a lot of sympathy,' admitted Leeming. 'I worked very briefly under the lady when she was manageress of the refreshment room on Exeter St David's station. Mrs Rossiter is a real martinet. My sympathy is reserved for the waitress there.'

'Would that be a Dorcas Hope?' wondered Smalley.

'Yes, it would.'

'I've heard all about her.'

'Have you spent much time with Mrs Rossiter, then?'

'I've spent as much as I can spare. But please don't ask me to give you a medical diagnosis. That's Dr Swift's prerogative. All that I can tell you is that she's in the clutches of a fantasy and won't be talked out of it. At the moment, alas,' he said, glancing up at the crucifix, 'she's beyond the reach of spiritual help.'

'When will it be possible to visit her?' asked Colbeck.

'Dr Swift will make that decision. Mrs Rossiter will certainly be in no fit state to receive visitors for some time.'

'Has she talked of the murder with you?'

'Oh, yes,' said Smalley, tolerantly. 'She's talked and talked.'

'And does she know that a suspect has been arrested for the crime?'

'I informed her of it this morning, Inspector.'

'What was her response?'

'It was rather violent, I fear. She said she wanted to be at the execution.'

'Then she hasn't been to one before,' said Leeming, ruefully. 'I've had to watch two or three. They're grisly spectacles. If it was left to me, I wouldn't allow women to be present.'

'I wouldn't allow any member of the public to be there,' said Colbeck. 'An execution should take place behind prison walls. It's wrong to offer it as a form of ghoulish entertainment.'

Smalley nodded. 'I couldn't agree with you more, Inspector.'

'What else can you tell us about Mrs Rossiter?'

'I have hope for her. I have definite hope.'

He went on to give them a succinct description of his sessions with Agnes Rossiter and an explanation of his role at the asylum. They were both struck by his intelligence, humility and dedication. Some of the staff they'd seen had been grim and unsmiling and they'd heard howls of despair echoing along the corridors. Canon Smalley was an island of calm in a sea of pain and desolation.

When the chaplain finished, Colbeck thanked him for giving them so much time, then led Leeming out. On their way to the exit, Colbeck was interested in the paintings, but the sergeant simply wanted to get out of there as quickly as possible. Once back in the fresh air, he filled his lungs.

'I couldn't breathe properly in there,' he complained.

'Yes, there was an oppressive atmosphere.'

'Canon Smalley is a brave man.'

'He's a good man, Victor. Only someone as selfless as him

could take on the chaplaincy. Bishop Phillpotts chose well when he appointed him.'

'That's the first kind thing I've heard you say about the bishop.'

'Well, he has rather tried my patience.' As they headed in the direction of the station, Colbeck sighed. 'How much longer will we be here?' he asked. 'I'm so eager to get back to London. I'm needed there.'

'If you accepted that Browne was the killer, we could leave today.'

'Not while there's unfinished business.'

'Are we still trying to link Michael Heygate or Woodford to the murder?'

'No,' said Colbeck, 'we're still hunting for a barn owl. Only when we've found it will we get to the bottom of what's been going on. Then we can pack our bags and I can return to the arms of the dear lady I'm about to marry.'

The journey to Exeter resolved itself into a continual list of complaints. Forced to travel on the broad gauge of the GWR, Andrews poured scorn on everything he could. He criticised the locomotive, the driver, the upholstery in the carriage, the speed at which they travelled and the regularity with which they stopped. Nothing outside the window diverted him from his diatribe. The beauties of Bath went by unseen and the commercial majesty of Bristol went unnoticed. Madeleine, however, saw everything that went past, taking especial interest in Bristol because it was there that Colbeck had once rescued her from her kidnappers on a ship.

Having made the sudden decision to quit London, she began to have doubts.

'I hope that Robert won't be cross with me,' she said.

'We don't even need to see him, Maddy. We can just enjoy looking at Exeter.'

'Don't be ridiculous. I'm not going all this way to avoid him.'

'Well, I'm going in order to avoid Ivy Young,' he said. 'I want plenty of distance between me and that harpy. I wonder what Binnie would say if she knew what her sister had done.'

'I think you're better off without either of them, Father.'

He was wistful. 'So there's to be no second wedding?'

'Not unless you're prepared to propose to Mrs Young.'

He let out a groan of terror. Streaming through Devon, he was so preoccupied by memories of the two women he'd escaped that he forgot to resume his carping. Madeleine was able to close her eyes and luxuriate in thoughts of her forthcoming reunion with Colbeck.

Adeline Goss was beside herself. When they'd taken Bagsy Browne off to the magistrate, she'd had only the merest glimpse and was unable to get any message from him. Locked in her cell, she was helpless and there would be no chance of a daring escape this time. The man who'd rescued her was being charged with murder and the worst thing was that she really didn't know whether or not he'd committed it. Even if he was a killer, Adeline would not desert him and she racked her brains for a way to save him. In the end, she devised a plan and demanded to see Superintendent Steel. He talked to her through the bars.

'What have you done with Bagsy?' she asked.

'He's on remand in prison.'

'He didn't kill the stationmaster.'

'I know he didn't,' said Steel, sardonically. 'And I suppose that he didn't attack a prison warder or rescue you from custody or stab a senior detective in the arm in the process. He's completely innocent, isn't he?'

'There's no need to sneer.'

'We've finally nailed him, Adeline. He's going to hang.'

'No!' she exclaimed, rattling the bars. She made an effort to compose herself. 'I'd like to change the evidence I gave to you and Inspector Colbeck.'

'Do you mean that you're ready to confess that you're an accessory to the murder?'

'I want you to know the bleeding truth.' She bit her lip. 'I told you that I wasn't with Bagsy on the night before Guy Fawkes Day. Well, I lied to you.'

'I can't recall an occasion when you *didn't* lie to me, Adeline.'

'Bagsy was with me that night.'

'So you were his accomplice, after all.'

'No, we spent the whole night in bed together.'

'Was that *after* he'd killed the stationmaster?'

'He never went anywhere near Mr Heygate. Why should he?'

'It's called revenge.'

'Bagsy's idea of revenge is to break someone's jaw or flatten their nose.'

'He did a lot more than that to Joel Heygate,' said Steel. 'He all but took his head off. But now that we know you were with him all night, perhaps you could explain how you got the body from the scene of the crime to the bonfire.'

'We did nothing of the kind. We were in bed. I swear it.'

'You swore earlier that you never even saw him that night.'

She tossed her hair. 'I did that because I was angry with him.'

'How can you be angry with a man who got you out of a police cell?' asked Steel. 'You should have gone down on your bended knees and thanked him.'

'I did thank him, Superintendent. Then he told me what he was going to do.'

'And what was that?'

'He meant to leave Exeter – alone. I was being ditched.'

'That much I can believe – he never travels with baggage.'

'Who are you calling "baggage", you swivel-eyed bastard?' she shrieked. 'I was his best friend in the city. That's why he came to me.'

'Yet you denied that he went anywhere near Rockfield Place.'

'I told you – I was angry with him.'

'He's going to be even angrier with you when he hears the paltry excuse you came up with in a bid to save him from the gallows. Is that the best you can do, Adeline?' asked Steel. 'We both know that you didn't spend the night with Bagsy. We have incontrovertible proof of it. If you could've offered him an alibi, don't you think he'd have seized it? But he didn't, did he? He wouldn't tell us where he was that night but it certainly wasn't between *your* thighs. He was too busy killing Joel Heygate.'

Turning on his heel, he walked away and returned to his office.

Adeline smacked the bars in sheer frustration. Her plan had failed.

'I'm sorry, Bagsy,' she said. 'I did try.'

* * *

Bagsy Browne had been given a jeering welcome at the prison. Since the staff had all heard about the beating he'd given to Wyatt, he knew that they'd soon assault him in return. Browne was a familiar visitor to the old Bridewell in Queen Street but he was now remanded to the new prison in North Road. Built four years earlier on the same plan as Pentonville, it had almost two hundred cells, each of them containing water, washing bowl, bed, table, stool and gas jet. Prisoners were kept in isolation and subjected to the silent system. There was none of the banter Browne had indulged in at the police station. He was forbidden to speak to the other inmates. Left alone in the tiny cell, he sat on the stool and brooded on his fate. His would be the first execution at the new prison. Warders had taken delight in telling him that they were already placing bets on whether or not he would cry for mercy when he was dragged to the gallows. He showed no fear but his mind was in turmoil.

When a warder came to unlock his cell, Browne thought that he was being taken out to provide some sport for the staff. He'd been beaten up in prison before and had won the grudging admiration of the warders because he took his punishment bravely and never complained. In fact, he escaped any violent treatment this time. He was shown into a featureless room then locked inside it. Seated behind the little table was Inspector Robert Colbeck.

Browne was pleased. 'You got my message, then?'

'Why don't you sit down, Mr Browne?'

'I never thought you'd come.'

'In my experience,' said Colbeck, 'criminals often have an attack of honesty when they're facing execution. They realise that their lies are utterly pointless.' He indicated the chair opposite him. 'Sit down. I daresay it's a lot more comfortable than the stool in your cell.'

Browne sat down. 'Thank you, Inspector,' he said. 'I asked for you because I knew that Superintendent Steel would never listen to me. All he's interested in is the moment when the lever is pulled, the trapdoor opens and I start dancing in the air.'

'You're quite wrong, Mr Browne. Like me, the superintendent is interested in only one thing and that's justice.'

'Do you believe that I killed the stationmaster?'

'I think that it's more than possible.'

'Does that mean you're certain of it?'

'No,' said Colbeck, 'I'm very far from certain and that's why I want to explore the full ramifications of this crime. Don't get your hopes up, however. I'm not at all convinced of your innocence either.'

'That's fair enough,' said Browne. 'I can see it from your point of view. You think I might be guilty because I've been unable to give you an alibi for the time when Heygate was murdered. There's a reason for that.'

'The obvious reason is that you were the killer.'

'No, that's not it at all, Inspector.'

'Are you claiming that you do have an alibi?' Browne nodded. 'Then why ever didn't you produce it earlier?'

'I was protecting someone.'

'You're the one in need of protection, Mr Browne. If someone can account for your movements on the eve of Guy Fawkes Day, then he or she should come forward. Don't they realise the danger you're in?'

'It's not as simple as that,' said Browne, running a tongue over dry lips.

'It looks very simple to me.'

The prisoner fell silent and searched Colbeck's face. He was trying to decide if he could entrust confidential information to him. For his part, Colbeck could sense the man's embarrassment. Browne's natural truculence had gone and been replaced by a mixture of discomfort and shame.

'If I give you the name of a young woman,' he asked, quietly, 'can you speak to her in private and keep her out of this investigation?'

'That depends on what she has to tell me, Mr Browne.'

'I spent the whole of that day and night with her.'

'Then why didn't you say so earlier?'

Browne squirmed. 'The situation is awkward,' he said, looking down at the table. 'I didn't want Ad to know.'

'Ah,' said Colbeck, 'I think I see what you're driving at. When you were being harboured by Miss Goss, you betrayed her by sleeping with another woman. Now it all begins to make sense.'

'You still don't understand, Inspector.'

'I understand that there may – just may – be someone in the city who can vouch for you and prove that you were nowhere near the place where Joel Heygate met his death. If such a person exists – and I'm bound to wonder if she's simply a figment of your lively imagination – then she can come forward and save your life.'

Browne was intense. 'Ad must never know about her.'

'Come now,' said Colbeck, speaking man to man, 'let's be frank, shall we? Miss Goss has made no secret of the profession she follows and you seem to accept quite happily the fact that there are many other gentlemen in her life while you're absent. By the same token, she will surely know that you don't behave like a Trappist monk during the long periods when you're apart. In short, I don't think she'll be surprised at your interest in another woman.'

Browne raised his head. 'Yes, she will – very surprised.'

'Why do you think that?'

'The young woman was her daughter.'

CHAPTER EIGHTEEN

When they arrived in Exeter, the first thing they did was to carry their bags into the refreshment room. The long journey had left them tired and hungry. Caleb Andrews and Madeleine sat at a table and ordered a pot of tea and some cakes. Dorcas Hope soon brought everything across on her tray.

'Are you staying in Exeter long?' she asked, unloading the items carefully on to the table.

'We don't know,' said Andrews. 'It all depends on my daughter's fiancé.'

'He came here to lead a murder investigation,' added Madeleine.

'Oh, you must mean Inspector Colbeck,' said Dorcas, brightly. 'He's such a handsome gentleman, isn't he? We've seen a lot of the inspector here.'

'Do you happen to know where he's staying?'

'Yes, he and the sergeant are at the Acland Tavern in Sidwell Street.'

'Then that's where we ought to go, Maddy,' suggested Andrews.

'There's no need,' said Dorcas. 'I can save you the journey.'

'How can you do that, miss?'

'Inspector Colbeck will soon be here. I sent word to him that I've at last remembered, you see. And since I can't leave here for several hours, the inspector will have to come to me.'

'This is all very mystifying,' said Madeleine.

'It's connected to the investigation.'

'Go on.'

'Well,' said Dorcas, 'it's all to do with a diary that Mr Heygate – he's the stationmaster who was murdered – left behind. They searched the house but couldn't find it anywhere. Then Peter came to our rescue.'

'Who is Peter?'

'He's Mr Heygate's canary. I'm looking after him.'

'You're not making much sense, young lady,' said Andrews.

'I'm coming to the interesting bit,' said Dorcas, hands on hips. 'When I cleaned Peter's cage, I found the diary hidden inside it under a false base. And what do you think? I also found over two hundred pounds in banknotes.'

Andrews laughed. 'Is this some kind of joke?'

'No, sir – it's as true as I'm standing here.'

'It is,' confirmed Vesey from behind the counter.

'Do you see why I said that Peter came to our rescue?'

'No, I don't,' said Andrews.

'Neither do I,' admitted Madeleine. 'Is this diary going to be of help in the investigation?'

'It is now that my memory has been jogged. That's the whole point.'

'So the case relies on the assistance of a canary?'

'The owl is far more important.'

'Saints alive!' exclaimed Andrews. 'We've stumbled into an aviary.'

'Let me explain,' said Dorcas.

'I think you've explained enough,' suggested Vesey. 'Why don't you leave our customers to enjoy their r-r-refreshments and t-t-take further orders?' He indicated the three people who'd just come into the room. 'I'm sorry about that,' he went on as the waitress moved over to the newcomers. 'Miss Hope gets r-r-rather excited. She was a good friend of Mr Heygate, so she's very involved in the case.'

Madeleine gave an understanding smile but her father was more interested in sampling one of the cakes. She poured tea for both of them, then added milk and sugar to her cup. Colbeck's letters had said nothing about a canary and an owl. She looked forward to getting a clearer explanation of their role in the investigation. Meanwhile, she stirred her tea then reached for a cake.

'I feel better already,' said Andrews, munching away. 'I'm completely safe here. Mrs Young can't come and spread lies about Binnie.'

'You promised to forget both of them, Father.'

'I'm trying to do that, Maddy, but they keep popping into my mind.'

She nibbled her cake. 'Robert is going to have a shock.'

'And a very pleasant shock it will be.'

'I do hope so. He must know that I didn't come here to hamper him in any way. I just wanted to see him.'

'And I just wanted *not* to see Ivy Young.'

'She belongs in your past, Father, and so does Mrs Langton.'

'You're right as always, Maddy. I'm happier without either of them.' He looked around. 'I've never been here before. What do you think there is to see in Exeter? Apart from an owl and a canary, that is.'

'There's only one thing I want to see,' she said, 'and that's Robert.'

'His last letter said that they'd made an arrest. The case is solved.'

'Then why did he warn me that he'd have to stay here for a while? No, I think there are still a number of things to clear up.'

Eating their cakes and drinking their tea, they were able to relax. They'd already noticed the marked difference to London. Instead of a vast, bustling metropolis that stretched in all directions, they were now in a provincial city with expanses of open countryside visible. It was altogether quieter and less frenetic than life in the capital. Madeleine marvelled at her own boldness in coming to Exeter. She'd acted on the spur of the moment and been able to involve her father. He'd been an irritable travelling companion but had cheered up now that they'd reached their destination. Like him, she felt strangely liberated.

Madeleine was just reflecting how small and uncluttered the station was compared to the London termini when an express train arrived for a short stay before continuing on to Plymouth without any further stop. Passengers poured out, many of them in need of refreshments before they rejoined the train. The room was so full of people that neither Madeleine nor her father realised that they included Colbeck and Leeming who'd walked into the station as the express juddered to a halt. Vesey and Dorcas worked at full stretch to answer the needs of their customers. As most of them chose to sit at tables, very few people were left standing.

Madeleine finally noticed two familiar faces and leapt to her feet.

'Robert!' she cried out.

Colbeck was torn between delight and amazement. 'What are you doing here?'

'I came to see you, of course.'

'And so did I,' said Andrews.

Wanting to embrace her, Colbeck had to restrict himself to a kiss on the cheek while in public. He then shook her father's hand warmly. Leeming also gave them a cordial welcome, asking what the weather was like in London. The refreshment room was too crowded for them to have a proper conversation, so they stepped outside.

'This is a wonderful surprise,' said Colbeck, grinning. 'I can't tell you how pleased I am to see you. However,' he went on, 'I am still heavily involved in the investigation, so you'll have to excuse me for a while.'

'Of course,' said Madeleine. 'We didn't come to interfere.'

'Though you're welcome to my advice if you need it,' offered Andrews. 'What's all this about an owl and a canary?'

'I can see that you've been talking to Miss Hope,' said Colbeck. 'Victor will explain. Where are you going to stay?'

'The waitress mentioned a tavern in Sidwell Street.'

'That's where we've taken rooms, Mr Andrews. Victor,' he went on, 'why don't you find a cab and take Madeleine and her father to the Acland Tavern? I know they have spare rooms there. I'll meet up with you later.'

'Where are you going, Robert?' asked Madeleine.

'First of all, I have to speak to Miss Hope and I can't do that until the train is ready to leave and the refreshment room clears. It may well be,' he said, 'that she has some vital evidence for us relating to the scene of the crime. Once I've heard what it is, I have to catch a train to Totnes.'

She was concerned. 'Is that far away?'

'It's about thirty miles from here,' he replied, 'and though your father might believe otherwise, the South Devon Railway provides an excellent service.'

'It can't compete with the LNWR,' said Andrews, loyally.

'It doesn't try to, Mr Andrews.'

Madeleine was curious. 'Why are you going to Totnes?'

'I have to interview an important witness,' said Colbeck. 'In fact, I can't think of anyone more important, because the young lady may well be in a position to save a man from the gallows.'

One of the few advantages of being in his office was that Steel could not be subjected to ecclesiastical meddling there. If the bishop wished to see him, then he summoned the superintendent to his palace. He would never bother Steel at his place of work. That, at least, had been the situation until now. All of a sudden, Steel's bolt-hole was no longer secure. Bishop Phillpotts demanded to see him and came waddling up the stairs. Admitted to the office, he flopped into the seat opposite the desk and looked around with undisguised disdain.

'Is this the room from which our city is policed?' he asked.

'It's all that the Watch Committee could provide for me.'

'It's pathetically bare and lacking in character.'

'We can't all afford the expensive paintings that adorn the walls of your palace, Bishop. Besides, this is an office and not a place where I can sit back at my leisure with a slim volume of verse or an improving novel.'

Phillpotts eyed him shrewdly. 'Do you dare to poke fun at me, sir?'

'No,' said Steel, 'I just wish to point out that ornate decoration would be wholly out of place in a building that routinely houses criminals.'

'It's about one of those criminals that I've come to enquire. Is the villainous Mr Browne still under your roof?'

'He's been charged and remanded in custody at the prison.'

'Good – if there's no possibility of his escaping, I'm not in jeopardy.'

'You never were, Bishop,' said Steel, 'except in your own mind.'

'I know when I'm under threat, man,' said the other, tartly, 'and I'll brook no criticism from you or from anyone else. Withdraw that slur at once.'

Steel shrugged an apology. 'I do so willingly.'

'Tell me about Bernard Browne.'

'He prefers to be called Bagsy.'

'I never use nicknames, Superintendent. They smack of juvenility. I want to know what's happened to this fiend from the time of his arrest until now.'

Schooling himself to be patient, Steel gave him an abbreviated account of the arrest and detention of Browne. He stressed Colbeck's bravery in tackling the man and was complimentary about the way that the inspector had questioned the prisoner. When the superintendent talked about the parallel arrest of Adeline Goss, the bishop responded with his pulpit voice.

'Prostitution is a sign of moral turpitude,' he said, solemnly. 'Every brothel should be closed and their occupants driven out of the city.'

'One has to face reality, Bishop. Where there's a demand, there will always be a supply. It's not called the oldest profession for nothing.'

'Are you actually *condoning* this foul trade?'

'No,' said Steel, 'but I accept that it's a fact of life. I have great sympathy for the poor women forced to sell their bodies in order to survive. Adeline Goss is a good example. She was corrupted almost from birth. Instead of being condemned, such unfortunates ought to be helped and reformed.'

'Don't preach to me, Superintendent,' said the bishop. 'Let me come to the reason that brought me here. I was hoping to confront Inspector Colbeck and ask why he still has reservations about the glaringly obvious guilt of Browne.'

'Only the inspector can tell you that.'

'You don't share his doubts, I hope?'

'I certainly don't, Bishop. I want to see Bagsy Browne hanged. Justice will be done and this city will be cleansed of one of its most notorious criminals.'

'Have you any idea *why* Colbeck thinks the fellow innocent?'

'He's relying on his instinct.'

'Well, I rely on mine and it's infallible. That man is the personification of evil. Nothing will ever convince me that Browne is not the killer. He deliberately dumped the corpse outside the cathedral as a crude parody of a sacrificial lamb.

In short,' said the bishop, angrily, 'he mocked both me and the Church that I am appointed to represent. He deserves to die in agony.'

Colbeck arrived at the address he'd been given. It had taken him to a backstreet in Totnes where rows of anonymous terraced houses stretched for a hundred yards. It was an area of blatant deprivation. Many of the properties were in need of repair and there was accumulated filth on the pavements. Ragged children played games, a man sold salt and vinegar from the back of a rickety cart and mangy dogs scoured every corner in search of food. It was the sort of place in which Bagsy Browne would have moved without exciting any interest. Colbeck, on the other hand, aroused curiosity on all sides. Because people of his impeccable appearance were simply never seen there, he collected hostile glances, muttered comments and jeers from the children.

The front door was opened by a slatternly woman in her fifties, with a sagging bosom and unkempt hair. When she'd overcome her surprise, she straightened her shoulders, pushed strands of hair back from her forehead and offered him a calculating smile.

'Can we be of service to you, sir?' she asked.

'I'm looking for a young lady named Christina Goss.'

'Christina will be happy to oblige you, sir – at a price.'

'I'm not here to transact any business with her,' said Colbeck. 'I'm Inspector Colbeck and I'm a detective involved in a murder investigation. I believe that Miss Goss may be able to give me some valuable evidence.'

The woman was indignant. 'This is a law-abiding house,

sir,' she said. 'My girls have nothing to do with a murder. We may be poor but we have our standards.' She tried to close the door. 'You've come to the wrong place.'

He put his foot in the door. 'Are you going to let me in,' he asked, 'or must I arrest you for running a disorderly house?' Her ire subsided immediately. 'Miss Goss is in no way involved in the crime but she may know someone who allegedly is. All I wish to do is to have a brief conversation with her.'

After glaring at him for several seconds, she reluctantly opened the door.

'You'd better come in.'

Colbeck was admitted and taken up to a room at the back of the house.

Christina Goss was barely twenty, a shapely young woman with a striking prettiness and a clear resemblance to her mother. At the prospect of company, she flashed a smile but it froze on her lips when she was told who her visitor was and why he'd come to see her. She sat down sullenly on the bed. Left alone with her, Colbeck removed his hat and perched on a chair.

'Do you remember a man named Bagsy Browne?' he asked.

'I never ask them their names.'

'Oh, I think you know this man's name and I fancy you'll recall the night that he spent with you. Mr Browne was very generous to you, wasn't he? How many of your clients give you that amount of money?'

Her manner softened. 'Why are you asking about Bagsy?'

'He's sent you a message from prison.'

Victor Leeming took them to the Acland Tavern and arranged rooms for them. When they'd settled in, Madeleine and her father joined the sergeant for a discussion about the case. Careful not to give too much detail away, he told them enough for them to understand the references to an owl and a canary.

'That young waitress seemed like a nice girl,' said Andrews.

'It's very hard work in that refreshment room,' said Leeming. 'I should know. I took over her job while Miss Hope was being interviewed by the inspector.'

Madeleine grinned. '*You* were a waitress?'

'It's not what I expected to do when I became a detective.'

'It gives you another string to your bow, Sergeant,' teased Andrews. 'When you retire from Scotland Yard, you can work in a restaurant. Not that I'd recommend retirement,' he added. 'It brings hidden dangers with it.'

'The sergeant doesn't want to hear about your private life, Father,' said Madeleine.

'Perhaps not,' agreed Leeming, 'but I would like your opinion on something else, Mr Andrews. What's your view of the atmospheric railway?'

Andrews snorted. 'It was a disaster!'

'The inspector thinks it was a clever idea.'

'That's all it was, Sergeant – an idea. It should never have been put into practice. It cost a lot of money and ended in failure.'

'Don't listen to my father,' said Madeleine, good-humouredly. 'He doesn't approve of anything that wasn't used on the LNWR.'

'It's the finest railway company in the world.'

'Mr Brunel would disagree.'

'Brunel is an idiot. He lost a small fortune on the experiment of the atmospheric railway. That's no way to power a train.'

'All the same,' said Leeming, 'I'd love to have seen how it was done.'

'Then you should have been here when it was tried on the line between Exeter and Newton Abbot. It was abandoned after less than a year.' He cackled in triumph. 'It ran out of air!'

'Let's come back to the case,' said Madeleine, anxious to steer her father away from his ritual sneering at Brunel. 'Miss Hope told us that she was a good friend of the stationmaster.'

'That's correct,' said Leeming. 'In some ways, she was his best friend. He trusted her far more than anyone else.'

'Then his death must have been an appalling blow to her.'

'It was, Miss Andrews. Luckily, she's been strong enough to cope with it. She's controlled her grief and got on with her job. The same can't be said of Mrs Rossiter, I'm afraid.'

'Who is she?'

'She was the manageress of the refreshment room,' said Leeming, 'but not any more. They had to cart her off to the Devon County Asylum.'

It was only a stroll along the corridors of the institution but it seemed to do Agnes Rossiter some good. Canon Smalley accompanied her, pointing out some of the paintings on the way. When he took her into one of the workrooms, she saw dozens of women seated at tables as they sewed garments. None of them looked up at the visitors. Smalley escorted her back to her room.

'When will I go home?' asked Mrs Rossiter.

'This is your home for the time being.'

'My sister will pine for me.'

'I know,' said Smalley, gently, 'and we hope you'll be able to see her before too long. But you're not ready to leave our care yet. Dr Swift will decide when he can sanction your release.'

Mrs Rossiter gave a nod of acceptance. Sitting on the chair, she was lost in thought. Smalley took his leave. When he came out of the room, it was locked by the nurse waiting outside. After paying a visit to a number of other patients, Smalley then returned to his office to collect a book. With the volume tucked under his arm, he went off to the room occupied by Esther Leete. The door was locked and he had to wait to be let in by the nurse inside. Esther was not being restrained but she was under permanent surveillance. She was very subdued and showed no aggression when he sat on the chair opposite her. After talking to her for a while, he gave her the book so that she could feel it in her hands.

'It's full of illustrations,' he said to the nurse. 'I find that they often help to stimulate the patients.'

When he opened the book for her, Esther stared dully at a painting of Christ on the cross. As the pages were turned over, she took no notice of the other illustrations either. Then Smalley turned another page and the woman immediately sprang into life. Grabbing the book, she jumped up and hugged it to her chest. When the nurse tried to take the book from her, Esther fought back.

'Let her be,' advised Smalley. 'She can keep the book.'

'I think you'd better leave her alone,' said the nurse.

'I'll call back this evening. She may have calmed down by then.'

Canon Smalley let himself out and heard the door being

locked behind him. Esther Leete puzzled him. Her reaction to an illustration in the book had been so fierce and unexpected. What she'd seen was a painting of the Madonna and Child.

Colbeck was able to spend only a few minutes alone with Madeleine at the Acland Tavern. He was full of apologies for having to leave almost immediately.

'I understand, Robert,' she said. 'It's my fault for arriving out of the blue without warning.'

'It was the nicest thing to happen to me since I came to Exeter.'

'I simply had to see you.'

'You should have come alone,' he said. 'You don't need a chaperone.'

'Father had his own reasons for leaving London. I'm beginning to regret that I brought him with me,' she said, light-heartedly. 'He keeps arguing with Sergeant Leeming about the merits of the atmospheric railway.'

'I'll have to rescue Victor. We have some work to do.'

'Was your visit to Totnes successful?'

'I believe so.'

'Will it make any difference to the case?'

'It will make a great deal of difference. Our main suspect has been exonerated. We'll have to look elsewhere for the killer.'

She was dismayed. 'Does that mean you'll be here for a lot longer?'

'I'm not sure, Madeleine,' he said, guardedly. 'Much will depend on what Victor and I find this evening.'

'What are you hoping to find?'

He smiled lovingly. 'We're searching for an owl.'

* * *

Dorcas Hope had seen little of the stationmaster throughout the day. When she was about to go home, however, he was waiting to waylay her outside the refreshment room. Woodford had reverted to his old authoritarian self.

'If you want to earn my respect, Miss Hope,' he said, reprovingly, 'you can stop giving a false impression of me to Inspector Colbeck.'

'But I didn't do that, Mr Woodford.'

'You told him that I blenched when I heard that the diary had been found.'

'That's exactly what you did.'

'No, it isn't.'

'You turned quite pale.'

'I was delighted by the news,' he said, forcefully. 'Try to remember that.'

'I can only say what I saw,' she bleated.

'Leaving that aside, what were you talking to the inspector about earlier? When I walked past the refreshment room, you were poring over a map with him. Why was that?'

'I recalled what "M.V." stood for, Mr Woodford.'

'What are you talking about, girl?'

'They were the initials in Mr Heygate's diary,' she said. 'He discovered that barn owl near a place called "M.V." The inspector brought something called an ordnance survey map and I pointed out where it was.'

'Where what was?' he asked, impatiently.

'It's the cottage that Mr Heygate talked about.'

'He never said anything to me about a cottage.'

'It was his wife who really loved it,' said Dorcas. 'She'd always wanted to live there. Mr Heygate said that he wished he could have bought it for her but could never have afforded it. He pointed it out to me one day.'

'What was the name of the cottage?'

'It's called Meadow View.'

Leeming was unhappy about trampling through long grass in the half-dark. When he trod in some horse manure, he was even more discontented and stopped to wipe it off his shoe on a fallen log. It was a cold evening but the clear sky gave just enough light for them to pick their way along. Colbeck had memorised the route from the ordnance survey map. As they passed various landmarks, he realised just how detailed and accurate it had been.

'I walked down this lane before,' said Leeming, 'yet I found nothing. And that was in daylight. How can we expect to find anything in the dark?'

'That's precisely what Mr Heygate did.'

'He had the sense to bring a lamp.'

'We don't want to attract attention.'

'What if Miss Hope is mistaken?'

'She hasn't let us down so far, Victor. The stationmaster actually showed her the cottage one day. She was able to describe it to me.'

'The diary only said it was *near* Meadow View. We don't know which side of the cottage it is.'

'Then we search both,' said Colbeck, affably. 'Cheer up, Victor. In a sense, we're on a treasure hunt.'

'I know, sir. I stepped in some of it.'

They walked on at a moderate pace and checked every building that passed them in silhouette. Eventually, they came to a large ramshackle shed at the bottom of a garden surrounded by a fence. It was only one of a line of sheds in various gardens, each in differing stages of repair. Leeming had inspected almost all of them on his earlier visit and been unable to find any evidence of an owl having been there. He and Colbeck looked along the line of sheds, wondering where to start. A voice came out of the gloom, then a figure approached the fence.

'You look lost, gentlemen,' said a man. 'Can I help you?'

When he got close, they saw that he was a beefy individual in his forties with a craggy face. He gave them a half-smile and spoke with a local accent.

'We're looking for Meadow View,' said Colbeck.

'That's a bit further on, sir,' said the man, appraising them shrewdly. 'It will take you less than two minutes to walk there. As you might have guessed, it has a nice view of the meadow. Look out for a horse chestnut tree,' he continued. 'It might not be so easy to recognise in this light but it's the biggest tree you'll come across.'

'Thank you for your guidance.'

'Is everything all right, Howie?' called a female voice.

'It's my wife,' he explained then raised his voice to answer her. 'Everything is fine, dear. I'm just giving directions to two gentlemen.'

'Dinner will be ready soon.'

They could only see the woman in dim outline. As she came forward, she was carrying a lamp in her hand. After taking a close look at the two strangers, she turned around and retreated into the house. Her husband glanced after her.

'May saw you through the bedroom window,' he told them. 'She's got better eyesight than me and spotted your hats. I was sent out to see who you were.'

'We won't hold you up from your dinner,' said Colbeck, one hand on the fence. 'We're sorry to disturb you. Come on, Victor,' he went on. 'We must find Meadow View. Look out for the horse chestnut.'

'I'd rather look out for horse manure,' said Leeming, grumpily.

The man laughed and waved them off. When the detectives walked away, he watched them until they vanished into the darkness, then he went back into the house. Colbeck and Leeming, meanwhile, went as far as the designated tree and paused beneath it. The meadow was off to their right. The sergeant was perplexed.

'Why did you say that we were looking for Meadow View?'

'I didn't want to arouse his suspicions.'

'Do you think it was in that shed that the stationmaster saw the owl?'

'No,' said Colbeck, 'not unless he climbed over the fence and trespassed on their garden, and I don't think he did that. I ran my hand over the fence. It's built with relatively new timber and reinforced with stout posts.'

'He wants to protect his property. I'd do the same.'

'There's more to it than that, Victor. It was the wife who interested me.'

'She was just a blob in the dark, sir.'

'Didn't you notice her lamp? It was unusually large and heavy. That's why she never lifted it up to her face. I'd have expected her to come out with an oil lamp or even a large candle.'

Leeming showed real interest at last. 'Do you think it might have been the missing railway lamp?'

'It's a possibility worth exploring,' said Colbeck. 'Add up what we know. There are two people excessively sensitive about anyone near their property. Both of them immediately came out to confront us so that they could weigh us up. There's a tall fence that's been recently constructed, yet the shed is falling to pieces and they've made no attempt to repair it. I find that significant. Finally, there's a lady carrying what may turn out to be a stolen lamp. On the basis of that evidence, I'd say we have cause to investigate.'

'What are we going to do, Inspector?'

'Give them plenty of time to start their meal.'

They waited a quarter of an hour under the boughs of the tree. Then they walked slowly back to the place where they'd encountered the man. Colbeck took a closer look at the fence and saw that it had cost money and effort. When he indicated to Leeming that they were going to climb the fence, the sergeant was at first alarmed. Chest high, it was a daunting obstacle. In spite of the cold, Colbeck shed his hat, coat and waistcoat before hauling himself to the top of the fence and hooking a leg over it. Rolling out of sight, he reappeared and crooked a finger for Leeming to follow. The sergeant took off his coat and hat and tried to do exactly what the inspector had done but he was neither as lithe nor as fit as Colbeck. It took him three attempts before he finally got a leg over the fence. Colbeck was waiting to steady him as he lowered himself down. They moved across to the shed and peered in.

'I don't see any owl,' whispered Leeming.

'Neither do I, Victor, but then I never expected to. This is not the shed to which Heygate referred. The one with the owl is closer to Meadow View.' He peered into the gloom. 'But I do see something else.'

It was an old handcart with sacking on it. Colbeck felt his way around it to make sure that it was serviceable. Then he led the sergeant back into the garden. As they walked furtively towards the house, Leeming tripped over something and had to stifle a curse as he fell. His knees were covered in fresh earth. What he hadn't seen was a small mound. It was next to another mound, overgrown with moss. Colbeck bent down to investigate the parallel mounds. He and Leeming were still crouched down when two figures were conjured out of the darkness. The woman was holding a lamp and the man was pointing a shotgun at them. There was menace in his voice now.

'I had a feeling you might come back,' said the man, standing over them. 'Hold the light up, May. Let's see who these nosy devils are.'

'Put that gun down, sir,' suggested Colbeck.

'Shut up!'

'You're right, sir,' said Leeming as the lamp was held near his face. 'I think it *was* stolen from Mr Heygate.'

'Heygate was too inquisitive,' said the man. 'If he'd minded his own business, he'd still be alive now. You made the same mistake that he did.'

Ready to pull the trigger, he aimed the gun at Leeming. Colbeck immediately snatched up a handful of earth and threw it into the man's face, distracting him completely. The gun went off but it discharged its shot harmlessly into the air. Leeming was galvanised into action. He dived for the man's ankles and brought him crashing to the ground before hurling himself on top of him. The woman was no mere bystander. She raised the heavy lamp with the intention of smashing it down on Leeming's skull. Colbeck stopped her just in time, seizing her wrist and twisting it until she was forced to let go of the lamp. It fell to the ground but she was not finished yet. Surprisingly strong, she grappled with him for minutes, kicking, screaming, biting and spitting at him. Evidently, she was very accustomed to a brawl and gave no quarter. Colbeck eventually slammed her against the side of the shed to take the fight out of her, then held her from behind with one hand around her neck and the other applying an arm lock.

Leeming was engaged in an even more desperate struggle against a man determined to kill him. Having failed to shoot the sergeant, he rolled on top of him and managed to hold him down long enough to get the shotgun across his neck. Pressing down hard on Leeming's windpipe, he tried to choke him to death. As the pain became more intense, Leeming put every ounce of his remaining energy into an upward shove, dislodging his adversary and making him fall backwards. It was the sergeant's turn to be on top now and the first thing he did was to wrest the shotgun away and fling it out of reach. The two of them traded punches and the advantage swung first one way, then the other. With the woman safely pinioned, Colbeck watched as the man finally shrugged Leeming away and tried to escape.

He got no further than the fence. Before he could scramble over it, he felt his legs being held securely. Leeming dragged him to the ground and pulled him over each of the two mounds in turn. Every time the man attempted to get up, he was knocked back down again by a well-aimed punch. In the end, drained of energy, he simply collapsed in a heap. Leeming reclaimed the shotgun.

An owl hooted nearby.

* * *

Dr Morton Swift worked long hours at the asylum. Though he owned a house only a mile away, there were times when he decided to stay at the institution instead of going home. He reserved a large room with an adjoining bathroom for his own use. It was far more comfortable and well appointed than the accommodation used by any of the patients. Much of the space was taken up by a double bed. When he finished work that evening, he adjourned to his private quarters. He was surprised when there was a knock on his door. Anticipating company for the night, he didn't expect his visitor to come so soon. When he opened the door, he saw that there was no compliant young woman outside. The trio of men comprised Colbeck, Leeming and Steel. The superintendent was holding handcuffs.

'May we come in, sir?' asked Colbeck, pushing him back into the room and following him in. Leeming and Steel came behind him. 'We must apologise for this intrusion but we've come to place you under arrest.'

'What the devil are you talking about?' demanded Swift, shaking with rage.

'I thought I was quite explicit.'

'Please leave at once. You have no right to barge in here.'

'We have every right, Dr Swift. Our duty is to enforce the law.'

'We've already made two arrests,' said Leeming, pointedly. 'Howard and May Gurney are both in custody. They're friends of yours, I believe. As you can see, they were stupid enough to resist us in the garden.'

He gestured to his filthy trousers and showed his dirty hands. Mention of the two names was a like a hammer blow to Swift. He was reeling. Trying to control his rising panic, he fell back on bluff.

'Don't listen to anything that Gurney and his wife tell you,' warned Swift. 'Both of them worked under me as nurses and I dismissed them for incompetence. They'll make up all sorts of weird tales to get back at me.'

'Two tiny bodies have been uncovered in their garden,' said Colbeck, regarding him with contempt. 'The most recent of them was buried there on the night that Joel Heygate was killed. In fact, it was the reason that he was murdered. He saw something that he shouldn't have seen and was battered to death as a result.'

'This has got nothing whatsoever to do with me, Inspector.'

'I think that it has, Dr Swift. The baby that the stationmaster saw was the murdered child of a young woman named Esther Leete, a patient at the deaf and dumb asylum. You were the father and you paid Gurney and his wife to dispose of the baby in the way that they'd disposed of the other child you fathered on a patient. Infanticide is a sickening crime,' said Colbeck, sharply. 'You incited it.'

Steel moved forward. 'I need to put these handcuffs on you, sir.'

'You can't touch me,' cried Swift in horror. 'I'm essential to this place. I cure people with disordered minds. I'm a noted person in my profession.'

'You'll be noted for other reasons in the future.'

'There's obviously been a gigantic mistake.'

'You're the one who made it, Doctor Swift.'

'Gurney and his wife have told us everything,' said Colbeck, icily. 'You suborned them and bought them that house in return for their services in getting rid of your unwanted progeny. When you heard that they'd killed the stationmaster, you helped Gurney to transport the body to the cathedral precinct on a handcart. But it's not just his word and that of his wife on which we rely,' he went on. 'There's the evidence of the two women you seduced and impregnated. One of them, I gather, was deaf and dumb. Could anything be more nauseating than the way you preyed on two vulnerable young women in your care?'

'Hold out your hands,' insisted Steel. 'Your career here is finished.'

'Come on,' said Colbeck. 'You shouldn't have been allowed anywhere near the patients in this institution. Gurney and his wife were nurses here until you realised they could perform a more useful function. You corrupted them.'

'They were corrupt enough already, if you ask me,' said Leeming.

Steel stepped forward and snapped the handcuffs on to Swift's wrists.

The prisoner hung his head in shame. The people he'd employed and trusted had clearly made a full confession. The game was up. He was destined to join them on the gallows.

Canon Smalley was so shocked by the latest developments that he hurried to the bishop's palace so that he could deliver his report. Plucked away from the dinner table, Phillpotts was in an irascible mood but it soon changed. When he heard that Dr Swift had been arrested and charged with murder, he refused to believe it at first and said that he had every confidence in the man. Smalley described the evidence amassed against the doctor and the bishop was stunned into silence for minutes. Finding his voice again, he pressed for detail.

'*Two* young women were involved?'

'Two gave birth to children,' said Smalley, 'but others fell victim to Dr Swift's charms. According to his accomplices, there were several females and, since they were patients kept in detention, there was nobody to whom the unfortunate women could complain. Dr Swift had complete control over their lives.'

'And over their bodies,' said the bishop with a shudder. 'The man has the cunning and instincts of an animal. The litany of his crimes is vile. He and his two accomplices deserve more than hanging.'

'I inadvertently saw something of his power over a female patient.'

'Did you?'

'When I first introduced myself to Esther Leete, the deaf and dumb girl, she was held in a straitjacket and unwilling even to let me talk to her. The next time I saw her, she was walking quietly by Dr Swift's side. In his presence, she was subdued. At the time, of course,' said Smalley, 'I was unaware of the full facts. Now that I am, Miss Leete's wild reaction to a painting of the Madonna and Child is explained. Like any mother, she wanted her baby back.'

'Dr Swift is guilty of inhuman cruelty.'

'He and his accomplices will pay for it, Bishop.'

'What about Bernard Browne?'

'He was in no way involved in the murder,' said Smalley. 'Other crimes will send him to prison for a long time but he's been cleared of the charge of killing the stationmaster.'

Phillpotts was disappointed. 'So Inspector Colbeck was right all along,' he said, sourly. 'In the teeth of the evidence, he championed Browne's innocence with regard to the murder. I hope he doesn't come to me for an apology because he won't get one. Browne should not avoid execution,' he said, vengefully. 'It would be a travesty of justice if he did so. Use your imagination, Canon Smalley. Isn't there some other reason we can find to hang the man?'

With Swift, Howard Gurney and May Gurney under lock and key, the detectives went up to Steel's office to toast their success with a glass of whisky apiece. Leeming was glad that he'd been able to overpower the man who'd actually battered Joel Heygate's head with the butt of his shotgun, Colbeck was pleased that he'd been able to save Bagsy Browne from an unjust death, and Steel was gratified that he'd been involved in the confrontation at the asylum. The superintendent was gracious in defeat.

'I should have listened to you, Inspector,' he said with admiration. 'You had doubts about Bagsy's guilt all long.'

'He was guilty of just about everything else,' Colbeck reminded him, 'and will have a very long sentence to serve. Your job, I fancy, will be a lot easier with him off the streets of Exeter.'

'How did you know that he had an alibi?'

'I didn't, Superintendent. But when a criminal facing the hangman requests an urgent meeting, I'm always prepared to hear him out. As a result, I checked that he wasn't even in the area on the night of the murder and was satisfied that he was therefore in the clear. The very best way to exonerate one suspect, however, is to arrest and charge another – or three of them, in this case. Browne was in no way party to the crime.'

'What exactly was his alibi, sir?' asked Leeming.

'It doesn't matter any more, Victor,' said Colbeck, smoothly. 'He won't stand trial for murder, so that particular witness need never be called. We can draw a veil over that aspect of the case.'

Colbeck was relieved to be able to keep the name of Christina Goss out of the case, not least because it might have caused severe embarrassment to her mother. The story told by the prisoner had been confirmed almost word for word by the girl. She and her mother had parted acrimoniously years before. Not daring to mention it to Adeline, Bagsy had taken pity on Christina because she was left to struggle alone. Whenever he was in South Devon, he called on her in Totnes to give her money, asking for nothing in return but her thanks and her discretion. Browne claimed that she'd always looked upon him as a kind uncle in the past. On his last visit, however, he wasn't able to simply hand over the money and leave. Christina had admitted that she'd thrown herself at him and – like the red-blooded man he was – Browne had been unable to resist, even though she was Adeline's daughter.

In Colbeck's opinion, there was no virtue in recounting the details to the others, especially to Leeming. As a devoted family man, he would have been scandalised at the idea of someone having sexual relations outside marriage with both a mother and daughter. It was knowledge he could live more happily without.

Colbeck finished his whisky. 'It's time for us to leave,' he said. 'The case is closed. We're keen to return to London and you, Superintendent, will be thrilled to see the back of us.'

'I can't thank you enough,' said Steel, exchanging a handshake with each of them in turn. 'Without you, we'd have hanged the wrong man and Dr Swift would have been able to carry on seducing defenceless women at the asylum.'

'Before I go,' said Colbeck, 'may I remind you of a wager we made?'

'You may indeed, Inspector. I'm more than willing to pay you the five pounds I owe you,' said Steel, opening a drawer and taking out money. 'I'm also returning the sovereign I won unfairly from you earlier. It's quite obvious that Bagsy *was* at the funeral, as you said.' He handed the money over. 'Forgive me for doubting you.' He drained his glass. 'Well, the murder might be solved and Exeter may soon be ridding itself of some despicable people but I do still have a serious regret.'

'What's that, sir?' asked Leeming.

'It's related to that information you discovered, Sergeant,' said Steel. 'I often used to go to the Crown Inn for a drink but you won't get me across the threshold if it's owned by Michael and Lavinia Heygate.'

'Oh, there's no possibility of that happening,' said Colbeck, confidently.

'How do you know?'

'I spoke to Joel Heygate's solicitor. He wasn't prepared to divulge details of the man's will, of course, but he did give me a broad hint. Very little of the estate has been bequeathed to Heygate's brother.'

'Then who is the main beneficiary?'

'She's the person who really deserves the money – Miss Dorcas Hope.'

* * *

Dorcas laughed as Peter flew around the parlour before landing playfully on top of her head. The canary then flew down to Maud Hope's knee. In the short time he'd been there, Peter had made a difference to their lives. He needed very little care, yet rewarded them with endless amusement. Peter had accepted that he would be a permanent guest in his new home and was happy with the arrangement. Hopping on to the table, he jumped back into his cage and stood on his perch, singing at the top of his voice. Dorcas was pleased.

'It's almost as if he *knows* that they caught Mr Heygate's killers,' she said. 'That's a song of celebration.'

Colbeck and Madeleine had really been able to talk properly for the first when they had breakfast together at the Acland Tavern. Thanks to Leeming and Andrews, who sat at a separate table, they shared precious moments alone. It was different on the train journey back to London. Though they sat side by side, they had their travelling companions directly opposite them in the compartment. It was only when Leeming and Andrews became embroiled in a long argument about the atmospheric railway that Colbeck felt able to speak more freely to Madeleine.

'Are you glad that you came?' he asked, squeezing her hand.

'Oh, yes,' she replied, 'and so is Father. He claims that the only reason you solved the crime is that we arrived in Exeter.'

Colbeck grinned. 'There may be some truth in that, Madeleine. When I caught sight of you in the refreshment room at the station, I had a real stimulus to press on with the investigation.'

'Why didn't you take me to Totnes? I've helped you in earlier cases.'

'I needed to speak to that witness alone,' he explained, careful to say nothing more about Christina Goss. 'In the event, her testimony was not needed.'

'It seems to have been a very difficult investigation.'

'I'm trying to put it at the back of my mind for a while, Madeleine, so that I can concentrate on the more appealing prospect of the wedding.'

'There's not long to go now, Robert,' she said, excitedly.

'I've been counting the days.'

'When you get involved in future cases, I won't have to mope at home with Father any longer. I'll be able to discuss an investigation with you.'

'I'm hoping that you'll do rather more than that.'

'So do I – it will be wonderful to work together.'

'It will have to be covert assistance,' he told her. 'Superintendent Tallis would never sanction the employment of a woman in the process of detection. It's in defiance of everything that he believes. I take a more practical view. Women are more than capable of committing crime – look at May Gurney, for instance – so why shouldn't they be able to solve it?'

'Is the superintendent still unhappy about your getting married?'

'It's not so much unhappiness as disapproval. That's why I won't be giving him a full report of our activities in Exeter.' He glanced across at Leeming, still quarrelling with Andrews. 'Victor can have that dubious privilege.'

Edward Tallis didn't believe in staying away from his desk simply because his arm had been wounded. He could still bark commands at his underlings and supervise the never-ending stream of investigations that were referred to the Detective Department. Pleased that the case in Exeter had finally been brought to a satisfactory conclusion, he was sorry that he hadn't been there in person to take charge and to grab some of the glory. Local newspapers would no doubt lavish their praise on the Railway Detective without even mentioning the person who assigned the case to him. Because of its sensational nature, details of the stationmaster's murder would be carried in national newspapers, so Tallis would be compelled to watch his detectives being feted while he was ignored. It made the wound in his arm smart.

All that he knew so far was what had been contained in a telegraph from Colbeck. The prime suspect, Bernard Browne, had been absolved of the murder and three further arrests had been made. Tallis longed to hear a fuller explanation. When he heard someone tapping on his door that afternoon, he hoped that it would be Colbeck, coming to give him a detailed account. Instead, it was Victor Leeming who opened the door with his usual feeling of dread.

'Good afternoon, sir,' he said. 'We've just returned from Exeter.'

'I've been waiting for you. Where's Inspector Colbeck?'

'He has an appointment with his tailor.'

'His *tailor*!' roared Tallis. 'I want him here so that I can question him. What on earth is he doing at his tailor's?'

'He'll be wearing a new suit at the wedding, sir.'

'I'm not interested in his private life, Sergeant.'

'The inspector sent me to deliver the report, sir,' said Leeming, taking a pad from his pocket. 'He was kind enough to make some notes for me.'

'I'm sorry that his kindness didn't extend to me,' said

Tallis, mordantly. 'I want to hear from the man who was in charge, not from his assistant.'

The sergeant was sufficiently hurt to forget his fear of the superintendent.

'I played my part, sir,' he said, stoutly. 'I was the one who overpowered Howard Gurney after he tried to choke me to death and I was involved in the arrest of Dr Swift as well. Inspector Colbeck was instrumental in solving the crime but it's unfair to dismiss me as if I just stood on the sidelines and watched. The inspector is always ready to pay tribute to what I'm able to do and I think it's time that you followed his example.'

Startled by Leeming's spirited retort, Tallis was chastened. He pointed to a seat and his visitor sat down, pad in hand. Tallis spoke kindly to him for once.

'You've earned your share of praise, Sergeant,' he said, benevolently, 'and I'll be the first to acknowledge it. Now tell me what really happened in Exeter.'

Involving only family and a small number of friends, the wedding was far too small an affair for such a large church. Those clustered at the front of the nave took up only a tiny proportion of the seats available. Colbeck and Madeleine were untroubled by that. They didn't notice anyone apart from the vicar who married them. They were both so elated that the only things they would later remember of the service were the exchange of vows and the pronouncement that they were man and wife. Madeleine was radiant in her wedding dress and Colbeck was at his most elegant. They were a striking couple. The two of them floated happily through the whole event, forgetting horrors in the recent past and thinking only of their future together. As they came down the aisle arm in arm, they distributed smiles among the congregation.

Some uninvited guests had watched the ceremony from the back of the church. Madeleine picked out two middle-aged women, seated together and ignoring the bride and bridegroom. Their gaze was fixed firmly on Caleb Andrews. When the couple came out through the main door, they were greeted by the cheers of well-wishers and curious passers-by. Running a thankful eye over them, Colbeck was met by a surprise. The sturdy, well-dressed man quietly withdrawing from the crowd was Edward Tallis. He'd come to give his tacit blessing, after all.

Colbeck was touched. It was a sign of progress.